To / Roy

THE OTHER SIDE
OF MORNING

STEPHEN GOSS

 FriesenPress

One Printers Way
Altona, MB R0G 0B0
Canada

www.friesenpress.com

ISBN
978-1-03-912301-4 (Hardcover)
978-1-03-912300-7 (Paperback)
978-1-03-912302-1 (eBook)

1. FICTION, HISTORICAL

Distributed to the trade by The Ingram Book Company

Table of Contents

DEDICATION

To those I have lost, who touched my life, made an impact, and moved on.

To my wife Laura, whom I love with all my heart, to my ever-supportive Mum and Dad, and to my extended family scattered like seeds across the vast reaches of our blue planet.

To my future—my daughters, Andrea and Robyn—and my grandchildren, Alexander and Brayden.

"The purpose of life is not to be happy.
It is to be useful,
to be honorable,
to be compassionate,
to have it make some difference
that you have lived and lived well."
—Ralph Waldo Emerson

June 20, 1756

John felt a great pressure on his back as the crowd was pushed and herded toward the entrance. He had no recourse but to move forward into the darkness, the first of 145 men and one woman, Mary Carey, to be unceremoniously packed into a room just eighteen feet wide and fourteen feet deep.

John's state of anxiety had been rising ever since he had contemplated the fate that awaited him and his charges. He knew the size and layout of The Black Hole and couldn't for the life of him fathom how all the prisoners would be able to fit. His anxiety now turned to sheer terror and nausea, and he vomited the moment he stumbled into the chamber. He had enough wits about him to make his way to the north end of the room, where he stood, hands clinging to the iron bars of one of the two small windows in the Hole. More and more bodies were piling onto him as the Moors prodded and shoved every last one of the prisoners into the room. He didn't think his back could withstand the pressure. He could hear the cries and screams of the other prisoners, many of whom would surely be trampled to death before their incarceration even began. *The lucky few,* he found himself thinking.

BOOK ONE

THE FOUR CROSSES
August 1732

Twelve days had passed on the Holyhead Road, a fortnight if you included the harrowing journey across the Irish Sea. Dr. John Zephaniah Holwell, a newly minted surgeon, stepped off the London-bound stagecoach with the help of a liveried footman, stretched out his back, and basked for a moment in the late summer sunshine. The weather had been a mixed bag of rain and mist for most of the journey, and the doctor's spirits were revived by the light breeze and gently scudding wisps of cloud overhead.

The coach had pulled into the track outside The Four Crosses Inn a short distance out of Shrewsbury, the county seat of Shropshire, and disgorged its travel-weary inhabitants: Holwell, two spinster sisters, and a barrister who had judiciously worn his wig and gown the entire trip.

The spinsters, giggling as they had all the way from Dublin, made a beeline for the Inn, as did the barrister. John chose to stand for a while outside the welcoming edifice, with its thatched roof and Tudor-style crossbeams. He watched as the footmen unloaded the luggage strapped on the roof, admiring their efficiency, and waited until the groomsmen led the four tired horses, now pulling a much lighter load, into the stable yard.

The first order of business now that he had taken in some fresh air and felt the warm sun on his face was to secure a room, call for a tub of hot water to wash away the day's grit, and then retire to the common room where he could enjoy a Shropshire ale, something he had been looking forward to from the time he had left Dublin and all its fine drinking establishments.

Once settled into his second-floor room, and while he was waiting for a tub of hot water to be sent up, he strode over to the bow window and studied the view. Fields, trees, wildflowers, and small cottages nestled into ash groves lay to the west in the direction from which he had just come; to the east, the Holyhead Road wound its way past a blacksmith shop and some small farms, and it then rambled across the River Severn into Shrewsbury proper. John could see the town's profile low on the horizon. Smokestacks, lonely sentinels of progress, were shadowy silhouettes against the greyish-blue late afternoon sky. The only prominent landmark was a church spire that rose imperiously above all else. *If the church itself were as impressive as the imposing spire,* John thought, *it would be something worth seeing closer.*

Life in Dublin, London, and Rotterdam — in almost equal thirds — had comprised his brief experience of twenty-one years. People bustling by on crowded roads; hackney coaches and grocers' carts vying for space on narrow, cobbled lanes; soot-stained roofs as far as the eye could see; babies crying; vendors of just about anything one could imagine, crying out and trying to outdo the hawkers beside them. This is what John knew, yet here he was in the middle of the English countryside in all its bucolic splendour, the landscape silent and peopled by trees, stones, and the odd jackdaw. Alien but beautiful.

Lost as John was in the vista outside his window, the sudden thudding at the base of his door startled him. He let in a young maid who was struggling to keep the heavy basin of hot water she was holding from spilling its contents.

"Beg pardon, Doctor. But 'ere's the tub of water you asked for. I'll set it on the washstand." In typical country fashion, she dropped the "h"; but John, who was always very proper in his speech, didn't mind. After all, she was a busty, red-haired, rosy-cheeked beauty, and he found himself following her bustling skirts all the way to the washstand.

"What's your name, miss?" John didn't want her to leave sooner than she had to.

"Callie, sir."

"As in Calliope?"

"No, sir. Just Callie."

She had a pretty, song-like voice. Totally unlike the incessant clucking of the spinsters when they tried to drag him into conversation on the stagecoach. They clucked and giggled just like a chattering of chickens or a gaggle of geese. He laughed inwardly at the contrast.

"Well, Callie. Thanks for the hot water." John watched her as she completed her task. "That'll be all for now."

The maid exited primly, offering a slight curtsy as she did so.

A fire was blazing in the oversize fireplace, which was built into the north wall of the common room, when Dr. Holwell, refreshed and looking smart in his very new surgeon's jacket, stepped off the last riser of the stairwell leading down from the second-floor bedchambers. He spied a small table tucked into the far southeast corner of the public house, away from the heat of the flames, and made his way past a handful of roughly hewn, sturdy tables, some occupied and others not. The solicitor, still in gown and wig, sat by himself at a table against the north wall, devouring what looked like an entire leg of lamb, completely absorbed in his dinner. Beside him, a trio of merchants, mugs of beer in hand, chatted idly about the day's business. And then, much to his chagrin, he caught sight of the spinsters wildly gesticulating for him to come and join them. He pretended not to notice and made his determined way to the quiet corner table. He deliberately put his back toward the sisters and waited patiently to be served.

His hopes that Callie would be doing double duty as a serving girl were dashed when the barman, burly and leather-aproned, approached him and inquired after his needs. He ordered a bowl of stew and a pint of ale and settled back into his chair. He found himself looking ahead to his future in London and wondering what it would be like as a junior surgeon at Guy's Hospital, where he had studied under Andrew Cooper and where he'd take up his residency in October. He also looked fondly back to his recent trip to Dublin, which had been exhilarating. He had visited with many of his relatives, most of whom he hadn't seen since he was eight years old. He had enjoyed the company of his aunts, uncles and cousins and visited the house in which he was born, now occupied by his father's younger brother and his large, mischievous brood of children. His aunt had thrown a party in his honour the day before he was to depart, and there had been much drinking and merrymaking.

It wasn't long before a steaming bowl of stew with thick pieces of meat, chunky potatoes, root vegetables, and rich broth lay before him, as well as a large heel of crusty bread. He set to it with a hearty appetite and washed it all down with the golden Shropshire ale.

No sooner than the barman had cleared the dishes away and another mug of ale was on its way that a young, handsome couple flitted into the room via the main entrance and made their way to the table next to his. Much of the conversation in the room had died down, and heads had turned to watch their progress. By the bemused expressions on the faces of the locals, one could surmise that they knew these rather dashing youngsters and were pleased to see them. It was obvious from the demeanour of the young lady, and the solicitous arm around her partner's waist, that she was worried about him. She was lithe and decidedly graceful in her bearing. *Perhaps a budding actress or dancer,* John surmised. She guided the young man into his seat and settled herself easily into the chair opposite. From John's vantage point, he could squarely see the young beauty, her hair braided neatly behind her, and her startling, bluish-green eyes that held him quite captive.

The barman brought over a couple of drinks. "Hello Robert. Hello Miriam. Good day today?"

"Not bad." The young man responded. "The crowds are getting larger every day."

"Though you'd never know it by the take." Miriam chimed in. She continued to glance worriedly at her partner.

"Lots of skinflints around," the barman cajoled, "they all want to see something fantastical, but they don't want to pay for it."

The barman returned to his duties, which included drying recently rinsed mugs and replacing them on the shelves behind him. The interest generated by the young couple's entrance had waned somewhat, but John continued to keep a subtle eye on them, drawn to them but not wanting to be deemed rude. The young man, Robert, raised his mug to his lips, and it was then that John understood Miriam's concern. Robert's right forearm was badly scraped and quite raw; only a light strip of cloth, as if torn from an old linen shirt, had been wrapped about it, but had slipped down and was not of much use.

"What's happened to you?" John had gotten up from his table and quickly made his way to stand beside Robert. "Please excuse my intrusion. But I'm a doctor, and I'd like to help."

"It's nothing. Really. Just a scrape. Will heal in a day or two."

Miriam interjected, "Robert, let the doctor take a look at it. It looks worse than others you've had."

After further protestation Robert finally acquiesced. "It's just a scrape, doctor."

"And a pretty nasty one at that," replied John, eying the abrasion, which was starting to weep a little. "I'm Doctor Holwell, from London. I've seen many of these sorts of rope burns before. This is going to fester if it's not looked after right away. Come with me to my room for a few minutes. I have some salve and fresh bandages in my kit. We'll get you straightened away."

It was indeed a serious rope burn that Robert had inflicted upon himself, and Robert's trust in this stranger, who had so quickly sized up the injury, seemed well founded. He got out of his chair and followed the serious but smart-looking gentleman to his room.

Miriam had been quietly awaiting their return in the common room.

"Thank you so much, doctor." She carefully examined the dressing on her beau's forearm. It was neatly applied and looked far better than her earlier crude attempt. "This is so much better. Come sit down with us. Can we buy you an ale? That's the least we can do for your troubles."

"Thank you. I had already ordered another just before you came in. The barman must have hung onto it or served it to someone else in my absence."

"Good old Carson. He's a fine barman and the owner of the Four Crosses to boot. Comes across all gruff and no-nonsense, but under that barrel chest is a heart as big as Shropshire." She lithely sprung out of her chair and headed over to the bar to order the ale for the doctor and a couple of bowls of stew for Robert and herself.

"So, you're a steeplejack? Wherever did you learn that trade?" John opened the conversation.

"My da was a thatcher in Stoke, where I was born and raised, and as a young lad I used to scramble up onto roofs to take him and his mates water and thatching supplies. Trees, piles of masonry—in fact, I loved to climb just about anything. It drove my ma to distraction! If work needed to be done on a tall building, windows washed or such, they would seek me out and pay me to climb up and do the job. It was fun, and I could make a lot more money than my mates."

A mug of ale appeared in front of John. Miriam had returned just as spritely as she had left.

"Tell him about the church, Robert." She had obviously caught some of the previous chatter. "Robert had just turned fourteen, and he sprung for a small barrel of ale to share with his friends. I was invited too. Go on, Robert. Tell him."

"We were into the drink, and we got to braggin' and kiddin' around. I recall saying something like 'there's nothing on God's earth that I can't climb.' And then Joe chirps up. 'I'll bet you a new pair of boots you can't climb up the spire at St. Pete's.' That was what we called The Church of St. Peter ad Vincula. Joe's da was a cobbler, so we knew that he could come up with the boots if he had to. I immediately jumped up and said that we should all go right now, even though the dark was almost upon us, and that we'd see who'd be wearing new boots.

"Miriam, who'd only had half a tippet of ale, tried to talk some sense into me. She tried to get me to hold off until the next day, when it would be brighter. And I'm guessing she thought I'd think better of the whole thing when the ale wore off. But I was charged up, and nothing was going to stop me. We all agreed to meet at the church in a half hour, and I rushed off to grab a long coil of rope from my da's work shed.

"Before long, I had the rope tied to my waist and had scrambled up the stone structure, quickly finding one toehold after the other. Having reached the apex of the church proper, the situation changed entirely, and now I had to sort out how to climb the recently-erected wooden framework that comprised the steeple with what was then the largest cross in the county perched on top of it. For this purpose, I needed to loop a short piece of the heavy gauge rope, which was trailing below me to the ground, pass it around one of the beams, flip it up, and then shimmy up a couple of feet. Repeating this process and catching my breath at every crossbeam, I eventually reached the base of the cross. A cheer went up from the gang below. I had won the bet.

"Climbing up anything is always the easy bit. It's coming down that's tricky. And now it was even trickier than usual because of the dusk.

Looking up as I was ascending, at least the sky was clear and there was enough light to see my way. Now, looking down, there was nothing but darkness. I could barely make out my friends below. A funny feeling crept into the pit of my stomach; shudders travelled up my legs and—pardon my crudity, but—the feeling settled uneasily in my nether parts. For a moment, I thought I'd be sick, but the wave of nausea passed, and I screwed up my courage to make the descent."

Robert briefly interrupted his tale to take a long draught of his ale.

"A Highwayman's knot is a self-releasing knot, and one of da's apprentices had taught me how to use it. Basically, the standing part of the rope remains passive while the knot is being tied. You hold up the first bight then transfer your grip to the second and third bight in succession. The hitch then needs to be carefully tightened. Having accomplished this, I firmly gripped the load-bearing rope and started my descent hand below hand. As I gained confidence in the belay, I increased my speed and progressed nicely past the end of the wooden structure. I could now feel the hard stones of the main building beneath my toes."

A painful expression now played on Robert's face. Miriam looked compassionately at him.

"About ten feet from the ground, I made a terrible mistake. My left hand slipped slightly, and I panicked, reaching out to grab hold of the rope. Unfortunately, I grabbed the standing rope, the one used to release the knot from where it was seated at the top of the spire. The knot released, and I went tumbling to the ground, quantities of rope spilling down onto me. My friends rushed over to where I lay crumpled on the ground. My head was spinning, and a fire was burning in my left ankle and knee."

Miriam now took over the narrative.

"When it became obvious that Robert was seriously injured, one of the lads quickly ran to Robert's house to fetch his da. His da came in short order, bringing along his oldest boy, Robert's brother Peter. His da's face was murderous as I explained the series of events that had led to this incident, but he quickly softened after more carefully scrutinizing Robert's predicament. It was too dark by this time to see much at all, but Robert's leg bent unnaturally beneath him—couldn't be missed. The two of them carefully picked Robert up and hauled him back to the house.

STEPHEN GOSS

I was sent to fetch the doctor, who wasn't happy to be bothered at this hour, as he was just about to have his evening port.

"Robert's left leg had been broken; the ankle was already three times its normal size. A large goose egg had also appeared on the back of his head, where he'd obviously smashed it on the ground.

"It took him a few weeks to recover, and even though he walked with a funny hitch for a while, it didn't seem to slow him down. Before long he was scrambling up buildings again."

"And I never did get my new boots!" Robert chirped up. "That was seven years ago. The next time I'm back in Stoke, I'm going to remind that weasel about it."

John revelled in the energy and pleasant conversation offered by the young couple. He pulled out an Irish clay pipe that he had recently purchased in Dublin, filled it with Iberian tobacco—very expensive at four shillings to the ounce and hard enough to come by—and the next couple of hours passed easily by.

He learned that Robert and Miriam were making the rounds, travelling to each of the large centres and putting on "climbing spectacles," as they called them. Robert would set up and execute a stunt, after which Miriam would dance around the gathered crowd and collect any coins they didn't mind throwing into her oversized satchel. They were able to make a tidy little sum doing this over the warmer seasons, and just as well, because come winter he would have to go back to Stoke and work as a thatcher with his da or as a steeplejack when the opportunity arose.

He and Miriam had been fast friends for as long as they could remember and were newly betrothed. Their travelling together was a rather scandalous topic back in Stoke, but neither of them gave a fig about that. As Miriam put it, "Let them wag their tongues as much as they want. We're just living the life they can only dream about! We'll get married sometime in the spring."

Here in Shrewsbury, they had set up their spectacle at St. Mary's Church where in the twelfth century, the city burghers had added a very large tower to the west side of the building. The spire, one of the tallest in all of England, reached 223 feet into the sky and looked east over the

10

Severn River. On the far side of the river was Gay Meadow, a pleasant tract of land where lovers strolled arm in arm and school children who were free from their schoolmaster's clutches for the day played roll the hoop or just ran about noisily. Robert had scaled the spire, tied a firm knot to the base of the cross, belayed down to the ground, hired a punt to take him across to Gay Meadow, and then firmly planted an anchor to the ground, to which he attached the other end of the rope. The rope then stretched down from the top of St. Mary's spire, spanned the Severn and terminated at the anchor 820 feet later. The stunt involved scaling the rope to the top of the church, attaching a chest harness to the rope and then, after a pause for effect, hurtling down to Gay Meadow. This was the most daring stunt he had conceived to date, and for the first two days, they had drawn pretty decent crowds. Today, he had sustained the rope burn when the "ingenious" brake system he had invented didn't quite work, and he had needed his arms to help slow his descent. Even with leather gloves and a long-sleeved shirt, the friction was intense.

Tomorrow was Sunday, and since the horses needed to be rested for a couple of days now that they had reached the halfway point on the journey to London, Dr. Holwell and his travelling companions wouldn't be departing until Monday morning. That being the case, Robert and Miriam invited John to witness their final performance.

Besides, as Miriam put it, "It couldn't hurt to have a doctor on hand!"

STEEPLEJACK

A more glorious morning couldn't have been imagined. John stood outside the Four Crosses digesting his breakfast of eggs and mutton hash, washed down with a mug of ale and luxuriating in the brilliant mid-morning sunshine. He was happy not to be stepping into the coach today, being jostled about and having to politely put up with the sinister spinster sisters as he was wont to consider them. No sooner than John had let these babbling creatures into his thoughts than here they were demurely walking toward him, followed rather sullenly by the wigless, gownless barrister. Would wonders never cease? More wonderful yet was the presence of Callie, John's red-haired maid. Evidently, Sunday was her day off, and she too was going to Gay Meadow to watch the climbing spectacle. A lively yellow frock set off by a light blue sash around her delicate waist gave John great hopes for a deliciously pleasant walk into town. Robert Cadman and his jaunty Miriam had come out into the sunshine, smiled at the assembly, and then spryly led the way down the Holyhead Road.

Church bells chimed not long into their walk, and birds took to the air in response. The church service would be under way in a few minutes, and by the time the Four Crosses' entourage had reached Gay Meadow, St. Mary's would be spilling out its congregation just in time for them to become part of the spectacle audience.

"Hopefully they'll still have some coins left in their purses after the offering!" chirped Miriam.

Callie, John, Robert, and Miriam walked together; the sisters, along with the barrister, trailed a little behind. When John cast a glance behind him at one point, he could see that a number of other Inn folk had joined them—various groomsmen, house servants, and miscellaneous others. They were, all in all, a motley crew. The fresh autumn air was exhilarating, and he found himself getting more and more excited about the spectacle to come. His dreams of the night before had been peppered with fleeting images of circuses and stuntmen and bear-pits. His was an adventurous spirit and the promise of today's events could do nothing but bring a spring to his step.

As they walked, they talked. Callie, however, remained quiet, and John tried to engage her in conversation, at first unsuccessfully.

"There's not much for me to say, sir. I was born and raised in these parts. Well, in Oswestry, that is. On the Welsh border."

"We stopped in Oswestry on the way down from Dublin. A beautiful little town nestled into the hills, isn't it? What's the name of that imposing castle just as you enter?" John already knew the answer but was hoping to keep Callie chatting.

"Oswestry Castle, sir."

"Please, Callie, just call me John. You're not the maidservant of The Four Crosses today. You're just on an adventure with the rest of us, on our way to seeing young Cadman here flying through the air and attempting not to break his neck. Tell me more about Oswestry."

And so, she did. John was surprised at how much of the history she knew, and his appreciation for her intelligence grew commensurately.

"The town was first known as Croesoswallt when it was part of the Welsh territory. Literally, Oswald's Cross. Don't ask me how to spell Croesoswallt. The Welsh way of speaking is daft, there's neither rhyme nor reason as to how they spell things—or say things, for that matter. The English called it Oswald's Tree and that then somehow slurred into Oswestry.

"It's said that in 1400 the Welsh formed a rebellion against King Henry 1V, and one of their first targets was Oswestry, which had become an Iron Hills fortress on the borderlands. The town was badly burnt and almost totally destroyed. The Oswestry of today really sprang up from those times."

The group had now reached the outskirts of Shrewsbury, and they turned onto Copthorne Road that led into Frankwell and then across the Welsh Bridge. The Severn River flowed south here and then curled sinuously around the town. The outskirts of Shrewsbury were quiet on this Sunday, but as they made their way down Bridgestreet, then Barker Street, then Bellstone, more and more activity could be observed. But as they entered Market Street, a wall of people met them, and market stalls sprawled higgledy-piggledy.

"I thought Wednesdays were the normal market days." John turned to Callie.

"Normally, sir, yes. But today's a special market to celebrate the local harvest. On the way back to the Inn, I'm going to stop and look around for a birthday present for my sister. Meg'll be eighteen in a couple of weeks. Carson has also asked me to pick up some Shropshire Blue and some fresh vegetables for the kitchen."

In the meantime, Miriam had unfurled a large sign which read 'Chapman's Climbing Spectakle' and was doing her best to drum up business for the coming event, hoping, of course for an even bigger gathering today at Gay Meadow or in the church gardens on the other side of the river.

Having jostled their way through the crowds, the merry group reached the wide avenue of Wyle Cop, the entrance to English Bridge. Once again they crossed the Severn and found themselves strolling a little more leisurely now through the Abbey Gardens. It wasn't long before they came out onto Gay Meadow, a wide-open space animated here and there by families and larger groups waiting for the spectacle to begin.

Robert Cadman strode resolutely to the anchor he had planted some days before on the northeastern edge of the meadow and began fussing with the knots, making sure all was as it should be. Satisfied that nothing had been tampered with, he stepped back and began making his preparations. At first, he pulled out a curious-looking leather harness from his pack and Miriam strapped it assiduously to his chest, a large metal hoop bulging out from the middle. To protect his forearms, something he hadn't considered before yesterday's folly, Miriam had designed a couple of false leather sleeves that she now tied about his wrists with leather thongs. Dark leather gloves, like those used by a blacksmith at his forge, then appeared and these Robert pulled onto his hands.

Then there he was, a curly-haired Adonis, standing regally on Gay Meadow, a modern-day knight with curious armour, gauntleted and ready to do battle with the apparatus in front of him.

The Four Crosses contingent found comfortable spots along the riverbank, where they would have an unimpeded view of the drama. Miriam began gathering in the crowd and waving the large sign she had once again unfurled. Even if citizens didn't know the exact moment when Robert Cadman would begin his ascent to the spire of St. Mary's Church, they would certainly spot him once he was on his way and turn their full attention on this madman as he defied the land-bound state of everyday human beings. Dozens of eyes would be upon him as he reached the spire and when he, their fair-formed Quasimodo, would eagerly scan the world around him from his perch. Instead of hurling stones down at the soldiers below, however, he would hurl himself down the cordage and plummet like a raptor swooping down on its prey.

The crowd on Gay Meadow had now moved closer to the river, and all eyes were on Robert, as he remained standing stoically by the anchor gathering his focus. A few children still ran about, not knowing quite what all the fuss was about, but they too stopped in their tracks when a hearty cheer erupted from the crowd. A subtle signal from Miriam had propelled young Cadman to action, and he clipped the metal ring to the rope, walked his hands as far up as he could, threw his legs up and around the line and then hand over hand began his ascent.

Robert's rate of ascent, Miriam pointed out, was about thirty feet every minute. He would stop intermittently to catch his breath. At 820 feet of rope, this monumental climb would last a half hour or more.

As Robert reached the edge of the river, all eyes were still on him, but as he progressed further over it, attention waned and people looked about and chatted idly, only glancing occasionally at Robert's form slowly disappearing into the ether.

Standing beside Dr. Holwell, Miriam's worried eyes never left her beau, but she casually drew John into conversation. "What about you, Doctor? You haven't told us much about you."

Sensing that Miriam needed some distraction to take her mind off Robert's dangerous stunt, John began telling her his story, such as it was. Callie too edged closer so she could hear about the doctor's early years and what had brought him to this place.

"Well, then," John took a deep breath before delving into his tale. "I spent the first eight years of my life in Dublin. My father was a respected businessman in the city, importing exotic goods from faraway places. He was so good at what he did that people in London took notice, and the Dutch East India Company hired him to be their representative in England. Not long before we were to leave, my younger brother, Edward, took ill and died. This made my father's resolve to move even greater, and he made his way to London with my mother and me tagging along.

"I was enrolled in Mr. McKenzie's Grammar School, and when my father discovered that I had a natural talent for classical studies, he decided to send me away to Iselmond on the Meuse, near Rotterdam in the Netherlands, where he had associates who would take me under their wing. I studied French and Dutch, and when my masters there put me to a study of mathematics and discovered my high aptitude for numbers, they wrote to my father and declared that I was now fit to make a career in the mercantile trade. My father journeyed to Rotterdam and fixed a position for me with a friend, Mynheer Lantwoord, a successful banker who controlled a fleet of ships plying the Greenland trade. My apprenticeship was to last five years, whereupon I was to be taken on as a junior partner in the enterprise. However, it wasn't long before the tireless hours and the hectic pace of the business wore me down and affected my health. My father retained the esteemed Doctor Boerhaave, and I recuperated well under his ministrations over a six-week period. When he declared that I was fit again, I resumed my work with Lantwoord's company."

Cadman was now two thirds across the river, and people on the far bank were taking more notice. John stopped to focus on Robert's progress. Miriam encouraged him to continue with his narrative.

"I couldn't seem to settle back into the life of a bookkeeper and found myself more and more distracted. I had made close friends with a young man who, like me, had hailed from Ireland, and we spent most of our off-work hours together, frequenting some of the local watering holes. One evening, as we were well into our cups, he told me that he was going to be returning to Dublin in a few weeks, and that I should accompany him. At first, I didn't think I could disappoint Mr. Lantwoord, not to say anything of my father, and I told my friend that it was not likely that I would go with him. But, as the days wore on and I felt more and more depressed about my position, I finally decided to do it. So, I turned in my resignation and headed for Ireland with my friend."

"But what about your father?" Callie chimed in. "He must have been furious. And probably worried to boot."

"It didn't take my father much time to find out what I had done. He easily ferreted out where I was staying in Dublin, what with all his kin scattered throughout the city, and before long, I received a rather curt summons to return to London.

"Enough time had passed upon my return home that my father's anger had dissipated substantially, but now, even more forbidding, his looks had rather turned to disappointment and disapproval. We spent much time talking about my future, and when it became evident that life as a bookkeeper wasn't going to suit me, he turned to his friend, Mr. Forbes, a surgeon in the Park located in Southwark, and cajoled him into taking me on as an apprentice. I was aghast initially at this seemingly random choice of occupation; but, as I began my training with Mr. Forbes and accompanied him on his rounds at the hospital and occasionally to patients' residences, I found it exciting, and I applied myself purposefully to the work."

John thought for a moment that he should apologize for this rather pedantic and expository telling of his story, but seeing the anguish in Miriam's eyes as she followed her lover on his dangerous ascent to the spire of the church, he knew this was a necessary distraction for her. He continued.

"My life again took a turn in 1729 when my father died after a brief but debilitating illness. It still pains me to think about it. Anyway, for a couple of years before his death, several of his business ventures had begun to fail, and that left but a small inheritance for my mother and me. Luckily, my apprenticeship with Forbes and the costs associated with it were almost at an end, and at the age of eighteen, I was ready to go to work as a surgeon's aide. Mr. Forbes recommended me to Thomas Guy, who was set to open a new hospital off St. Thomas Street, and he was looking to hire surgeons, nurses, and general workers for a host of other positions. Guy's Hospital was intended to treat the "incurables" that had been released from St. Thomas's Hospital because there was nothing more to be done for them. Thomas Guy wanted employees with strong stomachs and who weren't averse to using unorthodox methods.

"I thrived there happily for almost three years, and then I was granted my qualification as full surgeon and presented with the surgeon's jacket you saw me wearing yesterday. I was granted a three-month furlough and decided to head off to Dublin to visit some of my kin and the friend I had met in Rotterdam. I'm now on my way back to London to begin my medical practice at Guy's. I'm looking forward to the next chapter of my life."

Another burst of clapping and cheering directed everyone's attention to the spire of St. Mary's Church. Robert had successfully reached the apex and was stretching out his muscles, which must have been cramping up after his marathon climb. He sat down as best he could, his back to the base of the iron cross, and focused on the stunt ahead.

Miriam now pulled out her oversized satchel in anticipation of collecting money from the gathered crowd. She had already provided another of the Inn's maids with a cloth shoulder bag and had positioned her on the other side of the river by the church. Now she turned to Callie and asked her if she wouldn't mind doing the same on the Meadow. There were too many people for Miriam to do this work alone. Callie eagerly agreed and sorted out her market basket to be used for that purpose.

The sky was the light blue colour of the sea on a beautiful summer's day. Several varieties of small birds skittered here and there, while larger kites, higher and more effortlessly spilling the breeze beneath their spans, regally surveyed the crowds below. The town hall bell tolled noon. Robert stood up and all eyes were riveted to him, a solitary, spectral figure communing with the heavens.

Robert Cadman stepped off the precipice, his feet dangling in front and below him. His back arched backward as the metal hoop took the full load of his weight and he plummeted down. The crowd gasped in awe.

John found himself holding his breath, entranced by the spectacle. Robert was living the dream every schoolchild had—and perhaps many adults as well. What would it be like to fly? What would the birdman be feeling? What would be going through his mind?

As Robert approached the halfway point, he engaged the brake system he had rigged up and his descent slowed noticeably so that by the time he arrived at the eastern bank of the river, he was well in control of his landing. He alit on both feet to a thunderous round of applause, a number of the spectators rushing over to him with alacrity and congratulating him by heartily clapping him on the back.

Miriam, ecstatic that Robert had come safely to roost, now sprang into action and flitted happily from group to group, gathering in the coins they willingly parted with. Callie did the same and before long, the two of them waded back to the rest of their companions now protectively standing around Robert. By this time, he had divested himself of the contraption he had been wearing and was now sitting on the grassy riverbank smiling radiantly and catching his breath. Miriam's sack and Callie's basket were heavily laden with the day's take, and they were all in a jovial mood.

Miriam sat down beside her lover, draping her arms about him, and the two of them passed an intimate moment together.

"Well done, old chap!" The crowds were filtering away and John now came over to Robert. "Any ill effects?"

"Not as much as a rope burn, Doctor. But thanks for standing by."

"It was my pleasure. What an amazing performance!" John reached into his purse and took out a guinea and pressed it into Miriam's hand. The young couple was taken aback by the Doctor's largesse. Miriam stood up and hugged John, and the young daredevil also rose and pumped his hand. The guinea, these days worth twenty-one shillings, along with all the other coins they had harvested, would go a long way toward making this trip to Shrewsbury the biggest success of their "climbing spectacle" season.

The walk back to the Inn, with a brief stop at the market, went by in the blink of an eye, everyone in a carnival mood and wanting to talk about the stunt they had just witnessed. Upon returning to The Four Crosses, John took his leave from the group and retired to his room to rest a little and freshen up. He had made a date with Robert and Miriam to have dinner with them. Tomorrow, he would continue his journey to London, but this evening he wanted to spend as much time with the adventurous young couple as he could and throw back some more of the delectable Shropshire Ale.

"I'm afraid it's the end of our run this summer. Tomorrow we'll begin making our way back to Stoke." Robert was in fine form, and he had just been reminiscing about the many thrilling stunts he had performed over the last few weeks, Miriam having piped up every so often to set the record straight when he got some of the details mixed up. "First thing in the morning, we'll head over to Shrewsbury and recover the rope and anchor. We'll be hitching a ride from there thanks to a merchant heading to Stoke on business and who has agreed to give us a lift in his cart."

"Let's have a look at your arm, Robert. Let's see if the burn is getting any better." John came around the table and examined Robert's forearm. Where yesterday the wound had been raw and weeping, it was now scarring. It was still an angry red, but clearly on its way to healing. "I'll give you some of the salve to take with you." He directed this to Miriam. "Gently apply it to the wound each evening for the next several days, and wrap it lightly with a bandage. Take the bandage off in the daytime to allow the skin to breathe. The wound will heal more quickly as a result."

As John returned to his place at the table, Carson was laying out their supper. A large leg of roasted mutton, placed on a pewter trencher and surrounded by golden potatoes, sat in the middle of the table. Each of their own plates carried a hearty helping of leafy green vegetables. Supper was delicious, and for some time there wasn't much conversation. The inn patrons, of which there were more than usual for a Sunday evening, and some of the staff who had been eager to come over and congratulate Robert, now gave him some space.

Carson came by in due time to remove the supper plates when he could see that they had eaten their fill. "Supper's on The Four Crosses tonight, Robert. Your presence here has been a boon for business. All the locals have come by to see the notorious young Cadman and his beautiful assistant. I trust you enjoyed the victuals?"

"My dear sir. It was first-rate. Thanks so much for your wonderful hospitality." Robert raised his tankard and the three of them toasted the owner of the inn and then drank to his good health.

When Robert and Miriam had taken their leave after much hugging and handshaking, John took out his prized Irish Clay, carefully filled the bowl with tobacco, and gently tamped it down with his thumb. He lit the pipe and a pleasing wisp of bluish smoke rose cobra-like from the bowl. Sighing contentedly, he sat back in his chair.

Guy's Hospital
October 1732

Dr. Holwell could hear the coughing well before he entered Samuel Chapman's hospital room. It was the raspy, phlegmatic cough he had grown all too familiar with in his short time at Guy's. He put a handkerchief over his mouth. Consumption was one of several chronic conditions that St. Thomas's Hospital just wasn't able to cope with, so they happily shuffled all their 'incurable' patients to the brand-new Guy's Hospital, situated just south of the Thames, across from The Tower of London and just a hop to the West. If that wealthy March hare, Thomas Guy, wanted to set up a hospital for incurables, then just let him! So went the conventional wisdom of St. Thomas's directors.

"Good day, Mr. Chapman." John strode confidently over to the patient's bed. "How are you feeling today?"

As Mr. Chapman tried to respond through fits of coughing, Holwell took the patient's pulse and then moved his fingers over the sides of his neck, checking for swollen glands. Glandular degeneration, according to the esteemed Dr. Richard Morton, was a key to this particular pathology. The patient seemed to exhibit all the classic symptoms of phthisis, or consumption as it was more commonly referred to. He had been experiencing fever and night sweats; he had lost a lot more than three stone since the condition overtook him; and the most telling of symptoms, he had a chronic cough, bringing up bright specks of blood.

John had carefully studied Dr. Morton's seminal treatise on the subject, *Phthisiologica, seu exercitationes de phthisi libris comprehensae.* Although he had a fair knowledge of Latin, it was the 1720 English translation that he found most useful. Dr. Morton considered consumption an infectious "wasting disease" and hinted that the pathogen was somehow airborne, and people in close proximity to the patient were in the greatest danger of contracting it. This made a lot of sense to John and was the main reason for his wearing a handkerchief over his mouth and nose. He still hadn't been able to convince all of the other doctors to do the same, but he was pleased that most of the nursing staff had taken to this practice.

Mr. Chapman was resting a bit easier just now, and his coughing had abated somewhat. "What are my chances of getting out of this mess, Doctor? Poor Susan, my youngest daughter, she didn't make it past a fortnight."

John had had it ingrained in him by his old mentor, Mr. Forbes, that it was always best to be forthright, and so he didn't mince words with Mr. Chapman. "My good sir, you know that you have consumption. Last year alone eighteen percent of all deaths in London could be attributed to this scourge. Once you have contracted the disease, the mortality rate is fifty percent. There isn't any way of knowing if you'll be one of the lucky ones, but the fact that you've hung on for as long as you have is a good sign. The next few days will tell."

"May I accompany you to supper, Dr. Holwell?" John's smartly dressed colleague was already pulling on his coat. John liked to get out of the hospital for a brief time each day, and he greatly enjoyed the atmosphere of the Goose & Gander pub just down the road. He also looked forward to a little solitude.

"But of course, Dr. Treleaven. I'd be happy to have some company." He hoped his response sounded sincere; but the subtleties of his tone were quite inconsequential, as Dr. Treleaven was clearly preoccupied as they made their way across the courtyard, through the front gates of the hospital, and turned west onto St. Thomas Street.

"I wonder if I may consult with you about one of my patients?" John's colleague didn't wait for an affirmation before he delved into his subject's situation. "I have a male, twenty-six years old, who four weeks ago was the very picture of health; yet today, he is lying at Guy's, fading in and out of a coma. I believe I know what his condition is, but I would value a second opinion." He carried on. "Twenty-seven days ago, Mr. Sands experienced a sudden and intense fever accompanied by chills. He also complained of a severe headache. Then he developed a rash on his chest, which since has quickly spread to cover most of his body—except for his

23

face, the palms of his hands, and the soles of his feet. A few days ago, he slipped into a coma for the first time, coming out of it only briefly once or twice."

"Tell me, Dr. Treleaven, before the coma, did the patient experience a significant sensitivity to light?"

"He did."

"And did he display signs of dementia or perhaps fogginess and confusion?"

"That's quite right, Holwell. From your questions, I can guess that we're on the same page regarding Sands's diagnosis. Well, confirm it for me. What condition is the poor man suffering with?"

"Gaol Fever. That's the most likely situation. What's the man's occupation? Or what environmental conditions had he been subjected to before becoming ill? You know as well as I do that Gaol Fever typically goes hand in hand with an infection of lice, fleas, or harvest mites."

"I hadn't really considered the source of his illness, but now that you mention it Holwell, the cause is likely quite plain." The two doctors had entered The Goose & Gander and were taking their seats. "Sands is a night watchman at the debtor's prison in Cheapside. No paucity of lice or fleas in that ungodly place!"

The supper hour passed quickly, though there wasn't any more "professional" discussion about patients. John had quite warmed up to Treleaven and was flattered that the doctor, several years his senior, had deigned to consult with him. He decided that he wouldn't be so "lone wolfish" in his own approach to treating his patients as he had been up to this point, and that he would perhaps invite Treleaven to join him every so often in his suppertime jaunts. The other surgeons ignored him for the most part and a couple were openly hostile. How could such a young man, barely twenty-one years old, secure a plum posting such as this at a sparkling new hospital? And how dare he suggest changes to everyday practice and procedure that were not only given an ear to by the Board of Directors, but also in many cases adopted! These grumblings were aired openly in the doctor's refectory and were another reason John preferred to take his meals elsewhere.

"How's the young master doing?" This John addressed to the woman who was sitting stoically by her son's bed. The eleven-year-old had been admitted earlier in the day, having been run down by a grocer's cart in the middle of High Street.

"He's peaceful, doctor. The laudanum you gave him has put him to sleep. I'm glad of it."

John gingerly reached out and examined the boy, the humerus now set, and the arm resting in a sling. Satisfied, he said good night to the anxious mother and went about his evening rounds.

Handkerchief once again covering his mouth, Dr. Holwell checked on Mr. Chapman, his consumption patient, and then made his last visit of the day to Sarah Whitehead's room. The smallpox victim lay wretchedly on her bed, covered head to toe in scabrous pustules. A foul odour emanated from her vicinity, and no one dared sit with her to console her in her misery. John called the nurse to have her administer a sleeping potion to the young woman and when this had been done, he left the hospital, deeply breathing in the cold London air that was a tonic for him after the close and stifling quarters of Guy's Hospital.

A few minutes of brisk walking brought him into Southwark, not far from where he had been apprenticed to Mr. Forbes. He was feeling a little tired and was on the lookout for a cab. It didn't take long to spot a Hackney Coach pulled over on the north side of St. Thomas Street in front of the Roxanne Arms Inn, its coachman sitting patiently on the fore bench, silhouetted in front of the Inn's two large gas lamps. Thank goodness for the Act legislated by The Common Council in 1716! The act compelled "All housekeepers and innkeepers whose properties faced a street or lane to hang out on every dark night one or more lights to burn from six to eleven o'clock between Michaelmas and Christmas." The roads were treacherous enough at this time of year, even with the paltry illumination cast from these gas lamps. John hailed the hackney, and he could hear the coachwhip snap as the coachman prodded his horse into action and a few moments later the coach had been turned about and was now waiting for him to enter the cab.

As they turned right onto Borough High Street and approached London Bridge, John could feel the air getting colder and looking out the window he could see that a mist had begun rolling in. Large halos outlined the gas lamps provided by the Borough of Southwark that were positioned at the entrance to the bridge and the light seemed imprisoned by the fog.

London Bridge was, as usual, in a state of constant reconstruction. Small businesses with dormers overhead, having only been erected but a short while ago, were now being razed, at least on the city side, the London lawmakers having decided that the bridge should only be used for the transportation of people and goods. The coach made its way haphazardly through this mess and eventually spilled out onto King William Street.

The coach made better way on this broad boulevard, and it wasn't long before it veered east onto Monument, which angled back toward the Thames. Pudding Lane, with its small monument to The Great Fire of London, soon came upon them, and John, as he always did when passing this stone marker, had a funny feeling in his stomach thinking about this spot where the conflagration had begun on September 2, 1666. The angry inferno was then driven west by the wind, wantonly consuming a large portion of the city over the next several days. John closed his eyes for a moment as they traversed the crossroad. The busy day had caught up with him, and he nodded off.

He roused himself when the hackney stopped outside a stately row of whitewashed houses on St. Dunstan's Hill, alighted from the coach, and handed the coachman his fare. His mother would be waiting for him, tea and biscuits at the ready, along with a myriad of questions for him about how his day had gone. He loved his mother and still worried about her lonely existence now that his father had gone, leaving her with only the day maid to keep her company. The mist wasn't as heavy here, and the gaslight shone brightly in its sconce by the entrance.

Mrs. Amelia Holwell stood smiling in the coatroom welcoming her son home. She took his coat and hat and carefully hung them on the coat stand. John smiled back at her, gave her a hug, and then a peck on the cheek.

"Tea's ready in the drawing room. Would you like to freshen up a little first?" This is what she always said, and the routine of it was comforting.

"I'll be down in a few minutes." John headed up the stairs to his room to sort himself out.

Sitting across the charmingly appointed table with its starched white tablecloth and delicately laid out tea service, John looked searchingly at his mother's face. The years were catching up to her. Wrinkles had appeared around her sparkling blue eyes, and her hair, which had been a beautiful auburn, was now a matronly white. All this since her husband's death three years past. Mrs. Holwell poured out the tea and passed over a small tray of lightly sugared shortbread. She listened attentively as John recounted the events of the day, showing special concern for the young lad who had been struck by the grocer's cart. The concerns of his adult patients always made her sad, but whenever John spoke of his younger charges, she was almost always brought to tears.

"That poor mother. How horrible for her. Will her son be all right?"

"He has a badly broken arm and a number of other abrasions, but he'll be up and running down High Street again in no time," John replied, attempting to lighten the mood. "Children are resilient."

When they had finished their second cup of tea, Mrs. Holwell took away the tea service and tray coming back from the kitchen with a letter that had arrived for John written in a very pretty hand, and also with a notice from John's bank. Not wanting to look too eager to open the letter, he perused the notice first. It was to do with the new Coin Act that had just recently been enacted by Parliament. He read it aloud to his mother, as he was wont to do with most of his correspondence:

Dear Sir,

You are a valued member of our enterprise. As such, we are extending to you an offer to purchase any Broad Pieces (or halves or quarters) that you may still have in your possession at higher than standard market rates. To be precise, 27 shillings to the Broad Piece. As you are no doubt aware the use of the Broad Piece as legal currency in this great realm of England is no longer permissible and any contravention of the Coin Act of February 1732 may result in charges of treason, the consequent penalties, of course, being severe.

This offer that we are extending to you shall be in effect until December 31, 1732. It may be acted upon by you in person or discharged by your legal proxy.

Ever Your Servants,
Child & Co.

"I don't understand the reasoning behind the *Coin Act*. I've heard people talking about it, but to be honest, I haven't paid much attention." Mrs. Holwell looked to her son for clarification.

John was quick with his reply. "The simple fact of the matter is that gold coins are easily counterfeited, and the problem of fake Broad Pieces, or halves, or quarters, has become endemic. Revenue collectors, such as our bank, have been charged with buying up all the bona fide Broad Pieces that are extant. They are to be turned into the Treasury which, we are led to believe, will melt them down for other uses. The going rate for a Broad Piece has climbed to twenty-four shillings as an incentive for people to turn them in, so this offer from Child & Co. to its clients is really quite generous. I have already sold most of our Broad Pieces, but I do have a few in my safe box that I believe I'll now cash in."

"I see. And what about the other letter, then?" ventured Mrs. Holwell slyly. She grinned impishly at her son, who had been eyeing the carefully addressed epistle furtively all the while he had responded to her question about the Coin Act. She knew whom it was from, but she would have her little bit of fun anyway.

"I daresay it's from Miss O'Connor, judging by the hand. But I'll take a look at it by and by."

"Just open it, John darling. And don't keep us in suspense." The amusement on his mother's face made John blush and he reached for the letter opener that Mrs. Holwell had conveniently placed by the letter.

John read the contents of the letter, trying to keep his enthusiasm at bay. Ailish O'Connor was the very pretty sister of his Irish friend from his days in Rotterdam. He had met her when he had impetuously returned to Dublin with James and had been infatuated with her from the start. The two of them had gotten along famously, and it was heartbreaking when his father so unceremoniously summoned John back to London. Before he left Dublin, John found a way to be alone with Ailish for a few moments—not an easy task with her brother and parents constantly hovering about them—and had kissed her. Where the courage to do that came from, he wasn't quite sure. Nevertheless, he had jumped into it as he had jumped into things many times before. He hadn't been sure what her response would be, but blissfully she had kissed him in return and held him close. As much as John was distressed about having to face his father, he was giddy with the unfamiliar tumult of young love. The two of them agreed to keep in touch. This they had done, and when John visited Dublin recently, he and Ailish had immediately picked up where they had left off.

"Alice is accompanying her brother to London." John had teasingly taken to calling Ailish by her Anglicized name while he was in Dublin, and now the name had stuck. Anyone other than John who dared call her Alice would have incurred her wrath. "Alice writes that James has secured a position with the English East India Company, and he takes up his post at month's end. She will help him settle into his lodgings before heading back to Dublin in time for Christmas."

"When does she arrive?" Mrs. Holwell asked sprightly, more than pleased for her son.

"Thursday, October 24. James has taken a rooming house on Threadneedle Street, not far from Leadenhall where the John Company offices are located." He fell naturally into using the colloquial moniker for the English East India Company. "Alice has asked if I would call on her the following Saturday for tea."

"Then you must. And do invite them for dinner sometime shortly after they've settled in." Mrs. Holwell was already getting ahead of herself. "What shall we serve?"

LADY MARY WORTLEY MONTAGU

"That bitch! Who the hell does she think she is?"

Drs. Holwell and Treleaven turned their startled attention to the table across the refectory. The quiet of their mid-morning tea was now quite shattered.

"Who the devil are they talking about, Holwell? And in such violent terms!"

"No doubt they are referring to Lady Mary Montagu, who will be gracing us with a visit this afternoon. Treleaven, haven't you been reading the notices in the surgeon's lounge? Lady Mary has a meeting booked with the Hospital's Board this morning and has then asked if she can meet with the surgeons this afternoon. We are to be in the lounge for one o'clock."

"I'm not going to allow a woman—nor that woman in particular—to tell us what we should be doing as doctors!" The diatribe from across the room continued. "She has no medical training. She thinks because she contracted smallpox herself and then survived—did some hocus-pocus with her children that prevented them from contracting the disease—that she can waltz in here with her la-de-da's and tell us what's what! We might as well be entertaining a witch doctor come to sell us on the use of Black Magic in healing our dementia patients! Balderdash, I say!"

"Hear, hear!" Came the response from the speaker's companion. "What with having to put up with the young upstarts right here in our own hospital, now we are to be subjected to this harridan newly returned from her scandalous exploits in the Turkish Zenanas. Coffee shops, she calls them. Brothels, more like!"

John didn't react to the slight that he knew was addressed his way. Rather, he pushed away from the table, nodded goodbye to Treleaven, and headed for the operating chamber, where his new patient, a butcher who had wielded his cleaver somewhat errantly, was being prepped for stitches.

The doctors had gathered after luncheon in the surgeon's lounge. The wood-panelled room was dark but for a few oil lamps jutting out from the walls and candles standing freely on the small tables dotting the room.

"The Lady Mary Wortley Montagu," announced the Chairman of the Board of Directors. Holwell and Treleaven stood smartly to attention; some of the other surgeons rose more slowly, registering their annoyance at this disruption to their busy workday by 'this woman' that they had little use for.

Lady Mary strode confidently into the room, proffered her coat to the Chairman, and took the seat offered her. Everybody sat except for the Chairman.

"Lady Montagu has spoken with the Board this morning about the means of preventing smallpox that she came across during her travels in the Ottoman Empire. She has convinced the royal surgeons of the efficacy of this method and knowing that we have a large number of smallpox patients, the numbers growing all the time, she has asked permission to speak with you about the procedure, which she hopes Guy's will adopt. The Board has granted her request to address you, and here we are. I now give Lady Montagu the floor." The Chairman took his seat.

"Good afternoon, gentlemen. I know this imposition on your time is rather out of the way and perhaps unsettling for some of you, given that it is engendered by a mere woman."

As Lady Montagu began her address, John took a shine to her immediately. She had astutely anticipated the tenor of the room and didn't mince words.

"While attending Lord Montagu in his role as British Ambassador to Turkey, I had much occasion to visit medical institutions and to speak with practitioners. As you can tell from the scars on my face, I once had a personal encounter with smallpox. That was in 1715, and the effects are still to be seen seventeen years later."

She must have been a great beauty once, John mused. She was regal in her demeanour, with a lithe, handsome figure. What a shame about the scarring!

"There were smallpox cases being dealt with in their hospitals, but nothing on a scale such as we have seen here in England. I enquired about the treatments that were offered and was quite startled to find out that they were spending most of their time on preventative measures and not necessarily on the treatment of smallpox once it was contracted. Rather forward thinking, I should say. They were using a concoction manufactured from smallpox pustules and blowing this powdered substance into the nasal passages of their citizens. The court physician, Dr. Maitland has refined this treatment into a procedure we call 'engrafting.' Engrafting is the process of using the live smallpox found in the pus of a smallpox blister, distilling it, and introducing it into the scratched skin of a previously uninfected person, rendering the subject immune to the disease."

"Really, Lady Montagu." One of the surly doctors, who had spoken up vociferously in the refectory that morning, couldn't hold his disdain any longer. "You would have us infect otherwise healthy people by introducing smallpox into their systems? Our wards, which are already bursting at the seams, will be unmanageable in no time!" A stern look from the Chairman brought the desired outcome, and the surgeon shut up, his face still red with indignation.

Lady Montagu continued, never raising her voice and totally in command of herself. "If the smallpox is extracted from the blister of someone suffering mildly from the disease, the recipient may briefly encounter some uncomfortable symptoms. There may be fever and perhaps a headache, but given plenty of water to drink and a good night's sleep, the fortunate person rises the next morning hearty and hale as ever, and immune to the smallpox pathogen." Now she paused for effect. "I have had this procedure performed on both my children by the Embassy surgeon, Charles Maitland. Though both children have been in direct contact with smallpox, neither has contracted the disease."

Another surgeon, more politely this time, broke in with a comment. "That's a rather small sample size, isn't it? Perhaps your children would never have contracted the disease in any case."

"Perhaps not." Lady Montagu responded. "The fact is that the 'engrafting' procedure was innocuous, and it didn't result in any severe consequences."

John smiled wryly at Lady Montagu's ironic use of the word 'innocuous.' His knowledge of Latin informed him that the word inoculation literally meant "to graft" something. He would have to remember to point this out to Treleaven later on.

"Also, I have been successful in appealing to Princess Caroline to have the procedure tested at Newgate Prison, and the results have certainly reinforced my position. Seven prisoners, each bound for execution, were given the option of undergoing engrafting. If they submitted to the experimental procedure, they would be pardoned. All seven of them, as you can imagine, jumped at the opportunity. All seven of them came down with mild smallpox symptoms, recovered quickly, and were subsequently granted their freedom. The results were so dramatic that Princess Caroline has had the procedure administered to her own children." Lady Montagu wrapped up her dissertation. "Gentlemen, I would like you to consider engrafting as a means of preventing the spread of smallpox. Perhaps you could start with family members of smallpox patients who haven't yet contracted the disease? I will be happy to send Doctor Maitland to Guy's at your earliest convenience to show you exactly how the procedure works. Should you wish to read further on the theme, I would also recommend that you read the relevant chapters of my treatise on the subject, published, of course, under a pseudonym. I have left two copies with your chairman. And now, gentlemen, I will take my leave. Thank you for your gracious reception."

A wry smile upon her lips, Lady Montagu stood up (all present rising as was expected), accepted the fashionable coat she had given to the Chairman for safekeeping, and left the chamber.

The Goose & Gander Public House was as cozy as it could possibly be. The weather had turned rather nasty outside, wind blowing and sleet glazing the deserted streets, a harbinger of the snow that would undoubtedly fall sooner rather than later. The hearth was ablaze, and candles lit up the dark corners of the venerable establishment. Holwell, pipe firmly in hand, and Treleaven, fussing over his pint, had finished their meal. Their conversation had been light, touching on their patients' conditions and musing on the weather. Now they got to the topic they were really interested in discussing: Lady Mary Wortley Montagu, who had been with them that afternoon.

"She speaks passionately, does she not?" Treleaven opened the conversation.

"She does. She writes passionately as well. I have read her *Travels to the Ottoman Empire.* The peoples and the cultures that she writes about come alive in her stories. In particular one gets a very unique perspective on the plight of women. She certainly challenges the contemporary social attitudes toward women and the persistent stifling of their intellectual and social growth." John paused for a moment to tamp down his tobacco and relight his precious clay pipe.

"She's a brave woman, then. And I suppose she's able to get away with it because of her station. If she had been born anything but an aristocrat, she'd have been pilloried by now."

John had been thinking much the same thing. "Quite right you are, my dear chap. Quite right you are."

"She certainly puts her coin where her mouth is. I'll give her that. To have her own children engrafted! Can you imagine that? And to persuade Princess Caroline to conduct the experiment at Newgate. She has sturdier man parts than most men I know!" Treleaven took a quaff of his ale, savouring it before firmly placing the mug on the table.

"I do feel sorry for her, though," John added. "Her son is now back from the continent and is raising hell around London. It's one scandal after another."

"I hadn't heard. What's his story then?" Treleaven's interest was piqued.

"After the second time the young scoundrel ran away from Westminster School, his parents sent him away to the continent with a tutor, whose life he made a living hell, by the way. And then, just like that, he reappears in London to terrorize Lady Mary and her husband. He has been leading a life of frivolity and dissolution ever since."

"I know what I'd do," Treleaven ventured. "I'd have him publicly flogged, disinherit him, and throw him out on his ear."

"That's rather unkind, Treleaven. We don't always know what goes on in the private sanctums of a family's world, and neither of us are parents. We don't really know how we'd react in Lord and Lady Montagu's circumstances."

With that, Holwell and Treleaven sat silently for a time, John finishing his pipe and Treleaven his ale. Then it was time to get back to Guy's to conduct their evening rounds.

ALICE

Saturday hadn't come soon enough. John only owned two good jackets, and these he put on one after the other over his broad, muscled frame, each time examining himself in the armoire mirror. Mrs. Holwell, summoned to provide feedback on his sartorial choices, helped him make the final decision and refrained from teasing him, though she sorely wanted to.

"You look splendid, dear! From where did I get such a handsome son?"

At last John stood outside his residence, waiting impatiently for the hackney he had ordered earlier in the morning, and which was now just discernible at the base of St. Dunstan's Hill. Once it arrived, too slowly for his liking, he spryly jumped into the cab and directed the coachman to his friend's Threadneedle Street address. He perched on the edge of the bench, unable to relax back into the padded seat, his brain a-muddle.

Thoughts of Alice had been occupying much of his non-working hours. Each time he had encountered a pretty young woman, he couldn't help but compare her to Alice, with her long flowing locks and her beguiling smile. Alice's beauty always won out. And if he found himself engaged in casual conversation with said young woman, Alice's jaunty attitude and innocent way of smiling with her eyes, made his companion seem somehow duller and less interesting.

John had no doubt that Alice would receive him warmly. In fact, he had great expectations for the next few weeks. The prospect of calling on her, showing her the London sights, and introducing her to his mother invigorated him. Now that his career as a surgeon had been successfully launched and his financial situation was assured, why not pursue Alice more resolutely? John was sure his mother would approve of Alice and that, in turn, his young, Irish beauty would fall in love with his mother. How could she not?

Gracechurch Street turned into Bishopsgate, and then the coach was heading west onto Threadneedle. With his Alice preoccupation, John hadn't given much thought to Alice's brother. He felt a little guilty about leaving James out of his considerations. He had been a good friend since Rotterdam, and John did look forward to catching up with him this afternoon and perhaps sharing a few pints down the road. He did want to know more about the new situation James had procured and looked forward to hearing news of some of their mutual friends in Dublin.

The coach soon pulled up in front of a townhouse in a busy but respectable row of such dwellings. Stone steps reached up to a welcoming entryway. As John's gaze travelled up the brick façade, dormer windows could be seen; two of them flush with the walls and one bowshot. The gable roof sported the ubiquitous London chimney pots, lonely sentinels that carried on for as far as the eye could see. John took a deep breath and stepped out of the cab.

John had thought about this moment ever since receiving Alice's invitation. He had pictured himself walking assuredly through the doors and Alice running toward him, crushing him with a bear-like hug. The kiss would be delicious and prolonged. This is as far as the scene generally played out, and this, as naive young men are wont to disregard, was not the reality of it.

"Glad you're here, old boy!" James greeted John at the door, heartily pumping his hand and welcoming him into the small boot room. "Ailish is in the kitchen getting the tea ready. She's been looking forward to seeing you." James was evidently aware of the attraction between his sister and his elegantly attired friend, though perhaps not quite having determined the depth of it. "Let me take your coat."

The two young men stepped into the narrow parlour, sparsely furnished, but comfortable enough. James loudly gibed to his sister, "Doctor Holwell has arrived. He has deigned to make a house visit. Why don't you come out and say hello?"

Alice appeared under the curved bulkhead of the kitchen entrance. She was dressed neatly in a Saturday frock, nothing fussy, but beautiful in its simplicity. Her hair was tied back in a green ribbon. John admired her for a moment and then walked over and gave her a gentle peck on the cheek. "How wonderful to see you in London. I hope you had a pleasant journey?"

"It was pleasant enough, but for the miserable rain the last two or three days."

"I hope you got the chance to stop in Shrewsbury? Such a charming town."

"Yes, and there was still a little babble about the daring Cadman among the locals. We walked down to Gay Meadow and tried to envisage the marvellous feat you so eloquently laid out for me in your last letter. I still can't believe the scope of the spectacle. It really must have been something to behold."

"That it was, my dear. By the way, I'm not sure what I expected, but it looks like you and James have been settled here for ages. How did you get this place in order in such a short time? You both must have been working like demons."

"Ailish has been a task-master. She's been barking out orders, and I've been running about fulfilling them," James cajoled gently.

"It really hasn't been that large a task." Alice intervened. "The place was more or less furnished when we arrived. We've just been doing some rearranging and fixing it up to our liking." With that, Alice retreated to the kitchen to fetch the tea, and the two men took their places at the table.

Alice bustled about, bringing in cups and saucers, quarter plates, a steaming pot of tea, and a platter of butcher's beef pies. She joined them at the table and for a time, they were silent, contentedly enjoying the repast, and just happy to be together as old friends. When the pies were all but devoured and the tea sipping ensued, they began to chat about friends and family. Alice was keen to hear about John's work at the hospital, and he eagerly obliged. He spoke about his patients, the other surgeons, and finished up with a recounting of the Lady Montagu episode. Both James and Alice listened avidly, occasionally peppering him with further questions.

"Tell me about your East India Company situation." John was intrigued with this new development for James. "We have been bombarded with news of John Company all over the world, and especially their growing trade in India."

"That's where the Rotterdam connection came in handy. My former employer there forwarded my name to the English East India people, who are in a real recruiting frenzy. They didn't even interview me; they just took the letter of recommendation from the Netherlands and forwarded me a promise of contract—with very generous terms, I might add. I took as long in considering the offer as it takes to pull back a pint of Black. I'll be working as a bookkeeper in the receiving department. The office is in Leadenhall Street, just around the corner."

"Da was for it right away, but Ma, she howled like a banshee when she heard." Alice rose to clear the table.

It was time for John to leave, though he really didn't want to. "Listen, the both of you. Why don't you join Mother and me at St. Paul's Cathedral tomorrow? You really should see it now that the post-fire renovations have been completed. It's spectacular! There's a commemorative service at noon we were hoping to attend. Besides, Mother would love a chance to meet you."

Alice looked over at James, her eyes hopeful.

"If you still feel unsettled and think it's too soon to get out, I'll understand. We could see St. Paul's another time." John said this to be polite but hoped against hope that they would agree to accompany Mrs. Holwell and him.

"We'd be delighted to accompany you. But do remember we're novices in London, and we'll have to rely on your guidance as to getting around." James grinned broadly.

"Don't worry about a thing, old chap. You will be our charges tomorrow. We'll call on you at ten o'clock and go on together from there."

Having settled this, James went to collect John's coat, and Alice still stood by the table, tea service in hand and sporting a rather quizzical expression. James came back into the parlour. "I know that look, my dear sister. What's so funny?"

"Don't you think it's a little ironic that good Catholics like us are going to attend a Church of England service? Father Patrick wouldn't be very pleased with us."

James added, "Not to say anything about our parents."

"Oh well. It's nothing that a few paternosters won't remedy." Alice's quick retort, impudent as it was, surprised even her.

They all laughed happily. This is what John loved about Alice. She could be so free-spirited.

It had rained overnight. The roads were wet, and pedestrians scurried out of the way to avoid being splashed by cartwheels thundering through puddles of standing water. The sky was clearing this morning, and the remnants of a few clouds couldn't dampen John's spirits. The hackney stopped in front of the Threadneedle Street townhouse where James and Alice were waiting for them. John and his mother alighted from the cab and introductions were made. Alice curtsied to Mrs. Holwell and then went over and gave her a companionable hug, after which James removed the tam that he was wearing and politely shook hands with her.

"It's a pleasure to meet you, Mrs. Holwell. Your son has told us much about you." Alice's Irish intonations were a delight to the ear.

"And John has spoken much about the two of you as well. Most of it good."

"It's time we were off." John deliberately did not take Mrs. Holwell's bait, and the four of them got into the cab.

"I can't wait to see the cathedral. I've read about it and have seen lots of drawings." Alice directed this at Mrs. Holwell. "It must be quite an imposing edifice!"

"It is, and it has a long and rather interesting history. St. Paul's has existed for eons, but not always in the same form. Sir Christopher Wren was commissioned to restore the church building in 1666, but, as you probably know, The Great Fire of London completed what time and the elements had already begun, and St. Paul's was utterly destroyed, even as Wren's scaffolding was being set up. The building stood derelict and an eyesore for two years before demolition work began. Gunpowder charges were used at first to bring down the structure, and several workers died or were hurt in the process. The neighbourhood was up in arms because of the noise and damage to some of their properties. Battering rams were brought in to finish knocking down the stone walls, and finally in 1675, work began in earnest to rebuild the church. The 'topping off' of the cathedral took place in October 1708, and the building was officially deemed complete by Parliament in 1710. A commemorative service is always held on the last Sunday of October to celebrate the occasion."

"You sound like a guidebook, Mother." John enjoyed teasing Mrs. Holwell.

"Not at all, John." Alice had been listening attentively. "I find it all very fascinating."

John smiled broadly when their eyes met. A warm feeling swept through him. She really was a treasure!

The carriage was making its way up Cheapside. John and Mrs. Holwell peppered the ride with tidbits of history and the pointing out of various landmarks. They enjoyed playing the role of tour guide.

"While your headquarters are in Leadenhall, James, no doubt you will be spending some time in this part of the city. It's the financial heart of London." As John pointed this out and as they made their way further up Cheapside, the buildings became more formal. The carriage soon turned down south, and the vista opened up into a wide-open stretch of trees and grass. The back of St. Paul's Cathedral was clearly visible.

John knocked on the headboard and caught the driver's attention. "This will do."

The driver pulled up and let them off.

They were all standing on the damp grass as the hackney moved along. The quartet was quietly surveying their surroundings, quite in awe of the peaceful gardens and the domed cupola of the cathedral poking its majestic head into the clear Sunday morning sky. A girlish giggle from Alice caught them all by surprise.

"What is it, Ailish? What's so funny?"

Alice pointed to the name of the street prominently displayed on a signpost. "Paternoster Row," she blurted out.

Grinning, John filled his mother in on yesterday's little joke.

"We're a little early for the service. Why don't we take a stroll about?"

It was good to be stretching their legs, and they heartily agreed to John's suggestion. Before long, they were standing in front of a wonderful two-storey arch spanning the street. Narrower arches for pedestrians to make their way through flanked it on either side. Statues of Elizabeth I, James I, Charles I, and Charles II were ensconced in niches on the upper floor.

"What's the significance of this?" asked James.

"This is the Temple Bar Gate. Also designed by Sir Christopher Wren, it's constructed of Portland stone and is meant to mark the entrance to the City of London. It's situated on the ceremonial route used by the royals between The Tower of London and the Palace of Westminster." Mrs. Holwell paused for a moment and turned to her son. "John, why don't you fill them in on the more sinister aspect of it? Tell them what can be seen on occasion at the top of the arch."

"Citizens convicted of treason are often beheaded, their heads placed on pikes on the roof of the arch, ostensibly to act as a deterrent to any who may be considering such a nefarious act. It's always a horrific sight. Many people don't like this use of Wren's gate, but they don't dare speak up too vociferously in case their objections are considered treasonous."

Alice was aghast at this tidbit of information. "I don't like it either, John! And now I don't know how I'm going to get rid of this horrible image ingrained in my brain."

On this more sombre note, the foursome turned back and headed to the cathedral's entrance, whereupon they came across an elderly gentleman speaking to a small crowd. It was clear that he was speaking to them about Wren's architectural vision. They decided to eavesdrop on the monologue.

"As you can imagine, a design of this magnitude has its detractors as well as its supporters. Notice the gilded capitals and the heavy arches?" The gentleman pointed toward the building's classical architraves. "Much like those on St. Peter's Basilica in Rome, aren't they? It smacks of Popery for many Londoners; it's nothing like the many Church of England designs dotting the landscape of Great Britain. There were even those who called for Wren's head, believing that his new design was heretical." The guide took a long breath and continued. "But when most people look up at the splendour of the cathedral, their eyes are filled with unrestrained delight, and they marvel at the beauty and grandeur of it all." The misty-eyed way in which the old gentleman punctuated his thesis made it clear into which camp he fell. The group moved on.

Alice spoke up. "I'm certainly inclined to see it as marvellous and beautiful. Besides, maybe Father Patrick wouldn't mind us going in after all!"

As services went, the commemorative liturgy was as uplifting as it could be in such a dark, vaulted, cavernous space. Before filing out into the welcome sunshine, John steered his party over to Donne's Monument commemorating the celebrated poet and clergyman; it was one of the only monuments to have survived the Great Fire. John was a great admirer of Donne's poetry, and he always took some time in reading the inscriptions on the monument.

"Before the fire, these walls were lined with the tombs of medieval bishops and nobility. Alas, they are no more." John sighed heavily.

Mrs. Holwell turned and whispered in Alice's ear. "That's just fine by me. I can't bear to think of vaults filled with bones and God knows what else in this beautiful building."

"What's that, mother?" John hadn't heard Mrs. Holwell's remark.

"Nothing, dear. Let's find some tea."

Night Terrors

November was flying by. Guy's Hospital was a hotbed of activity. Smallpox cases were up, as were instances of consumption. John spent long hours at work, leaving home before daylight and cabbing home through the damp, foggy evenings. Even then, he managed to find time to spend with Alice. Sundays were especially precious to him, when he, Mrs. Holwell, Alice, and James went traipsing about the city delighting in the kaleidoscope of sights and sounds that was London. All the venues were new to Alice and James, but even John and his mother occasionally discovered something new or rediscovered a spot they hadn't thought about for some time.

Alice taking his arm as they crossed a busy thoroughfare. Alice giving him a flirtatious glance across the aisle of a cab. Alice reaching out to straighten the lapel of his jacket. A peck on the cheek as they said their goodbyes. John revelled in these innocent gestures. When he was with her, his senses seemed to be heightened; the air he was breathing seemed somehow fresher than it had ever been; the world held great promise.

Alice's departure date was too rapidly approaching, and John's brain was an addled mess trying to decide how he should proceed.

"Mother has arranged a dinner party for Saturday, two weeks from now." They had just returned to James's townhouse laden with fruits and vegetables from the new Covent Garden market, and he and Mrs. Holwell were about to head home. "We were hoping that you and James might attend? Mother has also invited one of our neighbours, Mrs. Pattison, and I'm thinking of bringing along one of my colleagues at the hospital."

James turned to Alice, knowing that she would be keen to accept, but stringing her along for the fun of it. "Ailish, that's December 6th. Don't we have something on that evening?"

"Don't talk rubbish, James. Other than you gallivanting off for drinks with some of your new friends on a Saturday evening, we are quite free."

Alice's response was sharp and quite animated, but then her initial annoyance with her brother wore off quickly when she determined that he was just toying with her. "Of course we'll be there, John. What time should we arrive?"

"Seven o'clock would work well. Dinner will be served at eight."

"Won't we be seeing you next weekend?" Alice gave John an alluring smile.

"Unfortunately, I'm going to be somewhat tied up for the next little while. But I'll see you on the 6th."

Mrs. Holwell gave her son a quizzical glance but didn't say anything just then.

On the journey back to St. Dunstan's Hill, John was very quiet. It was obvious to Mrs. Holwell that he was struggling with something, and so she broke into his thoughts.

"What's the matter, John?"

"I should have told you before this, Mother. On Tuesday, the eminent Royal surgeon, Doctor Maitland, is going to be making a visit to Guy's and is going to be instructing us on the engrafting procedure Lady Mary Montagu laid out for us when she visited."

"You told me all about that. But why such a worried look? It sounds like an exciting opportunity. One you've been looking forward to."

John shifted uncomfortably on his bench.

"What I didn't tell you is that I'm to be the guinea pig. Doctor Maitland is going to use the engrafting technique on me while the other surgeons watch."

Mrs. Holwell's face dropped.

"I have decided that if I'm going to be a champion for this practice, it would mean much more if I've submitted to the procedure myself."

"But what does that mean? How sick are you going to be? What if you actually get the smallpox?"

"Based on what I've read and what we heard about from Lady Montagu, I'll likely run a fever for a couple of days and have a smashing headache. By Thursday or Friday, I should be right as rain." John tried to make it sound as benign as possible, but his insides were in turmoil. "I'll spend a couple of nights at the hospital under Doctor Treleaven's care and be home well before the weekend. I'll need to recuperate a little, and so we won't be able to visit with James and Alice."

"I don't like this, John. James and Alice don't know anything about this?" The worry on her face spoke volumes.

"No, I didn't want to worry them unnecessarily."

"Son, I don't know what to say. Maybe you should rethink this rash course of action?"

"It's all arranged, Mother. Try not to worry. Besides, if I keep coming into contact with smallpox, as I invariably will at the hospital, there is a good chance I will contract the full-blown disease, and then who knows what the outcome would be?"

The hackney deposited them in front of their house, and they both made their way inside, acutely sober and deep in thought.

Dr. Maitland, the Royal Surgeon, was impeccably dressed. He took off his surgeon's jacket, ermine-lined for the cold winter months, and handed it to his assistant. He removed silver cufflinks from their buttonholes and the assistant, a dour young man in his twenties, dropped these into a small leather pouch made for this purpose. Grey garters to be seen just over his elbows were now put to use and held the doctor's rolled up sleeves well out of the way. While he was preparing for the engrafting procedure, the eminent doctor lectured to the assembled surgeons, and a few curious members of the Board who had opted to attend. He repeated much of what Lady Montagu had stated in her earlier visit and added more specific aesculapian details.

Dr. Maitland had been an enigmatic presence in the room from the time he had entered. His eyes, recessed behind bushy eyebrows, held everyone's gaze. Even the surgeons, who had been constantly cursing Lady Montagu's medical emissary in the refectory for the past several days, held their tongues and were quite caught up in the matter at hand. After all, it was one thing to deride Lady Montagu, a mere woman, and decidedly not of the medical profession; but Dr. Maitland was a revered member of their order, and they treated him with deference while he was in their company.

John had been lying uncomfortably on the trestle-style operating table.

Dr. Maitland hadn't touched him yet, nevertheless he was already perspiring anxiously with the anticipation of what lay ahead. He looked around at the audience. Dr. Treleaven's was the only comforting face among them. The others, especially the surgeons, seemed to be silently taunting him, as if to say what a fool he was for undergoing this daft procedure, and that it served him right, being the young upstart that he was. He was ashamed to think that he wanted his mother beside him — or, better yet, Alice. He was regretting not having told Alice about what he was about to undertake. What if he didn't recover from the engrafting, but contracted smallpox full on? He hadn't been fair with her.

Before he could entertain any further thoughts along this line, Maitland approached him, wielding a scalpel-like instrument, which he had removed from a canvas pouch that his attendant had made a show of opening up slowly and handing to him. Only this knife had a serrated edge rather than one that was honed and razor-sharp.

He took hold of John's left hand, held it up dramatically to the observers in the room, and pontificated. "In the Ottoman Empire, the smallpox inoculum is harvested from the crusts of pustules formed on the bodies of mildly infected patients. These crusts are then crushed into a powder-like substance and blown through a funnel into the nostrils of the uninfected recipient. Here in England, we have refined the procedure considerably."

All eyes were on the charismatic Maitland. His deep voice resonated in the small chamber. "Rather than blowing smallpox crusts into the recipient's nostrils, we use the pus-like matter taken from the pustules and drop this serum into an open cut or scrape on the recipient's hand, specifically between the thumb and forefinger." Maitland pointed to the location on John's open hand that he still held firmly up in the air. Into the doctor's free hand, the attendant placed a small vial filled with a viscous substance, and this too Maitland raised aloft so the assembly could get a good look at it.

John felt powerless. He was a puppet being manipulated by a willful conjurer.

Maitland now dropped John's hand and let it fall to his side. He pulled a wooden chair up to the gurney, sat down beside John, turning his full attention to the task. A beckoning gesture to the attendant brought him over to stand beside him, and Maitland commanded him to hold John's wrist firmly. He instructed John to splay out his hand and warned him not to flinch.

The scalpel, wielded expertly by Dr. Maitland, sliced sharply into the webbing of the taut flesh between his thumb and forefinger. At first, there was only a mild sensation of something not being quite right, like you would feel upon sustaining a paper cut. But then, when Dr. Maitland excavated the open wound to make it wider, the pain exploded onto him. It was all he could do to keep from crying out and from struggling to free his hand from the assistant's vice-like grip.

Satisfied with the fissure, Dr. Maitland uncorked the vial of serum and, using an eyedropper, syphoned a small quantity of it out of the container. The assistant dabbed at the wound and sponged up the blood that was flowing rather freely. One of the Board members observing the procedure was ashen-faced and had to be escorted out of the operating chamber. Dr. Maitland's focus never wavered. He moved the eyedropper over the red, angry cut and released a few drops of the serum.

The wound was dressed in a fresh plaster and then wrapped like a mummy.

"Under no circumstances should you remove the dressing or attempt to clean the wound." This was addressed to Dr. Treleaven, who Maitland knew would be overseeing John's convalescence. "If the regular pattern plays itself out, the patient will be normal for several hours. By some time in the night, he will feel cold, and he will be very thirsty. Make sure he is kept warm and is given fresh water to drink. A short time after this, he will start to run a fever that could be quite severe and could last for up to twenty-four hours. Apply cold compresses to his forehead. You will know that he is well on the way to recovery when the fever abates. Remove the dressing and apply a light bandage. The wound will begin to itch. This will be rather distressing for the patient, but do not let him scratch at it."

Dr. Treleaven assured Maitland that he understood, and just like that, the procedure was over. Maitland and his assistant gathered up all their paraphernalia and got set to take their departure. Just before they left, John spoke up although his voice was a little shaky.

"Thank you, Dr. Maitland. Please pass on our thanks to Lady Montagu as well."

"You are quite welcome, Holwell. Have someone send a message in a couple of days to let me know how you're doing."

John had been moved to a quiet chamber in the south wing, with the window overlooking the hospital garden. He was feeling good and rather guilty that he was just sitting up in bed when he knew the hospital was a hive of activity and his patients would be looking out for him. Treleaven had arranged a fortifying meal, and John set to it with a ravenous appetite. He scraped up the last of the gravy on his plate with a heel of crusty bread. After all, this would likely be the last full meal he would consume for the next few days.

When his supper tray had been cleared away, he opened up a medical journal he had been reading and tried to focus on it. Before long, his eyelids got heavy, and he nodded off.

Sometime in the middle of the night, he woke up and was sure someone had left the window in his room wide open. It was absolutely freezing. Treleaven had arranged for a night nurse to be stationed just outside his room, and she came in unbidden. John asked her to shut the window and was surprised when she informed him that it was already shut. She reached out for his right hand. It was cold to the touch. She walked over to a side cupboard and brought over a heavy blanket, which she carefully spread over him.

Shivering, he curled himself into a ball under the bed covers and tried to get back to sleep. Finally, when his teeth chattering abated, he knocked off.

Dr. Treleaven came into John's room early the next morning. He could tell that his patient had not had a good night. His skin was pasty, his eyes sallow, and beads of sweat appeared on his forehead as quickly as they were wiped away by the nurse.

"My dear fellow. How are you doing?"

"Not too bad, Treleaven," John replied stoically. "I've been shivering away but sweating profusely at the same time; a very queer feeling. And I can't drink enough water."

"Just as Maitland predicted then, eh? If the good doctor is right, I think you're going to be in a pretty bad state over the next little while."

A 'bad state' didn't even come close to describing the horror of the next few hours. The fever took full hold of him, and he writhed piteously on his bed. He was abysmally cold and then so hot he thought his blankets might spontaneously combust. A headache, the likes of which he had never encountered, set off sparks of light behind his eyes. It was so bad that at one point, he felt like getting up and smashing his cranium against the wall. He lost track of how many times he threw up. So many times that there was no more inside him to be disgorged. The dry heaves left him breathless, and his sternum complained bitterly.

Mercifully, he lost consciousness every so often. But when he did, he was assailed by terrible dreams. Cadman was flying through the air, not attached to his rope. Miriam was standing by a broken body, her pretty frock splattered in blood. Monsters and demons pursued him from all angles. He couldn't escape. His feet were rooted to the ground.

A full day and another night had passed. John only had a fleeting notion that Treleaven and a number of the other surgeons had come to visit him. At one point, he had thought that Alice had come to sit beside him, and then he realized that it had just been the night nurse, confirmed when she blushed profusely the next time that he saw her. What had he said to Alice's apparition? He was afraid to ask.

The fever and chills had let up but now his bandaged hand felt terribly itchy. He wanted to tear the covering off but didn't dare to do it. The itchiness spread across his entire body, and he began scratching himself all over. His skin would have been raw and full of welts had not Treleaven come in good time and threatened that he would tie up his hands if he continued. John was in agony. It felt like bloodworms were crawling across his body just under the skin. He didn't know if he could bear it for long.

A nurse was instructed to give him a strong dose of laudanum, and he was finally able to sleep fitfully.

Friday morning dawned brightly, and John was able with Treleaven's help to get out of bed. He drank a full tumbler of cold water and walked over to the window gazing raptly at the gardens. It was like he was seeing the shrubs and trees for the first time. A raven perched disinterestedly on the garden wall and John marvelled at the bird's glossy wings and its steely eyes. He sighed deeply. He had a new lease on life, and he was going to make the most of it.

A Proposal

John spent the weekend and a few more days at home recuperating. Mrs. Holwell fussed and bothered over him so much that it was almost a relief to be getting back to work. He didn't feel much worse for wear. A little lighter, perhaps, and more tired than usual at the end of each day. Recovering so quickly after the engrafting procedure was a vindication of sorts, and he made himself visible in the refectory as a constant reminder to the other surgeons. Their curmudgeonly 'harrumphing' had abated significantly.

Mrs. Holwell had baked a lemon tart for Dr. Treleaven, a little thank you for helping him through his ordeal. The two doctors sat in the refectory on Thursday afternoon, drinking their tea and partaking of the tart.

"That couldn't have gone much better, Holwell, could it have?"

"It's the worst headache I've ever had. I wouldn't want to go through that again. But all's well that ends well, I suppose." As John responded to Treleaven's comment, he reflectively scratched at the healing wound on his left hand.

"Tut, tut," Treleaven admonished him. "By the way, you don't seem to have any pox marks on your face. Are there any on other parts of your body?"

"Only a few on my chest. They can be very itchy, but I've been applying a salve to them, and the relief lasts longer each time."

A few of them would likely last for as long as he was alive, but better that than contracting the disease head on. It was almost time to get back to their rounds.

"Treleaven, don't forget dinner on Saturday. Arrive about seven if you can. I'm going to stay home that day and help Mother with the preparations."

"Remind me again who will be in attendance." Treleaven had stood up and was about to leave.

"Alice and James, who I've spoken to you about, and Mrs. Pattison, our neighbour. You, Mother, and I."

"Is there anything I can bring along?"

"Only your charming wit."

"Well, then! I'll be coming empty-handed." Treleaven chuckled off to his rounds.

"You're a widow?" Dr. Treleaven, sitting stoically across from Mrs. Pattison and wondering why he had been invited to this dinner — to make it an even number, he supposed — now became far more attentive. He sat up a little taller in his chair and paid closer attention to the smart looking, middle-aged lady he had to this time found handsome but only mildly amusing.

"Yes, Charles has been gone these two and a half years. Dropped dead in the middle of the road, poor chap. They said he must have had a defective heart."

"So sorry to hear that, Mrs. Pattison. My condolences."

"Thanks for saying so, Doctor. But I've had my time to grieve, and Charles's ghost doesn't haunt me as often as it was wont to do. Anyway, enough of all that. Tell me about your practice."

Dinner was in full swing. John was pleased at how the evening was progressing. Mrs. Holwell had outdone herself. After a creamy leek soup, she had served a terrine of quail served with butternut squash and an array of other late fall vegetables. A flaming pudding was now ablaze at the centre of the table. Alice clapped her hands in glee, and all the other diners vociferously showed their appreciation. The serving maid removed the pudding once the skittish flames had disappeared. She would return shortly with slices of pudding neatly displayed on dainty china plates.

John glanced contentedly about the table. Dr. Treleaven and Mrs. Pattison were getting along famously and were engaged in a lively conversation, the good doctor more animated than John had seen him in a long time. His mother was chatting gaily with Alice. James was the only one of the guests who seemed a bit reticent — introspective, in fact. He had hardly said a word all evening. John would have to draw him aside to see what was going on with his friend.

The pudding came out and conversations were lulled as they devoured the festive treat.

"What do you put in your pudding, Mrs. Holwell? It's the best I've ever had!" Alice was savouring the last little bite on her dessert fork.

"It's an old family recipe, my dear. Someday, perhaps I'll share the whole process with you. Suffice it to say that it is comprised of mutton, shallots, fortified wine, a mixture of spices, and plenty of dried fruit. A little brandy poured over the whole pudding allows one to set it alight."

Doctor Treleaven chimed in. "Bravo, Mrs. Holwell. It is a veritable triumph!"

The maid was efficiently removing the dessert plates and the party had fallen into some more conversation. Tea would be served soon. John asked Alice to tell them about how she had spent the last few days, and she regaled them with an account of a long day walking down to the Thames with James. She described in great detail the sights, sounds, and smells of the London streets and the waterway. She couldn't get over the contrasts they had observed. The wide roadways lined with stately trees and then the narrow, dirty lanes with musty leaves scudding about in the breeze, and smells of stale and rotting vegetation, not to say anything of the teeming masses of unwashed humanity. A mist had hovered over the Thames, and this had reminded her of Dublin and the Liffey River winding its way through the heart of it.

Tea was served, and now it was Alice's turn to enquire about John's past few days.

"You were a little mysterious about why you couldn't join us last weekend, John. Can you share with us what you were up to?"

Mrs. Holwell turned to John, alarm showing in her eyes.

"I feel badly that I didn't tell you my plans earlier on. But I was afraid you'd be overly anxious for me." And John was off, relating the entire episode of Dr. John Holwell, guinea pig, leaving nothing out. The look on the faces of Alice and James was nothing short of startling. Alice was especially ashen, and a few tears escaped her pretty eyes. Even Mrs. Pattison was affected by the unexpected tale.

"You do seem a little more drawn-out than before. Are you sure you've recovered fully?"

"Quite, my dear Alice. The procedure has been such a success that I'm going to recommend it to all of my family and friends, and, of course, to most of my patients."

"Not on my bloody life." James was quick to respond.

"Never mind that for now. I'll have plenty of time to get you used to the idea now that you're in London."

An odd look of pain flickered across James's brow, and John was now quite certain that something was amiss with him.

"Please excuse me for a few minutes, everyone. I'm going to stretch my legs after that delightful dinner and take a puff on my pipe outdoors. James, would you care to join me for a bit?"

"I'll come out for a stroll, but I daresay I won't share your pipe."

This drew a few chuckles from the rest of the group, and the two men got up and headed to the anteroom to get their jackets.

"You're what?" John stopped dead in his tracks. He spluttered and choked as the tobacco he had been swilling about his mouth now inadvertently ended up in his lungs.

"I'm going to India."

"Why? When?" John was so flustered that he didn't know which questions to ask and which he wanted James to reply to first.

"John Company has been recruiting bright young entrepreneurial fellows to go to India and manage their trade there. Fortunes can be made overnight for enterprising men, and I intend to be part of it all. My superiors have encouraged me to take advantage of the opportunity. There will be a sailing in early February."

John didn't know how to respond, and so he started walking again.

James had quickly and firmly bleated out his news, but now his voice changed. He was quieter and more conspiratorial. "I spoke to the recruiting officer about you."

John stopped walking again.

"When I told him that you were a surgeon, his eyes lit up instantly. He said that while John Company doesn't hire surgeons, the military doctor in Fort William recently retired and was looking to sail back to England. When the recruiter was in Calcutta a few weeks ago, there had been talk in the military command about searching for a new medical recruit. John, you'd basically be a shoo-in if you wanted to go. Think about it, man. We could conquer India together! And…"

"Whoa! Hold on a minute." James was picking up the pace again. He was in the middle of waxing eloquent about the virtues of India, a land of spices and exotic animals and treasures beyond imagining. "You sound like a recruitment pamphlet. Besides, I've just embarked on a new career with Guy's. I can't just drop everything and leave."

James, perhaps regretting his overly exuberant approach, became more tactful. "Sorry, old chap. I'm just so excited about this prospect, but I know it's a lot to drop on you all at once. All I ask is that you'll consider it. I'd love to have you along. Just like in the old days."

"Have you told Alice about this, or your parents?"

The two men had turned about and were heading back to the house.

"Not yet. I still have to think about how to do that."

"I'm sure they'll be thrilled." The sarcasm in John's voice couldn't be missed.

The dinner party was reaching a successful conclusion. John volunteered to go outside to hail a cab for his two friends. Alice suggested that she accompany him. While harbouring James's secret would make it awkward for him to be around Alice, he still welcomed her company.

The two of them stood in front of the gas lamp, peering off into the distance.

"What a delightful dinner, John. Your mother is so gracious and Dr. Treleaven seems like such a good friend."

"He is indeed. And you, Alice. You looked like a dream this evening in your green dress. Green is a perfect colour for you."

He casually took her hand in his and silently hoped no cabs would come in sight for a little while. A gentle squeeze from her soft hands sent a small electric shock through his system, and he knew that his feelings toward Alice were reciprocated.

"I know how much you love the theatre. The Theatre Royal is hosting its Grand Opening tomorrow in Covent Garden, and William Congreve's *The Way of the World* is going to be its very first production. As it happens, the Lady Mary Montagu has sent me an invitation to come along and to bring a friend if I like. I know it's rather short notice, and you're probably in the middle of getting ready for your return to Dublin, but I'm hoping you'll be my companion tomorrow. It is going to be an epic event, and anybody who's anybody in London will be there."

Alice turned toward John, her eyes lighting up. "I don't know much about the play, but I've seen the beautiful marquee in front of the new theatre in Covent Garden. Of course, I'd like to go."

"What about James? Will he be okay with it?"

"I love James dearly, but the oaf doesn't have a cultural bone in his body. He'd rather be off carousing with his pals."

"You misunderstand me. I know James wouldn't enjoy an afternoon at the theatre. I meant to ask whether he would be okay with me taking you unaccompanied?"

"He won't have a choice, John. Leave it to me. I'll speak to him about it on our way home."

A cab came into hailing range, and John stepped onto Dunstan Hill Road.

"Great then. I'll call for you at 1:00 p.m. tomorrow."

James and Alice had departed. Mrs. Pattison had also taken her leave and now John was left with Dr. Treleaven and his mother, who began busying herself with the maid removing the tureens from the sideboard.

"You seemed to hit it off with Mrs. Pattison, Treleaven." It was a statement more than a question.

"Yes, a charming lady. Now I know why you invited me along, you young scoundrel. I did have a wonderful evening."

"Maybe you could call on her sometime?" John's success with Alice gave him the impetus to put forward this comment.

"Maybe, dear fellow. We'll see."

THE WAY OF THE WORLD

Covent Garden was abuzz with activity. Though almost none of the assemblage could afford to grace the inside of the Royal Theatre on this, its Grand Opening, the crowd was there for the panoply. Hawkers and sellers were in fine form, and pickpockets had been waiting weeks for this event. John Rich, actor-manager of The Dukes Company, could always be relied on for colourful antics and bombastic spectacles. What would he do to inaugurate his new building? Indeed, what would the good citizens of the town be wagging about over their ale and their tea on the long, dark December evenings?

The boisterous crowd was held back by heavy ropes and could only attempt to crush up to the front. As for those who weren't successful, they had to stand on their tiptoes or, as some of the more enterprising lads had done, find a perch on a stone plinth or other protuberance on one of the surrounding buildings. Occasionally, a roar would go up in the crowd when they spotted some member of the nobility or some well-heeled dignitary alighting from a cab, making his way into the Royal Theatre and wearing a well-dressed lady on his arm.

It was a cool, clear Sunday afternoon. The weather gods were smiling on the City of London this auspicious December 7th, and John and Alice revelled in their ride to Covent Garden. Alice's jaw dropped when she saw the crowds.

"I'm glad I'm not a noblewoman or a celebrity. I don't think I'd enjoy having to 'make an entrance' at every function I attended. I find this quite daunting, don't you?"

"It would be rather disconcerting, but I think I'll enjoy it just this once. It's not every day one gets an invitation to be part of such a grand event by a member of the royal establishment!"

"So why did The Lady Montagu give you this invitation? I assume it has something to do with the smallpox procedure?"

"Yes, she has been very grateful to see the engrafting procedure being championed by a city doctor, and especially one who has undergone the procedure himself. She was flattered that I had read her treatise on the subject and that I hadn't condescended to her like so many others of my profession had."

Once deposited at the entrance to the theatre, John invited Alice to take his arm, and they happily made their way into John Rich's spectacular thespian temple.

Upon surrendering the gilt-edged invitation to a rather gaunt and stern-looking usher, his demeanour softened immediately, and John and Alice were treated quite deferentially as they were escorted to the royal box. Rich tapestries, velvets, and chintz were everywhere in abundance, and the awe-struck young couple drank in the majestic interior as they walked reverently down the centre aisle. Once they reached the orchestra pit directly in front of, and partially underneath, the proscenium stage, they were ushered to the right, 'stage left' as John rather pedantically informed Alice, and were taken through a heavily brocaded curtain and up a small flight of stairs to the Royal Opera box. Of course, they didn't use the private entrance reserved for the royal patrons. That was an entrance from the side street that afforded privacy and allowed the King and/or his compatriots to enter the theatre unmolested.

The Royal Box was a two-tiered affair, with cushioned chairs and ornate coffee tables, now laden with vases of freshly cut flowers scattered on both levels. John discreetly pressed a coin into the usher's hand. He pointed them to chairs on the upper level and then quietly slipped out. John and Alice found themselves quite alone.

"Where's the Lady Montagu?" asked Alice.

"The royal patrons are generally the last to arrive. And, interestingly enough, by convention, the proceedings will not get under way until they have arrived and have been comfortably seated. Programs have been known to be delayed by upwards of an hour because, as you know, the royals are guided by their own whims and not tied to the schedules of mere mortals."

Alice smiled. "They can take as long as they'd like today. I'm thoroughly enjoying every minute of this experience!"

From their perch on the second tier of the royal box, they had an unimpeded view of the stage and the sprawling theatre complex. Delighting in the privacy of their box, they sat holding hands and watching the guests being ushered to their seats.

"It's quite the pageant, isn't it John? The men look so stately in their theatre jackets and top hats, and the women—why, they're divine!"

"Not as divine as you, dear Alice. You put them all to shame." John took the liberty of kissing her on the cheek.

Alice blushed.

"But there aren't any children. Why is that, John? In Dublin people often take their children to the theatre."

"*The Way of the World*, from the reading I've done about it, would not be suitable for children. William Congreve's plot is rife with illicit dalliances, cuckolded husbands, infidelity, and deception. It's also chock-full of financial and legal jargon, not really fodder for children."

"Then it's a rather risky enterprise for John Rich, don't you think? The King is not very fond of the theatre in the first place, so I'm led to understand, and he's definitely strait-laced."

"You're absolutely right about that. It's one reason King William will not be attending the performance himself. He's cut from a very different cloth than Charles was. Charles couldn't get enough of gaiety and frivolity! Court proceedings were so much more fun in his day, I'm told. No doubt that after this performance, depending on how the script is interpreted by Mr. Rich, there might be a lot of wailing and gnashing of teeth by the genteel public, who, while titillated to the core, will still frown outwardly and wag their fingers in sympathy with good King William, but once they get home, they'll romp naked about their bed chambers, flirting and cooing like Mirabell and Millament, the two protagonists of this afternoon's offering."

"Really, John. You're making me blush." Alice squeezed John's hand rather fervently. "But now I'm quite looking forward to the matter of the play!"

John was about to respond when the curtains to their right flung apart, and the Lady Montagu and her entourage entered the royal box. John and Alice sprang to their feet. There was no doubt as to who was in charge. Lady Montagu nodded politely in their direction, but then immediately set to organizing her group. She and her husband, the Ottoman Ambassador, took possession of the two central seats on the lower level. Her son, or so John surmised, stood beside his mother to the left. On the ambassador's right, an elderly dowager took up her post, rigid and brittle, perched uncomfortably on the front edge of her chair. Two female attendants and a young man, presumably a footman, came up the stairs to join John and Alice on the second tier.

Once everyone was in their allotted seats Lady Montagu turned to greet John and Alice and to make introductions. John bowed to Lady Montagu and to the other dignitaries seated below him and Alice curtsied gracefully. The pleasantries having been dispensed with Lady Montagu took her seat and all those standing now sat down. The Royal Box was now occupied, and the program could begin.

And so, it did. The double doors at the entrance to the theatre were thrown open violently, and Mr. Rich was paraded in on the shoulders of some of the players. In fact, the whole entourage came tumbling in, dancing, singing, and playing on their timbrels, fifes, and drums. A more colourful parade couldn't be imagined. Once Mr. Rich was deposited on the stage and the players and the musicians had sidled into the wings or disappeared into the orchestra pit, John Rich asked for silence, and he eventually succeeded in obtaining it. A long speech ensued in which the actor-manager of the Dukes Company thanked his patron, the King, for funding this wonderful new edifice and went on to thank his many other supporters. He began waxing eloquent about the state of the theatre in England, and perhaps like many other accomplished men of the theatre, went on a bit too long, only curtailing his speech when some disgruntled hissing and booing could be discerned emanating from the audience. He exited stage right in reluctant acquiescence with an ostentatious flourish of his feathered cap.

As far as John could tell the interlude was positioned somewhere after the third act. Lady Montagu took a sip of her wine, courtesy of Mr. Rich, and generously shared the bottle with each of the Royal Box guests. She stretched her legs and turned her attention to the young couple on the second tier.

"What do you make of the play so far?"

"The acting, the costumes, and the scenery are well done." John decided to be candid with Lady Montagu. "However, the plot is a convoluted mess. I can't keep track of who is having an affair with whom, or who once had an affair with whom! And there are inconsistencies in the characters, don't you think? Mrs. Wishfort, on the one hand, seems to be a very bitter, but astute woman; yet she also seems easily manipulated by Mirabell. And you, Lady Montagu, how are you enjoying the play?"

"I must say that I agree with you on the whole, Doctor. But I do see some very refreshing elements. For instance, have you noticed that there are twelve main characters in the play, six men and six women? And the women aren't just small players in the drama; in fact, they have prominent speaking roles. My hat goes off to William Congreve. His script is daring, and I dare say that it is moving the boundaries of theatre forward." Lady Montagu lifted up her wine glass and toasted the playwright. "To William Congreve." They all raised their glasses.

"And you, young Ailish. What does our Dubliner have to say about the play?"

John turned to Alice with a nervous glance and waited to see how she would respond. He needn't have worried. Alice curtsied to Lady Montagu and provided her commentary in a strong and playful manner. "I particularly enjoyed the scene in St. James Park where Mrs. Fainall and Mrs. Marwood are speaking about the loathsomeness of men. I thought they hit the mark rather spot on, don't you Lady Montagu?" The two women shared a conspiratorial smile. Alice prodded John gently in the ribs. John was impressed with Alice's boldness and was proud of how she was navigating this daunting experience, which even certain members of the nobility would have been cowed at.

The last half of the production was about to begin. A few last-minute stragglers rushed to return to their seats, and a hush fell as the ushers went through the theatre extinguishing the gas lamps.

The ruse to trick Mrs. Wishfort into agreeing to the marriage of Mirabell and Millament, thereby assuring Mirabell of Millament's £6,000 dowry, was successfully concluded. Act five focused on the two lovers. Mirabell and Millament, obviously smitten with each other, played coy and each took turns detailing the conditions under which they would agree to the marriage. The playing out of this prenuptial agreement was brilliantly conceived, the prosaic subtext of the financial and legal terms contrasting deliciously with the underlying sexual tension between the two. The romantics in the crowd were entranced, as were the solicitors and barristers. When the curtain fell, the theatre erupted in a swell of adulation and the players made their curtain call to a standing ovation.

It was late afternoon when John and Alice exited from the theatre, and the December dusk was almost upon them.

"Shall we have some supper hereabouts or would you prefer to be escorted home?"

Lady Montegu had sent up a bottle of the Rhenish wine they had tasted at the interlude, and this they had happily consumed over the last couple of acts. Feeling the effects of the alcohol, Alice thought it better that she be taken home. She absolutely didn't want to look the fool in public.

"I am hungry, though, and I'm sure you are, John. There are some provisions in the larder back at James' place. I can put something together for us there."

"Will James be at home?"

"No, he says I'm not to expect him until 11:00 p.m. at the earliest. An East India Company meeting, or something. When I asked him why they would hold a meeting on a Sunday night, he was very cryptic about it. In fact, he's been acting very strange lately, like he's harbouring a big secret or something. I'm a little worried about him."

"I'm sure whatever it is, he'll get it off his chest soon." John spoke in a conciliatory tone, though he knew full well what James's secret was and how devastating it would be for Alice and the rest of her family in Dublin. Not only that, but John had begun to entertain James's proposal concerning himself. Not earnestly, but whimsically, he kept telling himself. Nevertheless, the blowflies of his conscience were now buzzing about his head.

John removed his jacket and placed it gently over Alice's shoulders as they dismounted from the cab and walked toward the townhouse. They hadn't spoken at all during the ride home, content to just snuggle into each other, the wine and the salacious nature of the play working its amatory effect. Alice had dozed off briefly, and John had delighted in the soft fragrance of her hair resting against his cheek. He had so wanted to crush Alice into him and kiss her roundly on her lips but had thought better of it.

What happened over the course of the next couple of hours remained a blur in John's mind for a long time afterward. As soon as they had crossed the threshold into the front parlour, John had started to say how sad he was that Alice would be heading back to Dublin in a couple of days. Alice muffled him with a strong, sensuous kiss and drew him over to the sofa. John was taken aback but allowed Alice to pull him close to her. They stayed wrapped in each other's arms for a long, blissful time, not wanting the evening to come to an end.

John whispered, "I'm falling in love with you, Ailish."

Alice's soft and dreamy kiss was all John needed by way of response.

"James should be coming home any time now. We'd better rouse ourselves and have something to eat." Alice rolled away from him, sidled off the sofa, and righted herself. Before long, they were both sitting across from each other at the dining table devouring crusty bread and cheese.

They lingered over their tea, neither of them wanting the evening to end.

"I'd better be off before James gets home. Please pass on my best wishes." John retrieved his jacket and headed for the door.

"Write to me often, my love, and I'll write to you." Alice followed him to the foyer.

"Of course I will, Alice. I can't wait till I see you again. Have a good trip home. Give your family my love." And with a kiss, he walked sadly out of the townhouse.

Alice stood at the window a long while watching John make his way to the end of the lane so he could hail a cab back to St. Dunstan's Hill.

MORE PROPOSALS

John and James left Threadneedle Road and walked toward Leadenhall, where the English East India Company offices were located. The air was brisk with the promise of snow later in the day, and the two men were well muffled and mittened. An old clerk met them at the entrance to the recruiting office, took their names, opened the office door, and called out to someone hidden behind a desk in the small, dimly lit room.

"Master James O'Connor and Dr. John Holwell to see you, sir."

The two men were ushered into the room, and the door closed behind them. James was surprised to see that Mr. Chaplin himself was seated behind the desk. Sitting in an armchair just off to the side was a military officer.

"Welcome, gentlemen. Please take a seat." Mr. Chaplin pointed to two wooden chairs arranged in front of him. "I'm Mr. Chaplin, manager of the East India Company, and this is Captain Minchin, commander of the garrison at Fort William, in Calcutta."

The men shook hands all round, and John and James took their seats.

"Before we get to the matter at hand, I'd like to take this opportunity to commend you, Mr. O'Connor, for the fine work you've been doing in the short time you've been with us. Your supervisor has reported that you are a hard-working young man and a quick study, and that you are a fine addition to our East India enterprise. They will miss you here, but your skills and dedication will serve all of us well in Calcutta, where we have a thriving outpost. Now, as to your friend, Dr. John Holwell, he has asked to be interviewed for a post as a military surgeon. Hence, Captain Minchin is present to conduct the interview. You and I will now leave the two of them so they can carry on their business."

With that Mr. Chaplin and James stood up and exited the room.

A stiff military man, Captain Minchin was direct and to the point. "Your dossier, Dr. Holwell, is very impressive for a man of your fledgling years.

And your references, the administrator of Guy's hospital, Dr. Andrew Treleaven, and the Lady Mary Wortley Montagu have nothing but praise for your skills as a surgeon and your character. Indeed, their admiration for you is profuse. Now, tell me a little about yourself."

John, who had been nervous about this interview, settled in and spent a few minutes talking about himself. Beyond the mundane biographical information, John also spoke of his love of adventure and his desire for travel. Captain Minchin didn't interrupt him, but just scribbled notes in a small notebook.

"And what would my duties be, Captain?" John capped off his monologue with a question.

"As a military surgeon, you would immediately hold an officer's rank and have all the privileges that entails. You would be responsible for the health and wellbeing of our soldiers, as well as serving as a doctor to the prominent East India Company families that conduct their business in Calcutta. You would have an office in Fort William, and you would be responsible for supervising the other medical staff, such as nurses and one or two junior medics in the infirmary."

"If I'm successful in this endeavour, when would I be departing to begin my post?"

"We'll be sailing in early February. That would give you just over a month to get your affairs in order here. And…" Minchin paused for effect. "I'm pleased to say that the post is yours if you want it."

"When do you need my answer?" John's stomach was now in a knot, and he felt faint. This was all happening much too quickly.

"We'll need to know by Christmas. If your answer is no, then we'll have to scramble to find someone else by the time we leave."

"Then I'll let you know within a fortnight."

The interview now over, John strode out of the room to look for James and was happy to be outside in the cold afternoon gloom.

"He offered me the position, James. Just like that. I would have thought there would be a lot more competition for the position." John was striding purposefully toward the Angry Goose, a Leadenhall pub that James spoke highly of.

"While we were out of the room, Mr. Chaplin did tell me there had been a number of enquiries about the medical surgery position, and several of those applicants had been successful in being granted an interview. Congratulations, my man. Captain Minchin must have been very impressed by you!"

"Well, I suppose the references I provided helped in that regard, and no doubt Lady Montagu's letter played some role as well."

"So, did you accept the post?"

"I have two weeks to provide my response. I have a lot of thinking to do between now and then. Mother is going to be very upset. And then there's Alice. You know how devastated she was when you told her your plans! She'll be apoplectic should I decide to follow suit."

The Angry Goose was filling up at this hour, and John and James were lucky to find a small shelf they could prop up against with their mugs of ale. "Of course, the hospital administrators won't be pleased either." John had to shout over the din of the alehouse. "Having asked Mr. Randolph, the chief administrator, for a letter of reference has already given him a heads-up that I'm exploring other opportunities. No doubt he's shared this information with the others, including the venerable Thomas Guy."

"Perhaps, John. But you're so well thought of that I don't suppose they'd thwart your ambitions." James took a long draw from his mug, relishing the cool, hoppy liquid.

"Listen, James." John nervously approached the next topic he wanted to discuss with his friend. "You know how close your sister and I have become. Do you think she'd agree to marry me should I propose to her? Especially if I coupled the proposal with an invitation to come live with us in India?"

James almost choked on his ale. Numbskull that he was, he hadn't anticipated this line of questioning. "Codswallop, John. That's a question and a half!"

"I don't think I could bear being so far away from her. Dublin's far enough away from London as it is." His tone was perhaps more anguished than he had intended. "Besides, I have a mind to ask Mother if she'll follow up in a year or so and join me in India. There wouldn't be anything for her here. She and Alice would be good company for each other."

"I truly don't know how she'll respond, John. You'll have to write to her and ask. And the sooner the better. She'll barely have time to digest your letter before having to reply." The shock James had been subjected to had now diminished, and he became reflective. "Ailish in India, eh? Well, she is a free-spirited one and made of pretty stern mettle, there's no mistaking it." He buried his face in his mug and drained it to the lees. "What say you to another pint, brother?"

Dearest Alice,

I have started this epistle in so many different ways, not knowing how I should put my thoughts to paper, that I am now down to my last few sheets of vellum, the others balled up and strewn on the floor around me. My writing room floor is starting to look like the grounds of Covent Garden Market just before closing.

Let me begin by wishing you and your family a Merry Christmas. No doubt your younger sisters and your cousins are giddy with anticipation of the season, and your mother is busy in the kitchen preparing all those delightful confections I've heard James speak of.

We haven't had the opportunity to speak since you were here last, and since James shocked you all with his plan to deploy to India. I'm afraid I have a petard of my own to drop on you. I have been invited to assume the role of military surgeon in Fort William, the English outpost in Calcutta. After much deliberation, and with support of my mother and of my colleagues at the hospital, I have decided to accept the posting. My biggest regret is that you have not been here to work through this with me.

What has led me to this decision? To begin with, you know that I have always had a thirst for adventure. What could be more adventurous than sailing to an exotic land, coming into contact with flora and fauna that one has only read about, hearing the babble of strange languages uttered by people dressed in colourful and unconventional garb?

As a man of science and medicine, I also want to go with an open mind and learn some of the mysteries of the eastern medical tradition. The

Lady Montagu has convinced me that ours isn't the only way of doing things, that we have as much to learn from others as we have to share with them.

And then there's your brother. Wouldn't you all feel better knowing that James isn't alone in his enterprise, that he has a stalwart friend and confidant, one that can help to keep him safe (and grounded, I daresay)?

My darling Alice, I hope that you will give earnest consideration to what I'm about to say next. There isn't a day that goes by that I don't think of you. I yearn to be near you, to hear the lilt of your voice, to feel the gentle pressure of your soft hands in mine, to languish in the sight of your lovely green eyes. In short, I would like you to be my wife.

I understand that this proposal comes at an awkward time and in a rather awkward manner. But here's what I propose. I will travel to India, assume my post, and prepare to make a home there for us. In just over a year's time, I'll send for you. My mother has already agreed to pick up roots and relocate to India, and she'll accompany you on the journey. We can get married shortly after you arrive. You will be a wonderful companion for her on the voyage, and you can both help each other to adapt to your new home in India. She already loves you and would be ecstatic if you were to become her new daughter.

There it is, Alice. I realize that what I'm asking of you is monumental. I can only hope and pray that you'll accept me as your husband and will accompany me to a far-off and alien land. I promise you that if you are not happy there, I will return with you to England, and we can make a life here. I will always love you and strive to make you happy.

Write and let me know your thoughts. Unfortunately, our departure is set for early February, and so there isn't much time to have these things settled. Please say hello to your family and wish them all the best.

With all my love,
    John

BOOK TWO

A Fair Wind
February 1733

Metal scraping on wood. As tightly bound as the canon's runners were fixed to the floorboards, there was still enough play in them that they protested each time the ship yawed but a little. John Zephaniah Holwell, a newly commissioned medical officer, wasn't sure he'd get used to this unnerving sound. From accounts he'd read of voyages to India and from some of the other officers he'd spoken with who had made this journey before, he was led to believe that it could last anywhere from four to six months; so, get used to it he must! Brittania, a 560-ton, thirty-gun, three-masted Merchantman, had departed on February fourth and would arrive in Calcutta, God willing, sometime in June or early July, with its ninety-nine crew members and assorted passengers.

John lay quietly on his bunk staring at the low ceiling above him. The beams were large and well oiled, and a dusky light coming through the transom stern light played over the wardroom, casting fanciful shadows around his work desk, the operating slab perched on empty rum barrels, slop buckets in the corner, and James's hammock suspended across from the black metal canon. The Wardroom on an East India Merchantman, just abaft the mizzenmast, was typically assigned to volunteers and Land Officers. It was an oblong chamber that could accommodate six to eight men. In this case, it had been turned over to Chief Medical Officer Holwell to use as his bedchambers and his surgery. There was some turning up of eyebrows when he insisted that James O'Connor, private volunteer, be allowed to bunk in with him, but John was able to convince the captain lieutenant, a burly man with imposing sideburns, that James would be his medical assistant, and it was only fitting that he be in close proximity to him. John was learning quickly that life aboard ship was highly ordered, and that each person had his assigned place according to rank and/or station.

"Wake up, James! The ship's bell rang some time ago. Your breakfast will be getting cold. I'll see you on deck in a while." John walked over to his friend's cot and chucked him on the shoulder. The ship was listing to port, and John had to make an adjustment to his gait so he wouldn't topple over or go slamming into the walls of the cabin. Prevailing westerly winds coming across the Atlantic would make certain that this "listing to port" would last until they had reached the Western Sahara and the Northeast Trade Winds they'd pick up there.

John gingerly negotiated one tier of the Poop Deck gangway and made his way to the Coach Room, a long, narrow chamber amidships that served as an Officer's Mess Hall and a War-Room when that was necessary. He greeted several of the officers and received handshakes and warm smiles all around. It wasn't often that sailing vessels had medical officers of John's stature on board, and this made the officers and crew much more comfortable. On many vessels, a sailmaker with passable sewing skills would have done double duty as a surgeon, and many of the crew had angry, nasty scars to show for it.

A plate of tumbled eggs was set in front of him by a serving boy, and John eagerly tucked into it. This concoction of scrambled eggs, beans, and leeks was surprisingly tasty!

"Holwell, I'm impressed." John looked across the solid wooden table at Master Corporal Timms. "Three days at sea in this bucket and you still have an appetite!"

"Don't worry, Timms. We'll see what his appetite is like when we hit the equator and stall in the Doldrums, bobbing around like a cork!" Lieutenant Eakin shared a conspiratorial smile with Timms. "And then there's the cauldron off the Horn!"

Breakfast over, John made his way with the others further up the gangway and slipped out on to the Poop Deck, which was occupied by the helmsman and a few crewmembers controlling the sheets for the yards and sails of the main and mizzenmasts. This perch at the stern was the highest point of the deck and made for a great observation post. The crew tolerated the officers but weren't terribly friendly, especially when the landlubbers inadvertently got underfoot. John learned to stay out of their way, and he enjoyed leaning against the taffrail and peering out over the ocean, watching the gulls lazily following the ship's wake. He let the salty breeze wash over him, and he felt more alive than he had felt in a long time. In a while, he would scramble down to the quarterdeck and join James, who would have breakfasted with the other East India volunteers and a few private citizens making their way to India to join their families there. They would mill about relishing their time in the fresh, salty air and chat idly about the journey, or they would wax lyrical about the wondrous world they would encounter in India, and sometimes they would let their sentimental selves get the better of them and speak nostalgically about loved ones left behind or favourite haunts in their homeland.

James was chatting up a young woman, one of the very few on board, when John arrived on the quarterdeck. He decided not to interrupt their conversation and instead ambled over to a small group of civilians with whom he exchanged pleasantries. He learned that most of them were junior clerks with John Company, bound on making their fortunes in the spice trade. None of them knew what that enterprise would entail; nevertheless, they were full of vim and vigour and harboured some rather naive notions of what life was going to be like for them. John checked himself and had to smile at the irony of the situation. Here he was, passing silent judgment on these poor lads when he himself didn't have a clue about what he was tumbling headlong into. And there was courage here, no doubt. The sort of courage he had witnessed in Robert Cadman, the young steeplejack he had met in Shrewsbury. John found himself reminiscing about Robert and Miriam. He couldn't get over the fact that his encounter with them had taken place but six months past. It was only six months, though it felt like a lifetime.

A tall, thin man John guessed to be in his mid-thirties was standing against the railing and staring out at the waves. He was suitably dressed in serge trousers and a fisherman's knit pullover. John had noticed him before and had been puzzled by how aloof he had seemed, rarely engaging with his fellow passengers. John shuffled over his way.

"Good day to you, sir. I'm John Holwell, military surgeon and Brittania's doctor for the time being. It's a beautiful day, isn't it?"

"Lewis Mayne at your service. It is a beautiful day."

The two men stood side by side for a time in silence. When John realized that Mayne wasn't going to stoke the conversation, he decided to try again.

"What takes you to India?"

"I'm the undersecretary to the East India Company comptroller in Fort William. I'm returning to India after having presented my report to head office in London."

"How often have you made this journey?"

"This is my third trip, though likely my last. I'm going to be taking over as chief administrator in the next few months. The old chap is retiring and will be heading home shortly thereafter."

John was now full of questions. Here was someone who could fill in a lot of gaps for him about what he could expect to find upon reaching the Indian subcontinent. But his enquiries would have to wait. James was coming over to him, the young lady he had been talking with in tow.

"John, I'd like to introduce you to Susan Worthing. Her father is an army officer stationed in Fort William. She's moving to India to live with her parents."

"How do you do, Susan. I'm John Holwell, and this is Lewis Mayne."

Susan was a fresh-faced young woman with long flowing auburn hair that was now swirling about in the breeze.

"It's a pleasure to make your acquaintance, doctor. James has been telling me a little about you."

"Only the good things, I hope." John smiled broadly and then turned to Lewis.

"Perhaps you know Susan's parents, Lewis?"

Before Lewis could say anything, Susan offered, "My father's Sergeant at Arms, Henry Worthing, and my mother's Cecilia Worthing."

"Our paths haven't crossed often, but I do know your father. He's a fine gentleman and a good officer. Have a good morning, all. I have to go to my cabin and do some work." And rather abruptly, Lewis headed toward the stairwell.

Susan, James, and John remained for some time longer, chatting and getting acquainted. Susan was certainly a lively and animated creature and was full of stories about her time at a prestigious Naval Academy school in Suffolk. It was plain to John that James was enamoured with her, and though he wasn't quite ready to quit the invigorating morning air on the quarterdeck, he took his leave and left the two youngsters alone.

Rope burns, broken bones, stomach ailments, knife wounds, cat-o-nine-tails lacerations—these were just some of the situations John was likely to have to give his medical attention to over the coming weeks, or so he had been warned. Granted, it had only been a couple of days, but to date there had only been a few seasick civilians and one sailor with a rather embarrassing and itchy rash, no doubt picked up in one of the seedy brothels in Cheapside.

John slid his stool over to his desk, unstoppered his ink well, and pulled out some sheets of vellum. Before leaving port, he had decided to kill two birds with one stone. He would write to Alice every day, his letters serving to keep her well informed of daily life aboard the Brittania, and hopefully also to make up a sort of travel log that could be referenced in the future. And truth be known, this regular exercise was at least some way of communing with Alice.

Before setting pen to paper, however, Alice's last missive beckoned to him, and he dug it out of his travel chest. He carefully unfolded it and set aside the pressed flower, which remarkably still held some of its fragrance. It was probably the twentieth time he had read the letter, and he was sure it wouldn't be the last.

Dearest John,

Your letter of December 21 has set me (and my family, of course) in rather a tailspin. I don't know if I want to batter you with both my fists or hug the living daylight out of you? Both, I suppose. I wish we could have been together for a while so that we could have discussed this hare-brained scheme of yours. But now, of course, it's too late for that.

As for your proposal of marriage… I accept wholeheartedly! Yes, John, I will marry you. And yes, I will travel with you to India and see if we can make a life there together. I too have an adventurous spirit, and for many years, I've been jealous of the men in my life who have had the

*opportunity to travel and experience new places. I've always wanted that
for myself as well.*

*Ma and Da are in a frightful state about all of this. First James,
and now me! After recounting my trip to London and speaking so much
about you, I think they had a strong suspicion that I'd end up in London
someday. But I don't think that in their wildest imaginings, they saw
me moving to a land so far away! I have a lot of work to do to placate
them and to help them accept the circumstances.*

*Christmas has been a blur, and the countless comings and goings
of relatives, neighbours, and friends have been a godsend. My parents
haven't had time to mull about this sudden and tangled state of affairs,
but I think that once things settle down, we'll have plenty of time to talk
things over.*

*I'm happy that your mother has agreed to join us in India, and she
indeed will be a good companion for me. No doubt we'll make many other
friends and have a circle of people about us for support. I'm relying on
you to keep me informed about your journey and your status in India
once you arrive. I'm going to need lots of advice about what I'll need to
carry with me, clothes, household goods, etc.*

*I'm going to be taking this letter to the postmaster tomorrow morning,
and I'm hoping it gets to you before you depart.*

*I love you, John. The time we spent together in London was magical,
and I can't wait to be with you again. Be safe! And please pass on my
love to James. Give him a big hug for me (and a swift kick to his arse).*

Ever yours,
  Ailish

How happy he had been to read that Alice had accepted his marriage
proposal. And he still felt a warm glow pass through him every time
he read her letter. John folded Alice's missive, replacing the pressed
flower ever so carefully, and put it away in his chest. He then pulled a
blank sheet of vellum in front of him, dated the page *February 6, 1733*, and
began to detail yesterday's activities on board Brittania. The letter was
conversational, and he pretended that he was sitting across from Alice

and just talking to her. He pictured her opening his letters one at a time, reading them and then re-reading them, sharing his journey every step of the way.

Fifteen minutes later, there was an urgent knocking on his cabin door, and his train of thought was abruptly interrupted. He let in a couple of sailors who had one of their fellows propped up between them. They sidled through the doorway and deposited their charge on the wooden slab in the centre of the cabin. He was quite a sight! The right side of his face was bloodied and scraped raw, and his left arm was dangling at an impossible angle.

"We was hoistin a crate from one side of the deck to t'other. Ol' Charlie here weren't payin no attention. The yardarm buckler swung round and caught him full in the mug. As he went crashin down to the deck, his arm got all twisted up in the riggin and now as you kin see, it's hanging off his shoulder like he's been strung out on a wrack." The tall lanky sailor provided his colourful report, and then the two of them turned to leave. "Is there anythin you might need from us sir? We've got to be gettin back to the job."

"Yes. Please run up to the quarterdeck and find my assistant. His name's James O'Connor. Tell him I have need of him right away. Thanks. Oh, and by the way, what are your names? I'm going to need them for my records."

"I'm Sil, sir and my matey here is Jack."

"What about the injured man?"

"He's Charles Turnberry, sir. But he goes by Charlie."

With that the two sailors scuffled out of the cabin, and Medical Officer Holwell turned to give his full attention to the injured sailor.

CASA BRANCA

... And so darling, that's the news of the last couple of days. I'm sorry if it seems repetitious, but as you can see, life on board Brittania is highly routine. However, I'm sure you'll be more enthralled by my next missive, as we are about to drop anchor and spend a few days in the port of Casa Branca, a Portuguese outpost in Morocco. I've pressed Lewis Mayne for information about this ancient settlement, and though I've told you getting Mayne to say anything at all is like drawing blood from a stone; he has, it seems, finally given in and even warmed up to me, I believe. From what he tells me, the military fortress is highly ordered, but the surrounding areas are quite lawless and rather primitive. He has warned me to stick with the other officers and not to go exploring on my own. As contrary as that is to my nature, I promise you I will heed his advice.

So, farewell for now, Alice. I'll regale you with tales of this first port adventure upon my return to the ship.

Love as always,
John

After carefully putting away his writing materials and doing a little tidy up of his cabin, John scrambled up to the Poop Deck to take in the action as Brittania swung eastward, coming out of its broad reach, and finally running with the wind toward the ever-approaching coastline. The ship was now level for the first time in days, and it was a great relief to be able to move about the deck and not worry about toppling over. The light was waning as evening came on, and he could see flares from the parapets of the fortress and pinpoints of light from the surrounding town. The air was warm and the light jacket he wore was all he needed to be comfortable.

Mayne had informed him that Brittania would drop anchor about 200 yards offshore, and that when the time came, they would be shuttled to the dock in tenders that would be lowered to the water after having been released from their "gripes." The captain and his men would lead in the first tender, followed up by the officers and then the rest of the passengers and crew. A skeleton crew would remain aboard and then be relieved the next day, so that all sailors could have some shore leave.

As Brittania neared its anchoring point, the crew, all hands on deck, flew into action, some scrambling up the rigging to begin furling the sails, others taking in the slack from the hundreds of sheets that were being hauled in; still others beginning to work the anchor winches. It was a scene of controlled chaos, and John marvelled at it.

Like a great beast brought down by hunters, Brittania came to a slow halt, and the sounds of shrieking anchor chains and sailors bellowing orders faded into silence. It seemed like a satisfied sigh breathed up from the ship as Brittania settled into her moorings, and all that could be heard was the slapping of the waves below her gunwales.

The following morning, Lewis Mayne was more loquacious than John had ever known him to be. Maybe it was the subject—finance—that he could go on about *ad nauseum*, or maybe it was just a feeling of wellbeing and stability now that he was standing on *terra firma* in the port city of Casa Branca? John and Lewis were standing beside the dock waiting for James to arrive on the next tender.

"Ever since the second Treaty of Methuen was signed in 1703, Portuguese wines have been more readily available in England and at far lower prices than previously. Also, the treaty allows for English textiles to be exported 'tax-free,' a huge boost to the English economy."

John wasn't particularly interested in *The Treaty of Methuen*, a topic he had studied in depth as part of his apprenticeship in Rotterdam, but he allowed Lewis to natter on while he pretended to listen, and even as he surreptitiously scanned the vistas all about him, marvelling at the strange sights and sounds.

Not to seem rude, and intuiting that Mayne was eager to share his knowledge, John asked Mayne about the origins of the treaty. Mayne was happy to oblige.

"The first Treaty of Methuen made allies of Britain and Portugal, as well as the Netherlands, in the War of the Spanish Succession and ensuing Seven Years' War. Among other things, the treaty document established the number of troops that various countries would provide to fight the campaign in Spain. While the first treaty was political in nature, the second was economic."

Mayne was about to go on with his history lesson when John spied James waving at him from the tender quickly approaching the dock. He put his hand lightly on Mayne's shoulder, as if to say, "We'll continue this talk later," and he purposefully strode off down the length of the dock to greet his friend. He had to press his way through a throng of coffee-skinned men and women vying for the attention of the new arrivals, hoping to sell some of their wares. Brazen women, their bare bosoms bouncing freely and unabashedly, smiled leeringly at the male passengers, willing them to come and partake in their special form of hospitality. The passengers on this tender were of a genteel breed, and many of them, especially the few women, were obviously uncomfortable with this scene. John suspected that the sailors arriving on successive shuttles would have a very different take on things! He smiled wryly.

John took hold of Susan Worthing's arm when it was proffered to him by James and helped her onto the dock. James quickly followed, and together, Susan tucked safely between them, they made their way onto the shore.

The captain and a number of officers had headed up to the fortress to greet the Portuguese officials, with a strict warning to all others to remain by the docks until they received the "all clear" signal. Then, and only then, would they be allowed to move about freely in the surrounding town. While England and Portugal were on excellent terms at the moment, formalities had to be observed, and the ship, with its manifest, had to be formally presented to the Case Branca commander. Also, as a goodwill gesture, four sturdy sailors had been commandeered to haul two casks of Pusser's Rum up to the fort.

John felt that the ship still seemed to be moving under him as he stood aside with his companions. He wondered how long the feeling would last.

It seemed like an eternity, but eventually, a large Brittania ensign could be seen being waved about outside the fortress walls. John turned to Mayne and asked, "Where to now?"

"We'll head over to an establishment I remember from the last time I was here. We should be able to find some local food and some passable beverages there. Furthermore, the proprietor is quite the character. You'll enjoy meeting him. By the way, the Portuguese consider the whole area a part of Casa Branca, but the natives refer to their town as Anfa."

Mayne turned to the small group accompanying him and addressed them directly. "Ignore the locals who will be sure to assail us with all sorts of items for sale. The goods are worthless and of poor quality. Also, hang on carefully to anything of value you may have on your person."

Mayne had been right, and as they made their way north into the heart of Anfa, their progress was often curtailed by men, women, and even children dressed in dark flowing garments who accosted them at every turn and vigorously pushed merchandise under their noses. There were bits of colourful cloth, earthen cooking vessels, vegetables, and large flat slices of bread skewered on wooden sticks. Susan Worthing had to be pulled away from the cloth sellers and from children trying to grasp hold of her pretty floral dress. James had to be turned away from the offerings of food.

The party moved into a series of narrow, gnarly roads and eventually stood outside a small, but ornate building adorned with trellises covered in vine-like vegetation and flowers. Mayne led the way inside. The space was remarkably airy, and the walls were decorated with ceramic artefacts: larger-than-life mottled lizards, painted plates, utensils, and, rather randomly, a picture of a Spanish galleon. The proprietor, a slim man wearing a magnificent turban-like apparatus on his head, bowed gracefully as he met them at the entrance, and the small contingent followed him to a large table in the centre of the room. While the others were seated, Mayne went off with the proprietor toward the kitchen to make arrangements for food and drink.

Mayne returned and immediately fell into his pedantic habitude, a trait that John was beginning to find slightly annoying and rather tiresome.

As Mayne was their de facto guide and interpreter in this Moroccan adventure, there really wasn't much to be said; and, if John later on wanted to pick Mayne's brains about India and Fort William in particular, he would just have to put up with him.

"The owner's name is Aksil, which he tells me is a Berber name meaning 'strength and speed.' He says he's descended from a long line of Berber nobility. His ancestors settled in Anfa generations ago."

Susan Worthing interjected, "Who are the Berber's?"

"They are an ethnic group indigenous to North Africa, and their language is a dialect of Arabic."

Before Mayne could go on, a serving girl arrived bearing a tray laden with an ornate polished silver teapot on a brass foot. The handle and spout were slender and curvaceous, and the lid was adorned with a tiny, delicate finial. Teacups, also brass and silver, were laid out in front of each of them. Aksil approached the table, lifted the teapot from the serving tray, and poured out a stream of steaming dark liquid into each cup.

"Most Berber meals are accompanied by tea. We'll get to the stronger stuff later." Mayne lifted his cup and gingerly took a sip.

The others followed suit. John found the tea bitter, but very refreshing. Wonderful odours were emanating from the kitchen, and John was suddenly famished. All of them would welcome a change from the victuals on board Brittania, which hadn't been too bad for the first few days, but which in the last little while had consisted of hard bread and an ever-thinning salty broth with a few odds and ends thrown in.

"What's for dinner, Mr. Mayne?" This from James, who hadn't spoken much to anyone since stepping on shore, except, of course, to the young Miss Worthing, whom he had surreptitiously taken under his protective wing.

"When the food comes out, I'll ask Aksil to give us a run-down of what's before us. I just told him to bring out his best fare, and lots of it. I take it you're hungry, James. Don't worry, when this meal is finished, they'll have to roll us back to Brittania in wheelbarrows!"

This was the first sign of levity from the otherwise staid Lewis Mayne, and John could see that their leader was enjoying himself.

"Oh my!" This from Miss Worthing upon seeing the dishes upon dishes of food that were now spread across the table. The bowls of lamb stew, fresh green legumes, sauces, and pickles were almost too much to take in. And in the middle of the table, almost as if it had sprouted up from the centre, stood a large copper tureen piled high with a steaming, golden concoction sprinkled with herbs and cloves of garlic.

"Seksu, my friends, is the staple of Berber meals. Crushed wheat is mixed with water and oil and crumbled into little balls and then steamed. The serving boy will place a mound of it onto your plates. Then you can create a small hollow in the middle and add the various dishes to it. The sauces you can sample in smaller amounts. Do be aware of the reddish-brown sauce, the *matbucha*. It's a very fiery concoction of red peppers, garlic, and chili. Not for the faint of heart!" With a flourish, Aksil finished off his overview of the dishes spread before them, gave a low bow, and took his leave.

John wasn't sure he'd be able to move after finishing his meal. He sat back, wine glass in one hand and the other over his now bulging stomach. He listened to the others in the group commenting on one element of the feast or the other. He hadn't felt so satisfied in a long time. Lewis Mayne was settling the bill of fare with Aksil and had adamantly refused to accept any recompense from the rest even after many protestations.

The company left Aksil's establishment and retraced their steps to the dock. Not wanting to go back onboard so soon, they sat on crates watching the ship's crew haul barrels of produce and other victuals to the waiting tenders. John tamped his well-lit pipe, pressing the tobacco further down into the chamber, and creating a thick, creamy plume of smoke. There was almost always too much breeze aboard the Brittania to allow John the pleasure of smoking his pipe, so this little sojourn in Casa Branca was very welcome. As they watched the sailors sweating over their loads in the late afternoon sun, they offered little snippets of their former lives. Even Lewis Mayne recounted a brief anecdote about a particularly corpulent accountant in Fort William who had to have his office furniture moved outside the finance building because he couldn't get through the front door. This engendered a little chuckle from all of them.

"What's going on?" James stood up abruptly and pointed to a ruckus that was taking place a short way off, but which was coming nearer. Lewis Mayne quickly took charge. "Let's move off a bit, away from the dock. We'll see what the situation is from a distance."

The 'situation' turned out to be several ships' officers dragging two shackled sailors back to the boat. The sailors weren't coming peaceably. The air around them was purple with foul language, and James protectively turned Miss Worthing away from the scene.

"My guess is these two sailors got into the drink at a local establishment and then proceeded to make giant asses of themselves." Mayne went on with his exegesis. "They'll sleep it off in the brig and then face the captain's justice in a day or two, probably after we've left port the day after tomorrow. John," Mayne spoke ominously, "Make sure you have lots of salve on hand in your surgeon's kit. I fear the cat's going to be coming out of the bag!"

CALEB GRANTHAM

A flurry of activity on deck and a ghastly clanging of chains as the anchors were hauled up left no doubt that the Brittania was about to resume its southerly course along the western reaches of the African continent. For a few more days, the westerly winds would keep the ship listing to port, but then the northeast Tradewinds would pick it off the coast of the Western Sahara and gradually skew the Brittania and its denizens to starboard.

On the last shore day, John was able to take his small packet of letters and leave them with the port postmaster. When no one had been looking, he had pressed the letters to his lips and then to his chest before lovingly placing them on the postmaster's desk. He couldn't wait for them to arrive in Dublin and to have Alice read them. His next opportunity might not be for several weeks—that is, once they arrived in Cape Town.

Feet planted squarely and firmly on the deck between the fore and mid masts, Captain Caleb Grantham looked, for all intents and purposes, like he had sprouted amidships, his trunk firm and stout. The ship was his, and he was the ship's. He was a short, but barrel-chested man with massive forearms and stern, bushy eyebrows. His voice, canon-like, drilled through the very fibres of the crew, and they responded instantly to any orders given.

John looked around him. It seemed like the entire crew and most of the male passengers had gathered about the mainmast. He knew the few women passengers aboard had been instructed to stay below in their cabins. The crew was a sober lot, knowing what was about to transpire. Even the gentle sun, wispy clouds, and fair winds couldn't lighten their spirits. Two of their own were going to be subject to maritime law and would suffer the consequences of their intemperate behaviour while on shore leave in Casa Branca.

The two unfortunate sailors held in the brig these past few days on short rations were led in irons, arms tied cruelly behind their backs, up into the noonday light. They were positioned clumsily in front of the captain, both looking down at the deck and squinting mightily. Grantham reached behind him, not letting his gaze wander from the two miscreants, and retrieved a parchment that he began unfurling in a way that showed that he had done this many times before. The onlookers, who had been speaking in hushed tones, if at all, were now dead silent. The captain lowered his attention to the parchment and sonorously began to read the injunction.

"Able Seaman Griffen. Ordinary Seaman Wallace. Both of the Brittania." Grantham looked each of them squarely with steely eyes. *"On the 27th day of February, in the year of our Lord 1733, you were both arrested in the port of Casa Branca for drunken and disorderly conduct. Your actions have brought dishonour to the name of Brittania and to your fellow sailors. In the name of His Majesty, the King, I hereby sentence you, Ordinary Seaman Wallace, to thirty lashes, and to you, Able Seaman Griffen, eighty lashes; forty now and another forty, five weeks hence."*

Here Grantham deviated from the text. "Griffen, with your senior position on the upper deck, you bear the greater responsibility for what transpired in Casa Branca, and it is disappointing that you so negatively influenced Wallace, but only on his second turn of duty aboard His Majesty's fleet. This and your previous history of intemperance I have taken into consideration in meting out this sentence."

Grantham turned to several ship's officers standing nearby. "Officers, secure Wallace to the mast."

As the officers busied themselves with their unsavoury work, Lewis Mayne made his way to stand behind the ship's surgeon. He was discreet and measured in his speech.

"Dr. Holwell. This is your first voyage as ship's surgeon. There are a few things you need to know about your role when ship's discipline is being meted out. As surgeon, you must examine the prisoners after every few lashes. If you believe a prisoner is in jeopardy of his mortal life or in danger of suffering debilitating and irreversible harm, it is incumbent on you to stop the proceedings. The captain must acquiesce to you upon this matter. However, use this power carefully. If it is perceived that you are too easily swayed to stop the proceedings, it will make you few friends aboard the Brittania, especially among the officers."

Why hadn't anyone told him of this sooner? John suddenly felt very unsteady and quickly tried to recall what he knew about the use of the 'cat' and its effect on the human body. He knew that the 'cat o' nine tails' was about two and a half feet in length, was fashioned from three strands of rope, which were further stripped down, each into three filaments, and then all braided together loosely at the base. The device was designed to lacerate a man's back in a painful fashion yet would not lead to permanent damage if wielded correctly.

Still, lashes that strayed too low and wrapped themselves around the lower waist could cause significant harm to the recipient's kidneys or other organs. He had heard that sailors could die from receiving two hundred or more lashes. Splitting up a sailor's sentence into two or more sessions, as Grantham had done with Griffen, served several purposes. First of all, most sailors couldn't bear more than about fifty lashes in one turn. Also, part of the punishment was to be carried out when the ship was in a harbour in the company of the King's other vessels, so that the punishment could be observed by sailors from other ships and subsequently be used as a 'warning' for all. Finally, the re-opening of the lacerations after they had had a little time to heal would be even more painful with each successive flogging.

A slop bucket filled with fresh water and clean rags were stationed close at hand. This Surgeon Holwell could use to wipe the wounds and see the damage more clearly. It wasn't until sometime hence, and speaking about the ship's discipline some more with Lewis Mayne, that Holwell would discover Captain Grantham's benevolence and humanity. Not only would many other sea captains have sentenced the two sailors to even more lashes than Grantham had, but instead of fresh water in the slop bucket, there would have been briny seawater, which would have led to excruciating agony. This practice, Holwell learned, was the origin of the phrase "rubbing salt in one's wounds." But for now, this ordeal seemed awfully brutal as it was, and Holwell's legs were turning to jelly.

The first crack of the 'cat' made John jump even though he had been expecting it. A deep red welt appeared on the sailor's back, just below the shoulder blades. It wasn't until three or four strokes later, once the welts started creating their crisscross matrix, that the first few drops of blood starting oozing from the wounds; then, with each successive strike, blood would fly off the unfortunate sailor's back in random and fascinating patterns. While Holwell was repulsed by the sight of the flogging, his medical curiosity was also heightened.

Ten strokes in, he lifted his hand uncertainly and was almost surprised that the First Mate lowered the 'cat' and suspended his assault. John reached into the bucket, wrung out a rag, and ever so gently wiped the blood from Wallace's back. Wallace had cried out initially when the barrage of strokes had begun, but now he was quiet. He knew that the way he received his punishment would go a long way toward how he would be accepted by the crew, and, in fact, his status could even be elevated somewhat if he deported himself well. John wasn't sure what he should be looking out for, but seeing Wallace rigid and determined, he gestured to the first mate to continue.

The proceedings continued thus for some time. Wallace's thirty lashes having been dealt out, he now rested slumped over and sweating profusely. Holwell called out for someone to bring him water to drink and one of the cook's mates scurried away to one of the rain barrels, pitcher in hand.

Griffen, whose back still bore the reminders of a previous flogging, stoically accepted his punishment. Fresh lacerations over the existing scar tissue meant that blood started dancing off his back much earlier than it had with Wallace, and with more alacrity. It was much more difficult for Holwell to assess the damage being inflicted. He halted the proceedings a little more often than he had with Wallace, but after a scowl from Griffen following the twenty-seventh lash, John decided that he would allow the last thirteen to pass by uninterrupted.

What would it be like to suffer such pain and humiliation? John could only imagine what the two men must be going through! All he knew was that he never wanted to find out firsthand.

Grantham, a man of few words, simply barked out a last warning, which was aimed not only at the two broken sailors, but also toward the assembled crew. "You have witnessed the consequence of bringing shame and disrepute to the Brittania and, indeed, to the entire Royal Navy. You do so at your peril." He then gestured to the standing officers. "Remove these prisoners to the surgeon's chamber. When the surgeon has cleaned them up and examined them, take them bound and shackled to the brig.

They are to be kept for seven days below with short rations. They will, however, be allowed all the water they want to drink." With that he turned about smartly and walked off to his chambers.

The prisoners, cleaned up, and with a light dressing draped over their backs, were led away by four ship's officers. Holwell carefully scrubbed the table on which the men had been treated. It was only then that he felt light-headed, and a violent shuddering rifled through his body. He would have fallen to his knees had James not been nearby and guided him to his cot. He closed his eyes and tried not to think of the events that had just transpired. It was an exercise in futility. The harder he tried to block it out, the more intrusively the horrific scenes played through his consciousness.

"What you need is a strong drink." James was holding out a small tin cup, which John accepted gratefully. He downed the searing liquid in one quick draught. Feeling steadier, he motioned to James to pour another drink. James found a cup for himself, and the two of them sipped their drinks in a little more genteel fashion.

Intuiting that John didn't want to speak about the flogging, James cajoled him into "getting some fresh air," and the two of them went up the gangway and emerged on the Poop Deck.

RUNNING OUT THE GUNS

James and Susan Worthing were spending more and more time with each other. John was careful what he wrote to Alice about in regard to her brother. He was sure she'd approve of the liaison, but he didn't want to betray James' confidence. He found himself harbouring some jealousy in the budding romance nonetheless. He couldn't help but miss Alice terribly.

Not wanting to be in their way, John sought out Lewis Mayne in order to learn more about what would be waiting for them in India and on other aspects of the remaining sea voyage. Lewis had dropped his guardedness around the surgeon and seemed to actually enjoy their visits. John was sure to allow Mayne his pedantic diatribes just so that he would be more forthcoming about the topics that mattered most to him.

The comptroller-to-be had just finished a philippic about the vagaries of the slave trade in Orungu, a powerful trading centre in the country of Gabon, which they were sailing parallel to at the moment. John looked out at the dark, mysterious lands they were gliding past. He knew that sometime in the next few days, Brittania would hit the doldrums, and they would bob about like corks in a barrel. Just then, the ship came around a point of land and Mayne pointed out a river delta that was quite stunning in its aspect.

"Isn't that something, Mayne! It could be the entrance to Hades. The world bright and beautiful on one side and murky and dangerous on the other."

"That's the Ogooué River. It flows into the heart of Gabon."

"How do you know all these details, Mayne? You are a veritable encyclopedia!"

"As I have told you, I have completed this voyage more than once, and being a man of some curiosity, how could I not learn as much as I could about the world around me. Besides, you never know when some salient detail of the peoples and places one comes across in one's travels might hold some pecuniary value."

It really was all about finance for Mayne, though John was impressed nonetheless with his voracious appetite for knowledge and his ability to recall details as readily as Mayne was able to.

"It's lucky," Mayne returned to his Gabon colloquy, "that piracy isn't as common on this coast as it used to be."

"It was common?" Piracy was a topic he had wanted to address with Mayne for some time.

"It was indeed, especially in the time of Bartholomew Roberts, 'Black Bart,' as he was known to sailors in these parts. He was notorious for raiding ships off West Africa, and when the winds were favourable, he made runs to do the same off the Americas. He died at sea just off Cape Lopez, very close to here."

"How did he meet his end? Or is it even known?"

"Roberts captured a French frigate in April of 1721. On board was the Governor of Martinique, a French colony. The pirate was merciless with the crew of the frigate and even had the audacity to hang the Governor from his own ship's yardarm. This heinous act was the cause of his undoing. When word of this outrageous event got back to France and Britain, both countries made it a priority to find Roberts and bring him to justice; the French for obvious reasons, and the British so that Roberts couldn't do the same to one of theirs. In February of the following year, a British man-of-war under Captain Chaloner Ogle located Roberts' ship and pursued it. Off the Cape of Lopez, a violent sea battle ensued. When it became obvious that Roberts wouldn't be taken alive, they destroyed his ship and sent her to Davy Jones's Locker. Only a few unfortunate souls were pulled alive out of the water, and it was they that would, in years to come, recount the many tales of the treacherous blackguard that have gone down in maritime legend."

"Davy Jones's Locker? I have never heard that expression." Holwell had been held spellbound throughout Mayne's discourse.

"Suffice it to say, Bartholomew Roberts, most of his crew, and what was left of his ship, rest somewhere on the bottom of the ocean, perhaps even just below where we are now."

Mayne left off his narrative.

"I think it's time for the noon meal, so I'll have to tell you more about the pirate, Davey Jones, some other time. Most of his tale is purely legend and his story is ensconced in many myths and sailor's lore."

With that, John took a last searching look at equatorial Gabon and made his way to the Officer's mess for lunch.

Several days later and further south along the African coast, Brittania was languishing in the doldrums and with it, the spirit of the crew and passengers was languishing as well. As difficult as it had been to get used to the ship listing continuously to port or to starboard, and habitually feeling like one leg or the other was longer than its mate, this unsettled motion in the doldrums was far worse. One didn't know from moment to moment which way the ship was going to yaw and gape. And the groaning of the boards and the complaining of the masts in their stays was disconcerting. A light breeze would spring up for a half hour and then, just as suddenly, it would disappear. Without the breeze, the heat was oppressive. Even the type of injuries Holwell had to deal with as the ship's surgeon differed as a result of the changed condition. Instead of the rope burns and swinging tackle injuries, he was setting more broken bones and rationing out more tonic for seasickness, especially to the passengers or landlubbers, as some of the crew were wont to call them.

In order to keep up his own spirits, John wrote longer and longer missives to Alice and several letters to his mother. In them, he detailed the shoreline ever slipping past them. He delighted in describing the strange sights and majestic panoramas he had come across. He also spelled out in great detail the workings of the ship and the regimented life aboard Brittania.

There were thirty guns aboard Brittania, many of them twenty-four pounders. Several times now on their voyage from England, the guns were "run out" and the gun crews practised their craft. Now that the ship wasn't making much headway, Captain Grantham had decided to drill them tirelessly. Holwell found this exercise fascinating, and at every opportunity, he would talk to Mayne or to one of the gun captains and get as much information as he could about the firing of the guns. One gun captain in particular, a sturdy sailor who went by the name 'Smake', was particularly helpful in filling in the details for John. Once John was satisfied, he had the gist of it, he reported on it in a letter to Alice.

Even though Brittania is a stout ship and formidable in her aspect, what with her many gunwales, there is always the chance of pirates or privateers making a desperate attempt at capturing her and exacting a toll. Lest you be too worried about this, my love, Mayne assures me that these attempts are not likely to succeed. While there are faster ships than Brittania, there aren't many that dare come near her thirty cannon, and Captain Grantham has a fierce reputation as a maritime warrior. Besides, East India Merchantmen are bigger targets on their return voyages, their holds laden with treasures from the exotic East.

I have befriended a gun captain (as much as a 'landlubber' can befriend a sailor!), and he has taught me much about the firing of the guns. I will explain this phenomenon as much as possible while it's still fresh in mind. I find the whole exercise fascinating, though when the guns are fired, the noise is deafening. I have supplied James, Miss Worthing, and several of the other passengers with plugs of cotton for their ears. It is no wonder that many of the sailors who are members of the gun crews are losing their hearing. Indeed, it is futile to even attempt to make oneself intelligible to them for several hours after the exercises.

Mayne tells me that the Brittania is one of the best merchantmen at 'running out her guns.' To put this in context, the standard on a ship of the English fleet such as a man-of-war is the ability to fire and reload the guns every three minutes while in battle mode. This takes hours of practice and crack gun crews —one for each gun. Brittania crews can achieve this feat in about three and a half minutes, remarkable considering many of the gun crew members are but ordinary sailors, many quite new to this pursuit.

A gun captain and two or more crewmembers each with very specific assignments man each gun. The first man loads the cartridge and a wad of cloth. The next rams it home with a wooden 'rammer.' The gun captain feels for the piece of flannel cartridge with a small length of wire (a 'pricker'), which he places down the touchhole which is in the breech of the gun and then yells "Home!" when he makes contact. On the command "Shot your guns!" a round shot is loaded into the barrel followed by another wad and this too is rammed home.

Once the gun has been loaded, it is run out. The crew hauls on tackles until the front of the gun carriage is hard up against the ship's bulwark and the gun's barrel stands at horizontal attention through the gun port. Training the gun left or right is managed by another set of rope tackles and elevation is achieved using iron crows to raise the breech and then by manipulating the 'quoin,' which is a wooden wedge, in or out.

The gun, now loaded, run out, and sighted, is then primed. A mixture of fine powder and spirits of wine is poured down the touchhole using a priming horn. The gun captain, being satisfied with the sighting, raises his hand to signal that the gun is ready. In his other hand, he holds the linstock (a wooden staff at which one end is a soldering slow match kept alight in a bucket when not in use). On the command "Fire!" the linstock is brought into contact with the touchline setting off a small explosion in the pan as the priming powder ignites, which in turn prompts the main charge propelling the shot out of the barrel.

It is because of what happens next that I receive many casualties of the exercise. As the shot is expelled, a violent recoil is the result and the gun flies backward. The only element restraining it is a sturdy breech rope made fast to ring bolts set into the bulwarks with a turn taken around the cascabel, the knot at the end of the gun's barrel. As you might imagine, Alice, more than a few gun crewmembers, especially if they are not careful, will suffer broken toes and other unfortunate infirmities.

The gun captain commands "Stop your vents!" and the touchhole is closed by a gun crewmember wearing a fireproof glove placing his hand over it. Smake, the gun captain I befriended, tells me that this is to prevent gasses passing through the touchhole and consequently corroding it, which would render the gun unstable and infinitely more dangerous.

The gun is then swabbed out, with the other end of the rammer, wrapped in sheepskin, and soaked in seawater. This ensures that all the flame has been extinguished, and only then can the sequence begin all over again. A gun can be used three times in succession like this. On *the fourth, a wardhook (a large corkscrew-like instrument) is used to extract any cartridge remnants left in the barrel.*

And now, Alice, I must put away my writing utensils. Trying to write while the ship is bobbing about has made me feel a little nauseous, and I need to get some fresh air. The doldrums should soon be behind us (at least I hope that's the case!) and the Southeasterly Trades should pick us up and carry us on to Cape Town and the southern tip of Africa.

Good night and God bless, my beloved!

Ever yours,
*   John*

Cape Town

What a blessing it was to be out of the Doldrums and knifing along into the Southeast Tradewinds, the African shoreline flying past the Brittania, passengers and crew all in high spirits. It was a clear, hot day, and no doubt on shore African denizens would be basking in the tropical heat. But here, on deck and mid-ships, the breeze wafted them ever closer to Cape Town and kept them pleasantly cool.

"What's Cape Town like?" This from Miss Worthing as she, James, Holwell, and Mayne took a turn about the deck.

"A bit of a backwater, really, but exceptionally beautiful." Mayne strode over to the railing and glanced wistfully at the shore. "The town begins on the shores of Table Bay and then rises up to Table Mountain. You can just see the outline of it in the distance. The Bowl, as it is called, is where most of the business activity lies. Just away from the docks and the moored ships, merchants and traders conduct their business. There are a handful of independent businessmen, but by and large, the majority of them work for the Dutch East India Company. The Dutch settled in the Cape two or three generations ago and are the governing power in Cape Town. Farms and orchards become more prevalent as you leave the Bowl and head up the gentle slopes of the surrounding hills. Most of the labor is delegated to slaves, either from Indonesia or from Madagascar. One prominent family owns the majority of land on the slopes of Table Mountain. The Van Breda family lives in an estate, Oranjezicht, and is wealthy beyond measure."

"Orange view."

"What's that, John?" Mayne turned to Holwell.

"Orange view is the literal translation of Oranjezicht."

James piped in. "John and I spent some years in Rotterdam working for a concern closely tied to the Dutch East India Company. We picked up some of the language there. John, much more than I, of course, because he is very clever with languages."

"That makes a lot of sense. The Van Breda estate overlooks vast orange groves." Mayne was bemused.

John's brow was furrowed, as if he were searching for some small piece of information that was eluding him.

"Is the head of the Van Breda clan Pieter Van Breda, by any chance?"

Mayne replied, "I'm not completely certain, but that name does sound familiar."

The scene as they entered Table Bay and made their way to a mooring spot was unbelievably beautiful. Whereas on the open seas they had but encountered one or two other ships, they now looked out on at least a dozen vessels of various types and origin. There were barques not unlike Brittania, two-masted brigantines, and even a felucca that seemed oddly out of place in these southerly waters.

Once Brittania had come to a rest, its anchors taking hold on the silty bed of Table Bay, a bumboat was lowered into the water and Grantham, along with two of his officers, were rowed ashore to the customs house. There they would observe the usual formalities and pay the mooring fee, always a little heftier for ships not of the Dutch East India Company. The Customs House managers wouldn't scrutinize their manifest much though, at least not until the return voyage.

Mayne advised Holwell, James, Miss Worthing, and her dowager chaperones, a Mrs. Adams and Mrs. Simpson, to pack enough clothes for a stay of some two to three weeks. He also reminded them to gather together any letters they wanted to send to England.

"If I'm not mistaken, that brigantine two ships over from us is Captain Charles Rigby's ship, The Normanton. It's fortunate that we're crossing paths with her here. Your letters should reach London in a couple of months. Rigby, like Grantham, is a highly respected captain and fearsome sailor."

Mayne, as in Casa Branca, delighted in taking charge of this small group.

"I know of a cozy little rooming house on Bree Street that should have rooms for the six of us. It's just a bit off the mainstream and is nestled in a quiet little community at the upper end of the Bowl."

The further the group moved away from port and the lower reaches of the Bowl, the more dramatically the landscape changed. Slaves hauling goods along sturdy wooden walkways watched menacingly by their overseers overran the areas around the port. Within the Bowl itself, the buildings were claptrap and shoddy. Merchants hung about their front doors, and a few rough looking men loitered on the aprons of drinking establishments. As Mayne and his entourage made their way past these men, they felt unfriendly eyes following them. It definitely made John very uncomfortable, and he was sure the others would be feeling the same way.

As they progressed further away from the Bay, their path rose gently up and then became quite precipitous. The gridiron pattern of the lower Bowl streets became increasingly serpentine and less ordered, and they encountered more and more vegetation. There were shrubs and other plants John had never seen before. These included heath plants and reeds. 'Sugarbush' and 'Pincushion'; John would come to learn their names over the next few days. As a medical man and avid scientist, John had more than a passing fascination with nature and all it had to provide.

The confines of the ship meant that there was very little opportunity for vigorous exercise, at least for the passengers, and the group of six was quite exhausted by the time they reached the rooming house. Mayne paid the porters who had toted their luggage from the docks and then entered the building.

Mrs. Versluuys was a matronly woman in her forties. She bustled about the pretty little rooming house with its flower garden overlooking Table Bay. She made sure that her guests were comfortable in their rooms and charmingly informed them in her broken English that dinner would be served just before sunset.

John, who had been looking forward to puffing on his pipe, stole into the garden even before unpacking the few personal items he had brought along with him from the Brittania. James joined him soon after.

"Do you really suppose Wouter Van Breda, who we got to know in Rotterdam, is Pieter's son? I knew that scallywag was from a rich Dutch East India family, but he didn't ever talk about his connection to Cape Town." John was looking out over the Bay, entranced by the movement of ships on the water. The lowering sun was just beginning to leave golden tails of light on the peaceful expanse.

"I do remember once when it was bitterly cold outside, and while we were mooning over the same serving girl at Rink's Kroeg, that Wouter mentioned that he wouldn't be staying much longer in Rotterdam, but that he would be heading south to warmer climes to help out his father and siblings. I just didn't think south meant Cape Town! You were there that evening, I'm sure of it, John?"

"If I was, I don't remember that conversation. I've been thinking I'll pay Mr. Van Breda a call tomorrow. Want to come along?"

James smiled and replied sheepishly, "I think I'll pass. I've promised Susan that I'd accompany her to the markets and perhaps do a little shopping myself."

The two of them watched the sun slowly kiss the horizon and then they turned to go into the parlour for dinner, where inviting aromas and animated conversations awaited them.

John looked over the inviting platter of neatly presented fresh fruit that arrived just after the sumptuous breakfast. He had slept well and was looking forward to his first day in Cape Town.

"Why don't you come with us to the market today, John, and visit Van Breda tomorrow?" James had stood up from the table and was politely moving Miss Worthing's chair back and out of the way.

"No thanks. I'll head up into Oranjezicht and see what the Van Bredas have been up to. I need to stretch my legs, and the climb up to the orchard should be invigorating."

Because John had insisted on speaking to her in Dutch, rusty but intelligible nonetheless, Mrs. Versluuys had taken an instant shine to him. Now, however, her visage had clouded over.

"You want to go up to visit that *tiran*?" The innkeeper used the Dutch word for tyrant. "He's an insufferable idiot who thinks he's the bloody king of Cape Town. He can be a treacherous man, so I would be very careful if I were you."

"How do I get there?" John was taken aback by Mrs. Versluuy's words but decided to continue on with his plan anyway.

"Just turn left outside the gate and keep walking up the road. You'll know when you've reached the orchard."

It was exhilarating to be out in the cool morning air and not worrying about keeping one's balance, though there were times when the terrain below his feet seemed to heave inexplicably. Holwell was amazed by the profusion of flowers and shrubs all around him, none of which he had encountered before. He made a mental note to write to Alice about them. Maybe over the next few days he could practise his sketching skills and give her a visual depiction of some of the more interesting flora?

The narrow well-worn dirt track continued up the southern slope of Table Mountain. Occasionally, John would stop for a breath and then he would turn back and scan the impressive vista below him. There was constant motion on the waters of Table Bay. The sky was crystal clear with wispy clouds hanging lazily about. The twitter of songbirds commingled satisfyingly with his thoughts. And every so often, a cicada-like chirping added staccato notes to the symphony.

Half an hour into his walk, he turned a corner and came upon a copse of gnarly, stunted trees. Out of this tangle of branches and limbs someone had carefully fashioned an archway that spanned the road. On the right side was a sign with its prominent, yet forbidding message, "*Verboden Terrein*." John was now faced with a dilemma. Should he keep going or should he turn back? Perhaps he should have sent a note by messenger announcing his desire to meet with Mr. Van Breda? Perhaps this wasn't even the Van Breda family he had had dealings with in Rotterdam? Holwell stood still for some time, nonplussed by this turn of events. He would be trespassing; but once he had met Van Breda, he could beg for forgiveness and ask for his indulgence, could he not?

Having made up his mind, he sheepishly stepped through the archway and immediately before him stretched orange trees as far as the eye could see. This had to be Oranjezicht. The orchard was magnificent. John took a deep breath and headed down the path that was now a little wider than earlier and much better cared for; the dark, baleful thoughts engendered by the sign quickly evaporating away.

A tall, well-built man, as dark as the midnight sky, wearing a loosely wrapped outfit seemingly crafted from one bolt of cloth suddenly appeared from behind an orange tree at the side of the road and stood directly in Holwell's way. John stopped, his heart in his mouth. He was just about to try some communication with the man when he sensed something or someone behind him. He turned and, just as he did, he was hit full force with a thunderous crack to the head. An explosion of light flared behind his eyes and then there was nothing.

Oranjezicht

Awareness began creeping back into his body. The first sensation was of a smashing pain at the back of his head. Instinctively he attempted to lift his hand to feel the damage, but his hands wouldn't move. They were tightly bound behind his back. He opened his eyes, and it was only then that he began to understand the full degree of his predicament. After John had been cold cocked, he had been unceremoniously dumped in a barrow, his hands and feet tied up. The barrow was being wheeled along the track through the orchard, one black man walking along the side and the other presumably pushing the barrow.

John groaned and tried to call out to his captors. Nothing but unintelligible sounds emanated from his mouth, which was dry and felt like it was stuffed with camphor balls. Eventually he was able to call out in English for them to stop and untie him. This had no effect, so he tried mightily to find the words in Dutch. Either the two men weren't conversant in either language or they were willfully ignoring him. John's supposition was the latter.

The next while was agony as the barrow made its way down the path. John was thrust on his side, and he had a limited view of the landscape around him. The jostling about made his head pound, and he was afraid the nausea he was experiencing would get the better of him. He didn't notice the mansion looming overhead until he was directly in its shadow. The barrow came to a standstill and one of the black men entered the edifice.

Moments later, John could hear sturdy footsteps on the veranda and then on the wooden stairs leading down. A tall grey-haired man loomed over him.

"*Goede God*!" came the exclamation in a thundering voice. "Tomas, Kira, what have you done?"

Even in his current circumstance John was pleased that he was able to understand the Dutch words.

"Look at the clothes this man is wearing. He doesn't look like a vagabond.

Quickly untie him and carefully bring him inside. Tomas, you run and find Sara. She will need to tend to him immediately!"

Inside the room it was cool and mercifully dark. A cold, wet cloth covered his head and some sort of waxy salve had been rubbed onto his chaffed wrists. A large tumbler of water and a partially full glass stood on a nightstand beside the bed he had been placed on. John carefully reached for the glass, sat up slowly and drank. A glass of water hadn't tasted this good in a long time.

Seeing the stranger stir, a matronly woman got up from her chair, crossed the room and approached the bed.

"Hello, sir." She spoke in a firm but pleasing voice, each Dutch syllable clear and easy to make out. "I'm so sorry you've come to us in such a terrible way. There have been vagrants and thieves about lately, and our farmhands have taken their protective roles much too seriously. I'm Sara Van Breda. Who do I have the pleasure of addressing?"

"I'm Dr. John Holwell, military surgeon from the Brittania, lately arrived from England. I was hoping to pay Pieter Van Breda a social visit and to have a conversation with him. I certainly don't have any ill intentions toward Oranjezicht or any of its inhabitants. Is Mr. Van Breda at home?"

"He is. But perhaps you should rest a bit longer? You took a rather nasty whack to the head."

"I think I'll be okay. The headache has already abated somewhat. Just give me a minute to straighten myself out and I'll be out in a moment." John wasn't sure at all if he'd be steady on his feet, but there was only one way to find out.

The story of who he was and what he was doing there was made a whole lot easier once he discovered that Mr. Van Breda spoke English. The two men were seated on comfortable rattan chairs on the expansive veranda, a wooden table propped between them, and laden with a pitcher of lemon cordial and a plate of delicate pastries.

"I do remember Wouter going on about two brash young Dubliners he had been spending some time with. Who was the other young man?"

"That would be James O'Connor, sir. By the way, where is Wouter these days? He isn't here by any chance? James and I would love to see him."

"Actually, he's down at our warehouse in Table Bay, dealing with family business. He'll return sometime this evening. You're lucky to catch him. He's back and forth to Rotterdam on a regular basis."

Pieter Van Breda had a deep, guttural voice, and his habit of running his hands through his thinning hair reminded John of his own father's proclivity. A brief wave of nostalgia washed over him as he remembered the parent he had lost not all that long ago.

"Where are you staying while you're here?" Van Breda ran his hands through his hair.

John smiled inwardly.

"We're staying at a lovely guesthouse part way up the mountain. Mrs. Versluuys is the proprietor. A charming lady. She doesn't speak English, but I'm pleased to say that my Dutch has come back to me quite readily."

A bemused grin spread across Van Breda's face.

"If by charming you mean stubborn battleax, then I can believe it! I've been trying for a long time to get her to sell us her property, but she'll have none of it. We've offered her a lot more than her property's worth, but she still won't budge. Her place would make an excellent inn for Dutch merchants and dignitaries visiting Cape Town. I have to admit, I admire her for her tenacity. When we meet, she likes nothing better than to spit vitriol at me, and I regret to say I give it back in kind. It's rather amusing for any people who happen to be nearby when we do cross paths. Beneath it all, I do believe we have a mutual understanding of sorts and that, in other circumstances, we'd be good friends. Her family's from just outside Amsterdam and made their fortune in the turf business. Sophie and her husband took their share of the family fortune and made their way to Cape Town. Unfortunately, not long after they arrived, her husband found himself embroiled in a conflict with some shipjacks down at the docks and one evening as he was walking back home, he was accosted and bludgeoned to death. Sophie decided to carry on by herself here in Cape Town and has made a very good life for herself in her establishment on Bree Street."

"She did say to beware of you and that you were a tyrant." John smiled. "Now I have some context for that remark."

John and Pieter spoke for some time longer, Pieter being particularly attentive as John detailed his life as a surgeon and his signing on with the English East India Trading Company. The day was wearing on and Van Breda lifted his long, lank limbs out of the chair he had been occupying. Holwell followed suit.

"I'm so sorry that you were treated so harshly by my men. I will be dealing with them. You must let me make it up to you somehow. Why don't you and your entourage come up for dinner tomorrow? I can have a carriage or two sent to pick you up. I'll make sure Wouter is home for the visit. No doubt he will be delighted to catch up with you and your friend."

"I'll have to speak to the group, but I'm willing to bet that they'll all be in for the visit. If you haven't heard otherwise by noon tomorrow, there will be six of us. When should we be ready?" John was readying himself to depart.

"I'll arrange to have you collected midafternoon. We can have a leisurely stroll through the orchard before dinner. By the way, please pass on my best regards to Mr. Versluuys," Van Breda offered wryly.

A much-humbled servant, Tomas, as John came to know him, pulled up in a smart two-seater brougham, pulled by a sleek-looking dappled horse. He jumped off the seat and offered Holwell his hand to help him climb onto the conveyance. They started down the path along which he had so ignominiously been pushed in the barrow.

John waved at Van Breda and his wife Sara standing beside him on the veranda. He put his head down between his hands, his headache starting to come back. He would have an interesting story to tell the others.

THE VAN BREDA'S

Darling Alice,

Oh, how I love to call you 'my darling'! This missive, along with the many other letters I've written since our sojourn in Casa Branca, should reach you in two or three months. The captain of the Normanton has kindly agreed to transport our mail back to England. Captain Rigby will depart three days hence.

Our stay in Cape Town has been very eventful...

John had begun to recount the episode of his first encounter at Oranjezicht, but quickly decided against it. There was no point in alarming Alice.

... Remind me to give you a fuller version someday as we sit drinking our chai (the Indian name for tea) on our veranda in our new home in Calcutta.

James and I encountered an old friend from Rotterdam days, whose family owns an orange grove on Table Mountain, among many other enterprises in this bustling port on the southern extreme of the African continent. Wouter Van Breda and his family treated all of us — James, Susan, her two chaperones, and Lewis Mayne — to a wonderful day at Oranjezicht. We dined on the expansive front lawn of their massive estate enjoying suckling pig, fruits, vegetables (many of which were quite new to us), and a plethora of other delicacies that I wish I could do justice to in the recounting of them.

We toured the vast orchard and picked ripe, plump oranges directly from an orange tree. On our return to the house, Sara (Pieter Van Breda's wife) immediately took charge of the women and took them into the parlour for tea. Conveniently, the Van Breda's had invited an

108

English-speaking neighbour lady to come by for the afternoon so that she could facilitate their conversation.

Pieter and Wouter spoke some English, and James and I could get along with our rusty Dutch, so we were able to converse with relative ease while sipping a most delicious orange liqueur distilled right on their property. We sat on oversized rattan chairs on the veranda watching the sun slowly sink into Table Bay and talked for some time about the Van Breda's operations in Cape Town and their involvement in the Dutch East India trade. Conversely, Pieter and Wouter were very interested in how James and I came to be travelling to India. They plied us with questions about John Company and because of our relative inexperience with the same we deferred to Lewis Mayne who responded to many of their queries, though we could tell he was being somewhat guarded in his exposition.

At one point, I had pulled out my good old Irish clay and was about to fill it with some of my ever-dwindling supply of Iberian tobacco. You can imagine my surprise (or maybe you can't!) when Wouter told me to hold off for a moment, stole into the house, and returned with a beautifully polished wooden pipe. He explained that it was from South America, made from the Brazilian Cherry Tree or Jatoba tree. While I carefully inspected his pipe, which was a rich, deep reddish brown in colour, he carefully unravelled a large plantain leaf that housed a small quantity of a stringy, rope-like substance. He broke off a piece about half the length of his thumb and offered this to me. I was to rub it out in my palm and put the resulting granules in my pipe. This was Portuguese tobacco, and if I liked it, Wouter would take me to a shop where I could procure some for the continuation of my journey. It was only fair that I offered him a bowl-full of my precious stock in return, and he eagerly accepted. We packed our pipes and settled back to smoke and continue our conversation. Wouter's tobacco was more pungent than what I was used to, but it had a nutty, earthy flavour that was most satisfying. I told him that I would gladly take him up on his offer to go to the shop that sold it so I could avail myself of some more.

The sketches accompanying this letter (which you no doubt have perused already) are of some of the local flora. Though they don't do justice to the actual plants, they should give you some idea of their beauty and peculiarity. It won't be soon enough, but some day I'm certain you'll experience this wonderful vegetation first-hand.

I don't know what James has told your family about his experiences to date, but let it suffice to say that your brother and Miss Worthing are getting on famously. I have no doubt that their relationship will flourish, and my instinct informs me that when next we meet, you'll have acquired a sister-in-law. Susan is a delightful young lady and James has been a consummate gentleman.

When you write, address your letters to me care of the English East India Trading company commander at Fort William in Calcutta. Of course, I won't receive them until sometime after I've arrived there, but I will be awaiting them anxiously.

Lovingly yours,
John

Wouter was a tall Dutchman, standing nearly six feet, three inches. The group had left the carriage just outside of the main port and walked southeast. Wouter's long, loping strides made it difficult to keep pace, but James and John did their best. Their host was in a jovial mood and peppered them with trivia about the local areas of interest. The houses here, shanties really, were dilapidated and in need of repair. The locals, a ragged-looking lot, gave the group a wide berth. They were families of slaves that had been transported to the Cape Colony to work the docks and to serve the well-to-do Dutch colonists.

Rutted tracks made footing rather precarious, and more than once, John felt his ankles buckle uncomfortably. Eventually they reached a row of low buildings, ramshackle shops that held who knew what merchandise. They were led inside the largest of these establishments. The anteroom consisted of low wooden tables surrounded by three-legged stools. A few shoddily dressed men sat about smoking crude pipes or some rope-like cheroots that Wouter explained was hemp laced with a cannabin substance. Suspicious glares greeted them as they made their way to a backroom that was artfully arranged and that was surprisingly unlike the topsy-turvy anteroom.

A beefy, corpulent man rather amusingly jumped out of the chair he was sitting in, knocking it over in his exuberance and scrambled over to Wouter, whom he obviously knew. The two men shook hands and exchanged some words that were wholly unintelligible to John. He could pick out a few words of Dutch with one or two English words thrown into the mix. They were taken over to a display of metal-hinged chests. The first one held a startling array of wooden pipes each nesting on a bed of straw. Wouter indicated that we could pick these up and examine them. There were a number of Jatoba pipes such as Wouter had been smoking and others made from various and sundry materials. James hung back, knowing how excited John was to look through the assortment and John eagerly but reverently began sifting through the collection. He set aside three of the most interesting pieces and asked Wouter to inquire about the price for all three. He knew that without Wouter there the cost would have been exorbitant, but after a brief session of haggling Wouter was able to negotiate a very reasonable price. The proprietor handed an assistant the pipes and he took them away to wrap them up in clever canvas socks.

The group then moved over to a burlap-lined crate full of the Portuguese tobacco John had tried at Oranjezicht. The proprietor inserted his pudgy fingers into the dark brown ropey mass and carefully gave it a good sifting. The aroma of the tobacco was heady and altogether enticing. After some more conversation between Wouter and the proprietor, John was told that the price was equivalent to a crown for a pound of tobacco. This was far less than the price of tobacco in London, and he eagerly agreed to purchase four pounds of tobacco. Wouter, in turn, decided to buy a pound for himself.

Another chest held a large quantity of the hemp that John didn't have any interest in, so the proprietor fastened the clasp on the crate, and the men were ushered into the anteroom. There they were seated at one of the tables and served very strong black tea, bitter but refreshing, nonetheless. A carefully wrapped sack with their purchases was handed to them when they got up to depart. John was over the moon with his purchase and walked out into the glaring afternoon sun with a broad smile on his face.

The entourage walked back to their cart and rambled on to an establishment Wouter directed the driver to take them to. There they lounged in a shaded alcove and were served a hearty meal washed down with cool ale dispensed from a large wooden vat.

Upon their arrival at the rooming house, John squared up with Wouter and insisted on paying for his pound of tobacco. As James was heading into the inn, Wouter took John aside and asked if he and James would come up to the house one last time before they departed; he had a proposal for them. Intrigued, John agreed, and the cart moved on up Bree Street on its way to Oranjezicht.

The autumn weather in Cape Town had served everyone well. Susan Worthing looked the picture of health and her two companions who had suffered remorselessly on the water had now come to life as they strolled the peaceful avenues surrounding Mrs. Versluuys' rooming house.

The layover in Cape Town was quickly coming to a close, and John was sad about it. As sad as he was, though, he was also looking forward with anticipation to the final stage of the voyage aboard Brittania as it made its way across the Indian Ocean to his new home.

A few days before they were scheduled to depart, John was summoned aboard the Brittania to witness the administration of the second set of forty lashes to Able Seaman Griffen. Brittania had stood proudly amidst a smattering of other vessels, including a number of His Majesty's, including the Normanton, which was soon to depart. Officers and several sailors from these vessels had been invited aboard for the occasion.

Griffen withstood his lashes without crying out, even though the five-week-old wounds had re-flowered, and the pain must have been excruciating. The dignity with which Griffen accepted his punishment almost brought tears to Holwell's eyes.

John applied unguents to Griffen's weeping back and carefully placed a plaster cloth over the same before he was led away to suffer in peace in the hold on short rations. Caleb Grantham had shown remarkable benevolence in putting off the flogging for several days after their arrival in Table Bay thus allowing Griffen to spend some time ashore with his mates. Many other captains, according to Mayne, would not have granted Griffen this little mercy.

The day before they were to depart, John and James hired a carriage to take them up to the Van Breda estate where they were greeted effusively by Pieter, Sara, and Wouter. Instead of lounging on the veranda, they were ushered into a study tastefully furnished with a large wooden desk and decorated throughout with artefacts from many parts of the world. They were seated around what had once been a captain's table from a sailing vessel and served more of the wonderful orange elixir they had been offered previously.

Sara left them after she had served them their drinks and Pieter got right down to business.

"From the time you arrived at Oranjezicht, and please do accept our heartfelt apologies for the way you were treated on the first occasion, we have been impressed by the two of you. Please don't be offended by this, and we can't reveal our specific sources, but over the last few days, we have gathered some intelligence about you both. John, your reputation as a surgeon has been confirmed by several of the sailors and officers aboard the Brittania. And James, we have been told that you are an up-and-coming clerk with sound business sense. We need men like you in the Dutch East India Company. We have a booming colony at Hooghly Chinsura, which lies some twenty miles north of Fort William. In the next year or so, Fort Gustavus will become one of only two posts that will be granted the right to trade directly with the Dutch Republic: the other being our colony in Ceylon. The trade at Fort Gustavus, as it is at Fort William, is primarily in opium, salt, muslin, and spices. Now we don't know what the terms of your remuneration are, but I daresay we will be happy to offer you both significantly more. And John, if your heart is not completely set on going to India, we would be prepared to set you up here in Cape Town with your own medical practice. There is an appalling dearth of qualified medical practitioners on the Cape."

Though it was obvious to the Van Breda's that this proposal had caught the two men completely by surprise, Pieter ventured on.

"Your time in Rotterdam will stand you both in good stead. Your fluency in Dutch, John, is quite remarkable, and James, it won't take you long to brush up on yours. The English East India Company will, of course, not be pleased by this, but we'll endeavour to do all that we can to protect you from any actions they may take." Pieter set his drink on the table in front of him. "Why don't the two of you take a turn in the orchard, and we'll resume our meeting in a little while. Take all the time you need to digest this."

John's heart was pounding as he strode off the veranda with James. The two men walked a bit before James opened up.

"We would be considered deserters, John. And besides, I'm not willing to lose Susan. There's no way I'm going to accept this proposal, no matter what money they're willing to offer!"

John quietly responded. With the turmoil going on inside him, it was difficult to speak.

"You're quite right, James. If I had known what they were about, I wouldn't have agreed to come up and see them one last time. Alice and my mother are planning to join me in India, and John Company has been good to both of us. We can't let them down."

The two men turned quickly around and headed back to the house. John was feverishly trying to formulate how he was going to deliver their verdict.

Pieter and Wouter were waiting for them on the veranda.

"Given how quickly you've returned, I'm gathering that you have decided to turn down our offer. We had to give it a try."

The even-handed, almost fatherly tone with which Pieter spoke immediately put John at ease.

"If it had been only the two of us to consider, we may have come to a different conclusion. But both of us have a lot at stake in this venture to Fort William, and our families are counting on us as well. We'd like to thank you for your proposal and your kind words, but we really do have to decline."

John reached out to take Pieter's hand and continued.

"No doubt our paths will cross at some time, and I know that I will welcome that. It may be that our interests will be in conflict in India, but if there is anything we can do for you that doesn't compromise our positions there, please don't hesitate to contact us."

Wouter shook our hands warmly.

"We have our carriage ready to take you back to your rooming house. In it, you'll find a case of our orange liqueur. Remember us when you sit down to enjoy it. Also, my mother has prepared a parcel of food for you that should stay well preserved for the next month or so. She says to keep it wrapped up and in as cool and dry a place as possible. Also, there is a letter of introduction for the commanding officer at Fort Gustavus should you wish to travel to Hooghly Chinsura. It will pave the way for a more amiable reception than the one you are likely to receive once they know you are working for the British."

With final farewells having been said, alongside voluminous hugs from Sara, James and John climbed into the carriage and were driven away from Oranjezicht.

STORMKAAP

"We must be at the southernmost point of Africa?"

John Holwell and Lewis Mayne were taking a turn on the taffrail. Brittania was slowly making her way out of Table Bay under skeleton sails and beginning to bear southeast.

"Actually," Mayne slipped easily back into his pedantic parlance. "The southernmost tip is at Cape Agulhas some ninety miles east of Stormkaap. We should be in sight of it in a few days."

"Stormkaap? I haven't heard that name before."

"Stormkaap is what the Dutch used to call The Cape of Good Hope. You'll see in short order why the name is so appropriate. Not long after we leave Table Bay behind us, we'll cross out of the Atlantic Ocean and into the Indian Ocean. The water here is always turbulent, and the winds can be fearsome. In fact, when we approach forty degrees of latitude, we'll be in 'The Roaring Forties.' It is so called because the wind howls unrelentingly up from the south, with no land to obstruct it. The captain will not sleep until we are well away from that area and Brittania is heading northeast and approaching Madagascar. By the way, Holwell, make sure to have plenty of the tonics you use to treat seasickness on hand. You're going to need it unless I'm greatly mistaken!"

The next few days were the most dreadful sea days any of the first timers had known. Large, heavy swells were the first sign that these new waters were less than benign. At least for a time, the wave pattern was steady and while it made for some queasy stomachs, what came next was almost diabolical. As the two great oceans met, the sea became a cauldron. People on board were thrown about and the captain sent orders for all passengers to stay in their cabins. The sails went limp and then whipped about with such fury that they almost sounded like cannon shot.

John made his way as best he could, medical satchel in tow, to make calls on the passengers and offer them whatever solace he could. James

116

accompanied him and he was a godsend. Unbelievably, he didn't seem to be as distressed as most of the others and John relied on him a great deal. Miss Worthing wasn't in a really bad way, but the same could not be said about her two elderly companions. The two of them were whiter than white, their hands clenched tightly to the bolsters of their cots. They were exhausted from ceaseless retching and long past the time they had anything more in their digestive tracts to disgorge.

When John and James weren't ministering to the passengers, they were called upon to set broken bones and treat nasty lacerations. Even some of the most experienced crew members needed the doctor's ministrations.

John ran into Mayne in the Officer's mess and received a quick update on Brittania's situation.

"I haven't seen the captain quite so worried. We've lost a number of upper spars, and many of the sails are in tatters. He's worried that we're being driven to a lee shore and is doing everything in his power to keep well away from land. When we find the nearest sheltered bay, he'll try to maneuver us there so some repairs can be affected, and we can get back on track. I've been in these waters a few times, and they've been rough, but this is by far the worst I've encountered. How are you holding up, Holwell?"

"I don't think I've ever been this exhausted. But I'm doing all right. It's a blessing in a way that I have so much work to do. I haven't had time to be sick myself. I took a nasty stumble down one of the gangways midships and have a nasty bruise on my shoulder that is turning from yellow to blue to black. But it's nothing serious. Thank God for James. He has been doing yeoman's service."

Having finished whatever cold lunch he could get down, Holwell got up and exited the mess so he could get back to work.

On the following day, in the early morning hours, a knock came at the doctor's quarters. Smake, the burly gun captain who had been such a font of information about running out the guns, stood smartly in the doorway.

"You must get dressed and come with me. The captain has requested your presence on the foredeck."

When John went to awaken James, Smake just shook his head.

"Just you, sir. I don't believe your assistant will be needed."

Getting to the foredeck took a matter of some time, but they eventually arrived, popping up on a scene that was hardly recognizable. A tangle of debris, broken spars and loose sail sheets had to be negotiated to get to the captain who was standing over a prone sailor with a few other crew members standing balefully around him.

"Holwell. Thanks for coming up. One of our crew has taken a grievous injury and we think he's likely dead. Could you please examine him and give us your report?"

John looked down at the prone sailor. When his eyes adjusted to the light, he took a sharp jump back. The sailor had a long shaft pierced through him just below the collarbone. His eyes were lifeless, and his mouth was a study in pain, agape, his lips a horrible blue and black. John steadied himself and put his fingers on the sailor's neck on the other side of the wound. In a few moments, he let go and came up for air.

"Dead. There is no pulse."

Caleb Grantham nodded and his second in command scratched a notation in a tattered logbook he had carried with him for the purpose. The captain had him read it aloud.

"Alan Watt, sailor, third class. Fatally wounded by a falling spar on the foredeck of Brittania. Time of death one hour after the morning bell. The 3rd of May 1733."

Grantham ordered some of his men to wrap the body in a shroud and then had them take it below decks.

"When we get to shelter, we'll have a service and put the poor soul to rest." The captain turned and strode off.

John went back to his cabin and related the incident to James as he was getting dressed for the day. The two men were quiet as they made their way to breakfast. The wind had abated significantly, and the seas were calmer.

Though Brittania was limping north like a tired old woman, it was nice to see passengers once more taking a turn about the deck. They were a little like the walking dead, pale and ashen-faced; nonetheless, they had survived the past few days, and a few smiles could be discerned.

"It's the white flags you have to be worried about in those waters, not the Jolly Roger."

Mayne held on to the railing, still somewhat unsteady on his feet. He had been responding to Holwell's question about what might be in store for them all as the voyage continued. Mayne hadn't realized that the question was meant to be rhetorical, or he had ignored the fact and so had plodded on.

"On the northeast side of Madagascar lies a pirate haven. Out of Antongil Bay the likes of William Kidd, Henry Every, John Bowen, and Thomas Tew have taken turns stripping European ships of their silks, cloth, spices, and jewels. Ostensibly, they have been conducting their spurious business as champions of the Libertalia, denizens of an anarchist colony founded some forty years ago under the leadership of Captain James Misson."

"What do you know about these anarchists?" Holwell's interest was now piqued.

"They were a group of pirates and some disgruntled sailors who were against the various forms of authority and social constructs of the day, monarchies, slavery, and of course, capital. They live as they like holding no allegiance to any country or government. They live off the booty they take from vessels that have no alternative but to run the gauntlet north of Madagascar. Instead of the Jolly Roger, which no doubt you have heard about, they fly white flags on their ships. They aren't as brutal as the Jolly Roger pirates, who would rob you of everything, take your boat or sink it, and not leave anyone alive. Rather, they consider themselves gentleman pirates, oftentimes just exacting a toll to pass. Encounters with them are costly but rarely fatal. They have been known to take hostages at times and hold them for ransom."

This was rather alarming information.

"What are our chances of escaping these pirates?"

"There are a number of elements working in our favour. For instance, we aren't returning from India with our holds full of exotic and valuable cargo, which would make us an even bigger target. Also, we have a particularly large ship with crack gunners on board and a captain who knows his business. The bastards will be interested in us, but they'll be wary all the same."

119

Later that evening, Brittania veered closer to shore where the navigator had espied a sheltered cove. The ship would lie stationary there for a day or two while the carpenters and sail makers worked frantically to get Brittania shipshape and ready for the last legs of her journey.

Passengers were happy to be out of the elements, but they were skittish nonetheless, looking nervously port side at the dark, mysterious African continent.

John had time to check on those passengers that had fared the worst in the rounding of the Cape, and he was pleased to see that most of them were on the mend. There were one or two exceptions and these he tended to painstakingly.

Just before they were ready to hoist sails and make their way north between Madagascar and the continent, the captain held a solemn service for the deceased sailor after which his body was consigned to the sea. He then called for a briefing in the chart room for all of the officers. Grantham stood stoically at the end of the large table and addressed the assemblage.

"Gentleman, many of you will have made this passage before, but I need to remind you that we must be on guard at all times. The gunners have been instructed to have their canons primed and to have their crews on standby at all times. At the earliest sign of trouble, the bell will be sounded, and all soldiers, officers included, must report to their stations armed and ready to engage. We will be sailing on a starboard course. If there are pirates about, they will come at us from the port side. We will make them rue the attempt."

When the briefing was over, John went to find James and the others of his party.

Miss Worthing moved closer to James, who protectively put his arm about her shoulders. The chaperones were wide-eyed as the surgeon filled them in on all he had learned from the captain, and earlier from Mayne. John didn't want to alarm them, but he thought it best to be forthcoming and he instructed them that should they hear the ship's bell ring continuously that they should immediately go to their chambers and stay there until the all-clear was sounded. Furthermore, they should have a little food and water in their cabin in case the action was prolonged.

On the third day out from the cove, the sailor on the crow's nest spotted a sloop veering out of a small bay sheltered by trees that Brittania had passed some minutes before. When it emerged fully into sight, the Jolly Roger flag was clear for all to see. The sailor called out the alarm and the ship's bells rang out. The crew sprang into action and soldiers rushed to their posts. John took his pistol out of his chest and jammed it into his belt. He raced to his post, where he and Mayne were stationed midships against the port rail.

"Why isn't there anyone stationed on the taffrail?" John's heart was racing.

"If the pursuing ship fires on us, the rear bulwark will be the largest target. The captain won't turn to meet her until she gets closer."

Just as Mayne had finished his explanation, they heard the first canon being fired. The pirate ship was still too far away, and the ball fell harmlessly in the water behind them. Moments later another shot fell so close that water splashed up onto the taffrail. At this time, the captain made a course correction. Brittania had been running with the wind at its back but now the ship was veering to port in a broad reach. The pirate ship was much closer now, and the next shot whizzed overhead shearing through the upper shrouds, just missing the main mast. Brittania was now close-hauled, heading southwest, bearing down on the pirate ship. Sensing the danger, the sloop corrected its course as well. Smaller and more agile, it too went into a broad reach and then quickly into a close haul. And then it made a mistake.

"What just happened?" John shouted out over the noise of the wind.

"They've gone into irons." Mayne shouted back, "The sails are limp. They overshot their close haul. We'll be beside them in an instant."

Sure enough, Brittania sped up beside the pirate ship, and her gunners let loose their canons in a resounding cacophony. Splinters of wood flew off in all directions and then the top of the main mast shattered. Screams and shouts could be heard over the water emanating from the wounded and dying. The Jolly Roger flag was reeled down, and the pirates had given up. Grantham gave the order to come about and shortly after that, Brittania was heading back to the north once more running with the wind.

Some days later, Grantham gave the northern shoreline of Madagascar a wide berth. Even then a white-flagged vessel could be spotted easing out of Antongil Bay. The bells sounded and the soldiers raced to their positions. Passengers scurried below to their cabins. Port side at his station midships, John sensed that somehow this exercise wasn't as frantic as the last. It seemed the Libertalia ship was just monitoring Brittania. They followed along for some half hour or so and then dropped off, having decided this target posed too much of a threat. Mayne and Holwell were at a distinct disadvantage, at least in the early going when it came to following the action. Madagascar was to starboard, and they had to look across the expanse of Brittania's beam and then try to see what was going on across the water.

The all-clear signal was given, and Brittania settled down to negotiate the crossing of the Indian Ocean. John spied birds, some with enormous wing spans that he had never seen before, and occasionally, small islands that slipped by Brittania green, but uninhabited, at least to Holwell's eye.

"Three or four weeks and we'll arrive at the southern peninsula of the Indian subcontinent. We'll pull into a couple of ports to conduct John Company business and then make our way north, up the eastern side to arrive finally in the Bay of Bengal and our home in Fort William."

Mayne addressed the entourage who were basking on the foredeck watching the mesmerizing dance of the bowsprit as it heaved up and down over the gentle waves. They were in good spirits having come through a very trying few days. Miss Worthing's chaperones, still pale around the edges, had recovered to a large degree. That was obvious to John as he watched them watch James with his arms around Susan, their faces matronly and disapproving.

Susan turned to face them all.

"I can't wait to see my parents!"

James gave her a comforting hug and the two of them strolled aft so they could be alone.

Up the Hooghly

Bombay, Goa, Mangalore, Colicut, Trivandrum, Cuddle, Pondicherry, Madras, Balasor. Mayne kept the group up to date on the settlements they were passing as they rounded the southern tip of India and made their way north along the eastern coastline. Brittania slipped into two or three of these ports so that mail could be delivered or collected. A few English East India merchants and a number of officers boarded at Cuddle where Fort St. David was situated. They would be carrying information and accounts to Fort William, a much larger and more important outpost.

Brittania had set sail on February 4th, and now it was June 20th, and they were coming under full sail into the Bay of Bengal. The excitement on board was palpable.

"*Kati-Ganga! Kati-Ganga!*"

This shrill cry came from one of the half-caste sailors working the port side of Brittania.

"What's he saying, Mayne?" John was standing on deck with his small party.

"*Kati-Ganga* is what the locals call this distributary of the Ganges River, which splits into the Hooghly and Padma and then flows into the Bay of Bengal. Fort William is but a short sail up the Hooghly. We should arrive at the fort in the early afternoon.

The air was stiflingly hot and humid as Brittania tacked herringbone fashion against the current of the Hooghly. The land, a tangle of brush and low trees, encroached them on both sides. After the open expanses of the Indian Ocean, this ever-narrowing passage was eerie and unnerving. Standing where he was on the foredeck, Holwell experienced a sensation of dread and foreboding. He had to make a conscious effort to breathe. And when he did, his lungs filled up with searing heat and he had to hold on to the railing for fear of collapsing onto the deck.

The sound of strange birds and whirring insects was all about them, and every so often an animal, or what John thought was an animal, let out an ungodly shriek from somewhere in the dense forest. The rest of his group had retired to their cabins to finish up their packing, and just as well because, the humans on deck were assailed by gnats and biting insects. John found himself constantly swiping away the menacing creatures, and already, a few nasty welts were appearing on his hands and on his face.

The closer they got to Fort William, the more life there was on the banks of the Hooghly. Washer women, their saris tucked inside out around their knees to keep them from getting wet, would stop wringing out their laundry or flailing the wet garments against large stones, which to Holwell looked like they had been placed there for that purpose, and glance up to stare at the imposing behemoth angling by them. Wide-eyed children gambolled by the water's edge crying out and waving to Brittania. Where the banks were gentler, water buffalo reclined on the reedy sand and let the cool Hooghly waters wash up against them.

Mayne informed Holwell that they were nearing Fort William, and so he went below decks to fetch his friends. The insects that had assailed them were still present, but in lesser numbers, and when Holwell and his group emerged topside, the ladies, Miss Worthing and her two companions, were wearing netting about their heads. They marvelled at the lush landscape as it slipped past. None of them could put names to the trees and plants that they espied, but they would get to know them as *sal* and *teak* and *peepal*; trees that provided valuable timber for building projects, material for artisans to carve into lifelike jungle animals, or for fashioning into exquisite furniture. Of course, it was also valuable in raw form to send across the oceans to England. Much of the riverbank was crowded with reeds and tall grasses, 'canebreaks' as they were known by the foreigners living in and around Fort William.

The excitement on Mayne's face was clearly visible as they neared the fort. He had been pacing impatiently on the taffrail deck. When he saw Holwell's entourage emerge from the bowels of the ship, he scrambled lithely down the gangway and approached them.

"The water here is brackish during the dry season, which won't last long now. Once the monsoons begin though the water becomes much fresher because of the run-off from nearby streams and rivulets."

Before Mayne could get much further in his exposition, a startled gasp came from the lips of one of the ladies. A large reptilian creature had slunk away from the bank and into the river just across from where the ship was.

"What was that?" cried James.

"That was a crocodile.'"

From the even tone of his voice, it was clear that Mayne didn't see the crocodile as an unusual feature of the Bengal landscape.

"A crocodile," marvelled James. "What other animals are in store for us?"

"Pythons, as thick as a man's waist and as long as a tall tree; Bengal tigers which periodically attack unsuspecting villagers outside the fort; clouded leopards that move so quickly when they're on the chase that you can't even pick out the spots which cover their flanks; elephants; and rare, but seen occasionally in these waters, Ganges river dolphins. Local lore would have it that the person who spies one will have a fruitful year. This piece of malarkey doesn't sit well with me. I spotted a dolphin a couple of years back. It turned out to be the worst year of my life. I lost my wife and only child to smallpox that year."

The excitement on Mayne's face, which had been so prominent moments before, was gone. Shielding his eyes from the group, Mayne turned about abruptly and walked away. It was the first sign of emotion John had encountered with Mayne, the first time he had ever broached such a personal topic.

The entourage didn't know what to say to each other. They just stared into the alien void until the gnarled vegetation of the riverside morphed into a large opening where a small village was laid out, and until they could see one of the imposing redoubts of Fort William looming up in the distance.

White Town, 1745

1 - Fort William
2 - The Park
3 - St. Anne's Church
4 - Omichand
5 - Court House
6 - The Avenue

7 - Lady Russell
8 - Burial Ground
9 - Mr. Holwell
10 - Cptn. Minchin
11 - The Hospital
12 - The Great Tank

13 - Witherington
14 - The Ditch
15 - The Cross Roads
16 - Play House
17 - Rope Walk
18 - Sgt. Worthing

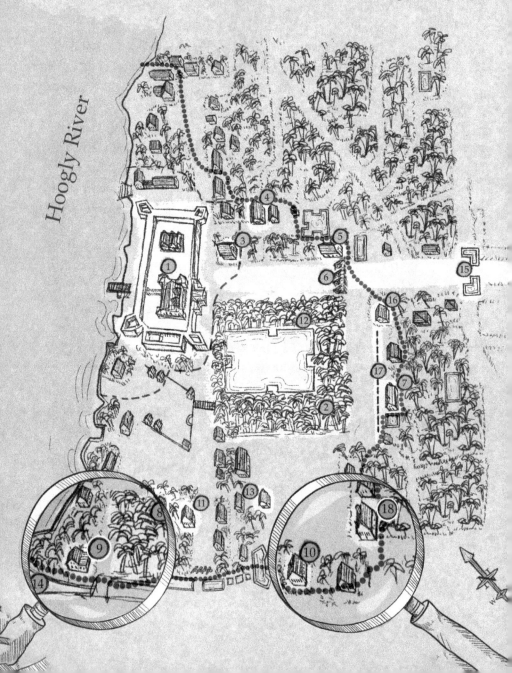

FORT WILLIAM, 1756

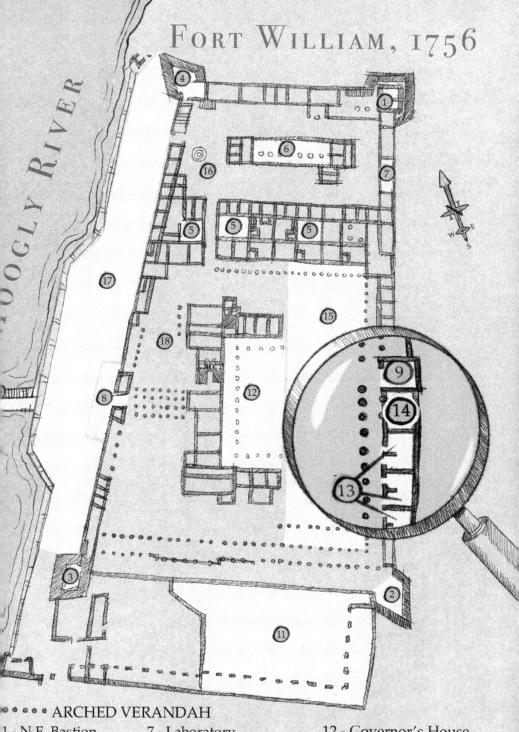

HOOGLY RIVER

BOOK THREE

ective View of FORT WILLIAM, in the Kingdom of BENGAL; belonging to the East India Compa of ENGLAND.

FORT WILLIAM

From the river Fort William was an imposing edifice, a vast, grey expanse that was obviously meant to keep invaders out. The ramparts that ran round the entire structure were stoppered at each corner by even taller bastions, each housing ten canons. It was in its time the largest such complex in all of Bengal. The governor, his family, his soldiers, his writers, and a smattering of other functionaries that occupied the Fort walked about and conducted their business secure in the knowledge that this place with all its fortifications and armaments could never be assailed.

Dr. Holwell's lodgings, surgery, and laboratory were in the far northeast corner of the fort, and they were perpendicular to the armoury, a long, low building continuously guarded by the Governor's soldiers. On the one hand, he was comforted knowing that armaments were plentiful, yet on the other, he was discomfited by his proximity to this cache of weapons as well.

The presiding surgeon, Samuel Godbout, had welcomed John heartily, and it was abundantly obvious he couldn't get out of Fort William fast enough. He spent an afternoon with John going over the lay of the land and explaining some of the administrative elements of the job to him. He was a short, thin man with a poxy face. A few years back, he had contracted smallpox and was lucky to have survived. His face was a canvas of devastation, though by his demeanour, one could surmise that he had come to accept his appearance. He introduced the new doctor to Samuel Chandler; the young surgeon's assistant John would grow to like and to trust.

Godbout's belongings having been removed to Brittania, he took his leave of Holwell, wished him well, and headed to the ship even though the departure was set for July 3rd, several days hence.

John was satisfied with how he had organized his surgery. His instruments had all been wiped down with alcohol and were neatly laid by in their canvas wrappings, placed logically on a wooden trestle near the operating table. A large ewer and pitcher for water stood at the ready just as one entered the room. The room's construction, as were the majority of buildings in the fort, was of wood, the roof shored up by stout beams. An old sail from some long-departed ship was pinned onto the ceiling directly over the operating slab. John had wondered about this curious chamber appointment, but before long, its *raison d'être* was made clear. Every time soldiers paraded overhead on the ramparts, as they were wont to do on a regular schedule immediately above his rooms, a shower of dust descended upon everything below, the lively motes dancing in and out of the fenestrated shadows created by the flimsy blinds covering the sole window whose aspect looked out over the armoury and the writer's rooms parallel to them.

The "writer's" rooms housed the many functionaries of the fort, especially the accountants who kept meticulous records of all Fort William's business transactions. There were records of trade with the local populace of Calcutta, with Sarfaraz Khan (the Newaab of Bengal), as well as 'bills of lading' related to the local ships which plied the Hooghly River, not to mention the East Indiamen like Brittania going back and forth to England.

James was newly housed in the writer's residence and seemed to find the accommodations acceptable, though a little spartan. John exited his room adjacent to the surgery and walked past the armoury on his way to James's lodgings. He passed the largest of the rooms, belonging to Lewis Mayne, the recently appointed comptroller of the fort, and knocked on the third door to the right. James appeared at the doorway and the two men stepped out into the searing heat of the day. The fresh shirt John had only just put on was already sporting perspiration stains under the armpits. Laughably, for the first couple of days at the fort, John had insisted on wearing his woollen surgeon's jacket, but the heat was unbearable and consequently he folded it up neatly and reluctantly stowed it in his travelling chest.

There was a lot to explore within the confines of the fort now that they had settled into their respective lodgings. James had already been out and about a few times, while John had been busy organizing the surgery and lab. He could act as a guide for his friend.

Having turned left, the two friends walked to the end of the writer's wing and turned left again passing through a narrow walkway which separated the residences from the officer's mess and the common canteen. While John often took his meals in the officer's mess, James was relegated to the other room. The two young men were still not comfortable with this arbitrary 'class' separation, but there was nothing they could do about it. It was much as it had been on Brittania. To top it off, the doctor had been invited to the Governor's palatial house for dinner on his second day in Fort William. He was to learn that the invitation would be extended on a fortnightly basis, usually on a Monday.

James and John hugged the western fortification wall to keep as much in the shade as possible until they came to the riverside entrance they had come through upon their arrival on June 20th. A sentry stood to attention when they came into sight and offered them a slight nod of the head as they slipped past him to the expansive wharf and the lazily flowing Hooghly. They walked onto the pier, with its wide landing steps and overhead crane and looked out at the landscape. The river, the colourful birds, the strange vegetation was all a feast for the eyes. John couldn't get over the trees across the river. Some were stunted and misshapen. Others were tall and stately. He did recognize the mangroves with their gnarled roots snaking sinuously out of the riverbank and into the water. And the palm trees, of course.

"I wonder how Miss Worthing is getting along in this heat?" James hadn't seen or heard from her since their arrival, and John could sense that he was anxious and pining for her company.

"Perhaps tomorrow we can go into Calcutta and pay her family a visit? What do you think?"

James eagerly agreed, and the two turned about and re-entered the fort.

They turned right, once again following the massive rampart and shortly reached the southwest bastion. They would have liked to climb up to gain a higher vantage point, but entrance to the bastions at each corner of the fort was manned and no one was allowed up except for soldiers on their rounds, gun crews maintaining the canons, or the Governor and his entourage. John, while an officer, was still an unknown quantity in Fort William.

At the southwest bastion they headed east, this time under cover of the long, arched veranda that spanned the entire south wing of the fort. Whereas the first part of their tour had been quiet with few people going about their business, now they were inundated with the noise of hammering and loud voices. James told John that they were passing by the carpentry shop and the carpenters were preparing wooden slats to be used to shore up bits of the Maratha Ditch. The ditch, he explained, was an additional fortification that would eventually surround not just Fort William, but much of Calcutta proper. It would act as the first line of defence if the town and the fort came under attack.

The carpentry shop occupied about a third of the expanse, and then the Export and Import warehouses took up the next two thirds. These were also busy, though there wasn't as much clamour emanating from within their thick walls. The warehouse was a holding ground for goods as they arrived from the ships, and for the exotic merchandise they were traded for courtesy of the Calcutta merchants and from the vast inner reaches of the Indian subcontinent.

The veranda now extended north along the eastern ramparts all the way to the writer's offices and residences, and in fact continued ninety degrees to run along their south side. Their northern walk took them past a primitive prison cell where drunken or unruly soldiers could be housed for a night or two, soldier's barracks, a guard house immediately adjacent to the Eastern Gate, and then the officer's quarters.

At the Eastern Gate, they stopped and turned into the central part of the fort taken up by the stately governor's mansion. The reddish dirt they had been traversing on morphed into a beautifully landscaped garden. Gardeners and other workmen tended the flowers and the carefully manicured grassy paths that led to the estate. Two immaculately attired soldiers guarded the stairway to the veranda that spanned the entire length of the eastern mansion walls, including its wings, which jutted out at right angles on each end.

John could now fill in some of the details for James as he had been in the opulent building on his second evening at the fort. He described the interior—at least the parts he had encountered. Lavishly embroidered rugs lined the floors. Exquisite candelabra were positioned artfully in sconces and on side tables; the tables crafted from exotic woods adorned with masterful carvings. Stately paintings, such as he had seen in venerable English buildings, covered the walls in the hallway leading to the dining room.

"The dining room, James, is absolutely breathtaking. At its centre is a massive dining table covered with the finest Irish lace tablecloth. A chandelier lit up with clusters of candles is suspended over the table. Rich brocades and tapestries depicting hunting scenes can be seen draped on three of the four walls. On the third is the largest tapestry that I have ever seen. It was a gift from the Newaab of Bengal, Sarfaraz Khan. The scene is a depiction of the throne room in his palace. The Nabob is seated on a cushioned throne and two Bengal Tigers lay one on each side of him, their leashes held by handlers standing nearby at attention."

James was suitably impressed, and it was with some sheepishness that John recounted the feast itself. He was quite sure that James would never be invited to partake in the Governor's largesse.

The two friends turned about and retraced their steps to the Eastern Gate. Turning left, they continued their walk under the trellised veranda past the officer's quarters and then veered left again coming to the south side of the writer's wing.

"Let's see if Mayne is in his office. We're going to need an escort if we're going into town tomorrow."

James led John to the largest office and John knocked on the wooden door.

Mayne called to them to enter, and they proceeded into the well-organized chamber. The comptroller was seated at his large desk, bookshelves and canvas filing boxes neatly arranged behind him.

It was clear that Mayne was pleased to see them. "To what do I owe the pleasure of this visit, gentlemen? I hope that you're settling in nicely."

"We are. Thank you." John got down to the request they had of him.

"We'd like to go into the town tomorrow and pay a visit to Miss Worthing and her family. We were hoping that you'd accompany us if you can tear yourself away from your work for a bit. Neither of us has been into Calcutta and I'm afraid we're going to need a guide."

"As it happens, I have a few calls to make to some of the merchants we do business with, and so I think that I could do that and find time to show you lads about. Shall we say ten o'clock? I'll meet you here, and then we can depart."

James and John took their leave, and each headed back to their respective quarters.

WHITE TOWN

Mayne tells us we'll never get used to the oppressive heat, just that we'll learn to cope with it.

John had picked up his latest letter to Alice from where he had left off the previous day.

I don't want to describe to you just how difficult it is to breathe when you're out of the shade—nor how humid it is—lest you should decide to abandon your decision to join me here in Calcutta. We are constantly wiping perspiration from our eyes.

James and I had a wonderful adventure today walking into town. I'm certain my words will come short in attempting to detail the extraordinary sights, sounds, and aromas we encountered.

At precisely ten o'clock in the morning (Lewis Mayne is nothing if not punctual) we stood outside of Mayne's office, each of us sporting a small rucksack. We struck out for the Eastern Gate, and having passed through it, turned immediately left onto a broad and dusty boulevard. To our right, directly across from the Fort is The Park, a large rectangular swath of green, which we're told comes alive each evening when British military families and other colonists take their evening stroll in the cooler part of the day. A large water reservoir, 'The Tank' as it's called, sits in the middle of it. When I closed my eyes for a minute, I could almost imagine you and me and perhaps my mother walking arm in arm down a wide pathway, where we'd happen upon James and Susan. We'd stop and sit on of one of the ornate wooden benches and carry on with some happy banter about the events of our day. (Please excuse this little fantastical digression. Whenever I see or experience new things, it feels like I am seeing them through your eyes as well. I can't wait until you're by my side!)

Directly in front of us was St. Anne's Church, beautifully spired and lovingly cared for, from the state of its trim wooden façade. (James and I have determined to visit the church some Sunday so we can see it on

*the inside and perhaps take in one of the Church of England services.)
In front of St. Anne's and leading east away from the Fort is a wide
road easily navigated by two horse-drawn carts. This is The Avenue,
and while James and I were drawn to its tree-lined magnificence, Mayne
kept us heading north toward the property of one Omichand, whom he
had some business with. Sadly, we walked past the west façade of the
church and then bore right past a collection of stately homes and small
businesses finally arriving at a large, rather opulent home surrounded
by palm trees. Beside the house was an office and storehouse, both done
up in the same style as the abode. This was Omichand's residence and
place of business.*

*Omichand is a comical fellow, though Mayne impressed on us not to
take him lightly. I hesitate at the use of the word 'lightly.' Omichand
is anything but light. He is one of the largest, most corpulent men I
have ever laid eyes on. The man must be nearly 23 stone! Can you
imagine it?*

*When he had completed his business with Omichand and we were on
our way again, Mayne gave us more insight into this larger-than-life
Jain merchant. The section of Calcutta we were walking in, populated
by English colonists and shopkeepers (The Park in the middle of it
all) is known as 'White Town.' Omichand is the only Indian native
allowed to live in White Town. He is wealthy beyond imagining, having
industriously (and unscrupulously) traded with both the Newaab
and the British. One cannot easily do business with the Moors except
through Omichand. This makes him a very powerful (and dangerous)
man, one you don't want to slight, and one you definitely want to be
wary of.*

*I asked Mayne what a Jain was and in brief (you know from
my previous letters how he can go on and on when he's on a topic
he's interested in) he told us that Jainism is an Indian religion
somewhat akin to Hinduism. Jains are ascetics and take vows of
non-violence, truth, respect for the property of others, sexual continence,
and non-possessiveness.*

*When I interjected and asked Mayne how a man with such wealth
and such appetites, and who was so cunning in his business ventures as*

Omichand obviously was, could be a Jain, he just shrugged and said it was a mystery to him.

Omichand's fortune and status were further reinforced for us as we walked by a palisade (guardhouse) just to the east side of his house and another in front of his warehouse. A burly, scimitar-wielding sentry was positioned at the entrance to each palisade. The scimitars were long and highly ornate. Mayne explained to us that they would have been acquired from Sarfaraz Khan.

We headed southeast and once again crossed The Avenue. We were now on Rope Walk. (How it got its name, I'm not sure, but when I find out, I'll be sure to let you know, dearest.) We walked by a playhouse on the corner of Rope Walk and The Avenue. I was taken aback. Mayne could see that I was astonished and explained that while the colonists were keen on the performance of theatrical pieces, the Indian population also loved entertainments of all sorts, and there were any number of such establishments in Black Town (the area directly north of The Avenue where the Indian population resides).

We strolled by Lady Russell's house (more about her later!). Rope Walk gave way to an open square, around which live many of the army officers and their families. It is in this square that Susan Worthing's mother and father reside.

"What if they aren't home?" Your brother asked rather wistfully.

"Not to worry," replied Mayne. "I sent a boy ahead of us this morning to the Worthing's with a note announcing our impending visit. I'm certain they will be pleased to receive us."

I'm sorry, I've had to take a break from my narrative. As I was writing to you, a young labourer was brought into the infirmary. One of the beams he had been using to shore up a section of the Maratha Ditch fell on him and crushed the poor fellow's shoulder. I've patched him up as best I could but once the laudanum wears off, he's going to be in a lot of pain.

So, where were we? Yes, we were about to arrive at Susan Worthing's abode.

As anxious as James was to take Susan into his arms, he rightfully held himself back in the presence of her parents.

Sergeant at Arms Henry Worthing and his wife Cecilia are a handsome couple. It's not difficult to see where Susan gets her fair countenance. They are also very gracious and welcomed us into their beautiful wooden home with a good deal of aplomb.

We sat in comfortable cane chairs and were served tea in grand British style. We talked about a great many things, and it struck me that the Worthing's would be fine companions for you and mother. They are cultured and well read, and Susan's mother, in particular, has a wonderful sense of humour.

The Worthing's insisted we stay for the afternoon meal, and we were treated to rice accompanied by two very savoury, but completely different dishes. One was a piquant pheasant cooked in what Mrs. Worthing called a 'masala' sauce. The other was potato cooked in ghee (a local cooking medium) and mixed up with green vegetables I have never encountered before and small black seeds. The meal was prepared and served by the family servants. They moved silently in and out of the room. It seemed to me that they enjoyed their work and took great pride in it.

As the afternoon progressed and we were sitting again in the cane chairs digesting our lunch, it became obvious to James and Susan that they wouldn't get any time completely alone. I was quite impressed by your brother. While he has never been the shyest of fellows, I still didn't think that he would take the bull by the horns and ask Mr. and Mrs. Worthing if he could call on Susan. But he did, and with a wry grin, Sergeant Worthing invited your brother (and me) to join them two evenings hence for a stroll around The Park.

Lewis Mayne had been very quiet over the course of the visit and seemed to be content to let James and I interact with the Worthing's. When I asked him why he had been so quiet, he just said that he didn't know the Worthing's all that well, and he wanted us to form our own opinions of the parents without his interference. Most of his business was with merchants, and he rarely had the occasion to visit with military families in White Town. He had enjoyed the visit and intimated that the good reports he had had of Sergeant Worthing and his wife had been reinforced.

On the walk back to the Fort, having now completely circumnavigated The Park, I asked Mayne about Black Town.

If White Town is unlike anything you've come across before, Black Town is totally alien, Mayne told us. He suggested that we wait for a few more days until we had become a little more acclimated to the heat and to the life of the Fort and of White Town before we ventured into the misery and squalor and mayhem that was Black Town.

And so, my love, I leave off this letter with a kiss. Brittania will hoist sail and make her way back to England in a few days. I will have a stack of letters and drawings for you (amateurish as they may be) in the care of Captain Grantham.

Looking forward to your letters upon the arrival of the next Indiaman!

With all my love, dearest Alice.
   John

THE PARK

It was Wednesday, June 24th, the day after their visit with Susan and her family and their first look at Calcutta, or at least White Town. On this day, Samuel Chandler, Holwell's new assistant, dressed in his finest clothes and, sporting a lively cravat, greeted Dr. Holwell at the entrance to the hospital located just to the southwest of Fort William. While John's rooms, offices, surgery, and laboratory were all within the confines of the Fort; the main hospital that served both military and civilian alike was just outside the imposing ramparts.

All staff that could be spared were also waiting at attention to greet their new supervisor. There were two or three nurses smartly turned out in their blue and white robes, as well as a number of day-to-day assistants, and of course servants. Chandler introduced Holwell to the nurses and the assistants and was about to shuffle him along to begin the tour of the rest of the facility when Holwell stopped him and asked to be introduced to the servants as well. From the looks on the faces of Chandler, the nurses and assistants, it was obvious that he had breached some sort of unwritten rule. Nevertheless, he persisted.

"This one's Katu; he's the bedpan *wallah*." Chandler pointed to a short, bald man wearing what to Holwell looked like an oversized man's shirt or perhaps and undersized nightgown. '*Wallah*' was a word he would get to know early on. As far as he knew, it simply meant "one who looks after or deals with." John offered his hand to the servant, who very meekly moved away from him while touching his own forehead with both hands.

"Sir, Katu is a Harijan, an untouchable, and he would be very embarrassed should you insist on shaking his hand!"

Holwell filed this piece of information away, knowing he would come back to it with Mayne or perhaps with the Worthing's tomorrow evening in The Park. Holwell let Chandler introduce the other servants, but this time made no move toward any of them lest he make any of them uncomfortable.

142

The hospital was neatly kept and airy and John was pleased to see that Chandler and the others took great pride in their work. The hospital was a long, narrow building that didn't take much time to go through. All the windows on the northwest side were wide open. They overlooked a burial ground very much in the English style, John thought, and accepted the breeze as it wafted occasionally over The Hooghly River. Each patient bed had a mesh netting ready to be draped around it, and no wonder — the myriads of flying insects would be sure to invade the hospital at certain times of the day.

There were not many patients in the hospital. John asked Chandler if this was a normal patient count or an aberration.

"It's quiet now. We're dealing with a few broken bones and few ailments brought on by advancing years. Just wait until after the monsoons, though. The country becomes a breeding ground for every disease possible, and we'll need all hands on deck."

"I keep hearing about this impending monsoon, Chandler. How bad is it really?"

"You know, sir, how in England it can rain incessantly and keep on for days at a time. Well, here, if the monsoon season lasts for two and a half months, we count ourselves very lucky. The water doesn't fall gently from the sky. It comes down in a deluge that's so powerful that it can flay the skin right off of your back. Roads and paths become rivers and streams, and getting about can be treacherous. You wait patiently for a slight break in the weather to dash out and look after your shopping or other outdoor errands. By this time last year, we were already in full monsoon. I'm betting that this year's season will be shorter but more intense. It will begin any day now, and it will go on until sometime in September."

Holwell's visit to 'his hospital' having gone quite satisfactorily, he exited the building and turned left onto a well-worn path leading into the cemetery. He read the names on the first few headstones. All English names he might have encountered back in London. The site was generally well tended, though the gravesites were overgrown and the markers in increasing states of disarray as he neared the Western edge of the compound.

Between the graveyard and the Hooghly River was an open tract of land where someone had attempted to establish a flower garden with rather mixed results. John sat on a stone overlooking the Hooghly underneath the shade cast by a mangrove palm and watched as the river lazily flowed toward its home in The Bay of Bengal. It was frightfully hot, and the air was still and humid, pregnant with the monsoon rains ahead. He let his thoughts drift to Alice and wondered what she'd be doing. His mother also came to mind, and he hoped that she was keeping well. As brutally difficult as it was to breathe in this suffocating heat, this was a very tranquil place and John felt instinctively that this would be a regular spot for him to visit, where he could sit and sort out the conundrums of the day.

When some time had passed and John knew that dinner would be ready in the Officer's Mess, he reluctantly got up from his perch and ambled back to the Fort.

"What is a Harijan, Henry? Yesterday when I went to make my first official visit to the hospital, I was introduced to a manservant who absolutely refused to shake my hand."

Cecilia Worthing gave her husband a knowing glance as the three of them strolled along The Park. James and Susan were several paces behind wrapped in pleasant conversation.

"A Harijan is the lowest hereditary status among Hindus. They are also known as 'Untouchables.' Typically, they are involved in work that is considered unclean. They deal with organic filth, bodily waste, and such. Some are involved in the butchering of animals, even eating some of the meat, which is an abomination to most Hindus. By nature, they are quiet when around others and quite self-deprecating. You would do best to leave them to themselves and only address them when you have a task for them to perform."

Henry Worthing was an imposing figure, tall and well built, and in other circumstances might have been considered a hard man. Yet here with his wife on his arm and his daughter in tow, his features were softened, and as he had been at their first meeting, he was amiable and soft-spoken.

"There are a good number of things you will need to learn about your new life in India, Doctor, and you would do well to observe and listen before jumping into something you don't quite understand. Now that is the only piece of advice that I'm going to impart to you." Henry chuckled.

"From what my daughter says, and I respect her judgment, you are a brilliant doctor and a fine, upstanding gentleman. I have no doubt that you will thrive here. And speaking of Susan, my wife and I are indebted to you for the care and support you provided her and her escorts while at sea. She has regaled us with many anecdotes about your exploits. We are looking forward to having you visit often and providing a first-hand account of your travels."

The heat of the day had dissipated a little, but John found himself wiping the sweat from his brow, which was trickling incessantly into his eyes. The company strolled along quietly for a time.

"Comptroller Mayne gave me some account of the politics here in Calcutta, but I have to admit I'm still uncertain of the situation." They had just turned right onto The Avenue and Holwell waited patiently for Sergeant Worthing to gather his thoughts.

"Well, you no doubt know that the population of Calcutta is predominantly Hindu, though you have already ascertained that even within the Hindu faith there is much stratification and significant diversity. The Hindus, for their part, are fond of us, and I think that they look at us as their protectors against their Moorish overlords. They provide us with most day-to-day merchandise — tea, rice, lentils, grain, etc."

"Don't forget, Henry, that they also provide labourers and servants to carry out our chores." Mrs. Worthing interrupted her husband, feeling a little left out of the conversation, John surmised.

"What of the Moors?" queried John. "Are there many in Calcutta? And how do they fit into the grand scheme of things?"

"A small percentage of the population is Muslim, and those that do live here are quite wealthy. They also tend to be standoffish and more than rude toward the Hindus. At this time, they have an easy relationship with us in and near the Fort. Most of them act as intermediaries in our dealings with Sarfaraz Khan, the Newaab of Bengal. His seat is in Murshidabad, almost 160 miles due north of Calcutta. The Hooghly River flows right by it as well. The only Hindu who rivals or even supersedes the influence of the wealthy Muslim families and merchants is Omichand, whom you've already met."

It wasn't long before they veered right onto Rope Walk and Worthing continued with his exposition.

"While the Hindus supply our everyday needs, the Moors supply us with exotic timber and the pelts of lions and tigers. Beautiful carpets, exquisite wooden furniture, and spices such as turmeric and cinnamon are sent down the Hooghly along with elephant tusks, crocodile teeth, and myriad other oddities."

James and Susan caught up with them as they passed Lady Russell's house. Lady Russell was a newly married lady in her mid-thirties. Tall and statuesque, she stood out, not so much for her beauty, though that could not be denied, but for her violent temper. Hindus, Moors, and the British alike gave her a wide berth.

The company had now come full circuit and parted ways in front of the Worthing residence, but not before agreeing to meet again in three days' time. The wistful look on James's face was almost comical but John decided not to have any fun at his friend's expense. Instead, he made small talk as they walked back to their lodgings in the Fort.

Black Town

Nothing in John Zephaniah Holwell's past had prepared him for this morning's experience. He stood in the middle of Bagh Bazaar with Lewis Mayne after a long and very exhausting walk north of The Fort through the heart of Black Town.

Misery, squalor, clamour, dust, heat, sweat, rich, poor, the unfortunate, the oppressed — all eddied about him along with swarms of flies. The flies seemed to defy the hostile sun to mill about the squatting fruit sellers, the vendors of fish, fowl, rice, herbs, and sweating vats of ghee. Dust pervaded everything and Holwell felt like it was coming out of his very pores.

Mounds of rice on threadbare cloths were spread out at the feet of rice sellers. Heaping piles of melons rested precariously on the dusty brown ground. Battered tin trays laden with sickly sweetmeats lay half hidden under a film of industrious flies and gnats.

Mayne looked anxiously at Holwell, who stood transfixed. He took him firmly by the arm and moved him out of the way of an approaching bullock cart.

"People come to the Bagh Bazaar from miles around to do their daily shopping and to trade with whoever is willing. It helps them to relieve the boredom and misery of their lives in the countryside."

John had hardly heard Mayne. He was having what he could only describe as a mild attack of the nerves. For a moment, he couldn't believe that he had chosen to come to this country. How would his mother and his darling Alice cope with this riotous place? Alice, leaving her emerald isle, and his mother leaving behind her stately home on St. Dunstan's Hill?

He took a few deep breaths and shook himself free from this state of asphyxia he had been hammered into by his surroundings. He tried to focus on the vibrant tapestry of life all around him and to put aside the dust and foulness and indigence that had been numbing him. He took a look about him with new eyes. The colours of the world around him were ones he had rarely, if ever, encountered.

The violence of a basket of oranges and the paler pastel hues of a heap of lemons suddenly made him thirsty, as did the green and brown tufted pineapples and the sliced pink and black-spotted watermelon. He turned to Mayne.

"Let's get something to drink, my friend."

The coconut *wallah*, his smile as wide as the gaps left by his missing teeth, used a mallet and wooden awl to punch two holes into the softer top of a coconut and handed it across to Mayne. Mayne passed it to John, and then waited for his coconut, digging out some small coins while he was waiting.

"Just lift it up to your mouth like this, Holwell, and drink."

Mayne took a long draught from his coconut. John followed suit. The liquid was surprisingly cool and sweet.

"Alice and my mother will love this drink, Mayne! I doubt they've had anything like it. By the way, how much did these coconuts cost? I haven't had to deal with any currency yet."

"I was generous and gave the vendor three and two, that is three *annas* and two *paisa*. An *anna* is one-sixteenth the value of a *rupiya*, and a *paisa* is one quarter the value of an *anna*. As money is my central concern as Comptroller of the Fort, I have become well versed in the local currency. In my research, I discovered that the *rupiya* is a silver coin that was to replicate the weight of 178 grains of cereal and was first introduced by Sher Shah Suri, a Newaab in the mid-sixteenth century. The Muslims have always been very clever in creating systems of measurement and husbanding their material assets. While it may be somewhat easier to get the better of a Hindu in the world of trade, the Moors are another kettle of fish."

Mayne couldn't help but slide into his habit of lecturing. John was used to it, and in any case, he had determined that Mayne's knowledge base was worth mining, especially if he wanted to be successful in his transition to this new world.

"What should we do next, Mayne?"

"Rak is the bane of our days here in Calcutta!"

Smake, the gun captain that had been so helpful in educating Holwell about the 'running out of the guns' aboard the Brittania stood before them on a filthy road they had been following back through Black Town on their way to Fort William. The men stood out front of a seedy establishment Mayne indicated was a brothel and arrack house.

"The sailors lose most of their wages drinking themselves into a stupor and then availing themselves of native harlots. Any money they don't spend on drink and women is likely to be pilfered by local ruffians."

Smake had a resigned look about him.

"I'm here to make sure these men get back to the ship without having to spend a night or two in the hole. It's only a few days before we take our leave and head back to England. We're going to need ever Goddamned one o' em on the sail back."

John heartily shook hands with Smake, and the two men took their departure.

"Mayne, what exactly is rak?"

"Arrack is a spirit distilled from coconut flowers or in some cases sugarcane blended with grain of one type or another. Production of it varies widely and there's no knowing how weak or potent it is going to be. Three or four glasses of it can put you into quite a stupor and your head will likely be pounding when you next wake. The sailors and locals simply call it rak."

"And what about the women? The ones I saw hanging about outside looked pretty poxy."

"This is one of those circumstances that we certainly shouldn't be very proud of, John. These arrack houses/brothels are all sanctioned by John Company, and we make a tidy profit off them."

The two men continued in silence through the rough, dusty streets of Black Town. John's profession had taken him to the worst sections of Cheapside and other notorious quarters of London, but he could never remember feeling like he was now. He could see the broad expanse of The Avenue ahead and its promise of White Town, and it was as if someone had taken off a huge weight that had been hanging around his shoulders. He was already thinking about how he was going to report this experience to Alice and his mother. He didn't want to scare them off; but he wasn't going to sugar-coat things either.

Mayne treated John to a lunch at one of the better eating-houses not long after they had crossed The Avenue. An unleavened flatbread toasted on both sides was served with potatoes blended with onions and green chilies, and some spice that John couldn't put a name to, but which was savoury and prompted a reaction that was quite exquisite. The aroma and taste consumed him, and he knew that he would be coming back here again to partake of this *jeera* potato dish.

A couple of minutes after they had departed from the eating house, it started to rain. Mayne picked up his pace and suggested Holwell follow suit. Fifteen minutes later, they arrived at the Fort looking and feeling like drowned rats, the cuffs of John's pants covered in red mud. The two men inhaled deeply as they walked past the guard at the East Gate, turned right toward their lodgings, and finally were under the cover of the arched veranda.

John turned to check on Mayne who, instead of looking disconsolate, had a sly grin on his face.

"Welcome to Calcutta and the monsoon, Holwell! I'll see you later."

MONSOON

Lading Brittania was a real chore in the relentless rain. John felt sorry for the sailors preparing the East Indiaman for departure. He felt even more sorry for the coulees lugging supplies and cargo from the storerooms and warehouses in the fort, struggling to cross the slick wooden pier and negotiating the treacherous drawbridge that angled down from Brittania's main deck. Sailors attached the heavier bales of goods to a sturdy wooden crane that swung out over the pier and onto the docked vessel.

John stayed out of their way, remarkably comfortable under the awning of the covered veranda. With the coming of the monsoon, the heat had dissipated a great deal, and if one were under some protective canopy such as he was here, the air felt fresh and cleansing. There hadn't been much for him to do these past few days. In the mid-morning, he would make the dash to the hospital and do his rounds. He would confer with his assistant and leave him any necessary instructions. Upon his return, and after lunch in the Officer's Mess, he would stroll to the South River Gate and watch the action on the pier and on Brittania, her men scuttling about her like a horde of army ants.

Two evenings prior to Brittania's departure, John sat with Grantham at dinner. He took his package of letters out of his satchel and passed them over to the ship's captain. It was a large bundle including letters to Alice in Dublin, to his Mother in London, and to Treleaven at Guy's Hospital.

"Don't you worry, Holwell. We'll see these missives safely over the waters."

Grantham had become quite fond of John, and the two men sat easily eating their meal and chatting about all kinds of things. The two men stood up slowly from the table and shared a hearty handshake.

"Grantham, if by some chance you happen to be the captain of the ship that brings my Alice and my mother to me, please look after them."

"I will, John. As if they were my own kin."

It was the first time Grantham had addressed him as John.

Days and weeks passed uneventfully, the routine broken occasionally by casualties of flooding accidents, building collapses, and the like, being brought in for medical attention. John spent countless hours with James and Lewis Mayne when he was available. He also attended the fortnightly suppers — banquets, really — at the Governor's quarters. Here he learned a good deal about the lay of the land and, in particular, Fort William's place in the grand scheme of things.

India was a patchwork quilt of fiefdoms, kingdoms, and confederacies as far as Holwell could make out. The Moghul stranglehold on India had been slowly loosening for the past decade or so. In response to his questions about the provenance of the Maratha ditch, especially the reason it had been commissioned, he learned about the Maratha Confederacy and its dominion over vast tracts of land north and west of Bengal. The Marathas, whom the locals called Bargis (a bastardization of the Marathi word for 'horsemen'), were always interested in expanding their land holdings and made incursions into the northwestern regions of Bengal and into Oudh, Rajputana, and Sind, and even Nepal, vast states splayed hodgepodge across the Indian subcontinent.

The Maratha Ditch was commissioned to try and hold the Marathas from venturing into Calcutta proper, should they succeed in venturing that far into Bengal. It was designed to be about nine miles long, an oxbow arrangement that began to the immediate south of the hospital and continued around The Park, then detouring sinuously around Omichand's Garden and finally enclosing Bagh Bazaar before terminating at the Hooghly River. Further to this secondary fortification, as it was considered by the East India Company, there was to be a stouter primary ditch, which began right outside the southern rampart of Fort William and encircled the Fort protectively. To date, about two thirds of the inner, primary ditch had been completed, and only the first mile or so of the planned secondary fortification.

When John asked about how real the threat was from the Marathas, he got two antithetical responses. On the one hand, a senior officer at the Fort, a Colonel Hatterly, in between mouthfuls of roasted pheasant, suggested that the fortifications were being put in place as a sop to the general populace. He believed that the Marathas were an ill-governed lot who weren't likely to succeed in any campaign against a much better organized British force. On the other hand, Babu, a prominent Hindu trader who had been invited on the aegis of Omichand, had a completely different perspective.

"*Sahib.*"

He addressed this to Holwell, but it was evident the words were directed to Colonel Hatterly, and a number of other officers that happened to be a part of the conversation.

"I have been into the heart of the Maratha Confederacy, and I can tell you that far from being ill governed and disorderly, the Marathas are fierce warriors, especially on horseback, and have highly experienced military tacticians guiding them. Chhattrapati Shahu, the Maratha Emperor, was a seasoned warrior himself before taking charge of the Confederacy in 1708. In his twenty-five years as Emperor, he has almost doubled the holdings of the Confederacy, and it is said he is still in his prime. My wife, Sahiba, still sings this cradle song to our neighbour's grandchildren when she is watching over them."

Most of Holwell's end of the table had grown quiet and was listening intently to the trader.

> "*Khoka gbhumalo, para juralo, barge elo deshe;*
> *Bulbulite dhan Kheyehe, Khozna debo kishe?*"
> "*Child has fallen asleep, silence has set in the locality, and the Bargi's*
> *have come to our lands;*
> *Bulbulis (songbirds) have eaten the rice grains, how shall I pay*
> *the tax?*"

"You won't hear this cradle song much in these parts, but I can tell you it is a common refrain in the villages and towns on the outer edges of Bengal."

Babu was about to continue speaking when he saw the look on Hatterly's face and stood down. The colonel's face had turned a deep shade of scarlet, and he rose from the banquet table.

"Balderdash and Poppycock, I say! Nothing but wives' tales and words to scare women and children."

With that he stormed off to the sideboard and helped himself to more wine, a task usually left to a waiting attendant.

Holwell had encountered this British sense of superiority before, but it was much more on display here in India among the officers of the East India Company. It was clear that they fully believed that most other nations were inadequate somehow — mediocre and fraught with weakness. When he thought about this carefully, he came to the nasty revelation that he had harboured similar notions of his nation's preeminence, and his conscience engendered an uneasy feeling about it in his stomach. He made a note to himself that he would search out this Babu and learn more about how the Hindus perceived the world around them.

It rained, and it rained, and then it rained some more, letting up, if they were lucky, for one or two hours per day. At these times, there was a great deal of dashing about. Servants ran to the markets, quickly buying up produce and goods that were barely visible under burlap swatches or coir mats. Children came out to play in the washed-out roads and ditches, racing their bamboo boats down the quick-flowing rivulets.

John loved the smell in the air in these brief interludes. The loamy aroma of the rich, red earth; the smoke from dozens of fires assailing his nostrils; the pungent, charcoal smell of Teenkona parotta being prepared for the evening meal in the canteen kitchen.

"It doesn't seem so bad right now, does it, my dear Holwell?"

John, James, and Lewis Mayne were taking a quick turn around the Park during a reprieve in the weather. Their boots would be mud red by the time they got back to their lodgings, but they didn't worry about it.

"But just wait! Over the next couple of months, we'll have almost thirty inches of rain, and you'll feel like you'll never be dry again. Water will have seeped into your chambers and your roof will leak. Walls and roofs will all have to be re-chinked when the monsoon mercifully comes to its end."

Holwell turned to Mayne, more than the monsoon on his mind. He had been thinking about his conversation with Babu and Hatterly at the Governor's dinner.

"Tell me, Mayne. Who are the Marathas that we are trying to keep out of Bengal and Calcutta in particular?"

"They are Hindus, primarily made up of two castes. The kshatriyas are a warrior caste, very colourful in their garb and very fierce on the field of battle. They hire themselves out as mercenaries to kingdoms that are in danger of being assaulted by northerners, such as the Afghanis who strike out from their centre in Kandahar and invariably try to increase their landholdings. The Maratha's price for this protection is usually a parcel of land or influence in the kingdom's governance.

The rest of the Marathas are predominantly members of an agrarian subcaste called Kunhi. They are servants to the Kshatriyas and make sure that their superiors are well tended to."

John didn't get to ask more questions of Mayne. The clouds opened up, and the three men had to make a mad dash back to The Fort.

EPISTLES

It had been almost eight months since John had been away from England. The last two had been especially miserable, as he and the other Fort denizens had remained holed up in their quarters waiting for the incessant rains to ease up. The only reprieves from boredom were the times they could cluster under the covered verandas and chat or at mealtimes when there was also some opportunity to socialize.

The sun finally made an appearance in mid-September, and another event was a godsend as well: the arrival of the Bedford, an East Indiaman, captained by a tall, hawk-eyed man, Captain William Wells. Bedford was a 440-ton vessel, a little lighter and hence more maneuverable than Brittania had been. She had arrived with ninety-seven of the ninety-nine soldiers with whom she had departed England, two of them having been killed in a skirmish with Barbary pirates early in the voyage.

At first sighting of the Bedford on the Hooghly River, as it made its approach to Fort William, the excitement at the Fort was palpable. With every new arrival, there would come an influx of new blood, young bucks wanting to make their fortunes, and sometimes families with eligible daughters. There might be sought-after English confections available to purchase in the Fort's canteen, and other British gew-gaws. But what excited the populace the most was the delivery of letters to the comptroller's office. At least one of Lewis Mayne's clerks would be assigned to receive and sort the incoming mail and to gather the post that was to go out on the return voyage.

Beginning the day after the ship's arrival, a long line up of eager civilians could be seen snaking away from the Fort. The sentries at the East Gate would only allow in a small group at a time, but even then, there was much congestion in front of the comptroller's offices. Soldiers and other military personnel were then allowed to join the queue on the following morning.

At the end of the first day of the mailroom being open, Mayne paid a special visit to John's residence and personally delivered a small but neat stack of correspondence. John eagerly took the parcel of letters into his hands and resisted the urge to abandon Mayne at the door and rush to his work desk so he could start reading. Rather, he exchanged civilities with Mayne and thanked him profusely for this particular kindness. He wouldn't have to wait in line after all.

When Mayne left—knowing how anxious John would be to delve into his correspondence he hadn't overstayed his welcome—John strode over to his desk, placed the parcel of letters neatly to one side, drew the candle nearer to the centre, and reached into an ornate sandalwood box to retrieve his letter opener. He lifted his pipe from its stand, tamped down the tobacco he had placed in the bowl earlier, lit it, and deeply enjoyed the first puffs of aromatic smoke.

He had waited months for word from Alice, and now that her letters were in front of him, he was hesitant to open the first one. He took his time arranging the correspondence, which he put into neat little piles. There were Alice's letters, a hefty dozen of them; missives from his mother he immediately recognized because of the beautifully flowing cursive script she was so fond of practising; and, his old colleague Dr. Treleaven had also included some correspondence. As well, there was a curious letter, in very formal script, and sealed with an official signet.

Where should he begin? He eagerly picked up Alice's letters and then impishly set them back down. He decided to tease himself by opening the very official looking envelope first. It was from the Lady Mary Wortley Montagu, the wax-embossed signet being that of her husband, the British Ambassador to the Ottoman Empire.

As was to be expected, Lady Mary was succinct and very direct in her approach. She hoped his voyage was going well (of course, at the time of her composition, he would likely have been in Cape Town), and once again thanked him for having championed her cause at Thomas Guy's hospital in London. Evidently as a result of the "engrafting" successes being witnessed, other hospitals in London were adopting the procedure, and there was a chance the smallpox epidemic in Britain might soon be somewhat manageable. To the main point of her message, she was requesting that Dr. Holwell keep detailed notes about the status of the medical world in India, especially in the treatment of smallpox and other such maladies. She would be curious about other medical concerns that he would routinely come across and subsequently any efficacious interventions for dealing with them.

John had thought a great deal about Lady Mary. Given her treatise on the handling of smallpox and her insatiable desire to learn more about the medical profession, he should have known that she would be interested in his experiences in India. He had indeed begun to keep detailed accounts of the medical cases referred to him including those he was dealing with at the hospital in Calcutta. He made a mental note to transcribe these in summary form for Her Excellency, the Lady Mary Wortley Montagu, and send them along on Bedford's return voyage.

Alice's letters were a delight to read. The first few were chattier than anything. She regaled him with stories of her family and life in Dublin. She had been keeping herself busy, helping her father with some of his administrative duties, and had been helping her mother around the house particularly enjoying preparing some of the family recipes and learning her way around the kitchen. She couldn't wait to share some of these culinary delights with John, *"after all, a doctor had to be kept well fed!"*

John would have to break it to Alice gently that in India the Western housewives didn't cook for their families; this duty was assigned to hired cooks. He would have to explain to her the delicate balance of economic life in India, something he was only now starting to get his own head around. The local Hindu population relied on work provided by the Westerners to make a living. Sometimes whole families were tied to the Britisher's households and serving them as cooks, dhopani's (washer women), ayah's (nursemaids), and general helpers. The notion of "servitude," which he had found quite revolting in England because of its connection to concepts such as snobbery, class distinction, arrogance, and superciliousness, was more complicated here. Certainly, some of the Westerners in Calcutta harboured similar notions to those back home, and it showed in the condescending way in which they treated the locals working for them; but, in many cases, the relationship between the foreigners and their employees seemed much more symbiotic and respectful. It was a confusing part of life here in India, and something John was very interested in exploring.

Alice had been tickled to hear about James's infatuation with Susan Worthing. She wanted to know much more about her and hoped John would keep sending reports about the two of them, imploring him to keep an eye out for her brother. In particular, Alice wanted details about Susan's physical appearance, her apparel, her *"bearing,"* as she put it. She had been reading her letters aloud to her parents, and they too were intrigued by this new development in their son's life.

The last two letters, dated March 22nd and April 4th, held some rather surprising news. On the 22nd of March, Alice wrote that she had been contemplating a move to London so she could be ready *"at a moment's notice"* to ship out to India. She had written to John's mother asking for her thoughts on the matter.

Her letter of April 4th was frenetic in comparison to the others. John's mother had replied to her earlier enquiry and had enthusiastically invited Alice to come to London and stay with her until they were ready to depart. Alice was now faced with convincing her parents that this was a prudent course of action. They understood that they'd be losing her in the not-so-distant future, but the immediacy of this development was not being taken well. *"John, I can't bear to hear my parents arguing when they think I'm out of earshot! I can't bear to hear my mother sobbing quietly into her handkerchief! It's tearing at my very soul!"*

In her letters, Mrs. Holwell also wrote to her son about the possibility of Alice coming to stay with her on Dunstan Hill Road. She was thrilled with the prospect. Her existence in London now that her son had *"abandoned her"* was very lonesome, and she looked forward to having another person about the place, especially her soon-to-be daughter-in-law.

She was full of news of the comings and goings of neighbours. Mrs. Pattison had become a soul mate of hers, and *"you're sure to be tickled by this. I have hosted several more dinners, having invited both Mrs. Pattison and Dr. Treleaven. The two of them are getting along famously!"*

The changes in John's world and the intensity of his experiences over the last few months had kept him from thinking too much about the pedestrian life of Dunstan Hill Road. His mother's easy banter about her neighbours and other goings on in the city was refreshing and left John feeling nostalgic.

As he got to Treleaven's missives, he wondered if he would mention Mrs. Pattison? In that he was disappointed. The good doctor was full of the news of Guy's Hospital, its doctors and patients, and the expansion of the "engrafting" program. He was happy to announce that most of the 'old guard' at the hospital had now *changed their tune* about the procedure. They still wouldn't acknowledge that the impetus had been borne from the research of 'that' woman and were quite happy to promote the idea as having been sprung from the eminent court physician, the esteemed Charles Maitland.

Now that the nasty weather had cleared up, John and James, and some-times Lewis Mayne, renewed their invigorating daily walks around The Park, often accompanied by the Worthing's. Overnight, or so it seemed, the world had gone from red bull dust seeping into every pore to water gushing in streams down every road and channel, to what it was now, a burst of colour. The world had come alive with flowers and grasses, so much so that The Park could almost be mistaken for a typical English garden. Ones senses were heightened, and Alice kept insinuating herself into John's conscious. And people had come out in droves. Holwell saw many characters he hadn't seen for several weeks. And then there was the birdsong. It too had returned full-throated and glorious.

One delightful morning, John couldn't resist calling on Lewis Mayne to take a walk about The Park. They stopped to listen to a bird perched on one of the many benches that lined the southern track. It had brown feathers on its back and a striking white underbelly. A red vent stood out in stark contrast beneath its tail feathers, matching two red dots sym-metrically placed under its shining black eyes. Its head was capped with a dramatic cowlick. John had never seen its kind at such close proximity, though he was sure he had heard its song.

"What bird is that, Mayne? It has such a distinctive call. So high-pitched, yet so haunting."

"That, my friend, is a *bulbul*, or as we English call it, a Persian

Nightingale. They make themselves quite scarce, so when one has the privilege of seeing one this close-up, it's a real treat. There is a saying about the bulbul. Should you wake up to the sound of a bulbul's call, your day will be full of promise."

In the evenings, he spent hours drafting responses to the letters he had received and in collating and summarizing his medical notes for the Ottoman Ambassador's wife. How he should advise Alice and his mother about making plans for their departure from England he wasn't quite sure, but he would consult Mayne and James to get their input.

James too had received letters from home, and the two friends spent considerable time comparing notes.

"What have you been telling Alice about Susan and me? We had only known each other but briefly before you could have sent anything from Casa Branca."

"Don't worry, brother. There's a lot more about the two of you in my letters from Cape Town. Just wait till those arrive in Dublin!"

James gave his friend a playful push.

PESTILENCE

Medical calls for Dr. Holwell were increasing by the day. Mr. Chandler, his hospital assistant, had warned him of this. Once the monsoons had dissipated, and the saturated earth slowly absorbed the moisture, standing pools were left everywhere and became stagnant. Mosquitos bred in them by the billions, and their larvae crawled out of the ooze and transmogrified into adults, some pesky, but benign, others carrying disease and contagion.

Ague and Marsh Fever were the biggest culprits. John was called out time and again to visit patients, who were experiencing severe shaking chills, high fevers, profuse sweating, massive headaches, nausea, vomiting, abdominal pain, and diarrhea. Some of the most serious were transferred to the hospital, where netting was secured around their cots, and hospital staff was kept busy trying to make the patients as comfortable as possible. Most of them recovered within a couple of weeks, but some poor souls never made it. They were restored to their families so they could be properly buried. Fresh graves could be seen popping up outside the windows of the hospital.

On his occasional forays into Black Town, John regularly came across Hindu funeral processions. If the deceased was from a well-to-do family, the body would be completely cremated, and the ashes would be spread in a place sacred to the victim. This was often Kati-Ganga, the Hooghly River, given it was a hallowed tributary of the mighty Ganges. Funerary urns would be solemnly carried by close family members down the ghats, steps leading directly into the river that women often used to launder their families' clothes, and the ashes released into the Hoogly often by the eldest son, if one existed, or by the father or closest male relative if the departed were a child. If the victim was from a poor family, only a small portion of the body would be incinerated, and the ashes scattered, the remainder of the corpse to be buried in a communal pit.

If it wasn't ague or Marsh Fever, then it was another devastating condition that resembled those ailments at first, but then mutated into something quite different and very frightening. The high fever would abate, but the poor victim would be left in agonizing pain, feeling like their bones were breaking even as they lay supine in their beds or on their pallets. There didn't seem to be a name for this ailment; at least Dr. Holwell hadn't come across one yet.

John wracked his head about this malady and tried to see if he could find out anything more about it from the medical texts that he had brought with him. But they were devoid of any commentary relating to a condition such as this. He had heard about practitioners of Ayurvedic medicine among the local population in Black Town, and against the protestations of Samuel Chandler, his assistant, Lewis Mayne, and even Henry Worthing, he decided to seek out one or two of them and inquire about this disease.

"Vaidyas are men who practise Ayurvedic medicine. There is one in particular here in Calcutta who seems to have an elevated standing in the community, one Sarasthra, though our previous Company doctor, Mr. Godbout, didn't think very highly of him at all. We are going to search him out. He has a stall just off Bagh Bazaar." Lewis Mayne had been roped into taking Dr. Holwell into Black Town to find a local practitioner who might have some knowledge of the insidious ailment he was so curious about. John would need a translator. With his facility for learning new languages, he had started to pick up a lot of Bengali words and phrases, but his understanding of the complex nuances of this language was still very rudimentary.

"The only would-be purveyors of medicine Godbout looked down on even more sneeringly are the folk practitioners who exist in multitudes across the city. They don't follow any written texts, and their treatments are based on superstition and blind faith. They sell their concoctions in the markets and on street corners. So many gullible locals are taken in by these charlatans, and they spend their hard-earned money on potions and elixirs that for the most part make them even sicker. At least the Vaidyas are working from a script developed over centuries."

The two men were striding along at a healthy pace, and John was pensive as Mayne enlightened him about the state of local medicine.

"Other than some of the Indian soldiers or those who are patients at the hospital, why haven't more locals, especially the wealthier of them, availed themselves of our medical expertise? There is no law written or unwritten, as far as I'm aware, to prevent them from doing so?" John had been thinking about this for the last little while.

"The natives are very distrustful of our British doctors and our Western ways. It's only after more and more Indian soldiers sailing on our ships have been exposed to Western medicine that they spread the word back home and give a modicum of credibility to what we do and how we do it. Still, they prefer to see their *vaidyas* or *hakims* or some of those witch doctors I was speaking of earlier."

"*Hakims*? What are they?" John had never heard this term.

"*Hakims* are who the Moors go to for medical assistance. They practise what is called *unani*."

Here was a word Holwell was familiar with. Indeed, the Lady Mary Wortley Montagu had discussed *unani* at some length in her dissertation of medicine in the Ottoman Empire. This was a system of medicine that sprang up from the Quoran and other holy treatises of the Islamic world. While it shared some similarities to the Ayurvedic tradition, especially in its advocacy of natural, organic treatments, it was also very concerned with right living and prevention of disease. The Unani tradition, as Ayurveda, went back centuries in its development. John would have to search out Unani practitioners as well to help round out his knowledge of Indian medical traditions.

Holwell couldn't wait to get back to his chambers in the Fort so he could collate the copious notes he'd taken that afternoon. His visit with Sarasthra in the Bagh Bazaar had been exhilarating. Once the Indian ayurvedic had finished with the patient he had been dealing with, a woman with a reddish rash all over her face and the backs of her arms, he carefully washed his hands in a bucket kept close for that purpose. Only then did he acknowledge Mayne and Holwell by pressing the fingers of both hands to his forehead before extending them out in a welcoming posture. The simple gesture of washing his hands after his interaction with his patient was encouraging to Holwell. At least this Indian doctor valued hygiene.

The three men sat under the shade of a banyan tree, and it was all

John could do to keep up with his note taking. Through Mayne, he had asked about two of the medical conditions that had been cropping up insidiously ever since the monsoon rains had ceased. He had only got two thirds of the way in describing the symptoms of one of the ailments when Sarasthra politely raised his hand and said, *"Myaleriya."* He then went on to enumerate several treatment possibilities. John had to interrupt on several occasions so that he could get as close an approximation to the spelling (though it would have to be phonetic for the time being) of the herbs and preparations Sarasthra was talking about.

The second condition, the one characterized by excruciating muscle and joint pain, and the one with the higher mortality rate of the two, Sarasthra called *"Hara bhanga ibarra,"* or "bone-breaking fever," as Mayne translated it. For this condition as well the small, wiry ayurvedic provided a litany of treatments.

As the men sat and continued their discussion, a beautiful woman in a simple but beautiful sari had served them hot water in mudden cups, into which Sarasthra crumbled some leaves he removed from a small container.

"Is this tea?" John had asked.

"Hartake leaves, grown in the upper reaches of the great mountains to the north, when crushed and mixed in hot water, will keep your body strong and protect you from disease. This you should drink once or twice every day." At least that was the gist of what Sarasthra had to say on the matter, according to Mayne. In a display of humble benevolence, and after quietly speaking to the woman who had served them the hot water, she left and then returned with a small packet of the hartake, which the Ayurvedic presented to Holwell.

On their way back to the Fort, John was effusive about this interaction with Sarasthra.

"Why was he so accommodating? I assumed that he'd be more reticent about sharing his knowledge with foreigners."

"First of all, I am well known in the community, and Sarasthra, wanting no trouble with the Fort, has deigned to treat me with the respect accorded to my position.

"Perhaps more genuinely, Sarasthra is a true ayurvedic, and he believes that we should do anything we can to help people. If by educating you about certain remedies for treating common ailments, you can ease people's pain, he feels he has been of use. I did tell him you were the lead physician at the Fort. This altruistic philosophy, by the way, doesn't extend to the other quacks selling their powders and unctions in the market. They hold on tight-fistedly to their recipes and guard them as great mysteries that only they can unlock and only they can provide to their paying customers."

John sat at his candle-illuminated desk and carefully surveyed the list of all the ingredients he was going to have to research. As a man of science and medicine, this activity gave him a great deal of pleasure. While his list was comprehensive, he knew it was just the tip of the proverbial iceberg, and most of the words... Well, they were largely unintelligible. If they had been Greek or Latin, he could have parsed them etymologically, but there was no chance of that here. His eyes pored over the list.

Sapta parna ki Chala
Giloy
Matha/H Artke
Dhane Paani
Sukano la'u
Lokabala
Hemcaka
Pippali
Behera
Brahmi
Belgiri (Bhel Phala)

MURSHIDABAD

The Huntington, a small English East India trading vessel, tacked relentlessly up the Hooghly River, fighting the strong currents precipitated by the heavy monsoon rains of a few weeks past. John and Lewis Mayne spent countless hours on the deck watching the Bengal landscape slide by and talking about all sorts. Mayne provided a constant commentary on the towns and villages, especially in the context of their relationship with Calcutta. He had invited the Company doctor to accompany him on a business trip to Murshidabad, the centre of the Newaab's prefecture.

"Our relationship with Sarfaraz Khan is very important to us, and we must do all we can to maintain the terms we have with him, tenuous as they are. You would do well to see for yourself the scope of his empire and the position we are in when dealing with him."

"I'd like that." John had replied. "Also, I'd very much like to visit Hooghly-Chinsura, the Dutch trading post. I believe Fort Gustavus is about a day's journey north of Calcutta?"

Mayne had been taken aback somewhat by this request, and after a moment's hesitation, he addressed Holwell.

"Perhaps we can arrange that on the way back from Murshidabad. We have very little to do with the Dutch, and they have little to do with us as well. Yet it might be valuable to have you do some reconnaissance for us. You'd better take along the letter of introduction Mr. Van Breda gave to you in Cape Town. No doubt that could open up a few doors for you that most of us couldn't enter!"

Mayne had pointed out the fortifications of Fort Gustavus as they slipped by the site on the western shores of the river, the town of Hoogly-Chinsura spread out haphazardly to the north. John paid special attention to one or two beautiful dwellings and expansive gardens that lined the waterway. He also was quite taken by an ornate building, a temple, that was in its final stages of construction.

"I don't know anything about that edifice, John. You'll have to ask about it when we drop you off here on the way back."

His notebook always at the ready, John jotted down the names of the many settlements they sailed past and included detailed descriptions of the salient landmarks. His botanical journal was filling up with sketches of the diverse flora they came across. Mayne was intrigued by John's attention to these details, but he could only add but a little to the explication of these species.

As the vessel passed by, children splashing in the shallows and washerwomen rinsing their linens in the fast-flowing Hooghly and then beating them against large rocks as if exorcising demons, stopped what they were doing and stared out at them, the ship a novel respite to their everyday experience. In the distance labourers in the fields could be seen tending their crops and teams of bullock carts rumbled leisurely down rutted pathways. Hundreds of colourful birds wheeled overhead and in the more forested areas the screeching of monkeys and occasionally the roar of a lion were eerie reminders that this wasn't the bucolic countryside of his English homeland.

At night, when the Huntington was anchored in a quiet elbow of the Hooghly or moored at one of the docks in some small trading settlement, John and Lewis Mayne would take a turn about the deck. They would look up and marvel at the panoply of stars that populated the sky. The smoke from John's pipe would rise sinuously into the cool evening air. At these times, the two men rarely spoke; they just luxuriated in each other's company and in the exotic world in which they found themselves.

According to Mayne, the sailing to Murshidabad would take about ten days, the return trip would be about half of that. On the final evening, John pulled out his notebook and scanned the names of the settlements they had passed. He marvelled at the words, some which slipped easily from his lips, others, more alien, that tripped him up.

Barrakpur, Chinsura, Kalgami, Jirat, Payradanga, Baghnapara, Dhatrigam, Mayapur, Katura, Bazarsan, Berhampore, and, of course, their destination, *Murshidabad*.

The only thing missing was being able to share these wondrous experiences with Alice. He pined for her as he stared out into the gloaming, wondering where she was and what she was doing. He whispered her name into the darkness and shuffled off to his cabin.

The waterway became busier, and more and more people could be spied along the shore. Murshidabad was a long, sprawling city bustling with commerce, and it was some time before the Huntington docked at the main wharf.

A runner was sent on to the English East India Trading Company's offices by Mayne to announce their arrival, and in short order, two palanquins were sent to transport them into the city. The contraption John stepped into was a covered litter, little more than a box with a cushion to sit on. Two lengthy poles extended beneath, and four wiry natives set to picking up the poles and as one began to make their way through the dusty lanes of Murshidabad. John had seen palanquins in Calcutta. Indeed, Omichand, the obese Jain merchant, could often be seen—rather comically, from Holwell's point of view—being shuttled hither and yon in a conveyance that was more ornate than the one he was in now. John, feeling very self-conscious, would have been happier to walk, but Mayne had assured him this was the appropriate way for them to get around Murshidabad.

As the palanquin made its way to the Company's offices, and as Holwell stared out at the wash of humanity streaming around him, he thought back to the many conversations he had had with Mayne about Murshidabad.

Murshidabad was the capital of the Bengal Subah in the Moghul Empire, and its jurisdiction extended across the Indian states of West Bengal, Bihar, and Orissa. It was a wealthy city, perhaps the most prosperous of all in Moghul India. Here the hereditary Newaabs had their seat. The state treasury was here as were the main revenue offices and the central judiciary.

This cosmopolitan city with a population approaching 700,000 people was home to many wealthy banking and mercantile families. European concerns, such as the English East India Company, the French East India Company, the Dutch East India Company, and the Danish East India

Company, conducted their business and operated bustling factories that were dotted across the vast precincts of the city. Murshidabad was a nexus of silk production and the centre of art and culture in the region. It was renowned for ivory sculpture and Moghul painting. Hindustani classical music flourished here, and Holwell was hoping they'd be able to sample it all.

It was midafternoon when they arrived at their first destination. Mayne had the palanquins wait outside while he and Holwell went indoors to hand over the mail that had been accumulating for the military members stationed in Murshidabad and likewise for the numerous functionaries of John Company. He introduced Holwell to the chief factor at the headquarters, a Stanley Millman, and then the two men returned to the palanquins to continue their journey to where they would reside in Murshidabad.

As the two men emerged from the expansive building, the palanquin carriers darted out from under the shade of a banyan tree and assumed their positions at each corner of the two conveyances. Mayne barked out the destination, and they were off. They were headed to the northeast quadrant of Murshidabad.

Before long, John spied an imposing yet striking building with two large, citadel-like towers looming at each corner of the façade. The whole structure was nestled in a grove of trees and lush greenery, a stark contrast to the red bull dust and coarse vegetation they had been traversing through. It was just as he had imagined what an oasis in a desert would be like. The road leading up to this oasis was wide, dusty, and busy, but as soon as they had crossed into the private sanctum of this edifice, it was like they had been magically transported into the world of Scheherazade, Sinbad, and Shahryar, characters he had fallen in love with as a boy from Richard Burton's collection of Middle Eastern folk tales published in 1704. He could still perfectly recall the look and feel of the book, which had sat in his father's library and now resided with his mother on St. Dunstan's Hill. The air was cool here and an air of languor enveloped him.

When Mayne dismissed the two litters, he strode up to John, who was standing entranced before the marble staircase leading up to the building's ornate main doors.

"Welcome to the Katra Masjid. This is where we'll be staying for the next couple of weeks. I don't usually stay here while in Murshidabad—the cost is rather extravagant—but I thought it would be a treat for you. Anybody of consequence who comes to do business with the Newaab stays here. The Newaab's residence is very near here, as is the Durbar, which is his noble court where formal meetings are held and discussions of state often supervene."

The aromatic fragrance of meticulously tended flowers rose from the garden outside his room as the surgeon luxuriated in a hot bath. The tub was made of stone and sat on four carved pedestals. An ingenious hole, stoppered by a rubber bung, kept the water in the tub until it was time to drain it. A narrow aqueduct cut into the tiles led away from the tub from just under the hole and made its way across the floor to a small opening in the exterior wall, where ostensibly the water cascaded down to the ground outside the building.

The Katra Masjid was a traveller's inn, a *caravanserai*, Mayne called it. 'Katra Masjid' literally translated into 'caravanserai mosque.' And indeed, as John would discover, there was a splendid Moghul mosque loosely attached to the inn. Before John had left Mayne to freshen up in his chamber, he had asked his friend about the crenellated openings in the two towers that framed the building. He learned that they were musket holes, more fanciful than functional, but which could be used if the Newaab's estate was under attack.

As he lay back in the steaming water, he mused about where his life had brought him. Life in India could be harsh, but it was also an exotic world, full of mystery and colour, with many elements of sheer, exquisite beauty. He closed his eyes and smiled. He couldn't wait to share this all with Alice!

That evening, the meal in the dining chamber was a feast he would remember for a long time. It reminded him of the luncheon they had enjoyed in Casa Branca, but even more lavish.

As they sat reclining on oversized, beautifully embroidered cushions around a low table laden with mutton *pilau*, spiced kebabs, *kuchumber raita*, and fruits of every description, Mayne was providing a steady commentary.

"Don't expect to eat like this every day we're in Murshidabad! I just thought I'd let you experience the gamut of what the Katra Masjid can offer its guests. While I'm at the East India offices, you'll have the chance to travel about freely, and you can eat in one of the many fine establishments in the city. You'll also want to avail yourself of some of the local delicacies offered up by street vendors. One of my favourites is the potato cakes served on plantain leaves with a tasty coriander chutney as an accompaniment.

"I have arranged for a local guide to help you find your way about Murshidabad. He will be waiting for you outside the gates in the morning. I'm going to retire early. Feel free to walk about the grounds this evening, John. Just don't go into the Durbar or into the mosque. There are strict protocols for entrance to those areas."

With that, the two men got to their feet rather sluggishly. Mayne went off to his room, and John went to fetch his pipe. He sorely wanted to stretch his legs and fancied a stroll in the beautiful gardens.

THE GRAND MASJID

The *masjid*, with its conical minarets, loomed imposingly before them.

"Katharu, can any Muslim worship in this mosque? Or is entrance restricted?" John stood beside his guide, a slim, wiry man whose age he could only guess at.

"The Grand Masjid is restricted to the Newaab's immediate family, his guests, and some of the wealthier Muslim families who have some connection to Sarfaraz Khan. We are standing in front of the women's and children's entrance; the men's is to the right and around the corner from here." Katharu spoke quietly, but his English diction was unblemished and crisp. It reminded John of a grammar tutor he had once had in London. When he had met the guide in front of the gates to the Katra Masjid after a leisurely breakfast and heard him speak for the first time, he was completely taken aback. Katharu's very Indian appearance and the disparate nature of his English pronunciation had been difficult to reconcile.

Workman and artisans were crawling all over spidery scaffolding that stretched up the western portion of the outer façade. John stood and admired their efficient movements. He had a fleeting reminder of Robert Cadman scaling the walls of a church somewhere in the heart of England. Attention was being paid to a section of the marble wall sorely in need of repair. He had just turned to ask Katharu a question about the workmen when his gaze was drawn to a young boy smartly turned out, with tight-fitting pants and a colourful thobe thrown over his upper body. He was running toward the construction site, and a little way behind him was a young woman, her black shash billowing up behind her head. She was carrying an infant on her hips, and it was clear she had lost control of her son. It was an amusing sight at first, and then John felt a terrible sense of foreboding. A marble block was being hoisted by block and tackle, and the boy would soon be directly beneath. The mother had nearly caught up to her son when a loud cry went up from one of the workmen. The marble block had snagged on a piece of the scaffolding and had become dislodged from its harness.

John stood transfixed. He could see it all unfolding, almost as if the accident were happening in slow motion. The marble block balanced precariously in its basket and then toppled over. It smashed through the two wooden scaffold cross beams below which then came tumbling after the block. One workman, who had been standing on the lower footing, was sent flying about ten feet to the ground. The block plummeted to the earth just narrowly missing the little boy, but he wasn't so lucky evading wood, tools, and other debris that rained down on top of him.

The young mother was in hysterics, and two servants who had been following behind her now came to where she was standing over the prone and bloody shape of her son. The baby on his mother's hip was wailing.

John and Katharu raced over to the chaotic scene.

His training and medical experience set him immediately to taking charge. He yelled out commands, and Katharu translated for those around them.

John's first task was to have the boy's retinue and the other workers and bystanders stand back so he could assess the situation. This was easier said than done, especially for the horrified mother. Before he bent down to examine the child, he called to the worksite supervisor, who had moved to the forefront to attend to the worker who had fallen off the scaffolding.

"Keep him calm, but don't move him!" Katharu relayed the doctor's instructions.

Turning his full attention to the young child, John gingerly pulled some of the fallen debris off his head and lower body. He checked the boy's pulse and was happy to see it was strong. His eyes were glazed over, the lids only partially closed and fluttering erratically. The lad wasn't quite unconscious, but he was almost there.

John checked for broken bones or other signs of distress. Luckily, barring a few scrapes and abrasions and a nasty welt above the boy's left knee, he seemed to be relatively unscathed.

Before he could even ask Katharu to have someone bring some water and clean linen to him, a woman from a nearby fruit stand came forward with a bucket of water and a cloth that had been covering some of her fruit. John was concerned about the piece of cloth. It did look clean and smelled clean when he put it to his nose, but who knew what contagion might reside on it. He tore the cloth into two pieces and dipped one of them into the bucket of water. Then, deciding to take a chance, he used the wet cloth to gently wipe the boy's head, washing the blood away from his eyes.

"The boy will be alright," he had Katharu translate for the mother. "But he will need to be watched carefully over the next few hours."

The site supervisor had been doing a reasonably good job of keeping the fallen worker calm. John now went over to where he was lying on the ground. The worker was moaning and holding his ankle that was twisted awkwardly and was swelling up enormously. Katharu came over to them and John used him to communicate.

"Besides your ankle, is there anywhere else you're feeling pain?"

The man at first was wary of John, but after Katharu said a few words to him he cooperated with the English doctor. The man's right elbow was banged up probably having struck a part of the scaffolding on the way down. He had also been winded by the fall but was slowly regaining his breath.

"Your back or neck isn't hurting, is it?" John was worried the man may have suffered a spinal injury.

"He hurts all over, Sahiba." Katharu forwarded the information. "But he says his back and neck are okay. It's only his ankle and elbow that are injured."

Two short slats of wood were handed to Holwell upon his request, and he used these as splints, employing the other half of the torn fruit seller's cloth to firmly bind them in place on each side of the workman's injured ankle.

Katharu translated for the site supervisor. "The doctor can't say for certain whether the ankle is broken or just that the muscles have been stretched out of shape. Once the swelling has gone down, take him to a doctor to have it examined. His elbow has been injured, and he may need to keep his arm in a sling for some time. If you bring him a piece of cloth about so big," he spread his arms apart expansively, "he'll show you how to create a sling."

While the cloth was being requisitioned, John turned his focus back on the young Moghul boy and his mother, who was sitting on the ground cradling her son's head in her lap.

"Katharu. Please translate for me." He waited while Katharu walked back over to them. "Your son may have a bad headache for some time. Keep putting cool compresses on his forehead but don't put too much pressure on it. When he walks about, he may feel dizzy or lightheaded. Keep him from running about. Have him rest in a dark, quiet, cool place. Bright light, full sunshine, and loud noises will likely cause him great discomfort."

As John was concluding his instructions to the mother who by this time was much calmer, seeing her son quickly beginning to recover, there was a disturbance among the swelling crowd standing and looking on. The wave of onlookers parted, and several burly, turbaned men quickly made their way toward the mother and child. Two of the men roughly grabbed hold of John while he was squatting by the child and hauled him to his feet. They were barking something at him. He had no understanding of what they were saying. When Katharu interrupted and attempted to translate, they quickly glommed onto him as well.

The child's mother stood up and whispered something into the ear of the nearest man holding onto John. His demeanour changed dramatically, and he ordered his men to release the two of them. The site supervisor also came over and spoke with the turbaned men.

"He's telling the Newaab's soldiers—that's who these men are—about the accident and your role in helping to manage the crisis. He is being very flattering."

One of the Newaab's men gently picked up the young lad, who was now fully alert and just crying a little. The others formed a circle around the young mother and her female retinue and knifed them through the crowd that was slowly beginning to disperse.

Cloth had been provided for the sling, and John walked back over to the injured workman and demonstrated the technique for folding it in half, then placing the damaged elbow into the triangular cradle and tying the two loose ends in a knot at the juncture of the neck and collarbone.

The site supervisor profusely thanked John and Katharu and then turned his attention to his workers with the aim of getting them to clean up the site and continue with their work.

The doctor and his guide made their way back to the Katra Masjid, stopping briefly to eat at a roadside stall. John ate the chapati and lentil curry with relish, but he had no appetite for exploring the city any further today. In insinuating himself into the situation this afternoon as he had done without a moment's hesitation, and given that the young victim was likely part of a royal family, had he overstepped his bounds? Could there be any serious consequences for him, or Katharu, for that matter? He would have to consider this later. Right now, he wanted nothing more than to take another refreshing bath, to smoke his pipe, and walk in the gardens as he had done the evening before.

"From your account, I'd say you've had quite the day, John!"

He and Lewis Mayne were seated in a comfortable lounge in a building just adjacent to the Katra Masjid. They were sipping on Arrack, an alcoholic beverage that was not allowed in the main building but was tolerated in the nearby precincts. It could be had in almost every quarter of Murshidabad. The coconut drink was sweet but strong. Just what Holwell needed after the day he had had.

"I hope the young lad is recovering? He seemed such a lively, rambunctious little boy. No doubt he won't be running about just yet. I wonder who he is and who his mother is? By their clothes and the deference paid to them by the workmen, and, of course, the turbaned soldiers that came to collect them, I'd infer that they were part of some important family." Holwell stared at the drink in his hand, occasionally using his thumb to displace some of the droplets of condensation that had formed on the metal exterior of the drinking vessel.

Mayne, who had been listening thoughtfully to Holwell as he recounted his adventure, responded. "I'd venture to say you're likely right about that assumption. The soldiers' rough handling of you tells me that this mother and her children are indeed close to the Newaab's family somehow."

"Thank God for Katharu. He was more than helpful in communicating with the workmen and the young lad's mother. I am also impressed by how steady he was throughout the ordeal. He didn't panic and just calmly did what I asked him to do. Mayne, you should have seen the chaotic tumult of the workmen's reaction to the accident. Many of them were scurrying about like madmen and yelling incoherently. What they could accomplish by this is a mystery to me. In any case, after the rest of our visit to Murshidabad, I'd like to ensure that Katharu is remunerated adequately."

"Never fear, my dear Holwell. He shall be paid handsomely."

The two men had paid their bill and were about to stand up when a young servant of the caravanserai slipped into the room and made his way over to the two Englishmen.

"Sahiba, there is a letter arrived for you." The servant handed Holwell a beautifully embossed letter, put his hands together deferentially, and then left the lounge.

"What could this be, Mayne?"

"I can understand Bengalese for the most part when I hear it; I'm far less proficient in the written word. If it's written in Persian... Why, that would make it even more unlikely I could decipher it. Maybe it's Urdu? Most of the Moors in India use Urdu as their primary language. We're going to have to find someone in the Katra to help us translate."

The excited administrator of the Katra Masjid held the gilded letter in his shaking hands. He read from it aloud.

"I, Sarfaraz Khan, Newaab of Bengal, Servant of the Empire, command the presence of the English doctor who treated my nephew this afternoon and who witnessed the accident at the wall of the Grand Masjid, tomorrow morning in the durbar immediately after the Fajar salah. As-salamu alaykum!"

"What is Fajar salah?" The magnitude of this request was just making an impact on John.

"It is the dawn prayer. You will have to leave your bedchamber early tomorrow morning."

SARFARAZ KHAN

John, Katharu, and Mayne waited anxiously just inside the entrance to the Durbar. The Morning Prayer was coming to its end. Soon, the Muslim men would touch their foreheads to the ground, stand up, and make their way out of the Grand Mosque.

This was but the second morning in Murshidabad, and John had been completely taken by the rapturous and haunting sounds of the muezzin's call to prayer, which could be heard five times each day emanating from one of the mosque's minarets. This morning's call had seemed particularly plaintive and exotic. It was a descant that he knew would remain with him for the rest of his life.

An official of the court made his way to the three men and ushered them toward the centre of the courtyard. The Durbar was a starkly plain quadrangle but with tasteful features surrounding it. At the exterior, tiny alcoves spread away from the open, marble courtyard, inviting spaces for two or three people to have a quiet, perhaps intimate conversation. Opposite to the public entrance through which the three men had come in stood a magnificent four-headed fountain that fed into a shallow pool.

Sarfaraz Khan, dressed in a stately black robe edged with gold thread work and an impressive black turban sporting a jade-green jewel at its centre, greeted his guests magnanimously in English. His greeting complete, the Newaab switched to Bengalese, one of his own retinue providing the translation.

"Sahiba, our deepest thanks for having accepted our invitation."

John had to laugh inwardly at this. The letter had been anything but an invitation; it had been a command.

"The young boy you treated yesterday is Afsin, our sister's son. Our sister and I are most grateful for what you did for our precious little warrior. He did have a headache for most of the day, but it was gone by his bedtime. He is already up and about this morning, chasing peacocks with his cousins."

The Newaab's demeanour shifted somewhat, and his tone became sterner.

"You and your Hindu servant witnessed yesterday's accident, and I would like you to describe it to me in great detail. If there has been any negligence on the part of the workmen or their leader, they will have to pay dearly for it."

John was convinced that yesterday's situation had been an accident. There were things he could recommend that would perhaps have made things safer for all concerned. However, he didn't think punishing any of the workmen or their supervisor would serve any useful purpose.

He carefully related the events he had been witness to and offered some of his advice should the Newaab be willing to listen to it.

"Of course, Doctor Holwell."

Somehow the Newaab had found out his name and his reason for being in Murshidabad. This was a man to be reckoned with.

"You are here with Sahiba Mayne while he is conducting business for the English East India Trading Company. You are the new doctor in Fort William, and we've heard many things about you. We would be most interested to hear what you have to say about making these construction projects safer. But first, let me send for the project manager so he too can hear what you have to say."

Sarfaraz Khan gave some instructions to one of his guards and he left promptly to do his sovereign's bidding.

The Newaab turned his attention to Lewis Mayne.

"I trust our mutual business interests are thriving, Sahiba?"

"They are." Mayne bowed low in response to the question. "Our trade with you and the Hindus has been very lucrative for all parties. We have now witnessed the successful sailing of several of our East Indiamen that have reached England with little to no hardship. We continue to thrive in Bengal under your auspices."

The next statements from Sarfaraz Khan, and the way in which they were delivered, caught Mayne somewhat by surprise, but he managed to think quickly on his feet.

"We understand that you are building fortifications around your Fort. What is their purpose? There are rumours that the English are trying to keep the Muslims out. We are also hearing rumours that the contracts you have with the Hindus are more lucrative than those you have with my Muslim brothers."

Seeing that Mayne had been caught unawares by this line of questioning, the Newaab quickly smiled and added. "We know that your position at Fort William precludes you from responding to questions of a political nature, but surely you can shed some light on the matters of finance."

"Newaab, I don't mind responding to both questions. As to the fortifications, they are known as the Maratha ditch. The Marathas, as you know, have been threatening to make forays into Bengal. The possibility of them attacking Calcutta, and Fort William in particular, has spooked the authorities. The ditch, when it is complete, will be there to protect our interests, and I daresay the interests of local inhabitants and Sarfaraz Khan's Empire alike. As to matters of a pecuniary nature, we show favour neither to Hindu nor Muslim. The rates of trade are identical. It is true that we do more trade by volume with the Hindus because they make up a larger portion of the population in and around Calcutta, but increasing our trade with the Mogul Empire is something we're always looking to do. In fact, ivory, silk, and artisanal furniture is in greater demand in England as time wears on. To that effect, I have instructed our operators in Murshidabad to source more of these and other wares from your agents."

"We shall see," countered the Newab. "We have eyes and ears throughout all our holdings."

Two of the Newab's guards came into the Durbar from a side entrance, the hapless site supervisor walking miserably between them. It became obvious to John that he had been kept prisoner overnight.

"Come before us." Sarfaraz Khan didn't mince his words. "This is the English doctor that was present at yesterday's disaster at the mosque. He has verified your account of what happened. It seems there is no blame to be laid for the accident. But the good doctor does have some suggestions for making your worksite safer. I would like you to listen to him and learn from his instruction."

"Yes, Newaab." The site supervisor bowed low a little more at ease knowing he wasn't going to be prosecuted any more sternly.

Sarfaraz Khan turned to John. "Doctor Holwell, if you please, provide your suggestions."

John looked to Mayne who gave him a slight nod of the head.

"Accidents will happen on occasion at worksites such as yours. Perhaps the strongest recommendation I have is that you create a barrier around the site, one that prevents the general public from getting too close to the activity, perhaps with signs posted warning people not to enter unless they have specific business with the work crew. Secondly, I would suggest that you always have ready access to bandages, clean water, and salves to dress mild abrasions. Furthermore, though I am not an engineer, it would seem prudent to me that you devise a way to keep pulleys and block and tackle apparatus a safe distance away from the scaffolding so as to allow unmolested passage of large building materials and avoid the kind of snagging that caused yesterday's accident. A small crane perhaps. And lastly, as site supervisor, I would keep a logbook of incidents so that they could be reviewed regularly with the intention of preventing the same sorts of mishaps from occurring time and again."

John wasn't happy with having to lecture the site supervisor so pedantically, but he felt that the present situation called for this approach.

"See that you put these suggestions into practice," the Newaab looked at the supervisor sternly. And then, as if to mollify him but a little he added. "I am looking forward to seeing your progress on the façade." He turned to his guards, "Take him to the kitchens, have them prepare a hearty breakfast for him and then let him get back to work."

"Now Dr. Holwell, Mr. Mayne. Please dismiss your servant, and the two of you follow me." Sarfaraz Khan turned about abruptly and started walking toward the palace.

Sarfaraz Khan's palace was stunning. The Newaab of Bengal led them through a curtained entrance into a large reception hall. Except for a throne-like chair elaborately decorated with carved sandalwood figures and upholstered with brass-studded leather coverings toward the back and centre of the chamber, the rest of the lounging furniture was comprised of oversized stuffed leather cushions. Once the Newab was seated in his chair, the two visitors were directed to a couple of the cushions. John felt awkward sliding into the pliable contraption he had been proffered. Once he settled back into it a little more confidently, he was surprised at how comfortable the cushion actually was to sit in. There was more than ample support for his back and thighs.

The walls were adorned with hunting trophies; lions' and tigers' heads with their beautiful pelts stretched behind them took up their positions on each side of a spectacular single-horned rhinoceros head, displayed on an angle and mounted on a large mahogany board.

Sarfaraz Khan, noticing what John's eyes were riveted on, spoke up, an eager gleam in his eyes. "Taking down that Greater One-Horned rhinoceros was the work of several hours and almost two dozen men, though I was fortunate to be the one to deliver the killing stroke. But enough of my boasting, let me offer you both some refreshment."

The Newaab clapped his hands and colourfully clad servants slid silently into the hall bearing trays of food and the most exquisite green and gold tea service John had ever seen. All these were placed on sandalwood trays ingeniously designed to fold up out of the way when not in use.

Copper plates were made available, and Sarfaraz Khan gestured for the men to help themselves. 'Some refreshment' as the Newaab had called it, turned into a sumptuous breakfast feast. Their host but nibbled modestly at a few morsels on his plate but was enjoying Holwell and Mayne's evident pleasure in devouring the food. John couldn't get enough of a dish made with scrambled eggs, spinach, red and green peppers, and a variety of spices he hadn't any idea about.

"I'm glad you're enjoying the *bid makhfuq*. It is one of my wife's favourites. And speaking of my wife, here she comes with my sister and her son, Asfin."

John noticed that the Newaab had stopped referring to himself in the third person once they had entered his abode. Beyond the responsibility of ruling an empire, he was also a family man and liked to keep his family life apart from matters of state.

Asfin ran to his uncle and jumped onto his lap, a grin prominently displayed on his face. Sarfaraz Khan squeezed the boy in his arms and ran his hands through his long, dark, curly hair.

"I'm sorry, *eazizi alzawj*, dearest husband. He wouldn't sit still long enough for us to have his turban put on." The Newab's wife spoke fluent English, and she stood regally before her husband. Even though her face was veiled, her deep glittering eyes mesmerized John. He was sure she must be a very attractive woman.

"Not to worry, dearest heart. Please meet Dr. John Holwell, chief medical officer at Fort William, and Mr. Lewis Mayne, English East India Company comptroller."

The Newaab's wife turned to where the two men had been seated.

"Please sit down, gentlemen." She summoned a servant woman who had been standing at the ready and took a carefully wrapped parcel from her hands. "This is but a small gift to thank you for your service yesterday. I offer it on behalf of my sister-in-law and my nephew, Asfin. We have recently taken delivery of some lovely bolts of silk. There is enough material to have two or three saris made for your wife."

John graciously accepted the gift. "Thank you, all of you, for this gift. As it happens, I am not married yet, but my betrothed will be arriving in India in a few months, and she will be most pleased to receive this gift. As for your nephew, I am thrilled that he has rebounded so quickly—children are resilient—and that he is running about delighting his family at every turn."

John sat down again, finding it easier each time he did so.

"Dr. Holwell, it has come to my attention that you are an accomplished surgeon in your own tradition, but that you are also interested in studying Eastern medicine. If that is so, I would like you to visit us again sometime soon, and I will make our court *hakim* available to you. There is much you could learn from each other!"

"That is very kind of you, Newaab. Perhaps I could stop by sometime in the next few days. Also, this time next year, could I make another visit with Mayne, and this time bring my new wife to meet you?"

Over the next few days in Murshidabad, John went about the city extensively with Katharu as his guide, also spending one stimulating afternoon with the Newaab's chief *hakim*, Mukhta bin Ali. He and Mayne had plenty of time in the evenings at the Katra Masjid to speak about their adventure at the Newaab's palace, as well as the state of trade between the English East India Company and the Moghul Empire. Mayne's business in Murshidabad having been concluded successfully, they boarded the Huntington and headed south, making easy way with the current.

"Well, Holwell." Mayne clapped John on the back as they watched Murshidabad slip away from them. "We'll have you in Hooghly-Chinsura before you know it."

HOOGHLY-CHINSURA

Without Lewis Mayne, navigating his way around Hoogly-Chinsura was daunting for John. He had two things going for him, though: the letter of introduction he had been given by Pieter Van Breda in Cape Town and his reasonably good facility with the Dutch language.

The VOC—or Vereenigde Oostindische Compagnie, known as the Dutch East India Company to the British—had found a stretch of the western banks of the Hooghly, a one- or two-day journey northwest of Fort William, which was ideally suited for the setting up of a trading post. The landscape and the weather were absolutely ideal. In fact, a string of European settlements sprang up along the west bank of Kati-Ganga (the local name for the Hooghly). John Holwell was reminded of the phrase Pieter Van Breda had used in Oranjezicht when referring to the location of Fort Gustavus: "Europe on the Ganges," he had called it.

Here the Dutch settlers found a perfect location for pleasure gardens and mansions, with wide steps leading down to the river. The mansions were known in Dutch as *bangelaers*, or playhouses, the term evidently derived from the Bengali state they were erected in.

John's time in Hooghly-Chinsura showed him, much to his surprise, that this was a trading post every bit as prosperous as Fort William. Dutch, Armenian, and native Bengali merchants became fat off the trade in saltpetre, spices, cotton, and indigo.

The first thing that had caught Holwell's eye when he had stepped off The Huntington was the artillery wall stretching along the eastern fortification facing the river with its massive cannons spaced about ten feet apart. No enemy ship would stand a chance against this formidable weaponry.

Dutch soldiers, at first abrupt and menacing, softened their demeanour when the British stranger replied to their queries in Dutch. They weren't used to a ship of the English East India Company, pulling into its wharves and disembarking a British civilian.

John asked to be directed to the Fort's administrative office. It was clear the soldiers weren't just going to send him into the precincts of Fort Gustavus on his own. One of the soldiers volunteered to accompany him, and they found their way through an entrance set imposingly between two canons and walked toward a sturdy, but utilitarian building in the central courtyard.

The arrangement of the Fort was somewhat akin to that of Fort William. Most of the barracks, storerooms, and work areas fed out from the sturdy wooden walls on the perimeter of the Fort and were lined with covered verandas, such as those he was familiar with in Calcutta. The biggest distinction between the two complexes was the omission of a grand governor's mansion at Gustavus. Where the regal house sat in the centre of the courtyard at home, here it was replaced by an administrative building, rather spartan in nature and surrounded by drill yards.

How was it that almost every Dutchman he had met was so tall and lean? John was musing on this as the chief administrator of Fort Gustavus stood up from behind his desk, stretching out his legs, which seemed to rise interminably up from the wooden floorboards. The curly-haired factor held out a long arm across the desk and firmly shook John's hand. John greeted him in Dutch and a friendly smile played across the administrator's face partially veiled by a full, but neatly trimmed beard.

Dr. Holwell retrieved the letter of introduction that Pieter Van Breda had given him and passed it across to the Dutchman. After perusing it, he strode out from behind his desk, put an arm about John's shoulders, and asked him to follow him out the door.

John understood that he was an interloper in Hooghly-Chinsura; perhaps not an enemy, but nonetheless part of a rival faction here in the Indian subcontinent. He decided that he would be forthright with Thijs Verhaven, the chief factor of Fort Gustavus, and disarm him with the cordial and easygoing charm he could adopt as the situation dictated.

The two men sat across from each other in a comfortable and well-appointed room that was quite obviously the officer's mess. Over mugs of hot tea, *ça* in the Bengali dialect, John allowed Verhaven to question him about the reason for his visit. When he seemed satisfied that the trip was simply to placate the Doctor's own curiosity and quench his insatiable desire to learn more about his exotic surroundings, and not to delve into the state of the fortifications at Fort Gustavus or to ferret out any trade secrets, he relaxed and fielded general questions about the state of local affairs in Hooghly-Chinsura. There was nothing disingenuous about his responses, and John felt like his understanding of this part of India had been enriched.

Verhaven left briefly so he could go and make some arrangements for the Doctor's stay. This allowed John time to pull out his ever-burgeoning notebook and add some of the details he had gleaned from his chat. It also gave him time to muse about Alice and his mother, and it was in this reverie that the lanky administrator found him upon his return to the mess.

Accommodations in a rooming house in the town had been secured for him and a company soldier had been assigned to him as a guide.

"I will also speak with our lead doctor, Dr. Bram Janssen, and have him liaison with you sometime tomorrow. I'll send word to the rooming house once I've established a convenient meeting time. Please say goodbye before you head off to Fort William."

The two men rose.

Holwell offered his hand to Verhaven. "Sir, I am most grateful for your kind reception and for spending so much time with me. I know that you are a busy man. I will touch base with you before I depart. I'm thinking that will be in three- or four- days' time."

Verhaven swept his left hand through his long curly locks and grinned broadly. "It has been my pleasure. A friend of the Van Breda's is always welcome here."

Upon exiting the Officer's Mess Verhaven introduced John to the soldier that would be looking after him during his stay. "This is Shem. He'll be taking you to your accommodations and he will be at your service should you need anything. He'll be happy to show you about."

He turned to face the smartly dressed, red-faced soldier. "Won't you, Shem? I'm sure you'll be happy to get away from your routine for a few days."

Shem didn't say anything. He just nodded, turned to leave, and beckoned the British doctor to follow him.

After settling into the rooming house, Shem took his charge on a grand tour of Hooghly-Chinsura. The number of splendid houses and gardens along the river was truly marvellous to behold. Not long into their travels they came across the nearly completed temple John had spied from the river upon their outward journey to Murshidabad.

"What building is this?" he asked of Shem.

This will be the Shamdeshwar Temple. As the legend goes, a local fisherman rescued a representation of Shamdeshwar, a form of the Hindu god Shiva, from the waters of the Ganga. A wealthy landowner and merchant decided to build a grand temple in honour of the Hindu deity near the waters he was said to have come from. It is still in the final stages of construction, so we won't be allowed to enter. You'll have to take in its beauty from here in the garden across the way." Shem could see that the doctor had taken out his sketchbook and wanted to commit the edifice to paper.

While Shem walked down to the river, John set up under the shade of a leafy tree and spent a good half hour sketching the breathtaking building from his vantage point. He dwelt for some time on the entrance that was made up of a very ornate series of arches adorned by frescoes and filigree designs. At the height of the uppermost arch that made up the third level of the structure was a cupola of sorts topped by a tapered finial. John put his sketching utensils back in his rucksack. Alice would have to see this!

Hooghly-Chinsura was a delightful town, cleaner and more pleasant in many ways than Calcutta. After a hearty meal, Shem walked Holwell back to his rooming house and bid him goodnight.

A note was waiting for him at the reception desk from Thijs Verhaven. He had arranged for John to meet the Dutch doctor at the hospital just to the north of the Fort. Dr. Janssen would be happy to attend him there midmorning tomorrow.

It was a real treat to be conversing with another doctor who quite obviously held the respect of the nurses and attendants at the hospital. Dr.

Janssen was sprightly in his mannerisms. His wiry frame darted hither and yon, a sharp contrast to John, who liked to think of himself as stately in demeanour and fluid in his movements.

After following Janssen for the better part of half an hour while he did his rounds, John looked forward to resting for a bit and comparing notes about the condition and treatment of some of the patients they had encountered. He was particularly interested in two patients who presented with smallpox-like symptoms.

Dr. Janssen seemed to have a broad understanding of the origins of the disease in India, stemming, as he said, from the Portuguese colonizers in Goa. An epidemic in the mid-sixteenth century was the demise of thousands of Indian citizens, especially children in that state. Understandably, Janssen was not familiar with the engrafting technique John had become familiar with at Guy's hospital in London. Janssen was intrigued by this development, and so Holwell laid out the basis for the practice and took great pains in providing an explication of the procedure. At the end of it all, he volunteered to send the Dutch doctor a copy of Lady Mary Wortley Montagu's treatise on the subject, along with the copious notes he had made.

The two men took lunch together, and they passed the time pleasantly chatting about the state of medicine in India. Holwell was shocked, though in retrospect he realized that he shouldn't have been, that Dr. Janssen thought very poorly of Indian medical practitioners. He couldn't make any distinction between the Hindu *vaidyas* and the Moslem *hakims*.

"Dr. Holwell, you have been in India but a short while, but you seem to have a better grasp of the situation here than I do after several years in this godforsaken country. I would be pleased to receive you here again sometime so we can continue our discussions."

At first, John wasn't sure about Janssen's sincerity. Perhaps he had been insulted by something he had said? The warm handshake and expansive smile that the Dutch doctor gave him upon their parting reassured him that this wasn't the case. "I look forward to the opportunity, Dr. Janssen. The next time, I hope to have my wife in tow."

Shem had been a very attentive guide. John could see that he had enjoyed his time away from his regular duties at Fort Gustavus. He had procured a ride to Calcutta for Dr. Holwell with a Dutch merchant who had business with the corpulent Omichand. The journey of approximately twenty miles would take the better part of a day.

On the evening prior to his departure, he stopped in to see Verhaven to thank him for the hospitality he had received. That night, he slept fitfully, dreams of Alice, Van Breda, Sarfaraz Khan, and smallpox all rolling together in a miasma of episodes. He rose early, washed himself thoroughly, and presented himself to the Dutch merchant. The morning was hazy; a low fog hung over the Hooghly. They set off south on a trunk road that was little more than a rutted cart path.

PERFORMANCE REVIEW

"You've been with us for six months now, Holwell. How are you getting on?"

John had been quite taken aback by this summons to the Governor's residence. After all, it wasn't one of his usual fortnightly visits. Mayne had allayed his fears somewhat when he told him that it was common for all the senior officers to be summoned twice a year for a performance review. A formal report would be written up with one copy going to him and another sent on to head office in London.

"I'm getting on well, sir. The hospital is well stocked, and with the able assistance of Dr. Chandler, we've been able to keep pace. In the aftermath of the monsoons, we treated many patients suffering from water-borne illnesses, dysentery, and the like. Smallpox is on the rise, and I'm planning to use a technique that is finally taking hold in London and should prevent a large outbreak. The process is still being perfected, and so I'll take things slowly in that regard. Besides, there isn't much I can do until the medical equipment and other supplies I've sent for arrive from London.

"I've had a thorough introduction to the Fort as well as the Park, and, of course, Black Town. As you know, Lewis Mayne was kind enough to invite me on his last trip to Murshidabad. That was an eye-opener! It gave me a better understanding of the Moghul kingdom."

"Yes," the Governor interjected. "I've heard quite a lot about your encounter with Sarfaraz Khan. I was chilled when I heard about it; His Excellency can be a daunting presence, but I'm happy your encounter was a positive one. What about your little escapade in Hooghly-Chinsura?"

Based on the sudden change of tone in the last question, Holwell understood that the Governor was not so pleased with this part of his adventure.

"In retrospect sir, I should have asked your permission to visit Fort Gustavus. You may not know that I have a close connection with the Dutch, having spent some years in Rotterdam as a young man. I have also made a friend in Pieter Van Breda, who is the de facto head of the

Dutch East India Company in Cape Town and who has close connections to the operation in Hooghly-Chinsura. I wanted to see first-hand how the Dutch enterprise in India rivals our own."

"You are quite right, Holwell. You should have asked my permission — a permission I would certainly not have granted."

The Governor paused for a moment, evidently considering something.

"Having said that, I believe this circumstance may prove quite useful. We could always use intelligence on the Dutch and how they pursue their business here in India." He turned now to the dossier in front of him on the desk. "And now let me fill you in on what some of the key people here say about your performance in your role as lead military surgeon in Fort William."

The Governor, a red-faced, middle-aged man with a paunch slowly forming around his belly, spoke at length about the reports he had had. These were all positive, some being embarrassingly effusive, and Holwell was feeling a little uncomfortable but quite pleased with himself, none-theless. The Governor's last words, however, were jarring and took him rudely aback.

"While your report to London will be exemplary, off the record, I would like to offer you a warning and some words of advice. I am not happy with how much time you are spending with the natives. I am told you've been associating with practitioners of Indian medicine and that you've introduced some of their suspect practices into our hospital. These men are barbaric, and they are miscreants, by all accounts. You are to stay away from them and focus on your English credentials. You may not have heard much about Dr. William Hamilton, one of your predecessors, but you ought to emulate the man. No doubt Dr. Chandler, or even Mayne, may be able to fill you in on Hamilton's remarkable successes here in India."

With this interrogation over, Holwell slipped out of the Governor's residence and, in a fog, walked back to his rooms.

Later that evening, in the quiet and dark of the Fort, a light could be seen emanating from the surgeon's chambers. John was wrapped up in a letter he was penning to his darling betrothed.

We have recently witnessed the celebration of Diwali, or Dioyali, as the Bengali's pronounce it. Alice, you would have loved it, and I can't wait until you're here so you can experience this spectacular and colourful affair that goes on for five days. There is dancing in the streets; every shop and bazaar table is adorned with shimmering paper or multicoloured drapery, and at night… Oh, my darling, at night the city is full of little lamps, their flames flickering about in the breeze. It's more than magical! And food… food is prepared in large vats for family gatherings and for sharing with others. The aromas are intoxicating. Sweets of every description are laid out on tables in the market. I can't say I'm overly fond of them; they do tend to be too sweet for my taste, but they look enticing.

Babu, a Hindu trader I have come to befriend, and whose intelligence I have come to admire, told me that the Hindu festival of Diwali or festival of lights celebrates the story of King Rama's return to Ayodha after he defeated Ravana, by lighting rows of clay candles.

Your brother James and Miss Worthing are evermore wrapped up in one another. James is always the gentleman, and it is obvious that Sergeant and Mrs. Worthing are very fond of him. I probably shouldn't be telling you this, but I did spy James steal away quietly with Susan during one of the Diwali candle lighting ceremonies in The Park. He had his hand around her waist, and I daresay he gave her a peck on the cheek.

Well, dear, I should be off to bed. I've had a long day; but, just one more thing. I told you about my performance review and that it had gone well. However, I didn't tell you how disappointed I am in the governor and a number of the senior officers. The way they treat the Indian populace is disgraceful. They think them nothing but unintelligent savages. Servants who work hard for them and are loyal to them are castigated relentlessly or, at the very best, ignored. The Governor is not happy with me for attempting to learn more about ayurvedic medicine from the local vaidyas, or indeed the medical techniques of the muslim hakims. HE WILL NOT STOP ME! In the next few months, I am going to search out a place for us to live away from the Fort. I have my

eye on a little parcel of land near the hospital and by the Hooghly River.
It's a lovely, serene spot. I know you will love it. And Mother will too.
*   And now, I really must be off to bed. Sweet dreams. I can't wait for the*
Devonshire to arrive, and with it, I hope for more letters from you.

John burst into James's quarters with a letter held high in his hands, his
heart beating vigorously in his chest.

"Have you received your mail yet? Have you heard the news?"

James jumped up from where he had been sitting on his cot. "What
news, brother? I can't pick up my mail until tomorrow."

"They've booked passage on the Brittania. All of them! The sailing is
tentatively booked for late February."

"What! Who is all of them?" James was now as excited as his friend.

"Alice, my mother, Dr. Treleaven, and Mrs. Pattison, the widow from
next door on St. Dunstan's Hill. Evidently, Mrs. Pattison made up her
mind to leave London and accompany Mother and Alice. I suspect it
didn't take Treleaven long to agree to accompany Mrs. Pattison. He is very
sweet on her, so my mother says. They should arrive in July sometime!"

"Perfect, just in time for the monsoons. At least we had a few weeks
before they began in earnest. There's no way I'm going to sleep right now,
John. Why don't we take a turn around the Park?"

The days leading up to Christmas were a blur. John wasted no time in
negotiating for the parcel of land next to the hospital. There was a lot of
work to be done. First, some of the land would have to be cleared. Then, a
house would have to be erected. Not a wooden house, John conjectured,
but a proper brick house like some he had seen in Hooghly-Chinsura. Of
course, it would not be as ostentatious as those mansions, but it would be
a house fitting for the head surgeon of Fort William and his wife. Also,
rooms in one wing of the house would have to be set aside for his mother
and a separate cook house and servants quarters stationed behind the
main building would have to be erected.

The weather in Calcutta in December was absolutely wonderful. The
days, while hot, weren't overly so, and the evenings brought with them
cool breezes. A walk about the Park necessitated the wearing of a cardigan

or light jacket. Finally, John could comfortably wear his woollen surgeon's jacket.

The 22nd of December was a bright, clear day, and after having enlisted Lewis Mayne to accompany him, the two men made their way to the Zamindar's offices in Black Town. The English East India Company, as a result of some deft diplomacy, had recently acquired the office of Zamindar in Calcutta, historically bequeathed to minor royal families of the Moghul Empire. This gave them greater control of the local population. The Zamindar would have complete jurisdiction of the municipal, fiscal, civil, and criminal affairs in Calcutta. In criminal matters, he had the power to fine, flog, and imprison. However, a higher authority would hear appeals of a 'capital' nature when the lash could be inflicted to death.

Business of a more mundane nature, such as the granting of a deed for a parcel of land, was handled by the Dewan, a ministerial officer reporting to the Zamindar. In 1723, the office of Dewan was granted to Govinda Ram Mitra, known by the populace as "The Black Zamindar." He was known to be a stern man, but fair-minded and astute. It was obvious that he wasn't cowed by dealing with Lewis Mayne or John Holwell, even though they were high functionaries of the British military establishment. John was impressed that Govinda Ram didn't treat them with deference, but rather as he would any common petitioner.

After presenting the Dewan with all the relevant particulars about the plot of land that Dr. Holwell wished to purchase, they were asked to wait in the vestibule. A servant offered Clay mugs of ça to them, and they had some time to sit and chat.

"Tell me about Dr. Hamilton. The Governor said that I should be taking a page out of his book. What did he mean by that?"

Mayne considered the question and, in typical Mayne fashion, matter-of-factly delivered his exegesis.

"Hamilton was the head surgeon at Fort William until his death in 1717. He was a very competent doctor and made a name for himself because of one rather remarkable circumstance. He saved the life of Emperor Mohammed Farraksheer, a powerful magnate in the Moghul Empire, who was suffering interminably with distemper and who looked to be on his deathbed. His ailment baffled the skills of the Imperial physicians, and Hamilton was brought in as a last resource. His ministrations resulted in the emperor's recovery. The emperor was able to marry a young princess to whom he was betrothed, and he was forever grateful to Hamilton."

"That must have resulted in Hamilton gaining much notoriety. I can see why the Governor would hold him in such high esteem." Holwell was taking little sips of the hot tea.

There was a sardonic grin on Mayne's face. "Yes, it did bring him much notoriety, and it went straight to his head. He was an intolerable prick thereafter, by all accounts. He put down Indian medicine and its practitioners at every opportunity and constantly wielded his holier-than-thou attitude."

Almost an hour had passed before they were summoned into Govinda Ram's office. Copies of the land title in Bengali, Urdu, and English were made available to Dr. Holwell. Copies would, of course, be filed in the registry office. John paid the fee to the Dewan's clerk, and the two men headed back to the Fort.

The Fort would be almost deserted, Mayne told his friend, because the officers and regular army alike were on furlough as of today for the week-long Christmas break. They would be at the arrack houses and brothels in Black Town. John could look forward to a formal meal at the Governor's mansion on Christmas Day. There would be roasted goose, buttery potatoes and yams, and other delicacies from the home country. All manner of distilled spirits would be on offer, and there would be much merriment.

It was surely something to be anticipated!

SPRING 1734

"Time is the nurse and breeder of all good." Holwell had studied literature in Mr. McKenzie's Grammar School in London, and he had become quite fond of Shakespeare. This quote from *The Two Gentlemen of Verona* came to mind at odd times; in retrospect, whenever he was in anticipation of something or other.

July couldn't come soon enough, bringing with it his darling Alice. Dwelling too much on it would be an agony, and so he threw himself into his work and his many passions outside of it. He delved with gusto into the design of his new residence and hired labourers to clear the land, making sure to leave shade trees wherever practicable.

He spent long days at the hospital, and with Dr. Chandler's help, refined many of the institution's systems and procedures, making them as efficient as possible. In particular, they revamped the record-keeping practices so they could catalogue the various diseases and infirmities they dealt with and commensurately the regimens and medications that had been used and each of their respective successes and failures.

In the evenings, by candlelight, he would study Urdu, Bengali, and Arabic. He would take note of those elements of each language that confounded him and these he would ask about when he met with native speakers.

When he became saturated with this study of languages, he picked up his sketch pad and fleshed out the anatomy and physiology of the myriad plants he had encountered. In a separate notebook, he kept track of the ubiquitous insects such as ladybird beetles, leafhoppers, rice bugs, water striders, scarabs — some benign, others not so much.

The politics of the region fascinated him. On his walks about the Park with Mayne or the Worthing's, or when he met Babu, the Hindu trader, for ça in one of the local tea shops, he would ply them with questions about the state of current affairs in Calcutta and India in general. He was also fascinated by the many offshoots of the Hindu religion and those of the Moors, and he loved to learn about the colourful celebrations that seemed to take place almost every other day.

Warier now about his association with the ayurvedics and the hakims, given the Governor's admonishment, he still met with them surreptitiously. His list of plants and mixtures with medicinal properties was ever growing, and these he carefully recorded and set aside to be tested when he had the opportunity. His laboratory adjoining his quarters in the Fort was strewn with all sorts of carefully labelled plants, powders, and insects impaled on hemp sheets or suspended in jars filled with formaldehyde.

"You're an exhausting friend to hang around with." James and Susan Worthing had just taken a turn about the Park with John. "But that's always been the case, hasn't it, my dear fellow?"

Spring arrived, and with it came the oppressive heat. Workers who had been hired to build his house arrived early in the morning, took a lengthy break at midday, and resumed their work in the evenings when the breezes off the Hooghly made labouring outside more tolerable.

On an evening late in March, after a long shift at the hospital, Holwell wandered over to the building site. Rather than seeing a team of labourers busy with the construction of the outer walls, John was surprised to see the men standing and sitting about. The foreman was in the middle of a heated argument with the man responsible for providing the clay bricks. He strode over to the two men.

"What seems to be the problem, here?"

The foreman, his face flushed and keeping his gaze fixed at the brick man, spewed out, "The last batch of bricks this idiot has brought us is *chi chi*!"

Chi chi, Holwell knew, as the Bengali word for shit.

"What's the problem with them?" The manufacture of bricks, John knew, was a rather straightforward process, as it had been for eons. Not much could go wrong. Dig up clay. Grind it into a fine powder. Mix it with water to make a thick, malleable paste. Form it by hand into bricks and them leave them out to dry under the hot sun. Finally, fire them in a kiln made for the purpose, and then let them sit for some time.

"These bricks haven't been baked for nearly long enough, or if they have, then they haven't been left to cure. They're too green. A slight knock with a mallet, and they fall apart!" The accusation burst out almost as if it were a curse. "Here, let me show you." The foreman picked up one of the bricks, set it on the fresh mortar of the section of wall that was being built, and gave it a slight rap with the mallet. The brick disintegrated.

John wasn't impressed. He turned to the brick man. "You'll take this last batch of bricks back to the brickyard and bring us a proper batch. I'll speak to the manager of the brickyard personally."

The brick man didn't speak English, and John's Bengali wasn't yet sophisticated enough to relay this message, so the foreman translated. John knew the translation wasn't verbatim; he recognized some of the colourful Bengali invective that peppered the foreman's words. The stricken looking man walked morosely back to his bullock cart, dug behind the seat for an earthenware jug full of water, took a swig, gathered his men, and had them start reloading the bricks. His boss would not be pleased!

The next day, having recruited Mayne to accompany him, Holwell made his way to the brickyard that was north of the Fort and nestled hard upon the river. Though he was still a man of rather youthful years, John had learned the value of tact and diplomacy when dealing with people, especially in circumstances that had the potential to become heated. With the brickyard manager he was firm, but not histrionic. Mayne just stood to the side and observed the interaction. The manager was apologetic and started to list several excuses for the delivery of substandard bricks. He was inundated with requests for his product because of the building boom that had been going on for some time in White Town. The delivery team had taken the bricks from the wrong pile, those that were still curing, and so on and on.

Holwell put up a hand to stop the fawning manager. "Enough. The reasons for the mess-up don't matter to me. Have your men deliver the proper bricks, and do so as quickly as possible. I'm paying for workers that are sitting idle."

On the way back to the Fort, Mayne chimed up. "John, you were too easy on him. I'm sure you could have renegotiated a better price for the bricks as a result of his blunder."

"You know me, Lewis. I am a fair man. I'll give him a chance to right the situation, life will go on, and, in the bargain, I will not have made an enemy. If the problem persists, then I'll make his life miserable. By the way, thanks for coming along with me. I know how busy you are."

"Not to mention it, John." Mayne grinned, and the two men carried on.

Rather than taking their usual constitutional about The Park, John had invited Mr. and Mrs. Worthing, and, of course, James and Susan, to visit the building site. It was a warm evening in April, and flies and other insects were buzzing about. As they walked and talked, the ladies used fans to keep cool and swat away the buzzing pests. The men, rather comically, just used their hands.

Progress on the main house was coming along nicely, and the Worthing's seemed impressed.

"I think this will be a lovely spot for you and Alice once you're married. And for your mother, too, John." Sergeant Worthing was walking through the walled partitions of each of the rooms. The site was still open to the sky waiting to be capped by a corrugated metal roof.

"Speaking of that, sergeant. What would you say to Alice and Mother being your house guests until the house is ready—and the nuptials finalized, of course? Susan brought this up to me as a possibility a little while back. She mentioned that you might have a spare room that could work. Of course, I'd be happy to compensate you for the inconvenience."

"Nonsense." This came from Cecilia, Sergeant Worthing's delightful wife. "No compensation will be necessary, dear. We'd be happy to have the company, wouldn't we, Henry?" She turned to her husband with a beguiling smile.

"It's settled. There will be no argument from you, sir." Sergeant Worthing continued on with his inspection of the property.

"I'm also on the lookout for a residence for Dr. Treleaven and Mrs. Pattison. If you can think of some place that might suit them, I'd be indebted."

John wasn't expecting such a prompt response. This time, it came from Susan. "Father, what about that little grey house on the east side of The Park? It's been sitting empty for the past while."

Sergeant Worthing thought quizzically about the suggestion for a moment. "That belongs to Lady Russell. You are aware she lives in the grand house beside it. I don't know if she plans to sell it or keep it so she can expand her own abode. Though why one woman and a husband who's almost never home would want with a larger place, I don't know. Besides, you know as well as I do what a tyrant she is. I shudder at the thought of even approaching her about it!"

"Don't worry about that Sergeant Worthing. I'll speak with her." John was pleased to have a lead.

"No, son. And please, just call me Henry. I think it best that I speak with her myself. We've known each other for a long time."

As the date of the Brittania's arrival neared, and as the Calcutta heat radiated ever more intensely, John's dreams became increasingly vivid and ever more tangled. In one such dream, he was strolling along the green at Gay Meadow, with Alice inexplicably by his side, watching the daring Robert Cadman shimmying up the wire to the steeple of the church. A commotion among some of the other observers drew his attention to Cadman, who had somehow been released from his harness and was now hurtling to the earth below. He tried to call out to Miriam, whom he could see hadn't been focusing on her fiancé, but nothing would come out. He stood silent and immobile, rooted to the ground.

This dream morphed into the refectory at Guy's Hospital. His colleagues were rudely pointing in his direction and sneering at him. He was looking for Treleaven. At first, he couldn't be spotted, but then there he was framed in the doorway of the refectory, his face distorted and full of pockmarks. When had he contracted smallpox?

When he awoke from these dreams, his bed sheets would be soaked through, his hair a tousled mess. The heat in his rooms, even in these early hours of the day, was unbearable. He would quickly tear the sheets off his bed and drag them outside to a laundry line, and then go for a brisk walk to the loading pier so he could feel any breeze that might be wafting over the Hooghly. He found himself looking forward to the cool and cleansing monsoon rains, though in the back of his mind, he knew that once they were present, they could be as dispiriting—and maybe even more so—than the oppressive heat. How were Alice and his mother ever going to handle this?

BOOK FOUR

New Arrivals

Brittania had been expected sometime in the third week of July. John had taken to spending as much time as possible at the site of his new house, which was almost completed now, peering out over the river and hoping to catch a scrap of Brittania's sails in the breeze. James would stop by every so often as well and join Holwell in this vigil. The two men talked about Alice, the impending wedding, John's mother, Dr. Treleaven, and Mrs. Pattison. It was no surprise to John when James declared on one of these occasions that he was going to propose to Susan and that, if she said "yes," perhaps they might have a double wedding?

"You will be broaching this with the Sergeant and Mrs. Worthing, I hope, before putting the question to Susan?" John turned to face James.

"John, I don't remember you doing the same when it came to proposing to my sister. Why, you didn't even have the decency to ask me for permission!" This proclamation was accompanied by a wry smile. "But of course, I will."

The two friends continued with this lighthearted banter as they returned their gaze to the Hooghly, squinting out into the evening light, willing the appearance of Brittania and the arrival of their loved ones.

The third week of July presented itself, and John's excitement was palpable. He had given explicit instructions to the foreman at the building site that if Brittania were to be sighted, he should send someone to the hospital immediately to let him know of the development.

The fourth week of July was now upon them, and John was increasingly excited, but a tinge of foreboding had started to creep into his thoughts as well. Sensing this anxiety, Susan insisted on accompanying the men as they sat by the river or, more often than not, as they paced up and down impatiently.

"Do you think she'll have changed much, James? It's been a lifetime since we've seen her." John was in such a state of anticipation, and his thoughts were scattered in every direction.

"It's only been a year and a half, John. Mind you, Ailish was but a young girl when we left. No doubt she's blossomed into a young woman?"

"And what about me, James? Have I changed?"

"Of course, you have, brother. Nobody could have the experiences we've had in the last while and not be changed by them. You're physically stronger now, and far more serious, but oh-so-much uglier!" James playfully nudged his friend.

The monsoon arrived, at first with grey skies and small droplets of rain, and then perversely in diabolical torrents. Life moved indoors, and John made the mad dash each day to the hospital and then back to the Fort. He tried to keep busy in the evenings with his work and his studies but concentrating was ever more elusive. Why hadn't Brittania arrived? Had something gone horribly wrong? Were his mother and Alice and all the others languishing somewhere in peril?

On August 12th, John had just finished splinting a broken arm. The patient had slipped on some wet scaffolding and fallen a few feet to the ground, his arm having been caught awkwardly underneath him. As he finished up with the sling James rushed into the surgery hall, his garments soaked through, his boots trailing a stream of water and most decidedly out of breath.

"Brittania has been sighted a few miles up the estuary! She's having a hard time making her way through the downpour and the interchangeable winds. She should pull into the dock sometime this evening!"

John finished up with his patient and with a calmness completely belying the tumult inside him, called for an attendant to clean up the mess created by the waterlogged interloper.

"Let's go back to the Fort, James. We need to make provisions for transporting our guests to the Worthing's. We'll also need to inform Henry and Cecilia of their impending visitors." He might have been placid on the exterior, but his heart was beating prodigiously in his chest.

John spotted her on Brittania's deck before she was able to find him out in the crowd and through the driving rain. He hailed her, and their eyes finally locked. His stomach was in knots. His mother stood beside Alice, somehow smaller than he remembered her, and he waved to her too.

It was an interminable time before the gangplank was lowered and the passengers were allowed to disembark. Alice sweetly took Mrs. Holwell's arm and helped her negotiate the slick wooden ramp. Treleaven did the same for Mrs. Pattison.

John couldn't wait any longer. He dashed past the coulees and port attendants. He gave his mother a hug and a peck on the cheek. She raised a hand to his face and gave him a loving caress. John then turned his attention to Alice. Water was streaming down the runnels of his tri-corn hat, and he thought to remove it before taking Alice up in a crushing and prolonged embrace.

He whispered into her ear. "You're here at last, my love. Welcome home." In a louder voice, he called out to the rest of his group. "Let's get out of this abominable rain!"

Finally, they were all seated in the Worthing's living room, a small but welcome fire burning jauntily in the fireplace. John looked about him. They were mostly all dry, except for Alice's long hair hanging in wisps down the sides of her pretty face, and the men's trouser cuffs, which were stained dark with rainwater and mud. A mad sprint from Brittania to the Fort had been followed by a frenzied ride by palanquin to the Worthing's residence in White Town. John had been worried about his mother and Mrs. Pattison because of the frenetic pace they had maintained throughout, but he needn't have. They both had managed heartily.

"Your boxes will be sent on tomorrow. It's quite too dark for the coulees to attempt the feat this evening." Lewis Mayne was standing under the arch of the parlour entrance, about to head back to the Fort.

"Where are my manners?" John had been so intent on the new arrivals that he had completely forgotten that Mayne had seen them all safely to the handsome wooden house on the southeast quadrant of The Park. "Let me introduce you all a little more formally to Lewis Mayne, the Comptroller of Fort William, and my very good friend. You will have heard of him in my letters, and no doubt you will have ascertained how important he has been to my well-being, both on our voyage to India and in regards to my current status in Fort William."

"Nonsense, John. I have learned a great deal from you and will always consider you an invaluable friend. But now, I should take my leave." Mayne gave a slight bow and left the room.

Cecilia Worthing made sure a hot mug of tea was comfortably nestled in the hands of each of her guests. She dismissed the servant girl, giving her instructions to follow up with some of the food that had been prepared earlier in the day. "While we're waiting for supper, why don't you tell us about your journey?"

Not knowing who should respond, the new immigrants glanced at each other. Dr. Treleaven, who had quite evidently taken the others under his wing during the course of the voyage, took the lead.

Well into their second cups of tea, and as the servant girl was setting out some food on the large wooden table in the dining area just off the drawing room, John, James, Susan, and the senior Worthing's, listened raptly to Treleaven's account. They heard about the rather uneventful journey to Casa Branca and then about a harrowing experience while Brittania languished in the doldrums. A two-masted schooner, having been commandeered by a Barbary pirate, stole out of an estuary off the West Coast of Africa, and taking advantage of the larger and slower Brittania, attempted to run her down. It was only because of Captain Grantham's expertise—and God's mercy, of course—that they were able to catch the schooner broadside with a terrifying barrage of cannon fire that saw her hobbling away back to her lair. Unfortunately, Brittania had taken a lot of damage to the transom athwart ships. Much of her stern had been splintered, and they were dangerously taking on water. Grantham guided his craft to a little-used port on the coast, and the ship's carpenters spent a solid week rebuilding what they could. A few men had been injured in the melee, and Treleaven had gladly offered his medical assistance, even though he was not a commissioned military surgeon on the voyage. Once the temporary repairs had been affected, Brittania made its way to Cape Town, where they sojourned for almost five weeks so proper repairs could be undertaken.

Sensing a shift in the narrative, Mrs. Worthing politely interrupted. "Please come over to the dining table. The food is ready, and I'm sure you're all famished. Dr. Treleaven, you can continue your account after you've all had something to eat."

John guided his mother to the table and then judiciously placed Alice so that he was between his two ladies. He hadn't had any time to speak with either of the two alone and was grudgingly coming to the realization that he wouldn't really have the chance until the morrow.

Dr. Treleaven and Mrs. Pattison sat across from them, as did James and Susan. Henry and Cecilia Worthing occupied the seats at each end of the table. There were all sorts of food on offer, most of which would not have been familiar to the British travellers. John provided a running commentary as each dish was passed around, and their china plates, the finest Mrs. Worthing possessed, began to fill up. There were little dumplings stuffed with potatoes and peas served with a mixture of mint and coriander chutney. John demonstrated how to take a dollop of savoury rice with raisins and shredded coconut and then place a ladle of a wonderfully aromatic curried chicken on top of it. Two varieties of flat bread were passed around, one soft and slightly puffed up, and one thicker and darker in colour. Finally, John spooned some curd blended with grated cucumber and tomato onto each of their plates, "so their palates could be cooled if the food were a bit spicy." As they began to eat, gingerly at first, and then with relish, John remembered to point out that if they came across whole cardamom pods, or cloves, or cinnamon sticks, that they should gently remove them from the rice and place them on the side of their plates.

As the meal wore on, they revelled in each other's company. John's heart leaped each time Alice's elbow grazed against his, and he was amused by how she kept glancing in the direction of her brother and the charming Susan Worthing. He made small talk with his mother and asked her about her last few months on St. Dunstan's Hill. The Sergeant engaged James about recent developments at the Fort, and Cecilia did her best to make sure Dr. Treleaven and Mrs. Pattison were included in the conversation.

A tray of colourful sweets was placed on the table, and John, hoping not to insult the hosts, politely cautioned the newcomers to partake but meekly of them. "They are very rich and very sweet. I would advise you to go easy on them. They are tasty, but your stomachs aren't used to Indian dairy products yet, and they may cause you some discomfort later on."

"You are quite right, my dear. I had forgotten this about our experiences with Indian sweets in our early days here. You may become quite fond of them, but I would concur with John. A small taste might be in order." Mrs. Worthing smiled at John, and he knew he hadn't offended her.

They slowly rose from the table and stretched their legs as they made their way back to the drawing room.

"I feel like I'm still on the ship," Mrs. Pattison remarked. "The floor seems to be moving." James, who was nearest to her, took her gently by the elbow and guided her to a chair.

The excitement of the past few hours seemed to have dissipated somewhat, and it became obvious to John that the travellers were beginning to show their weariness. "As much as we'd all like to hear more about your journey, I think it best that we call it an evening. You could all use a good night's sleep in something other than a ship's cot. James and I will call on you midmorning tomorrow, and those of you who would like to come to the Fort for a visit can join us then."

John and James said their goodbyes, hugging each of the ladies and shaking the gentlemen's hands. Alice's embrace was prolonged, and John reluctantly slipped out of her reach, planting a kiss on her cheek. The two men took their leave after profusely thanking their hosts for the marvellous meal.

They made a run for the Fort, the weather and their own tumultuous thoughts not allowing any opportunity for converse.

TRIPLE PLAY

Clouds were scudding across the sky as John and James made the trek to pick up their guests on the morning after Brittania's arrival. The rain came down sporadically, and it was gentler than yesterday and made moving around that much easier. Alice, Susan, and Dr. Treleaven were eagerly awaiting them and were ready for the day's adventures. John's mother and Mrs. Pattison had decided to stay back and recuperate a little more, enjoying the fireplace in the parlour and the cozy precincts of the Worthing residence on terra firma. Life on Brittania had been particularly difficult for them, and John understood why they might want to remain stationary for a while longer.

"We'll see you all a little later this afternoon, then." John took Alice's arm, and with James, Susan, and Dr. Treleaven following, they took their leave.

"It's so good to see you, Ailish. How are Ma and Da, and Clara and Siobhan?" James called out from behind them.

Alice stopped and turned toward her brother, embracing him in a bear-like hug. "It's wonderful to see you too, dear brother. All the family was well when I left them in Dublin. Your sisters were jealous of us and kept pestering Ma and Da to allow them to accompany me. Of course, they would have none of it. I got a letter from them before I departed, and they were full of good wishes for the three of us. They have sent along a few of your things that they thought you might want. When I'm able to properly unpack, I'll get them to you."

The quintet made the short trek to the Fort, keeping to the ring road and avoiding the Park itself, which was a muddy quagmire in this water-logged season. At the entrance, they turned right and headed toward John's chambers.

Standing in Holwell's crowded laboratory, Alice and Treleaven were overwhelmed. Every available space was filled with evidence of Dr. Holwell's scientific enquiries, such as specimen jars, collections of herbs, both dried and fresh, and corkboards studded with arrays of impaled insects. Neat stacks of parchment piled high, in some cases precariously so, occupied his worktable. There were diagrams and charts and notes; in fact, every wall was covered with elements of his work.

"You've only been here a year and a half, John! This looks like a lifetime of work." Treleaven, mouth agape, began making the rounds of the room, examining the displays; the ghastly, and in many cases repulsive, insects and assorted creatures really piquing his interest. Alice, meanwhile, went over to John's desk and began leafing through his stack of botanical drawings of strange plants, sometimes whole and sometimes in cross-section.

"These are beautiful, John. You are becoming quite an artist." Alice was flipping through his collection of *pteridophytes* or, as the non-scientific caption beneath the title clarified, *ferns*. "I absolutely loved the drawings you sent me from your time in Cape Town. Before I left London, I had many of them framed and sent them on to Ma and Da. There will be a little bit of you in their home in Dublin." She lifted her gaze and smiled lovingly at her fiancé.

"John, why don't I take Susan and Dr. Treleaven for a stroll around the Fort? I'm sure you and Alice would like a chance to catch up privately. We'll meet you back here in a half hour or so, and then we can make our way to lunch. Mayne has procured permission for any of our company to join him in the officer's mess. They're serving Irish stew, if you can imagine. I don't know if Mayne had anything to do with the selection, or whether it is just happenstance."

John, perhaps a little too eagerly, ushered them out the door and turned to finally take Alice into his warm embrace. As the others were making their egress, she was already moving toward John and in a heartbeat, they were entwined in each other's arms.

Time flew by as the two lovebirds held hands and responded to each other's queries, questions that each of them had been burning to ask of the other. Their eyes were firmly locked on each other and never did their hands part.

As the other three returned, Alice was recounting their stay in Cape Town, and her pleasant encounter with the Van Breda's.

"John," and here she turned roundly on her brother, "and you, James! Why didn't either of you tell me or Mrs. Holwell about the nasty situation surrounding John's 'grand entrance' to the Van Breda estate? Mr. Van Breda told us what had happened and was most sorry for it. You were hurt badly. We all were shaken up by the news. Are there any lingering effects?"

"Luckily, no. But we'll have a longer chat about it later. I'm sure Mother would like to hear more about it." And with that he ushered them out of his rooms and led the way to the officer's mess.

Over the next few days, John had no time for any of his personal pursuits. He spent the days in the hospital dealing with an ever-growing number of cases of dysentery and the evenings at the Worthing's' getting caught up on all the news of London, sharing stories of their travel adventures, and providing a rather animated orientation to life in Calcutta. On one of these occasions, Alice excused herself, went into the bedroom she was sharing with Mrs. Holwell, and returned with a clipping from *The Daily Post*, a prominent gazette from London. She passed it across to John.

"Oh my!" John's eyes were glued to the short notice that he held in his hands.

"I thought you might want to see this. A very tragic thing." Alice gave her fiancé a sympathetic look.

"What is it, John?" Susan Worthing could see that whatever the news was, it wasn't pleasant.

John spent some time relating his encounter with the young Robert Cadman and his beautiful Miriam in Shrewsbury.

"This is a notice of his death. It pains me to learn of it."

Before he was able to set the paper down James asked him to share the contents with all of them. Still shaken by the news and not trusting his voice, John asked Alice if she would read the notice aloud. She gently retrieved the article from John's hands and began to read.

Robert Cadman, a professional ropewalker and showman whose descent from the cupola of St. Paul's Cathedral, sliding face-first down a rope while blowing a trumpet earned him fame and the title 'Icarus of the rope,' has met his untimely end. On February 2nd of this year, he orchestrated a stunt in which he 'walked' up the 800 feet of rope that connected the 222-foot high spire on St. Mary's Church, Shrewsbury, from where it was anchored in Gaye Meadow below; he fired off pistols and performed tricks on the rope during his ascent. At the top, he fastened on a grooved wooden breastplate and launched himself in a 'flight' across a rope spanning the Severn River. The rope snapped when he was halfway across, and Cadman fell to his death, effectively ending the so-called flying craze of the 1720s. His monument at St. Mary's reads: 'Let this small monument record the name of Cadman, and to future time proclaim now by'n attempt to fly from this high spire across the Sabrine stream he did acquire his fatal end. 'Twas not for want of skill or courage to perform the task he fell. No, no, a faulty cord being drawn too tight, Married his Soul on high to take her flight, which hid the body here beneath good Night.'

John's mother walked over to console her son. He was a man who didn't usually wear his emotions on his sleeve. But now, while reveling in the beautiful Irish brogue of his darling Alice, he was also left numb by the contents of *The Daily Post* item.

Toward the end of August, the rains abated, and every so often, the sun could be seen. On a sunny Sunday, after attending a service at St. Anne's Church, John arranged for palanquins to ferry them all to the site of his new house. The roads were still a muddy mess, and he didn't want them to soil their Sunday finery. Even then, the combination of the sun and the moisture-laden air made for a highly humid experience. By the time they got back from their excursion, they would all need fresh baths, and their clothes would need to be laundered.

"Oh, John, it's lovely. Is this where we're to live?" Mrs. Hollwell smiled broadly. They were standing outside the expansive brick house after having walked down the curved flagstone path that led from the road to the property.

"It is Mother. Come on in and have a look at your rooms."

"What do you mean by rooms, son?"

"You're the mother of the head surgeon. You deserve your own sitting area and powder room and a bedroom. Of course, you'll have the run of the whole house, but Alice and I, once we're married, won't want to always be underfoot. You deserve your privacy."

John took his entourage on a grand tour of the residence. They began in the foyer or mudroom where the walls were lined with hooks for outer garments and low shelves were hung at a slight downward angle supported by cantilevered brackets. The boot shelves were slatted so that extraneous water and debris could slip through to the woven seagrass mats carefully positioned beneath.

Mrs. Pattison had bent down to start removing her shoes. John quickly interceded.

"Don't worry about that today, Mrs. Pattison. None of us has brought indoor footwear today. The floors are easily cleaned."

The group moved into a spacious living room. Alice immediately made her way across to the oversize bay windows looking out toward the Hooghly River. She was entranced. John came over to her and placed an arm lovingly over her shoulders.

"Someday, Alice. This little tract of land up to Kati Ganga will be a canvas for your garden. You can do anything with it you'd like."

"Kati Ganga?"

"It's what the locals call the Hooghly. Very appropriate because it is a tributary of the mighty and very sacred Ganges River."

Alice turned back to look at the expansive room.

"It's going to cost a fortune to furnish this room. There are nine adults in here now and room for twenty more!"

"We'll have to come up with a theme for the room, darling. You should start thinking about it." John was pleased with the effect his building project was having on those who were experiencing it for the first time. "Let's have a look at the study and then the bedrooms."

The study was in a space directly behind the living room. It too had windows opening up to the riverscape. Bookshelves, multitudes of them, were in various stages of construction lining the walls.

"This room is fashioned after the library at Guy's Hospital. Treleaven, I'm sure you can see the similarities? You and I spent many happy hours there reading and relaxing in the quiet moments between making the rounds and performing surgery."

Dr. Treleaven was impressed indeed.

"It's marvellous, John. I've no doubt you will be happy and productive here."

Once they had finished touring the bedrooms, a large chamber for John and Alice, another, more modest one for Mrs. Holwell, and a third guest bedroom, they came upon a smaller bedroom, which led back into the master chamber and in which John had left the ceiling beams exposed.

"What's this room, John? I hadn't really noticed it the last time I was here." Susan enquired.

With an impish grin John turned his gaze on Alice and replied, "Why, it's the nursery, of course."

Alice blushed.

They all moved into a stately dining room at the rear of the house. This seemed to have concluded the tour of the residence.

"There seems to be something missing, John." Mrs. Hollwell addressed her son. "Where's the kitchen?"

Sergeant Worthing piped in. "It's in the building behind the main house, Amelia, attached to the servants' quarters. Just like at our house."

John had never liked the use of the term 'servants' quarters,' but he let it slide for the moment. There would be time to have a fuller discussion of this later.

So far, so good, thought John. The four travelling companions seemed to be settling in quite nicely. The only one of the group who was experiencing anything like homesickness was Mrs. Pattison. Thank goodness Dr. Treleaven had agreed to join them. The budding relationship between the good doctor and John's old neighbour would go a long way to making life in India more palatable for the widow. The abatement of the monsoons and the earth coming alive, as it was with splotches of dramatic colour was also doing wonders to pick up everybody's spirits.

After a lovely dinner at the Worthing's one mid-September evening when the gathering took their places in the drawing room, the sergeant made his way to the liquor cabinet and pulled out a bottle of very expensive brandy. Crystal snifters were brought out, and the deep amber liquid was meted out carefully and with a flourish.

"I believe James has an announcement he'd like to make." Henry Worthing turned to James and gave him the floor.

James stood up, brandy snifter held a little awkwardly in his left hand. He cleared his throat.

"I would like to announce that Susan and I are engaged to be married." While there was no need for him to be afraid — after all, he had received the blessing of the Worthing's and had already broached the subject with Susan — his voice nonetheless betrayed his nervousness.

Susan was beaming and stood up next to her beau, clasping her hand in his. James gave her a loving kiss, and then the room erupted with congratulatory exclamations. Warm handshakes and hearty hugs were the order of the moment.

The sergeant raised his glass and proffered a toast to the newly engaged couple. The assemblage echoed his sentiments and glasses were clinked.

Once the mirth had subsided and people had taken their seats, John rose slowly and with a quick glance at Alice, began to speak.

"I have witnessed James and Susan's relationship developing from our first days at sea more than a year and a half ago. It has been obvious to all of us who have known them as a couple that they are wonderfully suited to each other. Alice and I could not be more pleased for the two of them. I'm sure, at this time, as happy as they are, that James is missing his family in Ireland. They will be ecstatic once they've heard news of this event. I'm sure that James will correspond with them as soon as possible. At least Alice, his darling sister, is here to celebrate with them. I would like now to inform you all that Alice and I have set a date for our wedding. It will take place on the last Saturday of November. Having said that, I would also like to extend an invitation to James and Susan to join us in a double wedding on that occasion. James and I have discussed this possibility, and with the approval of Susan's parents, we are hoping that this can be the case." John looked earnestly at the Worthing's.

Henry and Cecilia Worthing removed themselves to the dining room and, in a few moments, returned with huge grins on their faces.

"John, Alice. If Susan and James are game, then so are we."

Again, there was another round of congratulations, and just as they were settling down, Dr. Treleaven took the floor.

"Mrs. Pattison and I are not getting any younger. We have determined to forge a life for ourselves here in India. Would you mind very much if we were to make it a triple wedding?"

While it was no secret that Dr. Treleaven and Mrs. Pattison were sweet on each other, this announcement did come as a surprise to all of them, with the exception, perhaps, of Mrs. Holwell, who counted Mrs. Pattison as a confidante.

Alice piped up before any of them could respond. "Just think, John — and you too, James and Susan — this would be the celebration of the year here in Calcutta! Let's do it!"

There was a hearty acknowledgement by all.

"After our brandy, I propose that we all take a turn around the Park. There is much for us to digest." Mrs. Worthing stood up and little by little the others followed suit, placing their empty glasses on the tray that was being brought round.

John and Alice led the way out the door into the promising Calcutta night. The evening air was fresh, and lamps were being lit all around the Park as dusk began to settle.

CHOLER AND KHOLERA

It was a lovely evening in late January. There was a light breeze reaching across the Hoogly to where John and Alice sat on the exquisitely ornate bench that had arrived just after Christmas, courtesy of Sarfaraz Khan. How he had known the date of Dr. Holwell's wedding was beyond John; on the other hand, as the Newaab had said, he did have eyes and ears all about his kingdom.

The Holwell's had just hosted a lively dinner party in honour of Sgt. Worthing's forty-fifth birthday, and it was a lovely respite now that the guests had departed, and they had the late dusk to themselves to just sit and look out over the river. John had had lamps, strategically placed throughout Alice's garden once he had seen her preliminary plans, which were now lit and providing a magical illumination between the house and the banks of the Hooghly; in the bargain, they were playing a bewitching dance in the willowy mangroves that dotted the property.

"I can't believe I'm actually here in India and that we're married." Alice's lovely voice seemed far away and deeply reflective.

John took a long, satisfying pull on his Irish clay pipe, letting out a rich, thick volume of smoke that sinuously wrapped about his face before being wafted away. "It is like a dream, isn't it, Ailish?"

John had taken to calling his wife by her Irish name, especially in intimate moments such as this. Why he had done this rather escaped him, but nonetheless he had, and Alice never commented on it, though it was obvious she enjoyed it.

"I'm so glad that we were part of the triple wedding. People in Fort William and White Town are still talking about it. There couldn't have been three more beautiful brides!" John took another pleasurable puff of the new pipe he had received from Alice as a wedding present.

"Nor three more handsome grooms." Alice interjected. "I'm glad you're enjoying the pipe, John. I purchased it on Grafton Street in Dublin just before I left for London to stay with your mother. When I saw the display at Kapp's Emporium, I knew right away that you should have one as a wedding present."

"It is a very thoughtful gift, Ailish. They had Irish clay pipes for patrons to smoke at the Hog's Head, one of the Public Houses I sometimes frequented on Fleet Street in London. The pipes were laid out on the bar and whenever a patron requested one, the proprietor would bring out a small hatchet-like instrument and would chop off a small section of the stem so that one had a fresh mouthpiece. When the pipes became too short to smoke, they were ceremoniously disposed of in the main fireplace. All of it rather quaint."

From the days before his wedding, John had been studying a disease that seemed to raise its ugly head not long after the monsoon rains had stopped. The locals referred to it as Bengal Fever. By Christmas time, he had recorded a vast body of cases that seemed to follow the same symptomatic journey—a journey far too quickly and devastatingly concluded by anyone's reckoning.

In the early days, patients would say they had lost their appetite and that they were experiencing a sense of lassitude, not even wanting to stand up and move around even a little. A heavy fatigue would set in, along with an ennui so deep that patients felt lost and depressed. They couldn't take in enough water. They suffered from 'dry mouth,' and if a doctor were summoned in the early stages, which wasn't always the case, they could discern lesions or white patches on their patients' tongues. And the hapless victims couldn't sleep, tossing and turning relentlessly, which made their dispositions even more ill-tempered.

From this stage, which lasted but a few days, the Bengal Fever patient typically became feverish. He didn't run a significantly high temperature, but there always seemed to be a sheen of perspiration on his forehead, even on the coolest of evenings. He suffered from loose bowels, and his excrement took on a ghastly pale green hue.

The aforementioned symptoms worsened in due course and ere long patients were experiencing seizures and suffering a great deal of pain which didn't seem to be localized to any particular part of their bodies. A very agonizing and terrible death followed anon in the larger proportion of patients who had reached this final stage. But a very few made it through, and those that did were mere shells of who they had been before the onslaught of the affliction.

Now in the spring of 1735, the number of cases of Bengal Fever had abated substantially, and it was becoming more and more obvious to John that this disease was likely waterborne, due in large part to the pools of stagnant water that hung around in the aftermath of the monsoon season's torrential rains.

He went often to the few medical books and treatises that he had brought with him from England and the tracts that had been so kindly sent on to him from Lady Montagu. In one of these medical journals, he came across the term 'kholera,' which was defined as "a type of disease characterized by diarrhea, supposedly caused by bile." From his early study of ancient Greek, he knew that the term 'khole' meant bile, and that 'khloros' referred to a colour, either pale green or greenish-yellow. 'Khole,' he also knew as the term for drainpipe or gutter, which, in hindsight, made sense if you considered the intestinal anatomy of a human being—a body's drainage system, as it were.

All these musings he shared with Treleaven as they strolled around The Park and with Mr. Chandler at the hospital. They agreed with him that the Bengal Fever they had been dealing with was likely an intestinal ailment brought on by ingesting contaminated food or drink. They made a plan to educate the denizens of White Town and the Fort about the dangers of preparing food with water from still ponds and from drinking the same.

Sitting comfortably in his study at home, John began to write a treatise on the disease. He titled it *Kholera Nosoi,* using the Greek term for the gods or spirits of plague, sickness, and disease. He then scratched out the '*Nosoi*' and replaced it with the Latin term, '*Morbus*'; *Kholera Morbus* had a better ring to it, and more practitioners would understand its meaning.

Things couldn't have been more right with John Holwell, what with embarking on this new, connubial adventure with his beautiful Alice in their lovely environs by the Hooghly River, and with the fecundity of his scientific research and writings. There was one exception, perhaps, and a rather large one at that.

John had known since his first performance review that the Governor wasn't pleased with his association with—and more so his collaboration with—Hindu ayurvedics and Muslim *hakims*. Not long after that review, when it became obvious to the Governor that his surgeon's fraternity with the odious natives wasn't going to stop, the fortnightly invitations to dinner with the Fort's leaders at the mansion had been curtailed. This was a cause of great consternation for John, but he was absolutely convinced that he had as much to learn from the local practitioners as they did from him and his Western colleagues. If that meant being at odds with the Governor, then so be it.

"What's wrong, darling?" John had just returned from a summons to the Governor's residence and Alice could see how perturbed he was.

"That paunchy scoundrel is at it again. He berated me for twenty minutes about collaborating with the enemy. When I told him that the Indian people are not our enemy and that they deserve our trust and that we ought to be working with them, his face turned a ghastly red, and he was so apoplectic that I thought he would suffer a stroke then and there. We had words, and I probably shouldn't have spoken to a superior in such a manner, but I'm sorry to say that I lost control of myself. He told me he was temporarily relieving me of my duties as head surgeon and that he would seek a more formal dismissal in his report to Whitehall."

The shock on Alice's face was plain to see. "What are you going to do?"

"I'm going to carry on as a surgeon at the hospital. I've been demoted, not sacked… yet. Chandler will take over my duties at the Fort. I suppose that in one way, it's a blessing in disguise. I can keep on with my research, and I'll have some time to sort out my next steps—our next steps."

BOOK FIVE

JEDDAH
1735

Alice and John stood on the deck of the Montagu, a 530-ton Indiaman headed for England via the Arabian Peninsula and Cape Town. At this moment, they were carefully making their way north to the Port of Jeddah, an Arabian city resting on the Western side of the peninsula and hard up against the Red Sea. They could already see the walls and fortifications surrounding the city, constructed there by Hassain Al Kurdi, the Governor (or *Wali*) of Jeddah, in the 15th century to protect the Muslim enclave from the Portuguese. While they couldn't see the moat surrounding the city yet, John knew to expect one upon their arrival. He had done as much research about Jeddah as he could before their hasty departure from Fort William.

Knowing that John wanted to take a hiatus from Fort William and Calcutta until a new governor was named, Mayne had spoken with the captain of the Montagu, a sprightly, red-haired gentleman by the name of Williers, and had persuaded him to take John on as ship's surgeon, at least until Jeddah. He explained the connection John had with the Montagus—indeed the ship was named after the Ambassador to the Ottoman Empire, Lord Montagu—and in particular to his wife, the Lady Mary Wortley Montagu. Williers was an astute man and surmised that the ambassador and his wife might hold him in higher esteem once they found out about his having aided Dr. John Holwell and his new bride, and that could only help his career aspirations.

John had his arm about Alice's waist. He sighed. He hadn't really considered taking Alice along with him. Who knew what Jeddah would hold for them? It was predominantly a male-dominated world and not always friendly to infidels, as they would most assuredly be considered. However, there was not going to be any stopping her from accompanying him. In response to his exhortation, she had responded vehemently.

"John, I will not be apart from you again—ever! We are but newly married. Your mother has the Worthing's and the Treleaven's to look in on her. She has lived by herself for many years, and she knows how to look after herself. Besides, we are only going to be away for a year or two at most. You've told me yourself that Fort William changes its governors as often as women change their minds. I'll not be left behind. You told me in your first letter proposing marriage that you looked forward to sharing many adventures with me. I am most certainly up for this adventure!"

And that had been that.

As they stood outside the charter house waiting to be welcomed into the city, John reflected on how this arrival in a new world was so different from his arrival at Fort William a couple of years ago. There was no Mayne or James here, and no position waiting for him. He and Alice were quite alone. All they had was a letter sealed by one of Sarfaraz Khan's clerks by the way of introduction to the Wali of Jeddah. They would not get a letter of recommendation from the Governor of Fort William, nor did John ask for one.

Watching the cargo of teak being unloaded from the Montagu, John and Alice wilted in the oppressive heat. John loosened his collar, and Alice energetically used the fan she had brought along from India to cool herself. Alice had never complained once about the weather or any of the myriad inconveniences she had encountered on the voyage. John knew he had chosen wisely. Alice was beautiful; she was charming; she was highly intelligent; she was unflappable.

They wouldn't find out until sometime later what Sarfaraz Khan had dictated to his clerk, but once the letter had been perused by the Port Authority, the Holwell's were treated with deference and efficiently whisked away into the precincts of Jeddah to a rooming house close to the Souk, a vibrant market in the old town.

The first few days in Jeddah were spent getting to know their way about the labyrinthine cobblestone streets and learning the local customs. After all, the last thing they wanted to do was to offend anyone! Alice quickly learned that she must wear a sober-coloured head covering and should let

John speak first if they encountered someone in the street or in a place of business. She also discovered that women didn't go out and about in the market for the most part until later in the evening. The afternoons were spent doing domestic work at home or resting. In fact, the normal rhythms of their day were quite disrupted. Men sat on carpets or benches in the streets, their long flowing *abayas* wrapped comfortably around them, from late in the evening until dawn, sipping tea and talking about the comings and goings of their city by the sea. The women gathered together with friends and children behind latticed walls, gossiping, repairing garments, or preparing food. The nights were cooler and much better suited to being social. The heat of the day was oppressive, and it was a more sensible time for people to sleep or to be in the darker and cooler quarters of their abodes.

The rooming house they had been directed to was architecturally similar to most of the buildings around them. The exterior walls were fashioned of stone with perforated screens that were both intricate and alluring. This shield of latticework kept the building's inhabitants in shaded privacy, where they could look out onto the street but not be seen by prying eyes. It also kept out the dust for the most part and allowed in a modicum of fresh air should there be a bit of a breeze about. John was absolutely fascinated by the buildings, which were far superior to anything he had seen in India, barring the Newaab's palace perhaps, in Murshidabad.

Building materials included coral stones mined from the reefs that lined the Red Sea and purified clay taken from nearby lake beds that was used as mortar for the setting of the coral stones and for waterproofing the floors and roofs. John was to discover that this technique was absolutely unique to Jeddah. Teak wood, with which the Montagu had been laden, was used for decorative enhancements, while interior walls were plastered with alabaster, which could be manipulated while damp into artistic and beautiful designs. But the biggest wonder of all for John, and something he would definitely take back to India with him, was the system for harvesting rainwater so that there was always a supply of fresh water on hand. Large tanks were constructed on rooftops that collected rainwater and moved it through pipes into a cavernous cistern built below the ground. Ingenious mechanical pumps could then be used to transport the cool water into the kitchens and perhaps the privies of the dwellings of wealthier citizens. He was already formulating plans for adopting this innovation and installing something like it in their home by the Hooghly.

One evening on a trip to the market, Alice remarked on how trusting the people of Jeddah seemed to be. When the Muzzein's call to prayer was broadcast, as it was five times each day, the shopkeepers left their shops unattended, and the stall merchants would simply cover their wares with cloth and go off to pray. The call to prayer was as magical and mystical as John had remembered it from his time in Murshidabad. It was part of the fabric of life here in Jeddah and something John would never grow tired of.

The Souk at night was a bustling hive of humanity. On offer were oils and unguents, bolts of cloth, cooking utensils, and food of every description. Heaps of spices were stacked on tables under colourful canopies, especially small hills of a rich, red spice called Summak. They discovered that this was a delightful and delicious spice sprinkled over vegetables or mixed into stews. It took some time for them to get used to the process of bartering and establishing a fair price for anything they wanted to purchase, but they soon became accustomed to it. Alice was a much more astute negotiator when it came to making purchases than John. John gave in too early and showed impatience when bartering, which had the unfortunate result of tipping off the merchants that he could be easily separated from his *riyals*. Furthermore, he often confused *riyals* with *girsh*, which were worth a mere fraction of a riyal. When Alice discovered that John had paid eighteen *riyals* for sea cucumbers that should have cost eighteen *girsh*, which amounted to more than twenty times their value, she didn't allow John to do any more of the day-to-day shopping.

In one of the many shops lining the Souk, John came across chess sets, some made of wood, others of onyx. He couldn't resist, and so he purchased an onyx set that he could someday display in his study at home. He had taught Alice to play, and this would give them something to do when whiling their way through the long evenings and nights.

John's Arabic was improving all the time and he set out to hire a tutor to help speed it along. Alice too was proving to be a quick study, and she would sit in the background listening to the instruction. She and John would practise at every opportunity.

After a late evening meal toward the end of July, John and Alice sat down to play a game of chess. Alice had never defeated her husband, but her game was improving steadily. As this game progressed, she was putting a great deal of pressure on John's major pieces. Luckily for John, he was just able to queenside castle and place his king out of jeopardy. But Alice's next move was devastating. She forked his rook and bishop with her knight. He couldn't have been more relieved when there came a knock on the large wooden door of the rooming house, suspending the game and putting off the inevitable first loss to his wife.

One of the most noticeable architectural features found throughout the old city was the beautifully carved teak doors that were adorned with intricate patterns and tinted with a wide spectrum of colours. Their rooming house was no exception. Some of the grander houses had large double doors. It was one way to display the owner's wealth to the outside world.

John made his way to the entrance and let in a man, a royal servant to be sure, by the carefully tailored jet-black *abaya* he was wearing, and the voluminous head scarf tastefully embroidered with silver stitching along the seams. The gentleman wished them a good evening in Arabic and presented John with a letter sealed with the embossed signet of his master, the Wali of Jeddah.

Alice came to stand beside him as he broke the seal and read the contents, which were in English, the letters flowing on the page penned by an artful calligrapher. This was an invitation for the two of them to join the Wali for tea at their earliest convenience. Reading a little further down the page, their earliest convenience meant tomorrow evening after the Maghrib, the sunset prayer as John knew it to be.

John was a little out of his element here. After telling the messenger that they would be honoured to accept the invitation, he didn't know if the gentleman would expect an offering of money for his services, so instead he decided to offer him some refreshment. The royal servant politely accepted a small glass of pomegranate juice that Alice fetched from the kitchen, and then with a slight bow, took his leave.

The two of them went back to the chessboard in the drawing room and, with a grand flourish, John toppled over his king, signalling his capitulation. Alice grinned.

THE WALI OF JEDDAH

The Arabic tutor was very helpful the next afternoon in providing tips for how to handle the protocol of visiting the Wali. As it turned out, John and Alice need not have worried very much. The Wali, a large, jovial man wearing brocaded slippers and a colourful turban with a black gemstone at its apex, greeted them personally in the marble atrium of his palace, which was magically aglow after sunset, a hundred or more lit tapers reflecting in three small pools of water symmetrically placed in the large chamber. His English was flawless. When Alice commented on his English language fluency, perhaps a little too forwardly, in retrospect, the Wali smiled at her and cheekily replied that, "I should hope so, having spent the better part of my youth at Eton College, playing cricket, eating mutton, and terrorizing the poor servants at Windsor Castle over winter break!"

This delightful and completely surprising response had the effect of immediately putting them at ease, and the rest of the evening flowed wonderfully.

"Typically, at this point, Dr. Holwell, I would be taking you into my audience chamber, and leaving the lovely Mrs. Holwell to the devices of my wife and her sisters in the women's quarters. But knowing how brash British women are, I believe I'll include her in our deliberations — should that prove amenable to you?"

John glanced slyly at Alice and remarked. "That is most kind of you, Mawlana Wali. My wife is an equal partner in all my affairs, though I assure you she will be on her best behaviour in your company."

"Now before we get down to business, we should have some tea."

The Wali clapped his hands twice, and a servant appeared, almost as if by magic bearing a silver tea service.

"I have arranged for a less bitter concoction than we are used to drinking here, and some milk too, if you like. Though you should be warned,

233

it's camel's milk; it's quite a bit richer than the cow's milk or goat's milk you're probably used to."

The servant poured out the tea into cups resting prettily on an amazing wooden table carved with intricate designs.

"Is this table from India? I recognize the workmanship." Alice spoke up.

"It is, indeed, a gift from one of our misguided cousins in Bengal. I believe you've met him. Sarfaraz Khan?"

John piped in. "Alice hasn't had the pleasure, but I have, Mawlana."

From somewhere deep inside his voluminous *abaya*, the Wali pulled out the letter from Sarfaraz Khan that the Holwell's had presented to the Custom's House at the port.

"Let's see." And he began to read the missive out loud, having glossed over the preamble, with its obligatory salutations and honorifics, and continuing with a remarkable extemporaneous translation into English.

> *"I present to you the eminent Doctor Holwell, who has been of great service to my family. Not only has he capably ministered to my nephew who was injured in a construction accident, but he has given us thoughtful guidance in the prevention of such mishaps in the future.*
>
> *My court physicians met with him at length and were greatly impressed, not only by his willingness to learn from them, but also by the medical knowledge he was willing to impart. By their account, he is a formidable man of medical science, and Fort William has been lucky to count him as their lead doctor.*
>
> *I urge you, inshallah, to take him into your employ while he sojourns in Jeddah. You will not be disappointed.*
>
> *Your humble servant, Sarfaraz Khan. Allahu Akbar!"*

"What do you say, Doctor Holwell? Will you take up a post as one of my court physicians?"

John turned to look at Alice. This was more than he could have ever hoped for upon leaving Fort William in such a hurry.

"Mawlana, I would be delighted to serve you. I don't know how long we'll be in Jeddah, but while we are here, I can think of no better occupation. You are most gracious."

"Doctor, you will find that some of our *hakims* will be less than welcoming; in fact, they are unwilling to trust an outsider, especially an infidel. That being said, they will know that you have my favour, and that should help. Now, let's retire to the drawing room, as you would call it. I believe a cigar is in order. And my dear Mrs. Holwell, I'm sure you would prefer to visit with my wife. She is looking forward to meeting you. No doubt you are acquiring some of our language? Perhaps you could practise—and indeed, my wife could practise her English as well. She doesn't get much chance otherwise."

Alice didn't want to be excluded from the company of the men, but she knew that the Wali's suggestion was but a subtle command. She didn't want to create a fuss, which would only cause embarrassment for her husband.

"Of course, your excellency." Alice wasn't sure if this was the proper address for the Wali of Jeddah. She should probably have used the term that John had used once or twice already, Mawlana. But nevertheless, it was too late for that. "I would be more than pleased to meet your wife and see how the women of the palace occupy themselves."

She had tried very hard to keep any note of sarcasm from her voice when she replied. The Wali gave her a knowing smile and called for a servant to accompany her to the women's quarters.

The 'drawing room,' as the Wali had called it, was an intimate chamber, the walls adorned with tapestries, and the floor covered with plush oriental rugs. Cushions were laid out around the room, and low tables were strewn between them. Water pipes stood smartly beside each table each with two hoses emanating from the colourful glass-blown bowls. One had the impression that one was in a *pashah's* tent located somewhere in the middle of the Arabian Desert. On a side table sat an impressive wooden chessboard with the two ivory armies opposing each other and ready to do battle.

The Wali noted John's interest in the chessboard. "Do you play the Persian Game, Doctor?"

"I do."

"Would you like to play a game while we smoke our cigars and chat?"

"I would love to. But tell me, Mawlana, where did you come by cigars? I haven't seen any in the *shisha* shops in the Souk."

"Nor will you find any. I met King Charles III of Spain not long before his conquest of Naples and Sicily but two years ago. We became good friends, and on several occasions since, he has sent me Tabacalera cigars, manufactured in Seville. He says they are far superior to the rolled dried leaves wrapped in cornhusks that passed for cigars before Tabacalera came to be incorporated. These new cigars, as you will notice, are constructed with proper tobacco filler, binder, and wrapper."

"I'm sure I'll enjoy one, though my experience with cigars is very limited. I am a pipe smoker and have been for some time. I've tried your shisha and do find smoking a hookah most pleasurable."

A servant moved the chess table closer to the gentlemen, who had by now ensconced themselves on cushions. Another servant brought in a small, intricately carved box holding the treasured cigars. When the servant opened the box for the Wali to take one, he magnanimously gestured that John should avail himself of a cigar first. After setting down the box, the servant handed the Wali an intriguing guillotine-like device that he dexterously used to lop off the end of the cigar. John declined to use the device, asking instead for the Wali to deal with his cigar in like fashion. The servant then brought over a taper and two small strips of cedar. John watched, fascinated, as the Wali touched the cedar strip to the flame and then brought the burning brand to his cigar and lit the foot while taking in puffs of smoke. John attempted the same, and while his inexperience with this technique was abundantly clear, he did eventually get his cigar lit.

"Now, to the game, Doctor. You are my guest so you shall have the white army."

The two men studied the board and John played his first move, shifting the Queen's pawn forward two spaces along the file.

As accomplished a chess player as the doctor was, he was no match for the Wali, who dispatched him in a rather embarrassingly short time.

"I'm afraid I've caught you by surprise, Doctor Holwell. We'll have to play again sometime."

When Alice and John left the palace together, it was almost midnight. In the distance, they could see the minaret of the Shafi'i Mosque lit up and looking translucent in the glow of massive torches. They walked along the eastern wall of the city and then turned toward the heart of Jeddah.

"So, Ailish. How did your time with the women go?"

"I rather enjoyed myself, John. The Wali's wife, whose name I still can't get my tongue around, was a much more accomplished speaker of English than the Wali led us to believe. We talked about a good many things. Jawaria, as she had me call her when she noticed me struggling with her Arabic name, wanted to know all about life in India. After regaling her with a fairly lengthy description of Calcutta and the Fort, I tried to make conversation with some of the other women sitting quietly on the periphery. You know the status of my proficiency in Arabic—none of them evidently spoke any English—and you would have been amused to hear their tee-heeing and tittering as I mangled their beautiful language. And how was your time spent with the Wali?"

John wondered where he should begin. "I smoked an incredible cigar with the Wali. Having been thoroughly spoiled by the experience, I am already regretting the fact that I'm not likely to have that sort of opportunity again. Cigars such as the ones we smoked are a rarity, at least in the hemispheres we reside in. Even if they were somehow available, they would be prohibitively expensive."

It was an eerie experience to be walking home this late at night and to have the roads and little squares chock full of men sitting in groups drinking tea. As they passed, the men grew silent and followed them with their gaze. The sky was filled with an eerie orange haze.

"We played a game of chess, too." This piqued Alice's interest, and she turned to look at him. "I lost. In fact, I was annihilated."

"I'm not surprised, dear. Yesterday by little old me, and this evening by the Wali of Jeddah, who probably grew up using a chess set as a pillow." Alice hadn't meant to be so glib with this response. But John took it in good spirit and laughed along with his beautiful wife.

They were nearing their residence.

"Jeddah is going to be an even more populace city in August, according to the Wali. Thousands upon thousands of people from the Arab world, and from all over the globe, will be descending on Mecca for the Hajj. Many of them will use Jeddah as a jumping off point, Mecca being in rather close proximity to the east of us."

Alice looked quizzically at her husband. "What is the Hajj, John? I haven't heard of it."

"There are five main pillars of the Islamic faith. One of those pillars dictates that every good Muslim, having their health and the necessary finances, will make a pilgrimage to the city of Mecca at least once in their lifetime. Once there they will perform certain rituals, such as walking counter-clockwise seven times around the Kabaa, which is a cube-shaped building in the centre of the main square. Perhaps you've noticed that when the Arabs pray, they all face east — that is in the direction of Mecca. In India, of course, they all face west."

The wooden door of their rooming house was before them, and the exotic fragrance of the bougainvillea creeper that scampered up the trellised walls was intoxicating, reminding Alice of the Honeysuckle plants, which grew in wild abandon by her home in Dublin.

"Well, here we are." John opened the door and led them inside. "The day after tomorrow, I'm to present myself to the court physicians."

THE BRINGER OF HAPPINESS

The scent of burning *oud* was increasingly more noticeable as one approached the palace compound; it emanated from the up-scale shops and some of the well-to-do homes. Alice had researched *oud* and its oil derivative because she was intent on taking some of this intoxicating fragrance back to India with her upon their departure. On one of her increasingly frequent visits with Jawaria, having developed a close connection with the Wali's wife, she discovered that *oud* was agarwood, and that its oil, when harvested, was very expensive. "More expensive than gold!" Jawaria had said. "At least it burns slowly, and a little bit goes a long way."

There were other bits of information she had gleaned from the palace women that she enjoyed passing on to John while they spent time together in the evenings playing chess, or when her husband took a break from his scientific pursuits.

"Did you know, John, that 'Jeddah' means 'grandmother' in Arabic? And that the grandmother that is referenced is none other than 'Eve.' You know, Adam and Eve! According to local folklore, Eve was buried in Jeddah. The burial site is known as 'the cemetery of our Mother Eve.' It's a small park that people can visit. We should find this park, John, and see what it's all about. What do you think?"

John replied cheekily, "I'd rather find Adam's burial site, Ailish, but I guess Eve's will have to do."

The Wali was as good as his word and had paved the way for Doctor Holwell so that he could work collegially with the court hakims. While he never did feel that he was counted as one of their equals, most of them treated him with growing respect. They were particularly gratified when he read to them from Lady Montagu's treatise on the treatment of smallpox in the Ottoman Empire, and then when he demonstrated the technique he had learned from the Royal Surgeon, Dr. Maitland, which had refined the process.

"So, instead of harvesting the smallpox from mildly diseased patients and pulverizing it into a powdered concoction and then blowing the powder into the nostrils of your citizenry, we make a serum of it and drop the liquid pox into an open wound, such as an incision in the palm of the recipient's hand, between the thumb and forefinger. We believe that allows the diluted smallpox to enter the patient's blood stream more quickly and more surely."

Seeing that the hakims found this method distasteful, John quickly interjected.

"I have undergone this procedure myself. As you can see, I am here to tell the tale, and even though I have worked in close proximity to infected individuals, I have never caught the disease. In England, the success rate for the prevention of smallpox, using this technique, is ever on the rise. You may want to consider transitioning to it yourselves. I would be more than happy to show you the process. Please don't misunderstand me. We are ever grateful to the hakims of the Ottoman Empire, such as you are, for putting us on the right track. Without your impressive body of work on this subject, we would still be losing an intolerable number of people to this devastating affliction."

Not every court physician with him that day was mollified by his exhortation, but he could see the wheels turning, so to speak, in a number of them.

Over the next few days, he entertained a plethora of questions about engrafting, and when he went home one evening, he shared this whole exchange with Alice. She hadn't thought much about John's personal experience at Guy's Hospital in relation to this engrafting procedure. What little she knew about it had come by way of John's mother in the weeks before their departure from England, though he had filled her in on some of the more salient details after her arrival in India.

Just as John was about to put Alice's queen in check, likely spelling out the end of the game after a relentless attack on her defences, Alice blurted out, "John, you have said that I should undergo this procedure myself. Why not do it here, as an example for your hakim brethren?"

John looked lovingly at his wife. "You would do that?"
"I do trust you with my life, darling."

If the good doctor's wife was willing to sacrifice herself—at least that's how the hakims chose to look at it—then why not let her? It would be a novel opportunity for them all.

Doctor Holwell had had a lot of practice rubbing out the pustules from the scabs of lightly diseased smallpox patients and then distilling the resultant powder into a viscous serum he concocted for the purpose. The Arab physicians looked on diligently as he worked, and a number of them were happy to give the process a go themselves.

On the appointed day, a large group of observers gathered in the operating chamber. Among their number was the Wali himself and Jawaria. The Wali had been briefed by his personal doctor and had expressed a fervent desire to be present. Jawaria wasn't going to let "her friend" go through this trauma all by herself—that is, with no woman to comfort her. On this basis, she was willing to attend the procedure, even though she had registered her opposition to the whole affair quite vociferously. The court physicians were visibly shocked that there should be a woman in the operating chamber, but given that it was the Wali's wife, none of them would be stupid enough to object.

"Alice will rest most comfortably in the women's quarters. We will be able to tend to her every need." Jawaria wouldn't hear of any other option for Alice's convalescence. "Doctor Holwell, you have described in great detail what we should expect, and we will follow your instructions to the letter. You and the royal physicians will have leave to enter our quarters as needed. No other males will be allowed within the precincts of the harem as per our normal protocols."

Alice was resting peacefully on a divan in the heavily curtained room she had been given. John couldn't have been prouder of how she had undergone the procedure, not showing the slightest hesitancy nor flinching when he put the scalpel to its use and opened up a wound in her palm. He squeezed her good hand, kissed her on the forehead and left her to the ministrations of Jawaria and the other ladies.

He made his way back to the hospital wing and spent some time debriefing with the hakims. They were a subdued group and, for the first time, invited John to dine with them after prayer.

Some weeks had passed since Alice's ordeal, of which she had come out "right as rain," as she put it, in a startlingly short time. It was getting increasingly difficult to get around in their rooming house in the central part of Jeddah. John's collection of medical books and papers, his sketches in various stages of completion, and the artifacts both of them had been collecting while touring around the old city occupied every nook and cranny of the dwelling.

The Hajj had begun and ended. Alice had been so taken with the pilgrimage and the thousands of visitors in the streets that one evening, she asked John to enquire about visiting the site themselves.

"We could go for a few days once the Hajj is over. It's only a journey of two or three days, I understand."

"In all your studying about the rituals that are performed in Mecca by the devout, I'm surprised that you didn't learn that non-believers are strictly forbidden to enter the Holy City. If by some chance an infidel is caught trespassing, a whole range of punishments can fall on his head. He might be flogged or fined heavily. And he most certainly would be shipped out of the country as quickly as could be arranged." Having delivered this piece of harsh news, John could see that Alice was quite disappointed. "We'll have to limit ourselves to Jeddah and its immediate environs, I'm afraid."

Not long after Christmas, which was a very solitary celebration for them this year, they were delighted to receive letters from Calcutta. To prolong the pleasure of these missives, they took it in turn to read each aloud, after which they would discuss the contents.

The first was from John's mother, Amelia.

They were pleased to note that Mrs. Holwell was feeling thoroughly settled in her new home. She had been busy, before and after the monsoon season, fleshing out Alice's garden design. She wanted Alice to know which plantings had been a success and which one or two hadn't quite worked out. She wrote of the regular gatherings at the Worthing residence and the delight she was taking in walking the park circuit whenever the weather allowed. Mr. Mayne and Sergeant Worthing had been most helpful in dealing with the contractors that were still finishing up little projects at the house. The monsoon season had been a benign one, as it turned out, and people were in good spirits. She prayed each night for her son and his new bride and was hoping that they found themselves in good health and were happy in their new adventures.

It was obvious that she had broken off from her letter writing for a while, because when she came back to it, she reported that she had received the letters they had sent and that she was pleased that all was going well for them, and that Jeddah must be a fascinating place to visit. She closed off by saying that she was looking forward to their safe return, "sooner rather than later," and cryptically that "James and Susan have some news to share with you, but I will leave it for them to divulge."

There was no denying now that James' and Susan's letters ought to be read next.

"Typical James," claimed the exasperated Alice. "He's content to let Susan do all the talking!"

When they had come upon the 'news' that Mrs. Hollwell had alluded to, both of them sported huge grins.

"We are pleased to inform you that you are to be Aunty Ailish and Uncle John. I am with child. The birth should take place, God-willing, sometime in May."

When they got to the end of that letter, they took a break so John could pour some wine and to toast the pending arrival of their niece or nephew.

"I suppose we should start thinking about making our way back home. I'd like to be present at the birth, and I'm sure you would as well, Ailish?"

John had not wanted to return to Calcutta until a new governor had been installed at Fort William, so he was ecstatic when he read Lewis Mayne's rather succinct note.

*"I'm writing to you to tell you that we will have a new governor at
Fort William as of January 1st. Governor Freke will take over from
that pompous ass who made your life so difficult. As I write this note, I
am just finishing off my five-year accounts, getting ready to send them
to England. I thought you might be interested in the numbers.*

*1730-1735 – The British East India Company in Fort William has
exported goods to the value of £717,854. As well, they have returned
£2,406,078 worth of bullion to the home office. That should give
you a fair overview of our exploits here in India. Quite the success, I
should think!*

*One thing further, the aggressive Marathas, who, as you know,
have motivated us to build a protective ditch around the fort, have been
wreaking havoc on the suburbs of Delhi and have been pressing at the
gates. As I write to you, I still haven't heard the outcome of the matter.
It is a tragic affair, by all accounts, no matter how it's concluded.*

*I hope that you and Alice are well, and that this news of a new
governor might spur you on to hasten your return. We have missed your
presence greatly.*

Earnestly,
Lewis Mayne

"What is that you're embroidering, Ailish? It's amazing!"

Alice had been painstakingly working away at a project for several
evenings now. The yarn interwoven in the canvas was slowly but surely
beginning to suggest lovely green foliage with purple flowers. The hoop
was now highlighting some flowing Arabic words.

"This is a parting gift for Jawaria. The flowers and greenery will surround the words *"Jawaria—the spreader of happiness."* One of her sisters
told me the meaning of her name. It's beautiful, isn't it?"

"That it is, my dear."

"John, have you thought about something you'd like to give the Wali
as a keepsake?"

"I have, darling. One of my main occupations these last few weeks while working with the court physicians has been to codify as much of the medical knowledge that I've gleaned from them. They are very sound men of science and medicine, but they are not very good at promoting themselves, nor are they good at sharing their techniques with each other, and especially with physicians outside of their narrow sphere in the palace. I plan to leave a bound copy of what I have learned with the Wali."

"I think that's brilliant, John. I'm sure he'll value it highly!"

Two weeks before their planned departure for India—"home," as they were fond of calling it now—the Wali threw a farewell banquet in their honour. Food was laid out on large trestle tables in the banquet hall. Entertainers of every description delighted the invited guests. Speeches were made and then there was a presentation of gifts.

Jawaria presented Alice with an ornate vial of precious *oud* so that when she burned it in her Indian home, she would remember her time in Jeddah. John was touched by the thoughtful gift of a caduceus, carved intricately from a block of pristine obsidian and presented to him by the Wali's personal physician on behalf of the hakims he had worked with. The Wali's gift was stunning as well. It was a *muhaddab*, a scimitar of incredible workmanship, which the Wali personally unravelled from a thick piece of oiled canvas.

It was now time for John and Alice to present their gifts. Jawaria was in tears when she unwrapped the beautiful piece of embroidery that Alice had crafted for her. The Wali too was overcome by John's medical opus. After leafing through it for a moment, he called over the head physician and placed the folio in his hands with a command to have two copies made of it, one for the court physicians and one for the palace library. The original copy he would keep in his own study.

On the day of their departure, March 22, 1736, nine months and ten days from the date of their arrival, John and Alice stood side by side on the transom deck of the Wilmington, a 530-ton Indiaman, captained by Charles Massey, making its way to India with its crew of ninety-eight souls and thirty guns. They watched the walled city of Jeddah slip into the distance, the haze of the day's heat obscuring the details.

BOOK SIX

John Zephaniah Holwell

CHARLOTTE

They were seated around the Worthing's sitting room — all but Alice, who was standing behind her sister-in-law rubbing her shoulders. Susan was due any day now, her belly full and well rounded. Her face was glowing. Everyone agreed that pregnancy suited her. John was talking about their time in Jeddah, and Alice would chime in every so often, filling in details or expanding on descriptive elements of his narrative.

When John stopped occasionally to take a sip of his tea, someone would invariably interject with a question. Cecilia Worthing wanted to know about the food they ate. Mrs. Holwell asked about the customs and ways of the people. James wanted to hear more about the Wali's court and the wonders of the palace. Treleaven had questions of a medical nature, and John told him that he would speak to him at length about this when they were alone, so as not to bore the others. He did share some of the saga of Alice's brave undertaking of the engrafting procedure that would engender, as he had predicted to Alice, a visceral impact on the gathering. He began the tale and then left off so Alice could finish the episode in her own words.

The monsoon wasn't upon them yet, so they took a turn about The Park once it became obvious that they all needed to stretch their legs. They then parted company, respectively heading to their own abodes. John and Alice walked a little way to the entrance of Fort William and said their goodbyes to James and Susan who were now living in the married quarters of the fort. Having deposited them there they continued to their lovely new home by the Hooghly.

Dr. Treleaven delivered Susan's baby, on 28 May 1736. The child being delivered, the navel-string being tied and cut, the baby was wrapped in a warm cloth and a woollen cap was placed on its dainty head. Doctor Holwell took the child from Treleaven's hands. He walked over to the attending doula and had her complete the ablutions. These comprised primarily of removing the *vernix caseosa,* or the "scurf," as the nurse called it, from the newborn's body. It was a waxy white substance to be found on the scalp, under the armpits, and in the genital areas of all newborns.

Holwell carefully placed the baby in the crook of Susan's arms, swaddled up anew. It was making little mewling sounds, as if it were annoyed at having been disturbed by the nurse and the soapy water she had used to cleanse it. Only then did he have the nurse admit James, who had been pacing about in the anteroom like a tiger in a cage. James walked in, went straight to Susan, and planted a tender kiss on her forehead. He looked at his child in wonderment, and a huge smile lit up his face. He still didn't know the gender of the baby, and Susan, sensing the unasked question, put him at his ease.

"Darling husband, let me introduce you to Charlotte. Isn't she beautiful?"

The sergeant and his wife had presented the new parents with a fine perambulator as a gift. It had large wheels to navigate the roads when they were muddy, as they often were at this rainy time of year. A canopy could be accordioned up when the weather was inclement or if the sun was too glaring.

Alice and Susan led the way around the Park, taking turns pushing the pram. The torrential downpour of earlier in the day had subsided to a light drizzle. James, John, and the Worthing seniors trailed some way behind.

"Tell me, Henry, what's been happening with the Maratha's in Delhi?" With the busyness of their return to Calcutta and the excitement of Charlotte's birth, John had pushed this question from his mind until now.

"It's been a bloody business, John. The Maratha's are still on the outskirts of Delhi, and thank God they haven't yet been successful in storming the city itself. But there are stories of innumerable atrocities that have been perpetrated on the poor dwellers in the suburbs. The marauders have burned shops and houses, murdered hundreds of civilians, and have generally run amok, raping and pillaging. Soon enough, I'm afraid, they'll turn their attentions to the south, and then God help us all!"

"Since our return, I've noticed more activity at the Maratha Ditch. But there's still a long way to go to complete the fortification around the Fort and even further to go on the outer ring defending Calcutta."

"Governor Freke is an able soldier, John, and he is putting all the resources that can be brought to bear on the project. Still, it's slow work, and we're all rather worried that the Ditch won't be ready when the time comes. Let's hope that the Maratha's will be spent by the time their attack on Delhi is over. If they do have designs on attacking Bengal, surely they'll have to take some time — years one can hope — before turning their vanguard in this direction."

One soggy morning in July, John received a summons from Governor Freke. He was elated. Not wanting to seem overly anxious about his position in Fort William, and, of course, with the English East India Company, he hadn't pushed for an audience with the new governor, waiting for Freke to play the first hand. This Governor was, by all accounts, cut from a very different cloth than the previous commander of the Fort. Even in their physical stature, they were miles apart. While the former was paunchy and red-faced, Freke was tall and stately, with a swarthy complexion. The previous governor had accepted his post as a sinecure, the result of sycophantic overtures to some nobleman or the other. Freke was a true soldier, having distinguished himself in many fierce battles.

Upon being shown into the Governor's office, John was immediately put at his ease.

"Would you care for a whiskey, Holwell?" Freke began moving over to the sideboard before the doctor's affirmative response.

Whiskey tumblers in hand, the Governor nodded to a small sitting area off to the side. John accepted the glass when Freke offered it and then took a seat.

"I must say, Holwell! For a man who has been in the East such a short time, you seem to have made a mark here. It would seem that you have a lot of admirers and, beyond that, people who are importuning me at every turn to reinstate you as Fort William's head surgeon."

"I'm sure you're exaggerating, sir."

"On the contrary. Besides overtures from Mayne, Treleaven, and Chandler, I have also received a most interesting missive from none other than the Wali of Jeddah by way of His Eminence, Sarfaraz Khan. The Wali holds you in very high esteem. He praises your medical skills and waxes rhapsodic about a manuscript you gifted him, codifying the medical knowledge of the court physicians. Sarfaraz Khan has also provided his own encomium, saying that he is in your debt." Governor Freke put down the rather official-looking letter he had taken into his hands. He grinned impishly. "Having said that, my predecessor's report was not very flattering."

Upon seeing the effect this last statement had on John, he immediately chirped up. "You're not to worry about that, old chap. There are many of his reports that have been contradicted by people I have come to trust. As of August 1st, you will be reinstated as the head surgeon and will assume all of the duties and responsibilities that title bears. Your salary shall be 2000 rupees per annum—a slight increase from what it was during your first tenure here, I believe?"

"I am grateful to you, sir. Though I would like to broach a rather delicate subject with you first."

"What is it, Holwell?"

"Sir, one of the sore points that existed between your predecessor and me was my work with Indian ayurvedics—that is, doctors—and their Muslim counterparts. I can only accept your generous offer if I have leave to continue with that enterprise. We have much knowledge to share with them, and I dare say, they have much to teach us as well."

"Holwell, those terms are acceptable to me with one proviso. That is that your work here at the Fort and in the hospital takes precedence."

With that, the two men stood up, clinked glasses, finished their whiskey, and concluded the meeting. On his way out, Freke called after him. "I have kept up with the bi-weekly dinners at my residence. I shall see you next Monday evening."

When John relayed the details of his visit with the Governor to Alice, she gave him a crushing hug. Maybe life could continue on now with some semblance of regularity? John had resumed his scientific pursuits, but at times, he had been listless and felt like he didn't have any particular purpose. Now, Alice wouldn't have to worry about finding little projects for her husband to pursue.

That evening, they decided to host Henry and Cecilia Worthing, Lewis Mayne, James, Susan, and the Treleavens for a celebratory dinner. James and Susan declined, however, not wanting to subject little Charlotte to such inclement weather. The gathering was a joyous one, and each party congratulated John on being reinstated to his post.

"I would ask each of you to keep this bit of news to yourselves." Lewis Mayne, having put down his dinner fork and pushing away from the table, had everyone's attention. "Governor Freke is about to proclaim a new edict that will mean some uncomfortable squirming about for some of our English brethren in White Town, as well as for some of the Fort William insiders. No English citizen shall undertake to do business with anyone who is involved in trade outside of the auspices of the English East India Company, whether on land or at sea. Anyone not complying with this directive will be subject to large fines and other discipline as the authorities deem fit."

"What has brought this on, Lewis?" While the impact of Mayne's words didn't seem to have made much of a dent on most of the group, Henry Worthing was quick to pick up on it. John too had been struck by this disclosure.

"I daresay I may have had something to do with this." Lewis Mayne looked about him. "Having received intelligence of a number of residents and soldiers who have pursued illicit trade with the locals and who have subsequently been pocketing money, not giving the King his due, so to speak, I prepared a report for the Governor. It seems the previous administration was being hoodwinked by these culprits or, perhaps even worse, willfully turning a blind eye to the goings-on. A lot of money has slipped through John Company's hands. Upon perusing my report, Freke was incensed and immediately took counsel with his senior officers. The new edict shall be proclaimed later this week."

John's mother led the ladies into the parlour where they could talk about topics of interest to them, and John ushered the gentlemen into his study, where they could probe Mayne with further questions about the situation he had described.

Later that night, snuggled cozily together in their expansive four-poster bed, listening to the rain and wind swirl about their house, John and Alice took delight in each other's company, and John fell asleep with a huge smile on his face.

THE CALM BEFORE THE STORM

While Holwell's reinstatement as head surgeon was gratifying for him, the first few months at work were fraught with ever-higher numbers of cases of Bengal Fever, or kholera, as he had taken to calling it. He worked tirelessly at trying to understand the disease. To help him with this endeavour, he conscripted Dr. Treleaven and Chandler. They meticulously investigated each case, not only reporting on the symptoms and the progress of the disease, but also thoroughly interrogating the patients and their families about what food or drink had been consumed and where the ingredients had been sourced. Later that winter, when the kholera epidemic had abated and John had had time to review all the notes, two common phenomena started to emerge. One was that most victims had become ill after consuming seafood. The other culprit was meat or vegetables cooked using contaminated water. All of his findings, he recorded in his medical journal.

This study of the sources of kholera had a very dramatic impact on John's diet and consequently on the diet of his immediate family. From the early Spring of 1737, and indeed for the remainder of his days, he barred his cooks from preparing the cuttlefish he was so fond of eating, as well as other molluscs, bivalves such as clams and oysters, and crustaceans, including shrimp and crayfish. When Alice asked him why there were some species of fish he would still consume, he rather pedantically replied that shellfish were in fact not fish at all. Shellfish, he opined, ate a diet composed primarily of phytoplankton and zooplankton and were more closely related to insects and arachnids. On the advice of respected *ayurvedics*, he also started a regimen of primarily vegetarian cuisine. In one of the many treatises that he composed and sent on to England, along with his other prolific medical journals, he spelled out the efficacy of a vegetarian diet.

It was a particularly hot June, and the Holwell's were enjoying some lemon tea in Alice's garden. John had taken the day off, and the morning had been spent pottering around the flowers and shrubs. As they got down to their work, a bulbul had alighted on one of the trees and began singing its plaintive song. Alice was entranced.

"That's a bulbul, dear, a Persian Nightingale. It is said that if one hears one singing in the morning, the day will hold lots of promise. I think we've just been blessed!"

In the heat of the afternoon, they sat resting under the shade of the mangroves. Just before they were about to head into the house, a messenger arrived from the Fort with a letter for Dr. Holwell. He recognized the seal and immediately broke open the document.

"What is it, John? Who is it from?" Both Alice and John's mother were intrigued.

After perusing the letter, and keeping his female companions in momentary suspense, he replied. "It's from Sarfaraz Khan. He has invited me to Murshidabad. And he says I'm to be accompanied by the lovely Mrs. Holwell, should that suit her."

"But, of course, that suits me, dear. When do we leave?" Alice's excitement was written all across her pretty face.

"Not having had time to reflect on this, I would say that we would probably have to wait until this year's monsoon has come and gone. Also, there's the small matter of having to make an entreaty to Governor Freke to procure his permission. Perhaps not such a small matter after all. I'll go and see him tomorrow if he's at leisure to meet with me."

John stood up and was followed into the house by Alice and the senior Mrs. Holwell. He made his way to his study. There was much to consider.

"The Governor will see you now." An efficient secretary opened the door to Freke's office and beckoned John in.

"Very fine work on this Bengal Fever business, Holwell." The Governor pointed to a seat opposite his desk. "You are getting to the bottom of it, I hear."

"Yes sir. I have already made my recommendations to the cooking staff here at the Fort, though I must admit they are a careful lot and are already running a most hygienic operation. When the soldiers get sick with the fever, it's because of something they've eaten while on leave in Black Town. I have made up some billets that can be posted around the Fort warning inhabitants about the potentially lethal consequences of eating food from less than reputable establishments and street vendors."

"Wonderful, Holwell. Though I must say, it's just one more thing to worry about. If it's not going blind by drinking too much arak or picking up some nasty venereal disease from the whores in Black Town, now it's Bengal Fever arising from the eating of contaminated victuals! In any case, what is your business here today?"

"I've come to petition you for leave to travel to Murshidabad. Sarfaraz Khan has sent me a personal invitation to visit him. I was hoping to travel with my wife in early September when the monsoon has let up a little. It means being away from my duties for several weeks, but the hospital will certainly be left in capable hands."

"I'm afraid I can't release you from your duties, sir." Freke waited for his words to take effect. When he was certain that Holwell was experiencing some discomfort, he continued. "While in Murshidabad you will carry on with your scientific explorations, and you will accompany Mayne to the Company's offices there to aid him in any way that you can." The relief on John's face brought a grin to Freke's face. "I have already given this some thought, Holwell. The Khan sent me word a few weeks ago, asking me to grant you leave to visit. I have agreed to this request."

Governor Freke stood up signalling the end of the meeting.

"I'm sorry, I need to cut this conference short, Holwell. I have a meeting of our Security Council beginning in ten minutes."

John shook Freke's hand.

"By the way, my good sir, there's one more thing you will do while in the Khan's palace. You will get your head around what Sarfaraz Khan and his generals are thinking about when it comes to their relationship with us in Fort William. I'll also need to know what their position is regarding the Maratha invasion of Delhi and whether they are anticipating any of this damned ugliness coming our way. Upon your return, I will expect a full report and will also ask you to address the Security Council."

As John was turning to leave the office, Freke made a rather cryptic comment that gave John a new and revelatory insight into this Governor.

"So let it be written, so let it be done."

John turned back toward Freke. "You are a student of history, sir. But I do hope you're not claiming to emulate Pharaoh Rameses ll in every aspect?"

The two men took their leave of each other, both of them smiling broadly.

On a wet and dismal morning in September, the barge carrying Dr. Holwell, Alice, Mayne, and other sundry Fort William emissaries drifted lazily downstream before gaining way, with its sails unfurled, and finally making sluggish progress up the Hoogly river. Despite the rain, they could make out John's mother waving farewell from under an awning in the garden. They waved back, John experiencing a pang of guilt at having left his mother alone yet again. When the prospect of the house had been left behind, they quickly stole away into the bosom of the ship to get out of the soggy weather.

At dinner that evening in the spartan dining room aboard ship, Mayne and Holwell were engrossed in a discussion of their respective missions in Murshidabad, the seat of the Newaab of Bengal. Tumblers of port in hand after the meal was over, they continued their dialogue, John pressing Mayne for ideas about how best to gather the intelligence that the Governor was after. Alice, meanwhile, had one ear pinned to their discussion and the other eavesdropping in on other conversations that were taking place around them. She was happy to be on a holiday with her husband and looking forward to being in the royal palace she had heard so much about.

Their days passed leisurely aboard the Sparrow, and John delighted in pointing out to Alice the many sights he had witnessed on his first journey north and west of Calcutta. The excursion was a therapeutic one for both of them, giving them time to reconnect and to be lost in each other's company.

Soon, the day of their arrival was upon them, and they set about preparing for disembarkation.

The Katra Masjid was everything John had said it would be, and Alice settled in comfortably. Mayne had taken lodgings in a hostel close to the English East India Company's headquarters and had bid them farewell after setting a date and time for John to meet him. The proprietors of the caravanserai and all its employees treated the English doctor and his wife with great deference. Not only did they remember John fondly from his previous stay at their establishment, but this time, they were none other than the esteemed guests of Sarfaraz Khan.

They spent the first afternoon strolling leisurely about the expansive gardens and then sat down to a sumptuous dinner in the banquet hall. The Newaab had been alerted to their arrival and sent an emissary to invite them to the palace two days hence.

On the following day, John reconnected with Katharu, the Hindu guide from his last visit, and the three of them spent an exhilarating day seeing the sights. Katharu was gracious enough to put himself at their disposal for the duration of their stay, and when John was busy at the palace or on Company business with Mayne, the Hindu guide agreed to accompany Alice to the shops and emporia that were known throughout the Bengal Subah for their unique and exotic merchandise.

After a second morning of traipsing about Murshidabad with Katharu, they returned to the Katra Masjid and prepared themselves for the royal visit. For this occasion, Alice had chosen a sari she had had crafted from the silk that had been gifted to her husband on his last visit. John stared at her open-mouthed as she pirouetted about in their chamber showing off the lovely green drapery set off with brilliant gold thread.

"You are a vision, darling. You look like a real Indian princess." At his remark Alice smiled at her husband coquettishly.

"Do I, dear?"

Holwell's rejoinder was playful.

"I have a mind to undrape you right now and take you to bed."

"I'm afraid that will have to wait, my love. We don't want to be late for our date with the Khan."

Having been a regular guest at the palace in Jeddah, and now having been welcomed into Sarfaraz Khan's palatial estate, Alice was beginning to wonder why the English citizens in Calcutta settled for living in such relative squalor.

"My dear Ailish, we are the lucky few who get to see how the grand pashas live. Most of our countrymen have never been within twenty feet of the outer gates."

John went up to the main deck of the Sparrow, marvelling at how easily it had caught the river's currents on its voyage back south, to smoke his pipe and contemplate the panoply of remarkable events during the course of their stay in Murshidabad.

Sarfaraz Khan had been more than gracious. The Holwell's had been invited to a truly magnificent banquet held in their honour; it was lavish in every respect. The Khan's wife had taken Alice under her wing, and they sat with the other women talking late into the night. Little Asfin gamboled around them with his siblings and cousins like young lion cubs, Asfin's accident of so long ago completely forgotten.

At the banquet, there hadn't been any talk of politics. John was peppered with questions about his time in Jeddah, and especially his association with the Wali. Instead, he had waited until his next meeting with Sarfaraz Khan to probe him on matters that Governor Freke was interested in. He learned that there was a wide net of spies cast about the extremities of Bengal and beyond to keep track of the borders. The Marathas wouldn't make a move without the Khan knowing about it well in advance.

"Bengal is the wealthiest province in India, Sahiba. There are other factions beside the Marathas who are interested in us. We become complacent at our peril."

The conversation slowly and cleverly had become interrogative.

"At our last meeting, we spoke of the Maratha Ditch that was being built about your Fort and the town. While we acknowledge that its purpose is to protect the interests of the English East India Company from marauders such as the Marathas, I must tell you that not all of my generals like the development one little bit. They are suspicious of it and see it as a shallow pretense for building up your battlements. They ask why you would need such fortifications when you have our protection as laid out in the charter your government has ratified with us. Relay this concern to your governor, and do tell him we are watching Fort William with all due circumspection."

Then, his mood had lightened and he had let John know that the palace hakim was very much looking forward to spending some more time with him. He had set up an appointment with him for later that afternoon.

The two men — this time with an interpreter present, though one wasn't really necessary, given Holwell's growing mastery of Urdu — discussed medicine at length. John had passed on his learning about Bengal Fever, which was evidently a growing concern in Murshidabad. The hakim, in turn, had shared a number of promising treatments for a variety of other local conditions. The two men parted on good terms, John at the last inviting the Muslim doctor to visit him in Calcutta.

Something had changed with the progress of the Sparrow a few days into the trip home. In the middle of the night, John sensed sluggishness and could hear the timbers groaning which was quite a departure from the gentle creaking that had been normal. This new cadence lasted until well into the mid-morning, when Holwell and Mayne had an opportunity to speak with the captain. They found him standing at the wheel under a gray and ominous sky.

"Our progress has been severely curtailed, sirs. In my many years of plying these waters, I have not encountered anything like it. Whatever was holding the ship back, though, has let loose, and we're finally back to our normal passage. You will also have noticed that the waters are uncommonly high, and there is a lot of flooding over the banks. Something has happened. I suppose we'll find out more at our next port of call."

The next port of call was Hooghly-Chinsurra. It was obvious at their approach that something was amiss. That something had laid waste to much of the port infrastructure. Soldiers were scurrying about in work details, removing fallen timbers and clearing walkways of debris that was scattered wildly about.

As they would only stop there for a few hours, John, Alice, and Lewis Mayne secured permission to make a quick trip to Fort Gustavus, where, as it turned out, Thijs Verhaven was still the commanding officer. He welcomed them into his office, but dispensing with all formalities, immediately stunned them by the news he had to report. Verhaven spoke and John translated, welcoming the chance to exercise his Dutch.

"On the night of October 11th, a violent hurricane struck the environs of the Bay of Bengal. There were torrential rains and incredible winds that wreaked havoc on all of us. The river surged and massive flooding ensued, and the Hooghly broke its banks. We had to quickly erect levees where we could. And then, on the morning of October 12th, we felt the earth shake, and buildings began to fall down around us. The tremors lasted for several minutes. I don't know what you're going to find in Calcutta when you arrive in two days' time, but I'd wager it's not going to be pretty!"

The Sparrow pulled away from Hoogly-Chinsurra and all the passengers stood about the deck looking out over the devastated landscape, stunned into silence. How Calcutta and the Fort had withstood the ravages of a double calamity—a hurricane and an earthquake striking hard, one event following so closely after the other—was more than they could contemplate.

DEATH AND DESTRUCTION

The wind was still up, and the river unsettled as they neared Calcutta. The degree of destruction on both shores had been ever increasing as the barge made its way to its home port, and the Holwell's held their collective breath as they negotiated the last bend. As they slipped past the Fort with their sails in irons and prepared for a reverse tack into the mooring, they caught a first glimpse of their house. It was almost too much to bear. The grotesque scene confronting them was worse than anything they could have imagined. Alice blanched as she looked out at her once lovely garden, now a tangled mess, and John stared, mouth agape, at the ruined structure that he had been so proud of. Only some segments of the brick walls remained standing, and the roof was gone entirely, almost as if some giant had lowered its massive hands and plucked it quite away. At once, his thoughts went to his mother. Was she alright? Where was she now? Feverishly, his immediate thought was to dive into the roiling waters of the Hooghly and swim the few yards to shore. Mayne grabbed hold of his shoulders, sensing John's reckless intent.

"Hold off, John. We'll be docked shortly. Then you can make a run for your house."

John's shoulders sagged once he realized the folly of what he had been about to do, and he held on to Alice, willing the ship to hasten its approach.

Mooring the Sparrow was a difficult and delicate operation. A good portion of the dock had been destroyed by the floodwaters, and they had to wait an excruciatingly long time for a makeshift gangplank to be hoisted on board. Alice squeezed her husband's hand.

"At the first opportunity, John, you run for the house. I'll follow up as best I can."

John looked into Alice's eyes. He could see the pain and turmoil hovering just below the surface. He knew he must look just as shattered.

"I will, Ailish. Please be careful when you make your way off the ship."

John didn't enter the Fort. Instead, he scrambled as quickly as possible along the riverside ramparts, climbing over piles of debris, and finally making a dash to the hospital grounds, the cemetery, and then at last to the lane leading into his property.

Three solitary figures waited for him at the head of the lane. James and Henry and Cecilia Worthing stopped him before he could make his way to the house. By their forlorn looks, he knew that his world was about to be shattered.

He took a moment to catch his breath and then asked the question that was uppermost on his mind.

"I'm very sorry to have to pass on this terrible news. Your mother has perished, John. At the height of the storm, when the house was falling down around her, she must have tried to make a run for a safer prospect. In the morning, her body was discovered under some fallen trees by the cemetery."

As the impact of the Sergeant's words hit home, Cecilia held on to John as tightly as she could. His body was wracked by sobs, fitful and uncontrollable.

Finally, he was able to speak. "Where is she now?"

Henry replied, "She's lying in the hospital morgue along with dozens of other poor souls who perished in the storm. We'll take you there when you're ready."

"Alice should be arriving shortly. I want to take a walk around our house before she comes. She will be devastated."

The Worthing's remained behind to intercept Alice, and James accompanied his friend as they picked their way carefully over fallen trees and other obstacles to the entrance of the house. Walking into what had been the foyer was quite disorienting, but once through, they slowly made their way, first into the drawing room and then into the other reaches of the broken building. One or two walls remained intact, their pictures and other wall hangings in place, just as they had left them. A small glimmer of hope presented itself to John as he surveyed his study. Much of it was still as it had been, including his writing desk, the cabinets housing most of the specimens he had collected over time, and even the scimitar which had been presented to him by the Wali of Jeddah, which was still resting in its glass case on the mantel above the fireplace. It was a strange experience to be in his favourite room, which was now completely open to the sky above.

John walked into his mother's bedroom. He looked over the jumbled furniture and many of her personal belongings, which were scattered grotesquely about, and once again he broke down. James stood beside him, and after a brief time, tenderly led him back to the study. The two men just stood in abject silence, there not being anywhere to sit down or anything to say. Eventually, they could hear the others come into the house and made their way to join them.

"The hospital's still functioning?"

Treleaven had intercepted the group as they entered the Admitting room. His shirtsleeves had been rolled out of the way, but they were stained with splatters of blood. His forehead gleaming with perspiration and his hair hanging unkemptly down the sides of his face, he was a dishevelled mess. John's question had been in earnest. The hospital, at least from the exterior, looked in a shambles. He looked about him now and could see that the interior was more or less intact.

"We had some work to do to clear the entrance, tidy up the surgery, and bail out the western wing. But as the roads were being cleared and more and more patients descended upon us... well, we have had to make do." Treleaven's response was clearly an understatement, and the poor man looked like he could fall asleep on his feet.

"When's the last time you got any rest, my good fellow?" John's voice registered his concern.

"I don't rightly know, John. Chandler and I have been at this almost non-stop for the past three days."

"We'd like to go in now and see my mother in the morgue. When we're finished there, I'll roll up my sleeves and take over while you get some well-deserved sleep."

"John, we'll be alright. You have much to attend to, and you need time to deal with your mother's passing."

"I'm sure the work will help me keep my mind off it, Treleaven. Alice will stay with the Worthing's for a while until we get things sorted. In the meantime, I should be here assuming my duties. Lord knows there's much to be done."

Wooden slabs lined the morgue — as many as could be fit into the smallish room. Makeshift curtains covered the windows, and only a few tapers were lit to try to keep the room as cool as possible. Nevertheless, the stench was terrible, and John surmised that it would be intolerable in another couple of days as the decomposition process went into full force. These bodies would have to be interred, and soon.

Alice had covered her nose with a light shawl, and Holwell drew a handkerchief out of his pocket to do the same. Treleaven pointed to a body wrapped completely in sail cloth four bodies in on the left side. He and Alice made their way down the narrow aisle and stood beside the corpse. John reverently pulled the material away from his mother's face. In his line of work, he was used to the mask of death, but now below him lay his own kin, and he trembled. Alice stood beside him weeping quietly.

There were bruises and abrasions all about her swollen face, and John feared the rest of her body was likely battered up to the same degree, if not worse. He asked Treleaven to leave him alone with his mother for a bit, and Alice left of her own accord, knowing this ought to be a very private moment for her husband.

From somewhere inside him, Psalm 23 came to his lips, and he mouthed the words while sobbing relentlessly.

James had retrieved their belongings from the Sparrow and had taken them to his rooms in the married quarters of the Fort for safekeeping. It was late evening on the day of their arrival, and a large group of them sat in the parlour of the Worthing residence. Cecilia Worthing had organized a late supper for them, and they had eaten their fill, not realizing how hungry they all were. Each of the assembled guests had offered his or her condolences to John and Alice, and the rest of the evening might have been a rather sombre one except for the delightful presence of little Charlotte who by now was ambulatory and exploring her surroundings when she wasn't tucked snuggly into the laps of her mother or father. As children are wont to do, she gravitated to her uncle and auntie, whom she could sense needed some cheering up. John bounced her for a bit on his knee and Alice sang a children's song she had learned in her youth in Ireland, something about a cat, a donkey and two pesky children. Charlotte laughed and moved to the rhythm of Alice's lilting voice. All eyes were on the little child's face and when the song was over, they clapped. Charlotte wheedled her way off John's lap and headed across to her beaming mother.

James piped up, "John, you still have your laboratory and bedroom at the Fort. Why not talk to Freke about settling in there?"

"Nonsense," blurted out Mrs. Worthing. "They surely must stay here with us in the interim. I won't hear of anything else."

Dr. Treleaven and his wife, the former Mrs. Pattison, had also determined to make a similar offer, living now as they did along The Park in the tidy little house they rented from the incorrigible Lady Russell. But seeing how adamant Mrs. Worthing was, they decided to hold off.

"We would be delighted, Cecilia. Though we don't want to put you out." John looked at Alice, and they both smiled at the Worthing's.

"It's our pleasure," intoned Mr. Worthing. "The house has grown rather empty. Cecilia will be happy to have some company, and Alice won't be far from Mrs. Treleaven or Susan at the Fort. You'll no doubt be spending your time at the hospital and rebuilding your house should that be your plan."

"It's settled then," said John. "We graciously accept your offer."

The Fort, with its sturdy ramparts and large beamed buildings, had fared reasonably well through the nightmare of the hurricane and the earthquake that had followed hard upon its heels. The dock had been destroyed, of course, much of it swept away in the rushing waters. In the days and weeks ahead, they would learn that the massive river surge had travelled sixty leagues up the Hooghly River, leaving devastation all along its path. John and Alice had seen first-hand the flooded lands and riverside structures turned to rubble. The veranda, which fed its way around most of the Fort's interior, had been destroyed and would need to be replaced once other priorities had been seen to.

John had just completed a briefing with Governor Freke and a few of the other senior officers. This had nothing to do with his trip, but rather was a run-down of what needed to be accomplished in the next little while. Once John had the situation under control at the hospital, he was to lead a foray into White Town, going house to house, business to business, to see where medical aid was still needed. Only once that was accomplished could he take his team further afield into Black Town and help out as best he could. He was asked to file a report of his activities every third day. The other officers were tasked with examining the fortifications and shoring them up as necessary, as well as seeing to the removal of debris, both in the Fort and in the vicinity of The Park. Furthermore, they were to provide Freke with a ranked list of restoration projects that would need to be undertaken.

Before returning to the hospital, John looked in on Mayne to see how he was getting on.

"This tragedy will be a costly one, I'm afraid. Revenues will be down considerably, and expenses will be through the roof. Once we have a clearer picture of the damage we've sustained, I'm to compile a detailed estimate of the costs to repair the Fort and create a budget that we can reasonably direct toward helping the British citizens in White Town. Luckily, my assistant had the foresight to protect my ledgers and other important papers from the elements. By rights, I should recommend an increase to his annual salary to reward his quick thinking and his loyalty."

THE BUTCHER'S BILL

The disaster of October 11th and 12th, 1737 would forever remain in the living memory of those who had experienced it. If one hadn't personally lost a close relative or friend, then certainly a neighbour had. In the aftermath, months of hard labour and trying conditions ensued for most people, especially for those residents of Black Town who didn't have robust structures in which to live and work. Most of their homes were made of mud and thatch.

John concluded his work in White Town expeditiously, but Black Town was another matter. His first foray into its precincts was an eye-opener. Bodies had been piled up here and there, and there were a constant series of processions led by grieving relatives meandering their way to the ghats and the constantly lit funeral pyres at the river's edge. Kati Ganga, source of water and food, washbasin and bathtub, had now become a grand and organic mausoleum. At least the current was carrying the effluent, ash, and bits of flesh and bone that had resisted the pyre's best attempts at incineration south and east, where it would deposit its baleful contents into the Bay of Bengal.

The major roadways had been cleared, but there were mounds of refuse piled up on their edges, most of it unsalvageable, though that didn't stop the wretched poor from rifling through the debris in the hopes of finding something useful to aid in shoring up their miserable makeshift shelters, which dotted the landscape and stretched on for as far as the eye could see.

Moaning, crying, and outright wailing provided a constant aural backdrop to their venture into the devastated town. John and his handful of men, primarily soldiers that the governor could spare, did what they could on that first day before heading back to the Fort. The evening was spent gathering more medical supplies and recruiting White Town civilians to join them on the morrow. Though it was against his better judgment, John eventually agreed that Alice should join him in his work. She couldn't be persuaded otherwise. While she couldn't really help with the setting of broken bones or the stitching up of torn bodies, she could be of great use in helping to calm the keening women and in marshalling their children.

Not all who needed their help would accept it. Many of the Indians were leery of the white strangers in their midst. There wasn't anything to be done about that. They could only provide assistance and succour to those who welcomed it or who were too far gone to care about who was helping them.

Many days were spent in this pursuit, and eventually there wasn't anything more Holwell's contingent could do without exhausting the supplies and resources that were badly needed at the hospital. John, determined to meet with the Zamindar, whose role included bringing some order to the Hindu population in Calcutta since the office had been taken over by the British. Govinda Ram Mitra, the Dewan that John would have preferred to deal with, had died, murdered in his sleep. John would have to meet with Ravi Das, the Zamindar himself, to see what was being done about a comprehensive municipal response to the present situation. In his time in Black Town, he hadn't seen any evidence of a concerted effort to organize its constituents. He had been brooding on this and had compiled a lengthy list of items to discuss with the Zamindar.

Ravi Das had been appointed Zamindar because "he could get blood from a stone." At least that's how Mayne put it. He was very adept at collecting the taxes owed to the Mogul Empire and the municipality, but as far as Mayne knew, Das routinely underreported the collected monies and pocketed the difference. There was no other way to reconcile his lavish lifestyle with the generous, but nonetheless modest salary he was paid as Zamindar.

On a hot day in late November, Mayne had agreed to accompany Dr. Holwell to Das' office, which was tucked away on the far side of the Bagh Bazaar. Mayne was sure Das had selected this site for his office to be as far away from prying eyes as possible. He would have to do something about that. The condition of the main roads was significantly better than they had been when John had first ventured into Black Town, but there was still a lot of misery and mayhem to be witnessed on the smaller offshoots, where the majority of the natives lived and worked.

Just before they reached the entrance to the Zamindar's office, Mayne piped up, "The man is a weasel. Just mark his demeanour when he sees that you've brought me along. He suspects that I know things about his operation that he doesn't want exposed to the light of day. He detests and fears me, I believe, and I would just as soon keep it that way."

Ravi Das was a big man. Not obese in the way Omichand, the Jain merchant, was obese, but a giant of a man, nonetheless. His eyes were remarkably small orbs nestled deep in their sockets and clouded over by dense eyebrows. He sat behind a large desk smoking a cheroot, the large pile of ash that overflowed the ashcan an indication of his addiction to the habit. Upon being let into his office, John witnessed an immediate shift in his body language from an aura of superciliousness to one of benign docility. John turned to Mayne and grinned.

"What can I do for you, gentlemen?" Das spoke in fluent English. "It's good to see you, Mr. Mayne. And this must be the esteemed English surgeon, Mr. Holwell, I presume?"

"This is indeed Dr. Holwell, and I'm merely here as an observer at the Governor's request. Dr. Holwell has asked for this meeting, so I'll let him take the lead." Mayne and Holwell took the seats rather reluctantly proffered them.

"Mr. Das, I have spent a considerable amount of time in the past few weeks tending to the medical needs of the Black Town residents following the recent catastrophe. In this time, I have seen little evidence of your municipal agents coordinating any kind of recovery effort in and about the town. That is part of your purview, is it not?"

"It is, sir. My men have been working non-stop behind the scenes. If you haven't seen them, it's because they tend to blend in with the local population. After all, it is to our advantage to know who we can still collect taxes from and who we can't."

"Your office, I'm assured, is much more than the collection of taxes, Mr. Das. What about the survey of buildings that have been destroyed and need to be replaced? More keenly, what about a survey of the residents regarding their immediate needs and consequent attention from your agents? I have seen none of this going on. People have been left to their own devices. Neighbours have been helping neighbours, but many of the residents are still struggling to eke out a meager survival. I have kept meticulous records of the people my group have helped and begun a register of the deaths that have been reported, but it is just a drop in the bucket I fear in the grand scope of the situation. Furthermore, there has been substantial looting and groups of lawless hooligans taking advantage of the situation. Women are being abused. Children are running about parentless and are left to scavenge for food and clean water. What are you doing about them? And then there's the matter of the ghats. Large quantities of body parts, not fully consumed by the funeral pyres are being wantonly dumped into the river instead of being buried as has been the custom!"

John had to pull back a little. He found himself becoming too animated and hadn't really intended for this first meeting with Das to be so accusatory.

"Your office, sir, should be more visible, and your constituents need to be looked after."

Das looked sheepishly at Mayne and seemed to direct his comments to the comptroller of the Fort. "With all respect, sirs, my office doesn't report to the garrison surgeon. We report directly to Governor Freke. He will receive a full accounting of our efforts here."

Mayne stood up. The meeting was at an end. He glowered at Das, and in no uncertain terms, put the Zamindar in his place. "Be well aware, Das, that we too will be making a full report to the governor. You would be well advised to get on with this business and to provide us hard evidence of your progress."

Without allowing Das an opportunity to respond, he turned and beckoned John to follow him out of the Zamindar's office. "Good day to you sir."

The Christmas season was now upon them at the Fort, though there was little evidence of celebration and gaiety to be found. Before going into the Officer's mess for a scaled-down Christmas luncheon, Governor Freke called a meeting of all his officers. He asked for reports from the men he had commissioned to take charge of various post-disaster efforts. Dr.

Holwell sat among them, listening carefully. Later that evening he would be able to share some of these details with Alice and the Worthing's.

There had been some structural damage to the Fort, albeit rather minor. One soldier on duty at the Maratha Ditch had been killed. He fell into the flooded ditch at the height of the hurricane and couldn't scramble up the slippery walls. His body was found floating in the murky water many hours later.

Thirty-four White Town citizens had perished, and many homes had suffered flood damage. Several houses and businesses had collapsed, and a great recovery operation had been undertaken. In all, two hundred houses along the banks of the Hooghly River had been destroyed. Many of those residents, at least from White Town, were being housed by friends or in makeshift shelters provided by the Governor. What had become of those waterside residents living in Black Town or in surrounding areas had not yet been determined.

Beyond Calcutta, along the waterways, there had been reports of thousands of ships, barques, sloops, boats, and canoes that had floundered in the storm. Some of them, even barques of sixty tons, had been carried two leagues off and had settled on treetops in the forest. Eight of nine English ships in the Hooghly at the time were destroyed, most of the sailors presumed dead. One of these ships had been carrying a new steeple for St. Anne's Church in White Town. This tall and magnificent structure had landed miraculously intact on shore, 'a beacon of Christianity shining in a savage land' according to one zealous officer.

When Holwell, was asked for his report, he laid out the status of the dead and injured White Town residents. He gave a full accounting of the role the hospital had played in dealing with the hurt and dying, paying special attention to the rites of burial that had been performed by the clergy. He also singled out Chandler, Dr. Treleaven, and their assistants for the yeomen service they had provided throughout.

While listening to his report of his group's efforts in Black Town, the officer's faces were ashen. They knew that things were bad in Calcutta, but hearing Holwell put numbers to the people they had helped and the deaths that had been reported made many of them blanch. After finally hearing from the Zamindar, and combining that information with his own records, he told them that the death toll in Black Town was in the neighbourhood of twelve hundred souls, and who knew how many more deaths had been accounted for in the areas lying just outside the town.

Governor Freke hadn't responded to any of the other reports, but when John had finished, he stood up to adjourn the meeting and gravely said, "That's quite the butcher's bill, Doctor! We are grateful for all your efforts and those of your colleagues. We are also saddened by the personal losses you and your family have sustained, and in particular the passing of your mother. I only met her once, but she struck me as a steadfast and resourceful woman."

John stood quietly looking over his mother's grave, his eyes roaming over the words on the freshly planted tombstone.

AMELIA HOLWELL

1689-1737.
"Always In Our Hearts"

Alice stood beside him holding on to his hand. The plot was in a peaceful corner of St. Mary's cemetery and could almost be seen from their house. It was early March in 1738, and they had just moved back into their quarters, though there was still a lot of work to do to set it to rights. The reconstruction project had given John an opportunity to introduce some of the innovative ideas he had discovered in Jeddah, such as the installation of a freshwater cistern and piping so that the water could move freely into the lavatory and into the cook house out back.

Alice reached down and gently placed a bouquet of wildflowers at the head of the grave. She turned loving eyes toward her husband. "Dearest, I have some news to share with you."

John's heart skipped a beat. "What is it Ailish?"

"I'm with child."

POLITICS

Holwell was making a name for himself, both at Fort William and in White Town. Since the time of the October natural disaster, he had proven himself not only a competent physician and hospital administrator, but also a gentleman well suited to managing civic matters. His organizational skills were exemplary, and his forthright and insistent manner was more than evident when he spoke his mind, which was often. What was even more impressive was that people listened to him, whether he was speaking of medical best practices or the most efficient ways to run the town council (or the Mayor's Council of White Town, as the Fort authorities called it).

In June, elections were held to select a mayor and town aldermen. John never quite knew how his name came to be on the slate of nominees, but there it was on the ballot card. He suspected Mayne, but it might also have been one of a half dozen other people. His first reaction was to decline the nomination, but after speaking with Alice, the Governor, and then some of his friends, he acquiesced and let his name stand. On June 22, 1738, he became John Zephaniah Holwell, alderman.

"Alderman Holwell rather suits you, dear. You still look as young and handsome as ever, but these days there's also a stateliness about you." Alice, wearing a casual gardening dress, was hanging clothes to dry in the open area of the garden.

"How am I supposed to do it all, Ailish? My duties as Head Surgeon, my science studies and writings, my obligations here with you and our soon-to-be family, and now civic governance?" He handed her some clothes pegs from a small canister.

"Given everything that you've been doing up until this point, I'm sure you'll now have a chance to relax a bit." Alice laughed out loud at her little jape and John soon followed suit. He looked lovingly at his wife. Pregnancy suited her to a tee. Her belly was noticeably rounding out, and her skin shone radiantly.

The meeting with Ravi Das in the fall had remained with John like a sore that wasn't healing. He implored Governor Freke to find a way to replace the Zamindar with someone less unscrupulous. Freke had been giving it some consideration.

John sat in his study, listening to the downpour outside his window. The monsoon rains had come early, forecasting a vicious season ahead. He was mulling over the best approach to a letter he was about to pen to Sarfaraz Khan requesting aid toward the effort of rebuilding Calcutta. Perhaps he could persuade The Khan that people with some stability in their lives would have an elevated ability to pay their taxes, benefitting all concerned.

Disturbing news was coming out of Murshidabad, and this made his task even more difficult. It was being said that the Khan had fallen out of favour with the Moghul establishment. He had taken to spending most of his time on religious matters to the neglect of the day-to-day administration of his state's sovereign holdings and that of his suzerainty. His titled underlings were tasked with looking after matters of state while he spent his time with the religious leaders. He had taken to fasting for three months each year, two more than were required by the observance of Ramzan, and spent his days in the Katra Mosque. This change in the Dawan of Murshidabad hadn't been obvious to John when he visited him last, but it must have been fomenting even then. To make matters even more confusing, it was believed that Sarfaraz Khan would soon be elevated to the role of Nazim of Jahangir Nagar, Dhaka as John knew it to be. If he couldn't manage as Dawan, how could he as Nazim?

With all these doubts raging through his mind, he finally composed his letter and had it sent on to Murshidabad. Would The Khan respond? He would have to wait and see.

It was the indoor season, a season most people dreaded, but not John. He was content to sit for hours at his desk, losing himself in the myriad projects he had underway, such as taking the latest results of his kholera study and incorporating them into his previous findings. His compendium of waterborne diseases was likewise expanding at a brisk pace. The Lady Mary Wortley Montagu had been in regular correspondence with him.

She was constantly sending him medical treatises from various and sundry parts of the world, which she had acquired through her wide range of contacts and the impressive reach of her husband. She wanted all that Dr. Holwell could send her of medical practice in India and was particularly intrigued by his writings pertaining to ayurvedic medicine and to that of the Muslim *hakims*. John had been touched when she had sent him a bound copy of his work, *On the Prevention and Treatment of Smallpox*. He had sent her his study of the disease as several disparate writings over three or four shipments. She had collated the material, connected the dots, so to speak, and had the resulting text published as a single volume. Seeing his work bound in hardboard and leather, with a proper title and his name beneath, gave him an enormous sense of satisfaction. He was sure to pull it off the shelf, where it occupied a very prominent spot, and show it off to any of his visitors.

When he tired of his medical research and writing, he spent his time refining the bylaws of the Town Council, which had been in a very rudimentary state when he took on his role as alderman. He argued vociferously at Town Council meetings that if their association were to be effective in meeting the needs of the populace, their by-laws and codes needed to be airtight. He convinced them all, though the others had neither the inclination nor the fortitude to work on this. Therefore, he took the initiative upon himself. On more practical matters he did have the help of one other alderman, a Mr. Lassiter, who had been a shipbuilder in his day and who now did yeoman work as a draughtsman in taking many of the plans presented by Alderman Holwell and making them not only presentable, but plainly operational. A case in point was the plan John had crafted for the building of cisterns, which he had had incorporated into the renovations of his own house and could provide a steady supply of fresh water for drinking or cooking, thus preventing some of the water-borne pathogens that could lead to illness or even death. Armed with Lassiter's masterful drawings and one or two ingenious improvements suggested by the craftsman, John presented these plans to the Council. Subsequently, he was given license to share these plans with the citizens of White Town. It was most gratifying to see houses starting to sprout water tanks on their roofs over time.

The monsoon ended and the saturated earth slowly dried up, leaving little pools of water wherever one walked. Sedges and other grasses sprang up all around, and colourful flowers dotted the lush and fecund landscape. People crawled out of their houses, and the regular marches around the Park resumed.

The anniversary of the hurricane and earthquake of October 1737 was nearing, and Dr. Holwell was sure that anxieties would be resurrected, that people would look to the skies and the Hooghly more often, hoping not to witness any of the harbingers of disaster that had presaged last year's calamity: the gathering clouds, the winds picking up from the south and east, and the rising water levels on the river.

Alice's pregnancy was at its apex, and her term was approaching rapidly. While he was quite capable of delivering the baby himself, John felt better allocating the task to Treleaven and Chandler, both of whom had far more experience in birthing a child. He would also hire the services of Kalpana Gupta, one of the doulas the hospital used on occasion, whom they had all come to respect. She wouldn't help with the birth itself, but would care for Alice postpartum, as well as handle the many other tasks that needed looking after and that she was so competent at dealing with. Dr. Holwell had always believed that it was wiser for a doctor not to be too heavily involved in the doctoring of people close to him unless in an emergency. It could get in the way of being dispassionate and coldly calculating when one absolutely needed to be.

Sarfaraz Khan had not responded directly to Dr. Holwell's letter. But it was obvious that he had read it and had taken it seriously. Building materials and stores of food began to arrive in Calcutta, courtesy of the Moghul overlord. John couldn't prove it yet, but he was certain the Zamindar was keeping some of it for himself, reselling it at a tidy profit.

Ravi Das had never once set foot inside the precincts of Fort William, and he never would. Freke had had enough of Das and sent a contingent of officers and soldiers to physically remove him from the Zamindar's offices. A new Zamindar, a half-caste who had shown great promise in Writer's Row, suggested by Lewis Mayne, was sent as a replacement, along with a junior clerk to act as his dewan. This appointment of Arvindh Khalen was

STEPHEN GOSS

Governor Freke's last official function before leaving his post to attend to family matters in England. The new governor of Fort William, having just arrived on the Exeter was Governor Cruttenden.

Other than having to say farewell to Freke, Holwell was well pleased with this set of events. Now there would be a new and fairer administration tasked with organizing the municipal affairs of Calcutta and Black Town in particular. John looked forward to his first meeting with Mr. Khalen.

On the evening of November 9th, a Sunday, after having met with Khalen and Mayne, John walked home from the Fort basking in the glory of a splendid sunset. He was looking forward to dinner with his wife. That wasn't to be. As he set foot in the foyer, Alice called out to him, "John, my water has broken, I'm going into labour!"

Two-and-a-half-year-old Charlotte sat daintily on a small chair John had made for the nursery, now pulled out into the drawing room for her to use. She held the newborn in her arms, her mother, Susan hovering ever at the ready to rescue it, should the need arise.

"I'm so glad you named her after your mother, John. She would have been so happy to be here right now." Mrs. Treleaven was standing beside Dr. Holwell and lightly placed her hand on his shoulder. She turned to look directly at the little bundle in Charlotte's care. "If you are anything like your grandmother, little one, you will surely be blessed."

Alice beamed brightly at these words. It was hard to imagine that not quite eight days had passed since the birth of Amelia. She felt a little washed out still, but she was gaining strength every day. "Perhaps we should put her in her cradle now, Charlotte? What do you think? Can you help me with that?"

Charlotte, in the way of two-year-olds, said, "Kay. Put her in cradle." The adults all were grinning as Alice gently took the baby from Charlotte's lap and led the youngster into the nursery.

Amelia having been deposited carefully in her little bed; Alice now looked about the cozy chamber. John had taken great care with the design and ornamentation of the small room that lay directly off their own spacious sleeping quarters. He had thoughtfully purchased a rocking chair they could use when Amelia woke at night for her feeding. A colourful woollen blanket John's mother had knitted for her "someday" grandchild was draped over it. Charlotte walked over to a chest in which there was a collection of toys including a rag doll. She picked it up. "You can play with that Charlotte, if you'd like. Come, let's go back to the others."

Cecilia and Henry Worthing had procured some delightful little cakes and tea biscuits from the bakers in White Town. These were being consumed with great relish.

"We're hearing, John, that the Marathas have invaded Delhi again. When you meet next with Governor Cruttenden or with Lewis Mayne, please obtain more details for us. We would be most obliged." The old military man put down his teacup and for a moment there was a slight pall in the room.

SEEDS OF DISCONTENT

Governor Cruttenden was a competent enough man, but entirely unambitious and incomprehensibly averse to living in the Far East. It was evident that he was but a stopgap governor, holding the position for someone more permanent. He had assumed the governorship of Fort William in the fall of 1738 and just a few months later he shipped out after welcoming the new governor, Mr. Braddyth.

Braddyth had been a sea captain whose exploits were many and whose reputation of being a hard but fair man preceded him. He strutted about The Fort as if he were taking a turn about the deck of an East Indiaman and when he paused to look out over the river at the docks, he stood feet planted firmly, slightly bow-legged, but almost as if he were sprouting up from the ground.

Most unexpectedly, about two weeks after he arrived, Braddyth found his way to the Holwell residence on a hot March evening.

"Holwell, I wanted to make your acquaintance. I met Mr. Freke in London at Leadenhall, and he had many complimentary things to say about you. I wanted to get out of The Fort and look around a bit, so I thought I would amble over here. I hope I haven't taken you away from anything pressing?"

"Not at all, sir. Please come into the garden and have a seat. I'll arrange for some refreshment. A cool lime cordial would go down nicely about now." John led his guest into Alice's lovely garden and then turned to head indoors.

When he returned, he found the governor closely examining the exterior of the house.

"You've a lovely place here, Holwell. It could almost be mistaken for a pleasant Yorkshire cottage. But pray tell, what's that tank doing on top of the roof?"

John was pleased to explain the tank and buried cistern and the piping used for the transport of water to various parts of the house. He also spoke at length about how he had come across such structures in Jeddah and how a system such as this could capture fresh rainwater and was, therefore, a significant preventative measure against stomach ailments, dysentery, and other more serious illnesses such as kholera.

Alice came out of the house bearing a jug of lime cordial, condensation already gathering on its gilded exterior, and two glasses.

John introduced his wife, and the two men took their seats on a bench and resumed their conversation. When Alice had returned to the house, Braddyth remarked, "Don't you have servants to handle these sorts of tasks?"

"We do have a cook and a lady that helps with the housekeeping, but they are only here during the day. We like to be as self-sufficient as possible. Alice and I don't like the notion of keeping servants. But we realize that many of the Indian families rely on the British for employment, and so we do hire locals to help as needed. We also have an *ayah*, which is a lady who helps with the care of our baby daughter, Amelia. I'm afraid too many of our compatriots here in India treat the locals with a great deal of condescension, and we are very saddened by that."

A slight lifting of Braddyth's eyebrows and wrinkling of his forehead made John wonder if he had overstepped his bounds a little. But the governor's response quickly put him at ease.

"That is very fair-minded of you, Holwell. In my short time here, I have noticed the very same thing. It doesn't sit well with me either. We are all God's creatures and deserve to live with dignity and with the respect of our fellow men. Holwell, please do me the honour of stopping by my offices the day after next. We can have a more formal conversation then, Governor to Company Surgeon."

The two men finished their drinks, and the governor took his leave. John was ecstatic. This was a governor he might be able to count on as a friend.

On the way to the Fort after a lively Town Council meeting, John was struggling with a dilemma. How was he going to deal with Lady Russell? She was a battleax, and she put up a stink about anything the council wanted to make in the way of improvements to White Town. He had to be careful because she was Treleaven's landlord, and he didn't want to foment any trouble for his friend. Lady Russell was blessed with a statuesque figure and perfectly coiffed hair, and she lived in the largest of the houses on the periphery of the Park with her second husband, the first having died of an ailment of the heart, no doubt brought on by the stresses of living with such a demanding creature, at least as far as the local wisdom had it. She always had much to say about local goings-on. She presided over the other homeowners, especially the ladies who she would invite every couple of weeks to elaborate tea parties; that is, if they were in her good books. Her words carried enormous weight, and she would have to be handled delicately, with kid gloves so to speak.

John's meeting with Braddyth in the Governor's Mansion went quite satisfactorily, though it ended on an ominous note. Dr. Holwell brought the governor up to speed on the workings of the medical establishment at the Fort, at the hospital, and in White Town. He also took the opportunity of discussing the workings of the Town Council. When Braddyth had asked all the questions he had of the surgeon, they moved on to speaking of other matters. John was anxious to know about the recent events in Delhi and wondered if Braddyth had any insight into the troubling situation there.

"We have been hearing rumours, sir, about another invasion of Delhi by the Marathas. The last incursion brought much death and destruction to the communities on the outskirts. Now we understand that the city itself is under attack." This was a topic uppermost on the minds of the local citizenry and John pressed for some information on the matter that he might share with the civilian population.

"The news is quite dire indeed, Holwell. I've only been here a short while, but our scouts have been extremely active and have been reporting to us on an almost daily basis. They have told us that people have been massacred in the thousands. When the Moghul leaders in Delhi refused to pay tribute to the Maratha Confederacy, and even after they acquiesced and changed their policy allowing them to do so, the Marathas continued on with their attack. Some significant people have been killed. Stewart Hamilton, a prominent English citizen you may have some knowledge of, is one of the casualties, as is Shuja Addeen Khan, the grand Newaab of Bengal. Though the Marathas are Hindus, Hindu and Muslim alike have been slaughtered indiscriminately." After a deep breath, the governor continued. "Work on the Maratha Ditch, which unfathomably under the previous governor remained at a standstill, has now been stepped up. No doubt the Marathas will turn their attentions to Bengal, and we may be in for quite a battle."

"If Shuja Addeen Khan is dead, then who is taking over as the grand Newaab?" John was aghast at this update. He knew the situation was dire, but he had no idea it was this bad.

"Sarfaraz Khan. Though that is rather disconcerting. He has little appetite for war, I'm told." He paused for a moment and then continued. "Prayer and contemplation will not defeat the Marathas. There are rumours that Aliverdi Khan is gathering his forces and will confront Sarfaraz. There is only one possible conclusion should that happen." Braddyth left the statement hanging.

John put voice to it. "Sarfaraz Khan will be annihilated, and we'll be under a new Moghul order here in Bengal. A less benign one, I'm willing to wager."

Amelia was a constant delight in the Holwell household. She was just over seven months old and had already begun to hitch herself around on her behind. It wouldn't be long before she was crawling. When Charlotte came to visit with her Ma and Da, she doted on the baby. John was constantly amazed at what young age a girl's maternal instincts seemed to kick in. Charlotte wanted to help with changing Amelia's nappies and wanted to kiss her on the forehead when Alice took her to the nursery to put her down for a nap. Though she was more hindrance than help, Alice patiently humoured her and graciously allowed her to be underfoot.

John often found himself gazing lovingly at his wife and reflecting on the many blessings she had brought to him. The lively girl he had courted ever so briefly in London had grown into a beautiful and intelligent woman and a wonderful mother. How could he ever have been so lucky?

May 28, 1739, dawned brightly. It was Charlotte's third birthday, and the Holwell's had agreed to host a party in her honour at their residence, James and Susan's quarters being too limited for such a function. All the usual guests had been invited, along with two other young couples from the Fort and their children.

Once the luncheon had been served and the cake devoured, the men went out into the garden to take some air while the women and children remained inside where it was a little cooler. It wasn't long before perspiration was accumulating on the men's foreheads, and a number of them could be seen furiously fanning themselves with whatever they had on hand. The conversation quickly turned to the theatre of politics they were all embroiled in.

"So there has been a coup in Murshidabad, and Sarfaraz Khan has been killed along with many members of his immediate family. Aliverdi Khan is now our Newaab." Henry Worthing spat this information out almost as mundanely as if her were reporting on the outcome of a White Town cricket match. "We're going to have to be on our guard."

One of the young soldiers James had invited spoke up. "I hope Braddyth is seeing to our fortifications. Our regiment is ever at the ready, but the Maratha Ditch is far from complete, and some of our canons are in need of replacement or serious reconditioning."

"I've heard," Lewis Mayne piped up, "that there is trouble stirring in Black Town. With the ascendance of Aliverdi Khan, the Muslim citizens have been pushing for a larger share of the trade with us. They feel that while the Hindu traders are making off like bandits, they are languishing very much in second place. Now might be the opportunity to press their advantage."

"And how do you see it, Lewis?" John was very concerned about this development.

"It's true that in a gross sense our trade with the Hindus is far greater. But we still do a lot of trading for fine goods, furniture, silks, and the like with the Moorish traders. I'm afraid that Omichand is playing both ends against the middle, though, and he's not helping our cause." Lewis was referencing the obese Jain merchant who acted as an intermediary for the Muslim interests in Calcutta.

"I think it's time to pay the Zamindar a visit. What do you think, Lewis? Are you up for a visit to Khalen's office?"

"That's a capital idea, John. We'll go to see him in the morning."

As the afternoon wore on, the women and children came outside to join the men. John and Alice placed themselves strategically by the riverbank that edged their property, lest any of the children wander too close to the fast-flowing Hooghly. Alice was curious about what the men had been discussing. She had always been more interested in the politics of the day and in the questions that occupied her husband and his friends than she was in the intrigues of the women's world. John admired this quality in her.

"Do you remember when we visited the Khan mausoleum in the Katra Mosque with Sarfaraz Khan?"

Alice replied quickly. "I do."

"I wonder if Sarfaraz and his family have been interred there as well, or if Aliverdi Khan has not granted them that honour?"

The question was rhetorical, of course, but it had brought to Alice's mind another memory of their trip to the mausoleum. "John, I've often thought of that young woman whose tomb we came across in that place. What was her name?"

"Azmunisa Begum. She was the cousin of Sarfaraz Khan. The story went that she had slept with a number of men while her husband, Murshid Quil Khan, was abroad collecting taxes, and would have each of her partners killed in the morning so they couldn't say anything about their illicit dalliances. When Murshid found out about what had been going on, he immediately ordered her sealed up alive in the mausoleum. A truly gruesome tale! I can understand why it still haunts your memory."

Even in the hot, humid conditions of this May afternoon, the recollection of this macabre anecdote sent shivers through each of them.

James and Susan thanked the Holwell's profusely for hosting their daughter's party and, in short order, the guests took their leave.

John and Alice stood arm in arm at the end of their lane and watched as their friends disappeared into the late afternoon haze.

FAREWELLS

The lovely wooden bench gifted to them by Sarfaraz Khan as a wedding present had been badly battered in the hurricane of 1737, but had now been restored to its former glory, with some enhancements in the form of metal sheathing on the tips of the arms which gleamed every bit as brightly as the brass accoutrements on an English East India sailing vessel.

John, pipe firmly ensconced between his lips, tobacco smoke circling about his head, sat staring out at the Hooghly River. The Dodaldy wouldn't be sailing into sight for an hour or so yet. In any case he had promised Alice that he would call her out once he could make out her stately prow and her tall masts. This would be a sad day for all of them.

Several years had passed since his mother's death, since the arrival of their first child, and since his election as alderman. These years had been good ones for the Holwell family, which now counted one more child. Amelia had been joined by her sister, Emma, in 1742. They were a study in contrasts. While Amelia was lively and playful and daring, Emma was a sober little girl from the very beginning. To get her to smile was a trial, a challenge that John and Alice took up with alacrity. Amelia too got up to all sorts of antics to see if she could make her sullen little sister light up or, God forbid, to laugh. Emma studied the world around her with interest belying wisdom far beyond her years. John and Alice both agreed that the gregarious Amelia would grow up to be an entertainer of some sort and that little Emma would be the scholar and take after her father.

Taking deep, satisfying pulls from his pipe and looking out at a large branch floating gently down the river, John pondered on the state of affairs in Calcutta. Fort William, and therefore the British citizens of White Town, was thriving. Wealth was accumulating by leaps and bounds, the annual receipts sent to Whitehall eye-popping, and growing exponentially. White Town was expanding; almost every lot around the Park was occupied, and the houses that were being built were massive. Senior officers and commanders of The Fort took turns, one after the

286

other, erecting mansions that boasted rooms for dozens of servants, and stabling for many horses. Most of these were at the south end of the Park, too close to Holwell's private yet more modest riverside residence, for his liking. Captain-Commandant Minchin's was one of these monstrosities, the same Minchin who had interviewed him for the post in the offices at Leadenhall, as were Grant's, the adjutant, and Manningham's and Frankland's and slightly smaller; but just as ostentatious, was the home of Lieutenant Witherington.

Things weren't so good in Black Town, which had been torn apart by mistrust and sectarian violence. John, though he didn't have the sanction of the White Town Council, did have tacit approval from Braddyth to get involved in the Indians' affairs. Mayne and Holwell made several forays to the Zamindar's office. They helped broker a tentative peace between the warring factions. Even then, Omichand had to be dealt with. He was in large part the fulcrum on which the uneasy balance rested. Twice the two British men visited him in his palatial mansion north of St. Anne's Church on the border of Black Town. Twice they were met cordially by the corpulent, ever-perspiring merchant in his luxurious gardens and were subjected to his silver-tongued denials about his involvement in the troubles that had erupted between the Hindus and the Muslims. He was a snake and would have to be watched closely.

John looked out at the river. Still no sign of the Dodaldy having left her berth at the Fort. He sighed. His mind wandered back to the tragic circumstances of a few months ago. Sergeant Worthing had gone to the Baagh Bazaar on one of his rare visits to the bustling market in Black Town. Unhappily, he and a companion had been caught up in an ugly exchange between a farmer and a stall owner. Who knew what the disagreement was about but the upshot of it was that the farmer had assaulted the merchant? Throngs of Bazaar stall owners descended upon the scene and the farmer quickly jumped onto his bullock cart and began to move away. The irony of it must have been laughable. Bullock carts moved at a rambling snail's pace and could easily be run down by any able-bodied person. Most unfortunately for Worthing, in the few moments the cart was free of the crowd, it managed to mow down the sergeant, pulling him mercilessly under its wooden wheels. He must have died an agonizing death as the crowd ignored him and set on the farmer who was surreptitiously beaten to death.

Poor Cecilia couldn't be consoled when she received the news from a local constable. Word of the tragedy spread like wildfire in White Town and in the Fort. John and Alice, having left their children in the care of their *ayah*, spent the evening with Cecilia, Susan, James, the Treleavens, and a smattering of other family friends. All evening, they took turns attempting to console Cecilia, who was intermittently wracked with sobbing and at other times just stared blankly in front of her. Six-year-old Charlotte was the only one able to get her grandmother's attention, and when she sweetly put her arms around her and told her that Papa was now in heaven and that he was being well looked after there, Cecilia drew her arms about the little girl and held her closely.

All that evening, visitors arrived at the door with gifts of food and words of solace. Gervas Bellamy, the senior Chaplain, came by and stayed long enough to say a prayer and to read a few short passages from the Bible. He had ended with Isaiah 41:10, *"Don't be afraid, for I am with you."*

In the ensuing days, Susan and Charlotte moved in with Cecilia, and sometime after that, James joined them there as well.

Don't be afraid, for I am with you. Those words, as much as anything else, were the beginning of a lot of soul-searching for "Dr. Holwell, man of science." He had become very reflective and went often to the Bible trying to understand the messages revealed therein. When he had finished with the Bible, having been reminded of the many lessons he had been taught at school and in church as a young boy, he moved on to the sacred Hindu teachings of Samsara, about the continuous cycle of life, death, and reincarnation, and Karma, the universal law of cause and effect.

Now he was studying the Quran. Alice was puzzled by this sudden change in her husband but decided to give him a wide berth, allowing him to spend long evenings in his study with his esoteric pursuits.

Then something had happened that made John put aside his religious musings for a time. The Marathas had attacked Bengal. The work on the Ditch went into overdrive, and the Fort was alive with activity, the taking stock of armaments, and martial drills.

Word had come to Braddyth that Aliverdi Khan had sent emissaries to the Marathas and was attempting to broker a peace with them. A good deal of Moghul wealth was put at their disposal, and this time, the tribute presented to the Marathas was accepted and thus effectively put a stop to their murderous exploits in Bengal. They could all breathe a sigh of relief, at least for a time.

John could see the tops of the masts before he could see the prow of the Dodaldy. He got up from his seat on the bench and went inside to retrieve Alice and the girls. It took some time for the ship to slip its berth and to begin its passage downriver on its way to the Bay of Bengal and to England.

Amelia didn't say anything, but she pointed to the deck where her friend Charlotte, accompanied by her mother, father, and grandmother, were standing looking out at them and waving heartily.

After Henry Worthing's death, Cecilia immediately began pining to go back home. There were still relatives on the outskirts of London, and she pledged, "to live out the rest of my days there," as she put it often enough, and always with a deep sigh.

Cecilia had made up her mind, and nothing was going to stop her. James and Susan had discussed this development at length and eventually decided to join the family matriarch in her return to Britain. They would make a life for themselves in London. Lewis Mayne would provide a sterling recommendation for James, and he would find a senior and well-paid situation in Leadenhall Street, where his adventures with the English East India Company had begun but a few years ago. "A lifetime ago," as James would put it. And as much as they'd miss their life in India, Charlotte would have better educational opportunities in England.

The group on the deck of the Dodaldy, a fine ship financed heavily by Charles Manningham and William Frankland, were now so close to the Holwell's garden that they could almost hold an intimate conversation with those on board. They called out their goodbyes. John and little Amelia responded vociferously. Alice, who had a frog in her throat, was in tears as she watched her brother and his family take the bend in the river and slowly disappear.

The four Holwell's stood on the shore for a long time. The tops of the masts grew fainter and then were lost to sight. Emma started to fuss, and they turned to go into the house. It was time for tea.

DESPAIR

May 21, 1744, marked a new era in the affairs of all Europeans in India. This was a direct result of the declaration of war between England and France. It would be a matter of weeks before the official declaration was made known to the denizens of Fort William, but well before word had arrived, flotillas of English and French war ships were speeding on their way to protect their various interests in the Indian subcontinent.

The British authorities in India should have known something big was afoot as early as February of that year when the English government had asked the English East India Company for a loan of £1,000,000. As well, for agreeing to a three-percent tax on all their revenue going forward, the Company would be granted a fourteen-year prolongation of their charter to keep plying their trade in India with the protection of the King's army. This had been confirmed by Act of Parliament and by the personal assurance of King George ll.

On the morning of June 21st, Dr. Holwell said his goodbyes to Alice and his two daughters and made his way to Braddyth's quarters at the Fort, where weekly briefings were now a regular occurrence. Even at this hour of the morning, the oppressive heat was stifling, and John perspired profusely as he navigated the dirt track to the ring road and then made his way into the Fort. He encountered Lewis Mayne, also on his way to the Governor's mansion, and the two men strode deliberately to the grand entrance. They acknowledged the two soldiers posted outside and then entered the building that was blissfully cooler than the heat of the courtyard.

The ornate meeting room was crowded. John recognized Manningham and Frankland and Witherington, who had taken seats close to Braddyth, and deliberately found seats for Mayne and himself at the opposite end of the large table. The mood in the room was decidedly uneasy. The French had been putting a lot of pressure on some of the British outposts in the south and worrisome news was coming down the pipe about the impending capitulation of some of the English forts.

When all the expected officers had arrived, Braddyth stood up from his seat at the south end of the table and began the morning's session.

"Gentlemen, war is upon us as you know. Last night I received a message from the governor of Fort St. George in Madras. He has informed us that a British squadron under the command of Commodore Barnett has arrived off the shores of Pondicherry. The French settlement there is preparing for a siege. They have trained their cannon on Barnett, but he is for now laying idly off the coast and out of harm's way.

"Nicholas Morse has taken over as Governor of Fort St. George as of late January. You may not have heard his name before, but you have heard of his great-grandfather, the notorious Oliver Cromwell."

Braddyth went on to discuss the preparedness of Fort William to withstand a siege, should it come to that. He asked for reports from several of his officers, including Lieutenant Witherington, who oversaw the garrison's powder-train. Witherington reported boastfully that there were more than ample stores of powder and shot and that the Fort could not only withstand a prolonged siege but in fact, because of the superiority of his fellow officers, they would be sure to be victorious in any military campaign. He was about to go on with his pontificating when Braddyth cut him short.

"Thank you, Witherington. But let's not be too full of ourselves. Our intelligence sources have repeatedly warned us that the French presence in India is not only growing, but their garrisons are well commanded. We underestimate them at our peril. And we do not yet know whom the Moghuls will side with. I have heard disturbing rumours that Aliverdi Khan has already drafted a few mercenary French soldiers to lead some of his battalions!"

By late September the diabolical rains had eased off, and Holwell and Treleaven continued what had become their ritual of walking twice around the Park at great speed each evening after the dinner hour. This had become such a routine that White Town citizens were now used to the two men energetically flying past them on the outside of the well-worn track and no longer bothered to stare after them with quizzical looks.

Holwell felt in the top form of his life, and he surmised that Treleaven was no slouch either. Both men had adopted a primarily vegetarian diet, and along with their vigorous daily exercise around the Park, John had also added a regimen of *pranayama*. Each morning before breakfast, he would go out to the garden and Alice could see him through the drawing-room window working through his set of controlled deep-breathing exercises.

Treleaven and Holwell were generally silent on the first pass of the loop, and then they would engage in whatever conversation they could while maintaining their stiff pace. Today the topic of the siege of Pondicherry came up, and Holwell filled his friend in on the latest developments. He was able to tell Treleaven that the French Governor, a Monsieur Dupliex, had appealed to the ruling Newaab of Arcot, Anwar ad deen, to help in holding off the British squadron. The Newaab had grown angry at the situation and had insisted there be no hostilities engaged in by foreign powers on his land. Barnett had left Pondicherry with his little armada and had sailed up the coast to Madras. No shots were fired, but the French knew they would be met with resistance should they have any designs on expanding their territory. While the Newaab had taken no side in the dispute, it was obvious to those close to the action that he was most displeased with the British show of force.

"What does that mean for us, Holwell?" Treleaven was breathing heavily, but he was very interested in this piece of news.

John thought for a moment and then replied. "It means that we are all sitting on a powder keg that could blow at any time. There is an uneasy truce and both sides are marshalling their forces for whatever brouhaha is likely to come."

This uneasy truce didn't last for long. While life went on in Fort William much as it had for the past many years, the hostilities resumed with vigour in the south. In 1746, Commodore Barnett was killed in action and his successor, Commodore Peyton, engaged a French fleet a few leagues from Madras. While there was no decisive victory for either side in that skirmish, the French landed a force in Madras and attacked Fort St.

George. Governor Morse was forced to capitulate, and the French flag was flown on St. George's ramparts, a terribly embarrassing moment for the British in India.

The Holwells were hosting a dinner party, and the dire situation to the south was the central topic of discussion. The *ayah* had put Amelia and Emma to bed in the nursery, and the adults sat around the drawing room sipping on some wonderful claret that John had been able to get his hands on courtesy of his friend Gervas Bellamy, the chaplain.

While the claret was doing its bully best to raise the spirits of the gathering, the mood in the drawing room was still morose. Lewis Mayne got everyone's attention when he informed them that Braddyth's tenure as governor was coming to an end and that a new commander, a Mr. Forster, was on his way to take over the running of Fort William.

"By God, I hope he's half the leader Braddyth is!" John was very animated in his response. He had been at the weekly officer's session that morning, and this news hadn't been divulged at the meeting. "That smarmy Witherington is still full of bluster about our superior forces here in India. How could he go on like that with the defeat in Madras and with the French still moving on the offensive? The French have proven to be more than resourceful, and their actions are deliberate and masterfully coordinated. Our Fort is in the hands of weak and pompous leaders, with the exception of Braddyth, of course. I fear for all of us should the French forces come knocking at our door here in Calcutta. And what does the great Aliverdi Khan have to say about any of this?"

While John had meant this last question as rhetorical, Lewis Mayne once again took it upon himself to respond. "Murshidabad is wary of us. But we are tolerated because our trade has been lucrative and is helping to fill the depleted coffers of the Moghul Empire. Their skirmish with the Marathas has left them in dire straits financially and they need us now more than ever. Still, Aliverdi Khan has watched us build up our fortifications and strengthen our forces here in Fort William and he is suspicious of our intentions. He has been known to liken us to a hive of bees whose honey one might benefit from, but if the hive is disturbed, those same bees might sting you to death."

There was a lull in the drawing room, and Emma, who hadn't been successful in falling asleep made an appearance. Alice stood up to deal with her, but John waved her back and volunteered to take Emma to bed and read her a bedtime story.

With that, the evening was over and the guests took their leave.

ENDINGS

Braddyth had been governor of Fort William for several years, but once again the ridiculously quick succession of men to the highest post insinuated itself. Forster came and went in less than the span of a year. Mr. Dawson succeeded him and then he too was replaced by Mr. Fetch in 1748.

"How are we supposed to plan for anything with this carousel of governors?" John was chatting with Alice as they strolled along the Park on a warm December evening. Amelia and Emma had run on ahead. "Thank God for the Treaty of Aix la Chappelle. That truce has put an end to this interminable skirmish with the French. Word is that Madras will be restored to the British any day now. At least we shouldn't have to worry about Fort William coming under siege. Contrary to the idiots running the Fort, I don't think we would have come out of such a conflict very well."

As the family was passing St. Anne's Church, John started to feel unwell. His stomach had been uneasy these past few days, and now he felt a terrible urge to empty his bowels. Luckily, the church was open, as it usually was so that people could go in and reflect and make their devotions. He darted into the quiet space. The subdued light and fenestrated shadows, which would have been a source of solace to him at most times, didn't even come into his consciousness as he darted to the latrine out back.

Alice and the girls were waiting for him across the road in the Park. "Are you all right, John?" Alice's worried look played clearly across her face.

"I'm fine now. Let's carry on."

When they arrived home, Alice gave the children over to the *ayah* to be given a bath and put to bed. She gently took her husband's hand and drew him outside to the garden. They stood looking out at the river and breathed in the refreshing evening air. Alice squeezed her husband's hand and spoke to him in a gentle voice.

"John, we are going to have another child."

Dr. Holwell looked deeply into Alice's eyes, and they melted into each other's arms.

Dr. Holwell was no longer an alderman. In the last White Town election, he had been chosen mayor. With that role came the responsibility not only of being the administrative leader of White Town, but also its de facto magistrate. This had meant that he had to put aside his medical duties and he no longer had the luxury of carrying on with his other scientific pursuits. Evenings were spent studying law and jurisprudence, and his days were spent adjudicating disputes, luckily most of them rather simple affairs.

Now his wife was with child, and, to boot, he had developed a nagging stomach ailment that often left him fatigued and rather distraught. He consulted Treleaven and the prognosis was that he had picked up some sort of tropical parasite that had inhabited his body and was playing havoc with his innards. He boiled tulsi leaves and drank the bitter tea. He tried a host of other ayurvedic remedies such as chewing on sapt parna ki chaal (Chinese tree bark), drinking giloy juice, ingesting hartaki powder dissolved in hot water, and finally dhaniya paani (fresh coriander leaves crushed, strained, and boiled). All to no avail.

His body was wracked by violent spasms. He couldn't eat anything solid. His dreams, when he actually slept, were nightmares of *Divine Comedy* proportions. He lost weight, his clothes hanging on him.

And poor Alice! Her pregnancy, which had begun in normal enough fashion, was now a source of great concern. Nausea and vomiting, which she had experienced in the early stages of her previous two pregnancies, this time just kept going—and, in fact, became distressingly worse. In March, she started to experience severe pain in her abdomen, and at last, after a fainting spell, she determined that she had to abandon her ailing husband so she could tell Dr. Treleaven what was going on with her.

Treleaven interviewed her in detail and conducted a physical examination. The strained look on his visage wasn't lost on Alice. She knew something was amiss.

"You must stop all your activity immediately and get some bed rest." Treleaven closed up his medical bag.

"But how can I? You know how sick John is. I need to be available to help him." Alice was adamant.

"Wait here a moment, my dear. I'll be right back." Treleaven left the sitting room in which he often saw patients and headed into the parlour to find his wife.

He returned with the former Mrs. Pattison, and the two of them informed Alice that they would accompany her back to her house and that they would live with them for a time to help with the children and to look after the adult "invalids." Alice knew that they were trying to lighten the mood, but she could sense the underlying worry in the two of them.

April, May, and June were even hotter than usual. Alice suffered interminably. John fared little better, though his symptoms were abating somewhat. When he was feeling well enough, he sat by Alice and carefully rubbed her back and pressed her swollen feet and spoke to her calmly. She was as white as a sheet except for her lips and her fingertips, which were dangerously blue. Occasionally, the *ayah* would bring in the girls one at a time to see their mother and father, and then they would go away to play or be fed.

The Treleavens were a godsend. The doctor was kept busy ministering to the two of them, and his wife had taken over the running of the house.

"Treleaven, have you noticed the colour of Alice's lips and fingers? I'm afraid she's cyanotic. If she's not getting enough oxygen, then the child must be being starved of it as well. What are we to do?" John stood up dejectedly from his bedside perch.

Treleaven looked at him closely. "My God, man. You must have dropped three stone. You're a scarecrow!" He bent over Alice. She was breathing lightly, too lightly for his liking. He abruptly asked Holwell to move back and took Alice's wrist in his hands, checking her pulse. His face dropped.

"We're losing her, John!"

It was mid-July, and the monsoon was at its diabolical height. While John still wasn't recovered from his ailment, he was well enough that Treleaven and his wife were able to go back to their own abode.

It was late at night, and John couldn't sleep. He was in his study reading all he could about caesarian procedures. The surgical delivery of a child had been well documented from Roman times, the name itself supposedly a reference to Julius Caesar's surgical birth. Though how this could have been possible was beyond John's comprehension. Caesarian births in ancient times were only practised when the mother was already dead or on the verge of death at the time of the delivery and as history reported, Aurelia, Caesar's mother, had lived on to see many of her son's greatest victories.

John heard a loud whining coming from somewhere in the house. At first, he thought it must be the wind outside making the tree branches 'sing' as they sometimes did. A moment later, though, he knew the sound was coming from Alice in the bedroom.

After the scare she had given them a few months ago, she had recovered to a degree, and it was now getting close to her birthing time. John had no idea what to expect with this birth. The baby didn't seem to be sitting right in Alice's womb, and occasionally, Alice would go grey and into a catatonic shock. At these times, she was virtually unreachable.

The whining continued and grew louder. Alice had gone into labour. John immediately roused the children's *ayah*, who had now taken to sleeping in a room beside the kitchen out back. He sent her off to fetch Dr. Treleaven and then went into the bedchamber to tend to his wife.

What he saw almost made him keel over. Blood had saturated the bed linens from her waist down. Alice was pale and gasping for air. John quickly checked to see if the baby were making progress through the birthing canal. Her stomach was even more distended than it should have been, and John couldn't see any signs of the baby's head.

John looked tragically at Alice's face. When she opened her eyes for a moment, he quickly sported a smile and clutched her hand in his.

"Is the baby coming, John?" She could barely get out the words.

"Not yet, darling. But it shouldn't be long now." He tried to keep up her spirits. "Can you give it a push and help it along?"

Alice gathered what strength she had left, her face a rictus of pain, and bore down. This she could only sustain for a few seconds before it became too much.

"Never mind, darling. When Treleaven gets here, we'll attempt a surgical birth. In the meantime, I'll give you some laudanum. That will help with the pain."

John left the room to find the medicine and when he returned, he knew it was too late. Alice was dead, her arm dangling lifelessly off the side of the bed.

When Treleaven opened the bedroom door, he was immediately overwhelmed by the stench of blood, sweat, and bodily fluids. He could see Holwell kneeling beside his wife's lifeless body and holding on to a newborn baby still struggling to breathe and to be set free from the umbilical cord that had insinuated itself around its neck.

Treleaven sprang into action. He surely but carefully took the bundle out of Holwell's hands and deftly unwound the cord and then severed it from its mother's body using a surgical tool still tinctured with Alice's blood. It was then that he saw the incision and knew that John had ripped the child from Alice's lifeless womb.

NOVEMBER 1749

John stood unsteadily on the Fort William dock waiting for the gangplank to be lowered so that he, his three children, Treleaven, his wife, and a wet nurse could go aboard. He had written to James and Susan twice in recent months. Once to inform them of Alice's passing and of the birth of his son, and once more to let them know of their imminent departure from Calcutta and their intention of returning to England.

As the Wilmington slipped its berth, Treleaven put his arm about his friend's shoulder. "John, some time at home will help you recover from whatever ailment you've acquired. And James and Susan can help you with the children. God knows Calcutta is getting to be a dangerous place for any of us."

"This is my home, Treleaven. This is where Ailish and my mother are buried. I'll go to England to see Amelia, Emma, and baby James taken care of, and to convalesce. And then I'll be back. There is unfinished business here to look after. I have a list of things to bring to the government's attention in London and likewise to the powers that be in Leadenhall."

As they sluiced by Holwell's house and garden, Mrs. Treleaven drew John close to her, sensing that the grief for his darling Alice was welling up in him anew. He gave her a gentle squeeze in return. "Don't worry, my dear. The chaplain will take care of the place while I'm gone. After all, Bellamy won't be too far from his beloved church, will he?"

With that he turned away from the railing and slowly made his way down to his chamber mid-ships.

BOOK SEVEN

THE LAST DAYS OF PEACE
1756

The years 1749 – 1756 were an absolute blur to John Zephaniah Holwell. Mercifully, he had little recollection of the voyage to England after Alice had died and when he was still very sick himself. He did remember spending countless dreary hours in his cabin and, in moments of lucidity, putting together a comprehensive scheme for reforming the court of the Zamindar in Calcutta. This he had presented to the court of directors in Leadenhall, and his plan was accepted piecemeal. Furthermore, he was granted the commission of Zamindar, and after seeing his children settled with James and Susan, with the promise of help from Treleaven and his wife, who had decided to stay in London, he returned to India two years later. His health had been greatly restored, his salary increased threefold, and he returned to Fort William in seventh place along the chain of command.

"Drake, we must not ignore Watt's warning! He is emphatic that Kissendass and his wife be expelled from Calcutta immediately. If we don't do this, we risk bringing down the wrath of Siraj-Uddaula. He is very upset that we have granted hospitality to one of his main rivals to the Murshidabad seat. Aliverdi Khan is on his deathbed. You said so yourself at our last officer debriefing. We shouldn't be seen to favour one heir over the other." Holwell was red-faced.

"I am a man of my word, Holwell. I agreed that we should allow Kissendass's pregnant wife to rest here and give birth before returning to their home. I will not renege on that promise."

To this response, John turned away from the governor and rolled his eyes. Why should Drake become a moral man now after all the immoral and ridiculously stupid positions he had adopted on other issues? When would this governor start to listen to his advisers and stop acting unilaterally or worse, continuing to take counsel with imbeciles like Manningham and Frankland, who were civilians with the sole motivation of extracting as much as they could from this country which they had no love for?

John stormed out of Roger Drake's quarters. He knew that the Governor's council was ostracizing him. With Aliverdi Khan about to leave this world and headstrong twenty-seven-year-old Siraj-Uddaula likely to succeed him, Fort William, in fact, all British enterprises in Bengal, would soon be put at considerable risk. But no one would listen to him. He sometimes felt like Cassandra, the Trojan woman who had the gift of foresight, but the curse of not having anyone believe her.

While most of the Fort's commanders treated Holwell shabbily, not least of which was because he was a constant pain in their backsides, the people that actually did the work in the Fort thought very highly of him for his thoughtful consideration of practical issues and his propensity to act when action was needed. The citizens of White Town—and more and more Indians living in Black Town, especially the Hindus—held the same high opinion of the Zamindar.

John strode quickly across the parade ground outside the Governor's mansion skirting a small contingent of labourers who were in a great sweat in the March heat, moving lumber to a section of the Maratha Ditch that was presently being worked on. So many years later, he mused, and the Ditch still wasn't close to completion. So much for British superiority and ingenuity!

His vigour had not only returned to the level it had been prior to his ailment; it had, in fact, been greatly enhanced, though he was decidedly more angular of aspect than he had been. Having now reached the east veranda, he found himself directly in front of the Black Hole. He wondered if any recalcitrant soldiers were housed therein. There were never more than one or two at a time, usually sleeping off a night of drunken debauchery. This was not the civilian gaol of the White Town settlement with its three cells, each furnished with a cot and a small writing table. The Black Hole was a dark room, 18'x14', with two tiny, barred windows that let in small slivers of light and a modicum of fresh air. It was always stiflingly hot and had been built almost as an afterthought under the ramparts of the eastern wall. A narrow ledge two feet off the ground had been built against one wall to allow its residents a place to sit or sleep, most uncomfortably at that.

John squinted through one of the windows. It took a moment for his eyes to adjust to the darkness, and he could see that the Hole was not presently in use. A nasty odour wafted through the grate, and he quickly pulled his head away and carried on to Bellamy's house.

Gervas Bellamy was the senior chaplain at St. Anne's Church and lived in the rectory next door on the northeast quadrant of the Park and directly across from Omichand's palatial mansion surrounded as it was by palm trees.

The two men sat on the veranda drinking tea. John had come on the pretext of a friendly visit, but Bellamy, knowing all too well that Holwell never just made a friendly visit, finally enquired after the purpose of his call.

"You know that we are harbouring Kissendass and his wife here in Calcutta. I've heard a rumour that they've settled into Omichand's house. I thought I would confirm that for myself. Have you seen them across the way, Bellamy?"

"I have, John. In the evenings, they take a stroll along the palm grove. They are always dressed regally, and a contingent of personal guards are never too far away."

John looked over to Omichand's compound but at this time of the afternoon there were only the usual gardeners and servants milling about.

"How's your family, Bellamy? Anna is growing into a beautiful young lady."

"She is, John. She just turned sixteen and is as tall and lithe as her mother was at her age. John, my youngest son, is twenty-one and has taken well to his posting as lieutenant at the Fort." Bellamy's countenance shifted dramatically. "Now Thomas, my eldest, is a different kettle of fish. I'm very worried about him, John. He is as morose and disinterested as John is lively and intelligent. We are always at odds. He spends far too much time and money on frivolous and unsavoury activities. You should know this having had to sentence him to time in the local gaol on more than one occasion. My wife, Dorothy, despairs for him every day."

The two men finished their tea and Holwell stood to leave. He was very fond of Bellamy and most thankful for his having looked after his house while he had returned to England. Gervas Bellamy was his closest friend in Calcutta, now that Treleaven was back in London, and the unfortunate Mayne having succumbed to a massive stroke two years back. Bellamy was twenty years older than John, who was now forty-five, and he had amassed a small fortune trading with the locals privately while preaching from the pulpit publicly. He also had the finest collection of claret and madeira in these parts, something he was fond of sharing with Holwell when the two men met of an evening.

As they walked off the steps of the veranda, Bellamy asked after Holwell's children. "Have you had any recent news of Amelia, Emma, and young James?"

"They are all well. The O'Connor's have a busy household in London. Amelia is seventeen, and, by all accounts, she is of great help to them in marshalling the other children along with Charlotte, who has always been an older sister to her. They are thriving in school, especially Emma, who I'm told is at the top of her class. And James excels at almost everything, especially in sporting activities. When they've finished their schooling, I'll look to bring them back to Calcutta, should they wish to come."

After shaking hands, John made his way back to his sanctuary by the Hooghly, the house still as beautiful as ever, but now quiet and ever so lonely.

THE GATHERING STORM

While peace had been affected throughout most of Europe, trouble between the French and English carried on unabated in the Indian subcontinent. Understanding that the new Moghul leader-to-be, Siraj Uddaula, had no love for the English, the French went about spreading rumours that work on the fortifications and on the beloved ditch in Fort William was all by way of preparing for the landing of a large British force in Calcutta. Nothing could have been farther from the truth. Yet, a mere ten days after Aliverdi Khan's death, when Uddaula heard this rumour, he was livid, and quickly sent out a demand to the English garrison at Fort William that they should immediately tear down any fortifications put up since the coming on of Aliverdi's sickness.

Governor Drake, pompous ass that he was, ignored the wise counsel of Holwell and a couple of other voices of reason, that he should send Uddaula a conciliatory response. Instead, he fanned the flames of Uddaula's anti-English passions by responding that, based on the situation in Madras in 1748, the Moghuls couldn't be trusted to help protect the rights of the English in India. They would have to protect themselves from the French and to that effect had built up their defences, especially along the waterside. Fort William would not be tearing down any fortifications.

Zamindar Holwell presided over a meeting of the White Town Council on a morning in late March. He rose to address the mayor, aldermen, and a few other local leaders, including the incorrigible Lady Russell, now on her third husband.

"Sirs, and Lady Russell. My intent is not to set you to panic, but rather to calmly consider what it is I would like to relay to you." Holwell had everyone's attention and proceeded. "As Zamindar and a senior officer of the Fort William garrison, I am privy to the goings-on of the Officer's Council. At the risk of breaking some trust with said council, I feel it is incumbent upon me to apprise you of a development that I believe puts each of us at considerable risk. Our governor, Mr. Drake, has effectively antagonized Siraj Uddaula, who, as you know, is the new Newaab in Murshidabad." Holwell stopped to take a sip of water, the heat in the room intensifying each passing minute. He went on to describe the circumstance surrounding the French rumour, Uddaula's message to Drake, and Drake's insanely ill-conceived response. "The upshot is that Uddaula, upon receiving Drake's letter, has been thrown into a fit of rage. Our ears and eyes in Murshidabad tell us that Uddaula is gathering his armies and that even at this very moment he is preparing to attack us." The effect of Holwell's words was electric in the Council chamber.

One of the aldermen, a Mr. Blessington, stood up and spoke over the noise. "Gentleman, I say let the devil attack us. We have a stalwart army, and our English military superiority will repel his advances. Before long that Moorish savage will be running back to Murshidabad with his tail between his legs!"

A few individuals of the gathered assembly cheered at this bombastic sentiment. Holwell called for order in the room and at last succeeded in settling everyone down. "It is foolish to underestimate the Moors. It is true that we have stalwart soldiers and some line of defence, but I'm not very satisfied with the state of our fortifications. I have seen first-hand many of our cannons rusting away near the docks. Only a few of our pieces, those on the bastions, are in good working order, but they are surrounded by embrasures that are terribly eroded and hardly fit to protect the gunners inside them.

"Not only that, but there are crack French military leaders, such as St. Jacques, who have joined the Newaab's army, and I can tell you that they are men of great military acumen, and we would be remiss not to be wary of them." A silence descended on the gathering.

Lady Russell stood to speak and comically all the men stood up with her as gentlemen were wont to do. She quickly gestured for them to take their seats. "What are we to do, Mr. Holwell?" Lady Russell had never used any honorific such as Doctor, Alderman, Mayor, Magistrate, or Zamindar when addressing John. He had never minded this, and in fact found it quite endearing. She sat down and waited for his response.

"All we can do is look after our own enterprises and our own homes.

Gather all the arms at your disposal and keep them at the ready. Make sure you have an ample supply of food and water, especially the basics such as flour, rice, and lentils. With any luck, though I have great misgivings, cooler heads will prevail in all this, and diplomacy will win the day." Holwell adjourned the meeting and was the first to leave the chamber.

Governor Watts was the garrison leader at Cossimbazar, one of the British outposts a day's ride from Murshidabad. On June 5th, word came swiftly that Uddaula's army had taken the factory there with no resistance and in the bargain had relieved the fort of the forty cannons in their possession. Watts was made a prisoner and forced to march on with the Newaab's army.

Drake called a war council. He was ashen faced when the emissaries he had admitted to the room reported on the size and sheer magnificence of the Moorish army. Uddaula's large cavalry was followed by massive herds of elephants, each bearing one or more archers. Thousands of foot soldiers and teams of oxen pulling cannons and heavy loads of cannon balls and food supplies through the rugged terrain followed these. Drake asked them for more specific information about the size of Uddaula's army. All jaws dropped at the report.

"From the time the rear guard reaches the point where the vanguard had been, sir, is nearly one-half day. Our best estimates put their numbers at 300,000 to 400,000 souls."

The emissaries were dismissed with orders to check on Uddaula's progress and keep Drake informed of any noteworthy developments.

"Gentlemen. We must look now to our defences." He turned to the Company carpenter. "Leach, take us on a tour of the fort. We must see where our attention needs to be directed."

Drake's Council strode out of the mansion with Leach leading them on.

The state of the Fort and its fortifications was abominable. It was even far worse than Holwell had imagined. The neglect could not be hidden. Places where guns could have been mounted were in such a state that when Holwell picked up a piece of wooden shrouding, it fell apart in his hands. The cannon carriages themselves were eaten away, so much so that twenty-six of them were deemed totally unusable. The next sight made Drake stop in his tracks as if he had been hit with a wooden beam. Fifty cannons, eighteen and twenty-four pounders, which had arrived in Calcutta three years ago, had been left derelict by the river along with a stock of rusted cannon balls. They hadn't been touched since the moment they had been unloaded. It was inconceivable that Drake had never encountered this scene of sad neglect before, but he acted like he was seeing it for the first time.

Leach continued with his tour and the terrible condition of the Fort was laid bare for the Council to see.

Lieutenant Witherington, in charge of the ammunition train, was sent for and queried about the Fort's reserves of powder. Holwell could tell that the lieutenant wasn't telling the whole story when he cheerfully told the Council that never in Fort William's history had there been such ample stocks of powder. It was what Drake wanted to hear, and he thanked Witherington for having provided some positive news to brighten up their day.

Drake detested the garrison commander, Captain Minchin, and yet he had no recourse but to ask him for a report on the strength of the garrison. Unbelievably, Minchin said he didn't know, but that he would immediately find the information and bring it back to the Council.

When Minchin reported back several hours later, Drake was fuming. At least seventy soldiers were being treated in hospital for one ailment or another. Twenty-five more had been sent to various outposts, almost all without the knowledge of senior officers. That left about one hundred and eighty men, forty-five of them Europeans, the others being a hodgepodge of half-castes, Armenians, and others.

One hundred and eighty men against hundreds of thousands of Uddaula's Moghul soldiers! Later that evening, Drake made a few decisions. The first two were so willfully blind to the potentially harmful consequences that they made the Council apoplectic. Manningham had been promoted to Colonel and Frankland to the office of Lieutenant Colonel. Minchin, who as garrison commander should have been given greater status, was so outraged that he didn't wait to hear the rest of Drake's pronouncements and immediately left the Council room. Manningham and Frankland were businessmen, living in the two largest houses in White Town. They were not military men. What would they know of leading an armed resistance?

The next was one of the few decisions that Drake voiced that actually made sense to the senior officers. Holwell would be assigned to the forming of a civilian militia. Captain Holwell would muster every able-bodied man in White Town and present the militia for duty and training in two days' time. As much as the officer's looked down on Holwell, they knew he was the only man among them that had a chance of convincing the citizens of White Town that a defence of the Fort meant a defence of their town.

Just before they were dismissed for the night, Lieutenant Witherington arrived asking to address the Council. Holwell knew what they were about to hear.

"When I told you yesterday that we had a very large store of powder, I was truthful. After examining our stores more closely, though, it seems that much of it is damp and unfit for use."

CAPTAIN HOLWELL'S DIARY

(June 8ᵗʰ to June 13ᵗʰ)

The evening before Addaula's assault on Fort William, John sat at his desk
in his study, looking up occasionally to glance at the peaceful Hooghly
River and Alice's beautiful garden. Alice would have been so pleased to
see the mature trees and shrubs in her wonderfully envisioned creation.
Sensing this might be the last night he would be able to spend here, he
had lit every torch outside the house. The effect was magical, the light
of the lamps dancing on the waters of Kati Ganga. He thought of his
darling Ailish and had to wipe away tears that were starting to stream
down his face.

Since news had reached Fort William that Siraj Uddaula was on the
move against them, Holwell had decided to keep a careful record of the
decisions that were being taken by Drake and the other senior officers.
Someday the ineptness of the Fort's leaders should be laid bare for the
authorities in Leadenhall and perhaps for the British parliament. This
written record might be the catalyst that accomplished that. He looked
back at his notes from the 8ᵗʰ of June to the 13ᵗʰ.

June 8, 1756

*(Drake's chambers) War Council – John O'Hara (chief engineer)
suggests that all the grand homes surrounding The Park should be
torn down, thus preventing the enemy from using the edifices as pockets
of protection from which to attack the Fort. I believe this to be a sound
suggestion. Manningham and Frankland (recently appointed Colonel
and Lieutenant Colonel of the garrison) vehemently oppose the idea,
not wanting to see their own glorious homes destroyed. After very little
debate, the suggestion is vetoed.*

I countered that at least a few of the homes along the eastern border of The Park should be destroyed so that the gunners could have a clearer view of the attacking army and give them open lanes through which they could fire. This, too, is vetoed almost immediately.

June 9, 1756

It has come to Drake's attention that the Newaab has issued an order forbidding all merchants and shopkeepers in Calcutta from supplying the British with provisions of any kind.

Upon hearing this, Drake has sent out an order, effective immediately, that all inhabitants of White Town should gather whatever provisions they have on hand and whatever arms in their possession and transport them with all due haste to within the confines of The Fort.

June 11, 1756

My mission to form a militia of civilians from White Town has been quite successful, totalling 250 men (including 100 British citizens). They have been put under the wing of commanders at the Fort, and by late in the afternoon, they paraded in grand fashion to be inspected by the governor and his council. This militia, along with the 189 men already at the Fort, and a smattering of 75 odd sailors from British ships moored close by on the Hooghly mean that we have a fighting contingent of approximately 515 men.

Later in the day, we received news that an exodus of Black Town inhabitants had begun in earnest. Thousands of Indians have fled into the countryside.

Drake has been apprised of two letters that had been intercepted on their way to Omichand from Siraj Uddaula. Omichand's treachery has been definitively exposed. Governor Drake has subsequently had Omichand arrested and housed temporarily in The Black Hole (the garrison gaol).

The enemy is reported to be 50 miles off.

June 12, 1756

Households in White Town have been left servant less. Those of you who might be reading this report far away from the Indian subcontinent may not realize how devastating this circumstance is for the townspeople; most of them having relied exclusively on these native men and women to do all the work for them. Most have never had to lift a hand to cook or to clean out the chamber pots or to do any heavy lifting. For them this may be the biggest disaster they have ever experienced.

Thank God for Lady Russell. I have butted heads with her on numerous occasions in my time as a White Town councillor and magistrate, but now I must report that she has been a godsend. She has organized all the women and set them working on filling sacks with cotton waste so that the parapet walls of The Fort can be heightened and so that the gun embrasures can be closed off so as to offer greater protection for the gunners. She has herded the children into several open rooms within the Fort's walls so they can be close to their mothers as they work.

June 13, 1756

Omichand's perfidious role in this sad affair cannot be overstated. Gervas Bellamy (senior chaplain of St. Anne's Church) had taken in a few female inhabitants not convinced by Lady Russell that they should move into the Fort. He reports that gunshots were heard coming from Omichand's estate and fearing the church was under attack; he herded his refugees to the opposite side of the building. When the gunfire ceased, he went over to the west windows and encountered a dreadful sight. Members of Omichand's harem, thirteen Hindu women and three young girls were marched outside the line of palm trees that bordered the property. (Here, I must warn you that the retelling of this matter is not for sensitive souls.) The first woman in the line tore her sari away from her chest, revealing her bare breasts. Juggernath (Omichand's personal guard) drew a knife from within the folds of his robe and buried it deep into the woman's flesh. Each woman in turn repeated the same action and each in turn was felled by Juggernath. He then slit the throats of the three children.

After surveying the bodies lying in the sun-scorched dirt, Omichand's burly Indian guard then turned the knife upon himself.

We haven't ascertained what precipitated this odious display, but it seems obvious to me that it is meant as a warning to all Hindus to stay away from Calcutta and not associate with the foreigners lest they suffer a similar fate. The gunshots earlier were simply to gain the attention of as many people as possible.

Even as I put pen to paper, another, even larger exodus of Black Town inhabitants is underway.

Uddaula's army is now camped at Baraset (fifteen miles from Calcutta).

Captain Holwell's Diary
(June 14ᵗʰ to 19ᵗʰ)

June 14th and 15th, 1756

I have reclaimed my old quarters at the Fort. It is late at night, and I haven't slept for nearly two days.

Preparations for the defence of the Fort have been madly undertaken. It has been determined by our spies that the first of Addaula's moves will be to lay an assault on Perrin's Redoubt (a small building which houses seven cannons, and which protects the Fort from the northeast) assuming it to be the easiest place for his gunners and elephants to cross the ditch. Twenty-five men will be stationed there under the command of Ensign Francis Piccard and the merchant ship The Prince George, which is now laying off the northern shore of the Hooghly River, will provide further cannon support. She has twenty-nine-pounders on her gun deck and a further half-dozen six-pounders on her quarterdeck trained on the enemy beyond the redoubt. This will give Addaula something to think about!

Several small battalions of soldiers will occupy some of the larger houses on the east side of The Park and will fire on the enemy from their respective vantage points.

All gun embrasures at the four bastions will be manned, each with two gun crews.

This is all well and good, but who knows how long our dry powder will last? Not more than a few days, I think.

We have been informed that Indian armies never fight at night and that they take a hiatus from approximately noon–3:00 p.m. each afternoon to avoid the worst heat of the day. We will have to use this knowledge to our advantage.

June 16, 1756

Siraj Uddaula and his army have arrived. They are encamped in a great arc around the city, most of their troops hidden in the surrounding jungle. Uddaula himself has taken up residence in Omichand's enclosure just across the Avenue from St. Anne's Church.

Just after 3:00 p.m. this afternoon the assault of Perrin's Redoubt began, as we had anticipated, and several thousand of the Newaab's soldiers attempted to storm the building. Our troops at the redoubt have been doing yeoman service throughout the day, and with the Prince George firing heavily into the Indian troops, they have managed to hold on. Only five of our men are confirmed to have died. Eyewitnesses have reported hundreds of casualties on the Indian side.

Well into the evening, cannon fire from the indomitable Prince George thundered across the common, hitting enemy targets in the jungle, a cannon firing every two to three minutes. We don't know what damage has been afflicted on the Indians, but Addaula's troops have stopped their assault on Perrin's Redoubt. We have either dealt them a grievous blow, or they're regrouping for another attempt in the morning.

June 17, 1756

Many precious Fort William souls have perished today. But it's rather quite remarkable. While our men have been struck down singly, here and there, I can report that hundreds, perhaps thousands, of Indian soldiers have been killed. Our cannon fire and musket fire are far more accurate than the enemies'. Nevertheless, our army of five hundred men stands against several hundred thousand Indians. Unless there is a miracle of some sort, I don't see how this is going to end well. There are calls for Drake to offer terms of surrender, and he has refused. In this, I am of the same mind. We may have to surrender, but before we do, Addaula needs to know that we are a force to be reckoned with. He is a man who abhors weakness, we have been told, and our fearsome resistance can do nothing but impress him. When the time for surrender comes, if we are seen as strong and not soiling our pants, he is likely to treat us more honourably.

No further attempt on Perrin's Redoubt has been made. My guess is that Addaula has discovered the section of the Maratha Ditch that has not been completed. Today he has trained his focus on this spot south of the Fort and his army has finally been able to breach the outskirts of White Town. The soldiers stationed in several of the houses came under heavy attack and by the noon hiatus; many of those men had been cut down. A few have been able to retreat to the Fort and now we are relying solely on the cannons at the bastions and musket fire from the walls.

It was with a sinking feeling that we saw Uddaula's pennant flying over Lady Russell's house and atop Minchin's as well. What will tomorrow bring?

June 18, 1756

This has been a terrible day, not only because of the privation our women and children have been dealing with and the heavy fire on the Fort by Indian troops, but also because of the reprehensible behaviour of our leaders, Governor Drake and Garrison commander Minchin. Drake and Minchin have made themselves scarce. No one has been able to locate them.

We were never prepared properly for this invasion. Careful diplomacy was all it would have taken to avoid the whole mess. Our few plans to protect the Fort have now disintegrated, and decisions are now being made on the spur of the moment.

I have other horrible news to report. Addaula has ordered that Black Town should be razed to the ground. Since early afternoon, the city has been enveloped in a blanket of thick, dark smoke. Calcutta is burning. My best calculation is that two thousand native women and children have stormed into the Fort trying to escape the conflagration. How they even managed to get past the enemy is beyond me. This situation has now added to the plight of the hundred-odd women and children from White Town who have taken refuge here. Lady Russell recognized immediately that the children must be moved into the Governor's mansion away from the arcade beside The Black Hole. She asked Janniko (a local fiddler) to play a musical game of 'follow the leader' with the children and whisk them out of harm's way into the Governor's ballroom. Drake had already denied this request from Lady Russell but a day ago, but now that he was nowhere to be seen, she made the decision to go ahead with this relocation anyway. Janniko was three quarters across the parade ground when one of St. Jacques' eighteen-pounders exploded into the Fort, the ball landing but six feet from the fiddler. As Lady Russell reported it, Janniko was spun high into the air and landed dead on the ground, a bloodied mess. Even amidst the mayhem and carnage of this event, Lady Russell was able to gather the panicked children and rush them into the ballroom. Blessedly not a single child was badly hurt in the explosion or in the mad dash to the governor's mansion.

We have all been living on very short rations of flatbread and lentils, eaten cold. A small quantity of rice has been fed to the children.

Sarah Mapletoft, the Assistant Chaplain's wife, went into labour today. Thank goodness Bellamy's wife, Dorothy, was with her. They sent out for Surgeon Gray and when he couldn't be found, they sent for me, but I was too late to aid with the birth. What a way for a child to come into this world!

When I arrived at the room she had been removed to, the stench was overpowering, and the heat was unbearable. Sarah lay on a small cot holding a healthy baby girl, swaddled in a dirty towel. The new mother's eyes were lifeless. She stared into space not taking in anything around her. This woman, always complaining about life in Calcutta and perennially sporting a very sour expression on her face, was now too tired and worn down by recent events to say a word. Mrs. Bellamy amazed me. With no medicines or instruments at hand, she had made do by removing Sarah's undergarments and folding them between the expectant mother's lower body and the straw floor so as to catch the newborn when it slipped from its mother's womb into the world.

I must leave off now. We are about to undertake a very sensitive mission. We have decided to secretly remove the women and children to two or three British boats anchored in the Hooghly. We will do this

*under the cover of darkness and with as little noise as possible in hopes
to avoid the Black Town refugees getting wind of this. If they see a large
number of people on the docks getting into budgerows, the stampede
will be on, and we'll have little chance of getting our human cargo
clear of Fort William. Lady Russell has undertaken to take charge of
the children.*

June 19

    *I'm sorry if my report seems scattered this evening. I am running on
nerves alone. Bellamy and I are holed up in Drake's quarters, Drake
having deserted us by making his way to the Dodaldy! We have found a
small quantity of claret in his credenza and are gratefully imbibing.*

    *The events of the day are too many and too confused to set it all out on
paper. But I'll see what I can do.*

    *There has been constant bombardment of the fort from the enemy
guns. Muskets were trained on our parapets and let loose each time
the enemy saw movement. Panic has started to set in in earnest. A
number of the soldiers, especially the half-castes, have found arak in
the storerooms and have been drinking themselves silly. Fights have
broken out.*

    *I called a war council in the absence of any of our other leaders, and
we met here in Drake's chamber. It came to our attention then that
Manningham and Frankland had accompanied the women and children
to the Dodaldy during the night's escape, purporting to look out for them;
and, it has become painfully obvious that they intend to stay onboard
and make their escape. Between the two of them, they privately own a
large share of the Dodaldy's enterprises, and so the decision to remove
the women and children to 'their' ship is entirely self-serving. The shame
of it!*

    *Drake was found in the middle of the night draped over some bales in
a lower storeroom. Witherington, the gunpowder captain, found him and
was able to rouse Drake from his drunken stupor. Quite unfortunately,
Witherington reported to the governor that there was no more viable
gunpowder left, and only a very small number of cannon balls. He had to*

shout this out to Drake, who was having difficulty communicating with him. A number of native women, hiding out in the storeroom overheard this exchange. Sensing now that they wouldn't be protected at the Fort any longer, they ran to tell others. Hundreds of the refugees from Black Town left the Fort in a stampede and ran north toward their blackened city. A number of them were gunned down by the enemy troops who used them, as it were, as nighttime target practice.

Bellamy's wife and daughter, Anna, have made it safely to the ship, but Bellamy is devastated. His eldest son, Thomas, was seen to shoot himself with his own pistol on the ramparts. I had to deliver this news to the chaplain myself.

I don't know if I should be flattered or aghast at what transpired next. The upshot of it is that the remaining officers have appointed me as the new Governor of Fort William! Can you imagine that?

Shortly after naming me as the new commander some encouraging news came to us from the Prince George, which had so valiantly, held the day at Perrin's Redoubt. The captain sent word that he would be able to swing by The Fort later in the day and would be able to take on the remaining denizens of the Fort. We could all make our escape down the Hooghly!

Cruelly, just as I began making plans for the escape, another messenger arrived to tell us the Prince George had run aground on a sand bar in the river. Using semaphores, they would call the Dodaldy for help in drawing her off.

One of the damnedest pieces of infamy in this whole affair was to play out over the next few hours as Drake, somehow now on board with Manningham and Frankland, denied the request for help. The Prince George would not be able to rescue the rest of us after all.

One final note before I try to find some sleep.

Peter Carey, a seaman on the Dodaldy, who had been recruited by our militia, came into our war council. He was devastated. He had expected to find his wife, Mary, aboard the Dodaldy with the other women. He had personally helped her aboard the budgerow heading out to the ship. Somehow, he had found a way onto the ship earlier today to say his goodbyes and to make plans and was devastated to find *that she wasn't anywhere to be found. He confronted Manningham who was immediately evasive. Eventually, Carey got to the bottom of the situation. His wife, who had been a full citizen of White Town, but happened to be half-caste, had not been allowed to board. She was unceremoniously put back on the budgerow and returned to the Fort. Upon Carey's return to the Fort, he had found Mary along with Lady Russell, who had refused to stay on board the Dodaldy if Mary were not allowed on board, holed up with some of the men in a room in Writer's Row. Poor Peter and Mary, who have been stalwart and upstanding citizens of White Town and who have been faithful servants to the English East India Company!*

Betrayal

Sunday morning dawned clear and hot. For the first time in a number of days, the smoke from the burning city seemed to have dissipated. Holwell sent Bellamy to gather the officers for another war council. In the meantime, he walked out to the southwest bastion and surveyed the situation.

It was heartbreaking to see most of the houses in White Town destroyed by the constant bombardment of cannon fire and musket fire. Those houses still standing flew the Newaab's banner, fluttering brazenly in the morning breeze. He thought sadly of his own house now likely overrun by the Newaab's men.

He walked along the ramparts to the southeast turret. A sudden hope sprang up in him as he looked out at the Hooghly. The Dodaldy could still be seen downriver. Perhaps if they could signal the ship to let them know they were capitulating and that they could all be ready to board the ship if it returned to pick them up. Surely Drake would show pity on those stranded at the Fort and do the responsible thing: rescue the soldiers and officers of his regiment!

The men stood around their new leader. A wild hope was in their eyes. One of the officers left to convey instructions to the signallers to hail the Dodaldy and pass on the message Holwell had ordered to be sent.

A junior officer spoke up. He had come across a small cache of powder that seemed still to be dry. He had hidden it and set a guard on it. Commander Holwell congratulated him on his resourcefulness and immediately sent the officer with one other of the group to recover the powder and get it to the soldiers. While they were waiting to hear from the Dodaldy they would fire another volley at Addaula and show him that they were very much alive and still dangerous.

The minutes dragged on. Finally, the signalling captain entered the room. The Dodaldy had not acknowledged the message in any way. It seemed obvious that a river rescue would not be forthcoming.

The members of the war council were livid and dejected in equal measure.

Using the last dregs of dry powder, the soldiers of Fort William gave the Indian army one last taste of British military ferocity. In less than half an hour, it was over. All the powder had been spent. When Uddaula's forces realized what had happened, the dam burst, and hundreds of Indians spilled into the Fort, looting and ransacking.

Holwell, knowing they could not continue without being slaughtered, and after discussing the next moves with his officers and other trusted deputies including the incorrigible Lady Russell, made his way down to The Black Hole to speak with Omichand. He would have Omichand get a message to Siraj Uddaula outlining the Fort's surrender and asking for terms of clemency. He dodged his way, several officers leading the charge, through the unruly throng, to the entrance of the gaol. The change to the once orderly courtyard was horrific. Bodies lay strewn about. Rats, which found license in the mayhem, had come out of their warrens and feasted on the dead, as did flies and other insects. When rioters disturbed the vermin, they stood aside or flew up for a few moments and then just as quickly settled back into their repast.

When Omichand exited the quarters, he had been confined to for the past several days, he was almost unrecognizable. The clothes of the obese Jain merchant hung loosely on his skin that was a sickly, pallid hue. The heat and the short rations had nearly killed him. Yet, when Holwell put forward his request, he listened attentively and surprisingly treated John with grave respect.

John had come to the point directly with Omichand. He lied and told him that the Fort had enough food and powder to withstand an onslaught for several more days. Messages had been sent to other British outposts and reinforcements were expected any time now. He would urge the Newaab to consider that his animosity had been levelled at Drake, not the entire British enterprise in Fort William and that Drake was no longer there. They had both shared in the wealth that came from doing business with the English East India Company. Why would he want to jeopardize that? While his excellence considered terms of the Fort's surrender, all aggression toward the Newaab's soldiers would stop. He, John Holwell, was the new Governor of Fort William and he would see to it. Omichand agreed to send the message to Uddaula.

After sending a messenger on his way, Omichand then very calmly went back into the Black Hole. John marvelled at this but then realized it was one of the few safe places he could retreat to in the surrounding madness.

It was now noon. Holwell and his men holed up in a room nearby and waited for word from Addaula. After an interminably long hour, Bellamy poked his head out the door and wildly gesticulated to Holwell that there was something he should see. The square was almost deserted. In the midday heat and dust, the riotous Indians had retreated to the jungle to take some respite from the hellish sun. A semblance of order had been restored to the Fort.

Entering the Fort from the East Gate was a well-guarded functionary sent by Uddaula. John and his men rushed out to meet him. The message from Addaula was that he would agree to consider Holwell's terms of surrender, but only if they agreed to stop fighting. This John assured him of and as the messenger, with his retinue, left the Fort, John felt elated. They might just get out of this alive!

Peter Carey suggested they find his wife, Mary, whose turn it was that day to prepare food for those still in the Fort. They found her in the Officer's mess and had one last meal together. Skimpy though it was, it seemed like a banquet to them.

Holwell and Bellamy took another walk along the ramparts, looking out over the river, still just a little hope that the Dodaldy had changed her mind and was even now tacking its way upriver to collect them, or that the Prince George had shaken itself off the sandbar and was floating downriver to affect a rescue.

John had just turned his gaze back to the Fort when a musket went off, shattering the quiet of the past few hours. Someone had taken a shot at Holwell. His men quickly looked about and tried to find the culprit. A group of men stood about, and Bellamy turned his attention to John.

"What kind of devilry is this? Those are Hedleburgh's men!"

Before he could say anything further, more shots rang out. The contingent of Dutchmen was firing their pistols wildly into the air. Some of Holwell's officers aimed at the group and fired the last few rounds they had left.

"Heddleburgh has betrayed us! He is deliberately fomenting unrest so that Uddaula will think we have broken our promise to keep the peace."

Holwell and Bellamy scrambled to the safety of Drake's mansion. On their way, they could see that many of their remaining faction had been spooked, and believing that the Indians were resuming their deadly march through the Fort, they attempted to make their escape any way they could, but especially out the West entrance by the dock. From there, no doubt, they would run along the river's edge and head south past John's house and into the jungle. Or they would attempt to pile into the remaining budgerows and head into the river. John could picture the mayhem—dozens of people trying to scramble over each other to get into the small boats. Many of them would drown. Holwell's attention was caught for a brief moment when he spied Lady Russell with several others in tow, heading out to the dock. He had a sinking feeling that he would never see that noble lady again.

Siraj Uddaula made his grand entrance into the Fort on the back of a festively adorned elephant. His retinue followed close behind and was splendidly arrayed. Holwell, Bellamy, and the officers that were left made their way down to the parade ground and made their obeisance to the Newaab.

He was in a furious temper. Through an interpreter, he determined who Holwell was and lambasted the commander for not keeping up his end of the bargain.

It was no use trying to explain the circumstances of the earlier disturbance. Uddaula was not in a mood to listen.

The Newaab then summoned his troop commander and had a discussion with him. When the British officers saw Roy Doolub come forth to speak with Uddaula, they were visibly shaken. Here was a man who had traded privately with them for a long time, but who had been poorly treated by Drake. He had an axe to grind!

It was Doolub that suggested to the Newaab that it was too dangerous to leave the British garrison, what was left of it, to roam the Fort freely while he decided on a course of action. Rather, every last denizen of the Fort and of White Town should be rounded up and incarcerated until the Newaab, at his pleasure, could deal with them.

The Newaab asked Doolub where British soldiers were accustomed to being held if they misbehaved. "The Black Hole," came the ominous reply.

Uddaula, without a moment's hesitation, said to lock them up there, and he turned his elephant about and left the Fort.

THE BLACK HOLE

It had been a very long day, and the dispirited group of officers was weary on their feet. Commander Holwell and his group waited in the evening heat for the Moors to round up all the prisoners. Roy Doolub took personal charge. Once this task had been completed, he returned to the garrison gaol and threw open the door. Panic and mayhem ensued.

John felt a great pressure on his back as the crowd was pushed and herded toward the entrance. He had no recourse but to move forward into the darkness, the first of 145 men and one woman, Mary Carey, to be unceremoniously packed into a room but eighteen feet wide and fourteen feet deep.

John's state of anxiety had been rising ever since he had contemplated the fate that awaited him and his charges. He knew the size and layout of the Black Hole and couldn't for the life of him fathom how all the prisoners would be able to fit. His anxiety now turned to sheer terror and nausea, and he vomited the moment he stumbled into the chamber. He had enough wits about him to make his way to the north end of the room where he stood hands clinging to the iron bars of one of the two small windows in the Hole. More and more bodies were piling onto him as the Moors prodded and shoved every last one of the prisoners into the room. He didn't think his back could withstand the pressure. He could hear the cries and screams of the other prisoners, many of whom would surely be trampled to death before their incarceration even began. *The lucky few* he found himself thinking.

Three or four officers, including Clayton, Lushington, and Cooke, the Company Secretary, were thrown in directly behind Holwell. They formed a phalanx around him and did their best to stop other prisoners from glomming on to the coveted window position, where breathing might be a little easier. Peter Carey, who had been standing in the courtyard with his hands draped about Mary's waist, was nowhere to be seen. With the side of his head pinioned up against the bars of the window, John could use one eye to see what was going on in the courtyard where the Governor's House was now engulfed in flames and the other to witness the Dantesque tableaux in the Hole.

A terrible noise exploded from the hapless prisoners as the Moors had to thrust the bodies of the last few men into the Hole so they could shut and lock the door. The door opened inwardly and so a swath had to be cleared to allow it to be closed. The bodies of several of the trampled dead, which were lying at the threshold, had to be shovelled further in as well. At last, the door slammed behind them and for a moment, there was stunned silence. It was eight o'clock on Sunday evening.

The animal instinct to survive was in full force. The orderly existence of their former lives in the Fort or in White Town was now a thing of the past. Men struggled to keep upright; to hold their footing; to take air into their compressed lungs. If they slipped or sagged with the exertion, they would be trampled and they would die, leaving just a little more space for the others. Each hapless neighbour became an enemy.

The stench was so horrible that men disgorged vomit uncontrollably. And they were sweating profusely, some trying to rip off their shirts to be more comfortable. This had a devastating effect. Bodies covered in perspiration and vomit became eely and so slippery that it was even harder to remain on firm footing.

Holwell could see those unfortunates who had crawled under the bench that lined the east wall, thinking that it would provide some protection, but who were now suffocating. Aghast, he watched as one man dug out a pocketknife from somewhere in his clothing and slashed the feet of the people standing near him, trying to get them to move away so he could breathe.

The minutes passed like hours. Clayton had succumbed to the weight of bodies around him and had collapsed. He lay dead at John's feet. More men were trying to get at Holwell to pull him away from the window so they could take his place. With every ounce of strength, he struggled to hang on, not knowing how long his body could withstand the strain. Outside the window was a young Indian staring entranced at the scene unfolding in the dark space. John begged him to come closer and pleaded with him to go and find someone in authority who could be made aware of their plight. He offered him a thousand rupiyas to be paid on the morrow if he would do that. The magistrate could be very persuasive and soon enough the man agreed. A thousand rupiyas was a small fortune. The man went away, though he returned a few minutes later telling Holwell that nothing could be done. The faint hope in John's chest was extinguished.

As more men continued to fall and more space became available, Holwell caught sight of his friend, Gervas Bellamy. His son, the young lieutenant, was guarding the old chaplain as best he could. They were pressed against the far corner of the prison. He also saw Peter Carey, his body draped over his wife, protecting her from the crush of human flesh. Seeing his friends brought him some courage, and in a mighty voice, which took most of the reserves of strength he had left, he called for silence in the room. He had to call out several times and eventually, and all too briefly, he had their attention. The people trusted John and he hoped he could offer them some hope and some solace. His stentorious voice rang out.

"Friends, we must stop struggling and fighting with each other. The more we do so, the less likelihood there is of surviving the night. Tomorrow will come, and with it, fresh air and freedom. We must remain calm. We must do whatever we can to stem every agitation of mind and body. Look to your neighbour, not as a threat to your existence, but as a friend who can help you get through this torment."

With that the room remained quiet for a time, barring the groans and the sobbing of injured and dying men. John used this lull to extricate himself from his position at the window, giving it over to a man behind him. He slithered and angled his way to the far side of the room seeking out Bellamy. His son was standing over him, but Bellamy was gone. John couldn't say a word, but he gently squeezed the boy's shoulders and then he moved on to find Peter and Mary. He could hardly see Mary hidden beneath the powerful body of her husband. He bent down and whispered into Peter's ear. There was no response. Using all his ever-depleting strength, he turned Peter's torso over. His eyes were lifeless. He too was dead. Beneath him though, Mary was curled into a fetal position, and she was still breathing. John replaced Peter's body with his own and then he passed out on top of her.

In his world of dreams, Alice and his children, even his mother, made an appearance. He sat on the bench with Alice, keeping one eye on their beloved Kati Ganga and the other on his children gambolling merrily in the garden. And then he was sailing down the river looking out at the shore, at a washerwoman beating her linens on a rock. He was in Gay Meadow standing next to Miriam watching Robert Cadman fly through the air over the river Severn. He was...

With the coming of the dawn, small slivers of light played through the bars of the two windows, fighting for egress through the bodies still pressed up against them. John remained blissfully unconscious until a loud banging could be heard at the entrance to the Black Hole. The door had been unlocked but there was great difficulty in prying it open, so many bodies having been piled up in front of it. At last, there was success and suddenly light flooded into the room.

John roused himself and surveyed the grotesque scene around him. He blanched at the smell. Every muscle in his body was crying out in protest as he attempted to stand up. He finally managed the feat, but his legs were like jelly, and he collapsed again. His hand came to rest first on Peter's body and then on Mary's. She shifted beneath him. Never was he so glad to feel movement from another human being. Mary was alive!

John picked his way to the entrance. A group of Addaula's men stood outside, horror written on their faces. The leader gave orders to one of his men to go and relay the circumstances to the Newaab. Water was brought for Holwell and slowly, one by one; other prisoners crawled out of the Hole into the morning light. Some of them started gulping down water until Holwell gently stopped them.

"Small sips, friends. Small sips. You'll only make yourselves more ill."

It was six a.m. on Monday morning, ten hours after the lock had been turned on the door to the Black Hole. Twenty-two men and one woman had navigated across the corpses of their friends and companions and breathed in the fresh morning air.

And then somewhere in the ether, they all heard it—a bulbul singing its glorious song, full-throated and unaware of the misery below. John smiled and put his arms around Mary.

Uddaula stormed into The Fort, this time on a horse. He surveyed the grisly scene in front of him and immediately sought out Holwell. There was no contrition in his voice, though he did say that it was never his intention for the prisoners to be treated so harshly, that Doolub would pay for his treachery.

The Newaab wanted to know where the Fort's wealth was kept. Rumours of vast treasures buried somewhere in Fort William had come to his ears. Physically and mentally, John was spent. Nevertheless, the cruel Newaab persisted in interrogating him.

Holwell wasn't aware of any such cache and told Uddaula as much. The Newaab searched John's face, undertaking to search out any prevarication. He turned to one of his lieutenants, ordering him to let the prisoners go free with the proviso that they leave Calcutta within the hour—all, except for Governor Holwell and three random prisoners, who would be taken hostage. And he wanted Doolub found and brought to him in shackles.

The sky was clouding over ominously. The first heavy drops of the new monsoon season hit the scorched red earth sporadically, leaving it looking pockmarked and violated. Siraj Uddaula took one last hard stare at John Zephaniah Holwell, turned his stallion about, and cantered out of Fort William.

FULTA

Some of the Newaab's men, who had just been employed in the unsavoury task of removing the dead from the Black Hole and in plundering anything of value from the bodies, were now assigned to transport Holwell and his three fellow prisoners to Omichand's estate. They roughly took hold of the miserable quartet and unceremoniously herded them into the back of a nearby bullock cart. John and his fellow prisoners spent a miserable day shackled together in a shed adjacent to their beloved St. Anne's Church.

The next morning, under a blazing sun, the prisoners were marched in shackles to the banks of the Hoogly. They languished in the heat for the rest of the day, no water or sustenance of any kind afforded them. All four men were covered in boils. Holwell knew that without treatment their suffering would only increase as the pus built up and sought release. In his restraints there was nothing he could do at present for any of them.

And then, early in the evening, the clouds built up and the monsoon rain descended in cruel waves. In a matter of moments, they went from suffering under the intense heat of the sun's incessant rays to bone-chilling cold that pierced them relentlessly. They cowered together as best they could and waited miserably for the morning.

It was June 23rd and the deluge had abated sometime in the early morning hours. The prisoners were taken aboard a boat headed for Murshidabad and thrust into the bilge. Their arm restraints had been removed but they were still shackled to each other by metal ankle irons.

It took some time for their eyes to adjust to the darkness around them. They could hear the men above getting the boat ready for departure. They could also hear the waters of the Hoogly slapping up against the sides. Once the clatter of the sailors above subsided, another noise insinuated itself. The best John could guess was that the bilge rats had come out of their hiding places and were now scuttling all about the watery hollow. It was an unnerving sound.

The boat was not a fast one. Nothing like the sleek Sparrow John and Alice had once sailed on to Murshidabad, a lifetime ago it seemed to John. For fifteen days the poor souls languished in the bilge. Without proper food and drinking water they could feel themselves wasting away. Only four times did someone drop some unsavoury rations down to them, and they had to survive on drinking the brackish bilge water constantly swilling about their feet.

The pain from the boils all over their bodies was excruciating. John found a splinter from one of the overhead beams and began the slow and careful process of lancing as many of the furuncles as he could. On his own body, the sores that caused the most discomfort were on his inner thigh, just below his scrotum. These he treated carefully, draining the pus, and spreading some of the tar he had been able to mine from the wooden ribs of the bulwark over the now open abscesses.

Throughout this long, miserable ordeal, John had time, too much time in retrospect, to contemplate the events of the recent past. Somehow, he had to survive; he had to live to tell the story of the Black Hole. The English East India Company needed to hear of Drake's treachery, and that of his henchmen. They needed to hear about the ruthless Siraj Addaula and to formulate an appropriate response. He had no doubt that should word of all these events come to the ears of those in authority in England, action would be taken, and immediately. The British presence in India would certainly be on a much different footing than it had been to this point. What that would look like was anybody's guess.

While in the bilge, he shared stories of his family, happy memories and sad, with his companions. They, in turn, spoke of theirs.

At last, on July 7th, the boat was docked, and the prisoners were taken to a common prison in Murshidabad. Life here was hard, but nothing like their experience aboard ship. They were fed meagre, but regular meals and given fresh water to drink. Little by little, they regained some of their strength. Even then their shabby clothes hung on them. John reckoned that each of them had lost well over a stone in weight since their ordeal had begun.

Almost a week went by before they were summoned before Siraj Uddaula. A strong sensation of déjà vu came over him as they were escorted into the precincts of the Durbar, the same courtyard in which he had first met Sarfaraz Khan. Uddaula was waiting for them, surrounded by a phalanx of guards and other functionaries. John could see that even the hardened, callous Newaab was taken aback by the sight of the emaciated men standing before him.

He didn't address Holwell and his compatriots but rather turned away from them to consult with the Frenchman, St. Jacques, and Roy Doolub, who now appeared to be back in Uddaula's good books. While John could piece together much of the conversation, it was blatantly obvious from their faces that they weren't in agreement regarding the subject of their discourse. In fact, Doolub was quite red in the face.

Uddaula, in a final burst of exasperation, bellowed at Doolub and St. Jacques that the prisoners were to be released immediately, before smartly pirouetting away from them and striding vigorously toward his palace. This pronouncement could be understood by all.

"What just happened?" Lushington, the youngest and strongest of the four men, asked no one in particular as they shuffled as swiftly as they were able out of the Katra Masjid.

Holwell replied, "I believe that Uddaula finally concluded that I really don't know the whereabouts of this mythical trove of treasure buried somewhere in the Fort. Also, based on his conversation with St. Jacques and Doolub, I have a sense that the young Newaab may be regretting some of his actions in Calcutta.

"What do we do now?" Lushington posed the question they were all asking themselves.

"We go to the Dutch East India offices and see what help we can find there. I'm afraid the English will have made themselves very scarce in the past few weeks." The men followed their leader through the labyrinthine lanes of the Moghul city, marvelling at the sureness of his direction.

Holwell had had no word of the Van Breda's for many years, yet here he was seated opposite his old friend, Wouter, in his office at Fort Gustavus.

"How long have you been in Hoogly Chinsurra?" Holwell couldn't believe his luck.

Wouter poured out some tea before responding. "A few months now. We have been terribly worried about you all in Fort William. While our interests here in India can sometimes be in conflict, we too know that Uddaula's wrath could just as easily have fallen on us. He is a rash young man, hellbent on having things his way, and God forbid that anyone dares oppose him!"

The two friends fell easily into conversation and John was over the moon when Wouter offered him a pipe and some tobacco. He hadn't had this luxurious pleasure for well over a month now, and he was immediately transported back to happier times as the cloud of smoke wreathed sinuously about his head.

"You and your men will rest here a few days. We're going to have to fatten you up a little or your countrymen aren't going to recognize you." An impish grin played over Wouter's face. "You say that the refugees from Fort William will have made their way to Fulta? That is but a two-day journey from here down the Hoogly. We'll see you safely deposited there. Now, my good friend, if there's anything you or your men would like, don't hesitate to ask."

"There is one thing, Wouter. I'd like to visit your doctor. My men have suffered a lot and there are medicines and some other supplies I would like to get my hands on." John stood up and after shaking hands with the tall Dutchman, made his way to the quarters he and his men had been assigned.

Fulta was a small jungle village seven leagues south of Calcutta and not far from The Bay of Bengal. As the Dutch ship turned the bend and Fulta came into sight, John's mind was in a turmoil. He wrapped his fists around the guardrail and squeezed ever harder. What sort of reception would he be given? Were those feckless deserters, Drake and Manningham there? Would they have re-established their authority over the rest of the refugees?

A general buzz went through the crowd now gathered on the shore once they recognized Holwell and his companions as they made their way down the gangplank. John recognized all the faces and was ecstatic when he saw Mary Carey's face smiling at him from within the crowd. She maneuvered her way over to him and, putting her arm through the crook of his, steered him toward a paltry shelter on the outskirts of the encampment.

Mary wouldn't let him speak until he had a plantain leaf piled high with a mound of lentils and some flatbread planted firmly in his lap. Between mouthfuls of the tasty dal, John asked her about her experiences since that fateful night in the Black Hole. Not once mentioning her personal travails, she related the tale of the survivors and how they had made their way by foot to Fulta. They had been received by the others with mixed reactions. The reunited families were overjoyed, but this was bittersweet as the news of the tremendous loss of life in the Black Hole also became clear to the Dodaldy's passengers.

When John asked her about Drake and Manningham, her face darkened at once. The two men had indeed established themselves as the ultimate authority in the camp and had taken for themselves the best materials and supplies with which to furnish their shelter. Not only that, but Manningham had been commissioned by Drake to go to Madras to report to the Governor there and let him know the details of the fall of Fort William so that messages could be relayed to England and ships could be sent forthwith to extract them from Fulta.

This last bit of news was devastating. John knew that whatever story Manningham relayed to the Governor would certainly not include his and Drake's shameful role in the desertion of Fort William and their cowardly refusal to come back for the remaining soldiers and citizens of White Town when they had the opportunity. In any case, there wasn't anything to be done about that now. That story would have to be told by him and some of the other survivors upon their return to England.

As evening drew on, John walked dolefully to the banks of the Hoogly and looked out over the water. He could hear the familiar noises of the forest — chattering monkeys, snorting water buffalo, and the roar of a lion. His thoughts went out to his children, and to James and Susan and Charlotte, and finally, to his beloved Alice. Just as he was about to return to Mary's shelter, he spotted a bird perched on the overhanging branches of a mangrove. He smiled. A bulbul was calling out to the night, its song plaintive and beautiful.

EPILOGUE

When the Governor of Madras learned of the events in Fort William, he marshalled his forces and moved to retake the fort for the English. In January 1757, six months after the events of the Black Hole, he accomplished this feat with almost no resistance. Siraj Uddaula had done what he had set out to do and had lost interest in the affairs of Calcutta.

Upon their arrival in London several Fort William officers, Holwell among them, provided eyewitness testimony to the siege and fall of Fort William. Holwell's account, in particular, was given great weight. The British authorities were horrified by the account and immediately set about preparing to exact revenge. Inexplicably, and maddeningly from the perspective of the Black Hole survivors, Drake and Manningham, along with others of their ilk, were let off very lightly and, in some cases, even regained their standing in the English East India Company.

The French complicity in the affairs of the Fort William disaster added to the tensions between the two countries. When news of The Seven Years' War reached Bengal and Siraj Uddaula became aware of another war between England and France, his distaste of the English found him squarely on the side of the French interests in India once again. This was to be his undoing. Robert Clive, the Commander of the British forces in the East, knew that many of Uddaula's officials didn't share the Newaab's proclivity toward the French. Clive secretly made a pact with Mir Jaffir, one of these officials, offering him the throne of Bengal, should he help the English destroy Uddaula. This was actualized at The Battle of Plassey on June 23, 1757, when Clive was given license by the British Parliament to attack Uddaula and make him pay for his aggressive and devastating actions in Calcutta.

Mir Jaffir became Newaab, Clive received a gift of £234,000 and was named Governor of Bengal, and the British became the de facto rulers of the wealthy state.

England, which had been until this time interested solely in protecting her commercial interests in the Indian subcontinent, now adopted a more political agenda and began insinuating itself aggressively and on a larger scale, infiltrating the governance and bureaucracy of the expansive country, brazenly extending its grasp. This was no colonizing mission, but rather an exercise of imperial dominance.

In 1758, John Zephaniah Holwell, having returned to India, succeeded Clive as Governor of Bengal, and held this position until late 1760. Eventually he returned to England and made a name for himself as an academic and lecturer. His knowledge was eclectic; he authored books about native systems of Indian religion, the efficacy of ayurvedic medicine, and was responsible for a plethora of other scientific writings. His children thrived. Amelia married a Mr. Birch and became quite the socialite about London. Scholarly Emma became the wife of the notable Doctor Swinney, and James signed on with The English East India Company and rose quickly in its ranks.

John Zephaniah Holwell died in England in 1798 at the venerable age of eighty-six.

ACKNOWLEDGEMENTS

I would like to acknowledge:

My wife, Laura, for her sensible, female perspective on this work and for being ever supportive.

Chris Hansen and the Burlington-on-Whyte family for providing me an ideal space in which to be creative and for their constant encouragement.

Cody Porter, thespian extraordinaire and man-about-town, for the careful reading of my draft and for furnishing me with valuable editorial suggestions. Thanks for the "Writer's Tears," my friend!

The people at FriesenPress for their capable and professional direction in getting this novel to publication.

CPSIA information can be obtained
at www.ICGtesting.com
Printed in the USA
BVHW070448080222
627832BV00002B/3